Also by Sophie Pembroke

The Princess and the Rebel Billionaire

Cinderellas in the Spotlight miniseries

Awakening His Shy Cinderella
A Midnight Kiss to Seal the Deal

Also by Cara Colter

One Night with Her Brooding Bodyguard
Matchmaker and the Manhattan Millionaire
His Cinderella Next Door
The Wedding Planner's Christmas Wish

Discover more at millsandboon.co.uk.

VEGAS WEDDING TO FOREVER

SOPHIE PEMBROKE

SNOWBOUND WITH THE PRINCE

CARA COLTER

MILLS & BOON

First Published in Great Britain 2021
by Mills & Boon, an imprint of HarperCollins*Publishers* Ltd,
1 London Bridge Street, London, SE1 9GF

www.harpercollins.co.uk

HarperCollins*Publishers*
1st Floor, Watermarque Building,
Ringsend Road, Dublin 4, Ireland

ISBN: 978-0-263-30004-8

12/21

MIX
Paper from responsible sources
FSC C007454

This book is produced from independently certified FSC™ paper to ensure responsible forest management.
For more information visit www.harpercollins.co.uk/green.

Printed and Bound in Spain using 100% Renewable Electricity at CPI Black Print, Barcelona

VEGAS WEDDING TO FOREVER

SOPHIE PEMBROKE

MILLS & BOON

For Ellie Darkins.
Thank you for all the years of writing support—
and for inspiring me to write a Vegas wedding
romance after reading *Falling for the Rebel Princess*!

CHAPTER ONE

IT WASN'T EXACTLY the first time that Toby had woken up in a strange hotel room without much memory of how he'd got there, but it was a long while since the amnesia of alcohol had affected him this badly.

The curtains were drawn haphazardly across the floor-to-ceiling windows, letting in enough sunlight to make him wince as he opened his eyes. Through narrowed slits, he surveyed his surroundings. Four-poster bed, without the roof. Soft down pillows that were helpless against his pounding headache. Walls covered in some sort of fabric-like wallpaper that screamed *I am luxurious!* at him. A glimpse of a marble bathroom through the doorway. And through that chink in the curtain he could see mountains in the distance—and knew instinctively that below him would be a view of the famous Strip, with the sun rising over it.

The Four Seasons, then. Las Vegas. One of the Presidential Suites. Yes, that made sense. Finn had said that if they were going to do Vegas they were going to do it properly, and booked them in.

Finn. He'd be in one of the suite's other bedrooms. He'd be able to fill him in on anything he'd missed. As long as his best friend was with him, nothing could have gone too wrong last night.

Except...if Finn had been there, he wouldn't have drunk enough to forget anything. Finn always kept a tight rein on their alcohol consumption—he claimed because it impaired their betting ability, but Toby knew it was really because of his father's own drinking, which was why he went along with it.

So maybe Finn *wouldn't* be able to fill in the blanks in his memory. Which meant he had to keep trying himself.

'You're not just some student out on the piss, Toby.' His older brother's voice sounded in his head, a reminder of his university days long past, the words unwelcome but the tone familiar and comforting all the same. *'You're a Blythe. The son of the Eleventh Viscount Wishcliffe. You're somebody. You need to act like it.'*

Except he wasn't any more. That much he remembered.

His father was dead. Barnaby was dead.

He wasn't the son of the Viscount, or even the younger brother of the Viscount.

He *was* the Viscount.

The unlucky Thirteenth Viscount Wishcliffe, thousands of miles from home.

He'd never wanted to inherit the title, or the estates and the responsibility that went with it. Had never expected to, with his father, brother and nephew all happily above him in the line of succession. He wouldn't have wished the pressure of it on his brother Barnaby, or eight-year-old nephew Harry either.

Toby had watched what the struggle to keep an old aristocratic name, reputation and estate going in the modern era had cost his father. After the second heart attack he'd begged him to consider other options—but he'd been shouted down.

Then the third and final heart attack had hit, and Barnaby had taken the reins. Toby hadn't been able to stay and watch the estate drain the life and energy from his brother too.

He'd never imagined that it would take him so soon, or Harry with him.

His jaw tightened at the memory, which only made his head pound more.

'Just one last adventure,' he'd begged Finn. *'One last night to cut loose and forget everything. I have to go home and take over the estate for real tomorrow. One last wild night in Vegas.'*

Looked like he'd got his wish, anyway. Even if his body was regretting it now.

The giant king-sized mattress shifted under him, making his stomach roll, and Toby realised, belatedly, he wasn't alone. God, how big were these ridiculous beds that he could lose an entire other person in one of them? Or how hungover did he have to be to not even check for company?

Finn had definitely left him alone if he'd brought a woman back with him. His best friend was no prude, but his current focus on his mission to regain everything his father had denied him had blinded him to romance, however brief. Besides, when they were out together the women always seemed to go for Finn first. Toby was very much a second choice.

The mattress hadn't moved again, so Toby assumed his companion was still asleep. If she was anything like as hungover as he was, it was probably for the best, so he didn't want to wake her. But he *was* curious. Like getting blackout drunk, one-night stands had also mostly been consigned to his university days. A decade later, he preferred more considered romances. Where both sides went in knowing exactly what to expect—a few weeks or months of fun together before they both moved on. At least that had been the case since Julia left him, marking the demise of his only real, long-term relationship—God, was it two years ago now?

Two years since the only woman he'd ever contemplated marriage with—proposed to, in a way—had walked out of his life and he'd barely thought about her since. He'd seen her at the funerals, of course, but other than that...her surgical removal from his life had left no apparent scars.

So. Who had he brought back with him last night?

Easing himself up on one elbow—slowly, so as not to disturb his companion *or* his hangover—Toby peered down at the mattress beside him. Long auburn waves of hair fanned out across the pillow, and a pale freckled nose peeked above the covers. Toby searched his faulty memory but couldn't find a name to put with the face.

She shifted in her sleep, turning on her side to face him. He took in the soft lashes against her cheek and the rosy lips pursed as if about to ask a question, before her eyes suddenly fluttered open.

Bright green eyes widened and her hand gripped the covers tighter as she stared up at him. Her left hand, he registered, as he spotted the silver band wrapped around her ring finger. Oh, God, he'd seduced a married woman. This was so much worse than he'd thought.

Autumn, his brain provided unhelpfully. *Her name is Autumn.*

Silently telling his brain, *Not now*, Toby searched for the words to get him out of this situation. Barnaby would have known them. Well, Barnaby would never have got into this situation in the first place.

'I—' he started, and stopped, shutting his mouth before anything stupid could fall out.

Autumn scrambled to sit up against the bedhead, pulling the sheet with her to cover all that bare pale skin he suddenly realised had to be under there. Skin he must have touched, kissed, caressed—and had no memory of.

The world was a cruel, cruel place.

He reached out a hand to try and reassure her, realised it would probably do the opposite and started to pull it back.

Then stopped as he noticed something else he really should have seen sooner.

The matching silver ring on his own left hand.

Autumn blinked awake, froze, and tried not to panic. The man in her bed—well, his bed, she guessed, as she didn't recognise the room—looked just as terrified as she felt, so that was something.

Slowly, she relaxed the muscles in her body one at a time and let the memories flow back in. She'd drunk enough last night that her head pounded and her mouth felt as if she'd swallowed a rat, but not so much that she couldn't remember the sequence of events that had led her to this place. And, despite the hangover, her body still reacted to the sight of him, a warm flush racing up her chest at the memories of their night together. Of his hands on her body, suddenly steady and sure. His mouth on hers…then working its way down her body…

Autumn pulled the sheet up quickly to cover her blush as much as her nudity.

From the way her companion—Toby, her mind filled in helpfully—was staring at the wedding ring she'd pushed onto his finger after several tries, some time after midnight, she suspected he wasn't remembering the same things.

Awesome. Looked like this morning was going to be *ideal*.

Marriage. What had she been thinking? Marriage was *permanent*. Or at least more difficult to get out of than the fun she usually let herself indulge in. Even surprisingly good drunken sex didn't justify *marriage*.

Except, of course, the sex had come after the wedding. She wasn't the sort of girl who made a habit of falling into bed with random British men she met at work. At least she could justify it to herself as being a one-night stand within the confines of the marriage bed.

Yeah, no. That didn't make it any better.

Grandma had always said that she was just like her mother, diving in head first, wanting everything at once, all or nothing—until she got bored and walked away. But even her grandparents probably wouldn't have predicted her taking it this far.

Granddad must be rolling in his grave right now.

Toby was still staring at her as if he'd never seen her before, so she decided she should probably start talking instead of imagining how bad her grandma's reaction would be, if she were still alive.

'Morning,' Autumn said softly. 'How are you feeling?'

'Like I got run over by a hearse, and they might be about to circle back and take me with them.'

She almost laughed at the pain in his crisp, proper voice. How could he sound so *British* even hungover to high heaven?

'Should I call for some coffee?' She kept her voice to a whisper, in deference to his head. Like it or not, she was going to have to deal with the guy today, until they sorted this mess out, and that meant not poking the hungover bear. Or whatever. Her brain wasn't up to metaphors yet.

Toby ran a hand over his chocolate-brown hair—it

hung a little longer than she suspected he usually kept it, since it seemed to be annoying him. Even at the altar last night he'd been shaking it out of his face.

The altar.

Oh, Jesus H Christ, she'd got herself into a real mess this time. But, in her defence, only to try and get out of a different, very real mess.

There was an old lady who swallowed a fly...

The old nursery rhyme about compounding errors ran through her head and she knew she'd be singing it all day, the way she used to make her grandfather sing it to her when they were working in the garden.

She just had to make sure not to compound *her* errors any further. Autumn was damn sure that if there was a way to make this situation worse, she'd find it. She always did.

Of course, she always got herself out of any mess she found herself in too. At least there was that. Look at the time with the Russian fire-eater. That could have been really messy, but she'd—

'Yes,' Toby said, interrupting her runaway train of thought. 'Coffee. That sounds…yeah.'

Clutching the thin white sheet to her chest to try and protect any remaining shreds of dignity she might possess, Autumn reached across for the phone and called down to Room Service, asking for their largest pot of strong black coffee. 'And maybe some pastries?' she added for good measure. Toby nodded, which was good. From what she could tell, they were at the Four Seasons—one of the Presidential Suites by the look of things—and Autumn definitely couldn't afford their pastries.

Toby could, though, if he was staying here. Even if he'd been down a little before they got chucked out of the casino where she worked—well, *had* worked until last night, anyway. Looked like he could afford to lose it, which was good.

If he'd married her for her money he was going to be *really* disappointed.

The giggle bubbled up in her, and there was just no way to stop it. Autumn pushed her fist—and the sheet—against her mouth, but the laugh came out anyway.

Toby shot her a censorious look, which only made her laugh harder, until she was rolling on the bed with uncontrollable giggles. Oh, it had been so long since she'd done something like this—something spontaneous and ridiculous and life-changing—just on a whim. She'd thought she'd forgotten how, after everything that happened with Robbie. It was good to know she still had it in her.

Her unexpected husband didn't seem quite so pleased, however.

'I'm sorry,' she said, wiping her eyes with the corner of the bedsheet. A little mascara came away with it. Great, she probably looked like a panda. 'But you have to admit, this situation is kind of hilarious.'

'Is it?' Toby raised one dark eyebrow as he stared at her, clearly horrified by her antics. Or just by her mere existence; it was hard to tell.

She stuck with her argument all the same. 'Well, yeah. I mean, I've been working in Vegas for over a year now, never had so much as a one-night stand, then you come along and suddenly I'm *married*!' She laughed again, but this time it died in her throat as she saw his expression.

It wasn't just embarrassment or discomfort or any of the things she'd expect to see on the face of her morning-after, one-night stand husband. It was downright horror.

'You know we can probably get it annulled, right?' Autumn tried to sound reassuring. 'I mean, this is Vegas. This has to happen all the time.' She'd never needed to look into the rules for ending an accidental drunken marriage, but surely there had to be some.

'Not if we consummated it.' Toby looked meaningfully at the sheet protecting her modesty. 'I mean, I assume we *did* consummate it?'

His hands, sliding up her sides, cupping her breasts. Her nipples aching against his palms. His kiss, as he slid home inside her, filling her… The memories were sharp and fresh—and distracting.

Stop thinking about sex. Married people never have sex anyway, right?

'Yes, we consummated it,' she said shortly, trying not to sound annoyed.

But really. How could he not remember? Despite their inebriated states, it had been some of the best sex she'd ever had in her life. Which, actually, might say more about the low bar she'd set for that. Perhaps it had been mediocre for him, and that was why he'd blocked it out. Unless…

Autumn blinked as some of the horror he was feeling settled onto her. She'd guessed that perhaps Toby didn't have *complete* memories of the events that had led them to his hotel room, but if he didn't even remember the night they'd spent together *at all*...

'Toby?' she asked cautiously. 'How much do you remember about last night? About why you married me?'

He met her gaze finally, his dark blue eyes totally serious. 'Absolutely nothing.'

A knock on the outer door signalled the arrival of coffee—thank God—and pastries to soak up last night's indulgences. It broke the awkwardness of the moment too, which Toby appreciated more than he could say. The horror in Autumn's bright green eyes was more than he could take.

Did she think he'd married her because they'd fallen in love at first sight? God, he hoped not.

But *she* obviously remembered their brief courtship, which meant she knew exactly what she hoped to get out of this union. If it was money, well, he supposed he could pay her off, distasteful as it seemed. If it was his title... well. That was less easily given.

Luckily Finn was nowhere to be seen as Toby pulled on a robe to answer the door and retrieve the refreshments. Tipping the porter, he wheeled the trolley into the bedroom himself and found Autumn sitting cross-legged on the bed, having donned the other fluffy white bathrobe from the bathroom.

He supposed they could have taken breakfast in the main room of the suite—the one with the sofas and tables and another stunning view over the Vegas Strip towards the mountains. But something about this situation made Toby want to keep it confined to the bedroom until he'd figured it all out.

Not to mention the fact that he didn't relish the idea of Finn walking in on this conversation.

Still, he didn't sit back down on the bed beside her, choosing one of the padded chairs by the window instead, even if he was more focused on the view inside the room than out.

'You don't remember anything,' Autumn repeated, even though he'd been perfectly clear the first time.

'I remember going out for a last night in Vegas.' Toby poured her a coffee and handed it to her, wincing as she leaned over to add copious amounts of milk and sugar to her cup. He also tried to avert his gaze from the way her robe gaped open as she did so. They might be married, but that didn't give him the right to ogle. Unfortunately.

'That guy must have hit you harder than I thought,' she muttered, which didn't bode well.

Autumn blew across the top of her coffee before taking a small sip. She looked so young, sitting there. But Toby knew from experience that young and beautiful didn't always mean naive, or honest. 'You don't remember going to Harry's Casino?'

He shook his head. 'Never heard of it. Is it on the Strip?'

'Just off. It's where I work. *Worked*,' she corrected herself.

Toby had a bad feeling about this. 'Do I have something to do with that sudden shift to the past tense?'

Autumn sighed and reached for a croissant. 'This is going to be easier if I just tell the story from the beginning, isn't it?'

'Probably,' Toby admitted, and sat back in his chair to listen.

The first parts he could have guessed. He and Finn had arrived at some dive casino and sat down at a table. He'd been drinking, Finn hadn't. Autumn had served them—or him. A lot, by the sound of things.

'So, basically, you got me drunk and took advantage of me?'

She rolled her eyes. 'No. Now, do you want to hear this or not? We're just getting to the interesting bit.'

Toby fell obligingly silent.

'You won a hand—your first in a while, actually; you weren't doing so well before that. Your friend suggested you should leave, but you weren't having any of it, so he left you there.' She looked disapproving of that, which Toby found a little endearing.

'You think he should have stayed?'

'I think a good friend would have made sure you got home safely.'

'And unmarried?'

'That too.'

Hmm. Maybe she wasn't as on board with this sudden elopement as he'd thought.

'What happened next?' Toby asked.

'You played a few more hands, had a few more drinks, lost some more money.' Autumn shrugged. 'Nothing out of the ordinary. But then you had another spectacular, unexpected, implausible win. You grabbed me around the waist to celebrate.'

Toby winced. 'Sorry.'

'I wouldn't have minded so much, but you made me spill my tray of drinks over the guy playing opposite you. Who also wasn't very sober, and got kind of mad about it. Then he accused you of cheating—'

'I never cheat!'

'Counting cards or whatever.'

'I've never been good enough at maths for that.' Finn was the maths whizz. Maybe that was why he didn't have the patience for sustained gambling. He was too good at calculating how bad the odds were.

Toby, on the other hand, just set himself a limit of what he was willing to lose and stuck to it. He'd just never considered adding his single man status to the list before now.

'He swung for you, you swung back, I tried to stay out of the way… I guess you can see how it went from there?' Autumn guessed.

'Partly,' Toby replied. 'Although not the bit where we ended up at a wedding chapel.'

She sighed. 'My boss came out, broke up the fight, fired me on the spot.'

The injustice of that rankled. 'But it was my fault, not yours.'

'Which you told him at the time, not that it made any difference. Anyway, you said you'd make it up to me. Help me find another job at one of the casinos. Which was a ridiculous idea, but you were so stupidly eager it was hard to tell you no. And you said you'd buy me dinner, and I was hungry, and it wasn't like I had anything better to do.'

'Still not seeing the chapel in this.' The trying to fix his mistakes, though, however misguidedly, well, that sounded like him, Toby had to admit.

'Obviously, none of the casinos were going to hire me on the spot, with you as my only, very drunken reference. This is where I started drinking, incidentally, so things are a little hazy after this.' Hazy was better than non-existent, though, so Toby kept listening. 'We ate dinner and drank a lot of cocktails as we came up with plans for my next career. You decided I was too good for this place, anyway. I think you wanted me to be a ballerina at one point. Even though I have two left feet and no training.'

'It was probably your grace,' he replied without thinking. 'Or those long legs.'

Autumn raised her brows at him. 'Yeah, you definitely mentioned the leg thing. Then and, well, later.'

Later. From the way her eyes darkened as she spoke the word, he knew she had to be remembering exactly what had happened later that night, once they were married and alone… He hoped it might spark a memory in him, but no luck. All the same, the room seemed suddenly smaller, the distance he'd put between them nowhere near enough to quell the heat that seemed to be rising around them from just that one word. One look…

He swallowed and she looked away, and the moment broke.

'Anyway,' Autumn went on, 'I declared I was going to leave Vegas, and we toasted to it, and you decided I should come to the UK to find work, except I didn't have a visa, and you said there was an easy solution to that and, well…'

'*That's* how we ended up at the chapel,' Toby finished for her.

Autumn nodded and reached for another pastry.

Toby slumped back in his chair, replaying the story she'd told him in his mind. While his memory of events was still mostly absent, bits and pieces of the night were coming back to him, and they tallied with her story—and the bruise he'd noticed on his cheekbone as he'd passed the bathroom mirror to grab the robe.

But there were still some things he didn't understand. For instance…

'You were obviously far more sober than me. Why didn't you say no?'

He held his breath waiting for her answer, praying that it wouldn't be something along the lines of, *I didn't feel I could*, or even, *I was scared to.* He knew himself well enough to know that, however inebriated, he would never force a woman to do anything she didn't want to. But *she* didn't know him well enough to be sure of that, and Finn told him he could be…overly enthusiastic when drunk. What if he'd made her feel like she had no choice, even if she did?

This was why he shouldn't drink. A viscount should never lose control that way. Both his father and Barnaby had both been very clear on that.

Just another reason he wasn't up to the job.

'Honestly?' Autumn shrugged lightly. 'It was just…

fun. I mean, it was crazy and ridiculous, but it had been so long since I'd just cut loose like that, and you were so excited about the whole thing. And I *was* drunk; don't get me wrong. Probably I wouldn't have done it otherwise.'

'Probably?' He couldn't keep the incredulity out of his voice. Who would only *probably* have not married a total stranger if she'd been sober? That didn't ring true.

Autumn's smile was lopsided, and it charmed him more than he wanted to admit. 'I've done more crazy spontaneous stuff. Nothing lasts for ever, you know. You have to go out and enjoy life while you can.'

He wanted to know more about the crazy spontaneous stuff she'd done, but there was something more pressing he needed an answer to first. Because there was one thing she hadn't mentioned once when recounting the events of the previous night. And he'd have thought it to be one of the most important factors of all. Which meant either she didn't know it, or she wanted to pretend it didn't matter.

He needed to know which one.

Toby took a breath and braced himself, because there really was no good way to ask this one.

'So, you didn't marry me because I told you I'm Viscount Wishcliffe?' he asked, and watched her eyes widen.

CHAPTER TWO

TOBY'S WORDS HIT her like a slap in the face. The sort of hit that knocked the wind from her, but only really began to sting as the seconds passed and the truth settled.

'You think I married you for your money.'

Maybe she shouldn't be surprised. It wasn't completely unreasonable. This was Vegas, where currency was king. She'd known him only a few hours before he'd dragged her to the altar. It wasn't like they had a long and loving basis for their nuptials, and one of the first things she'd known about him, even before his name, was that he had enough money to not care about losing it at the card table.

Then the rest of his words sank in.

'Wait. You're actual British aristocracy? Like *Downton* and everything?'

Toby shifted uncomfortably in his seat, the bathrobe falling open enough to give her a good look at his bare chest, sprinkled with dark hair, and remember how it had felt under her hands the night before. How he'd held her close against that chest, his mouth working at her neck, kissing down her collarbone towards her breasts…

Focus, Autumn.

'Wishcliffe isn't *that* big. But technically. Yes.'

'Then what the hell are you doing in Vegas? Shouldn't you be shooting grouse or visiting your tenants or something?' Her grandmother had *loved* period dramas about the British upper classes. When she got sick, they'd spent whole days doing nothing but living in that lost and now fictional world.

Nobody on those shows had ever got drunk and married in Vegas. Toby was ruining the dream. She was almost glad her grandma wasn't around any longer to see it.

'We don't actually live in the nineteen-twenties over there, you know,' he snapped back at her. She tried not to flinch, but possibly didn't succeed because he sighed and ran a hand through that floppy hair. Aristocratic hair, she told herself.

'Sorry,' Toby said more gently. 'I'm not… I'm on my way home to Wishcliffe now. To take up the title properly. That's why I was here, having one last wild night before I become the Viscount proper. And I didn't know if I'd told you or not. Because it turns out there are lots of women who had no interest in marrying a guy at all who suddenly do once he's got a title and an estate and some money.'

'I can see that.' It happened in the shows too. And, of course, when an old lord died and the next in line took the seat, it was always a big deal.

Hang on.

'Oh, God, Toby. Your father died! No wonder you were out drinking yourself stupid last night! I'm so sorry.' She knew how it felt to lose family, sometimes twice over. She could imagine the pain he was in right now, and her heart swelled with sympathy.

And she felt like a total manipulative bitch, marrying him when he was mourning. Taking advantage of his vulnerable state. Yes, they'd both been drunk, but he was the one dealing with grief and misery. *She'd* thought it was a bit of fun, and he'd believed it was…what? A chance to cling onto something in a world that had torn everything away? A spark of hope in a time of loss?

She had no idea. But she was sure that Drunk Toby had thought it was a hell of a lot more than she had. And that made an empty feeling open up in the pit of her stomach, one that no amount of pastries could fill. A stupid, fun Vegas wedding was one thing, but she sure as hell hadn't signed up for anything more.

Like marrying into British aristocracy.

Autumn's life philosophy was pretty simple: have fun and move on. In her experience, good things never lasted all that long anyway. Getting out before they got bad was always the safest policy. Besides, who knew what new adventure might be just around the corner?

That was the spirit she'd married Toby in. While he'd been somewhere else entirely, lost in his grief for his father.

God, could this be any more screwed up? She shot Toby another apologetic look, but he stared back at her blankly.

'What? Oh, well, yes. My father died about seven years ago, actually. My older brother Barnaby; he was Viscount. He—' Now he looked away from her, down at his hands, his voice notably softer as he spoke of his brother. 'Barnaby and his eight-year-old son, Harry, died in a sailing accident last year.'

Eight. He was only eight. The same age she'd been when her mother left her on her grandparents' doorstep, swearing she'd be back. Her life had started that day, in some ways. It broke her heart to think of someone else's ending at that same point.

But she could tell from the tightness in Toby's jaw, the tension of his shoulders, that it wasn't something he wanted to discuss further. She could respect that, she supposed.

But wait. 'Last year? How come you're only heading back now, then?' And did that mean he *wasn't* in the grip of sudden and unexpected grief when he'd married her?

Toby gave her a grateful glance for not digging for more personal details. 'I went back for the funeral, then took a year to sort out my own businesses and such, before I go back and take on the mantle of Viscount for the rest of my life.'

Oh, and he looked so happy at the idea of that. Not.

But then, he was the younger son. Grandma's shows had a lot to say about them too. He'd never planned on being the Viscount, she'd guess. Younger sons were the ones who went out and made their own way in the world—and had some fun along the way.

Now he had to give that up for duty. She could see how that could be kind of a drag. If it weren't for the fact that it meant he was richer, had more opportunities and a better quality of life than almost everyone on the planet, that was. That made it a *little* harder to have sympathy for him, she had to admit.

'Don't worry,' he said, obviously misreading her expression. 'I left *our* estate in good hands. I was going to stay after the funeral and take over the estate but…my sister-in-law was still living there. She'd been running it all with Barnaby and I didn't want to, well, kick her out. She said she liked the distraction of having work to do. Plus, I had my *own* businesses to tie up, so we struck a deal. I got a year to sort out my life, and she got another year at Wishcliffe, while we started the handover virtually.'

There was an uncertainty in his eyes as he spoke of

the deal that worried her. Was he concerned about his sister-in-law or the estate?

She shook her head. Not her problem. It wasn't *their* estate, whatever he said. She was not getting dragged into this British period drama.

'Okay, well, I see why we need to get this fixed quickly then. You probably need to go to London and find a proper wife to give you heirs and stuff.' Something else she had no intention of doing.

'Again, Britain is not actually stuck in the Regency period. We joined the twenty-first century with the rest of you.' Autumn shot him a disbelieving look, and he amended, 'Well, at least the late twentieth.'

'The point is, you can't be married to *me*. And I don't want to be married to *you*.'

Which made everything a hell of a lot simpler, really.

'You really didn't know who I was when you married me?' he asked, not accusingly, but more like he just needed to hear it one last time.

'Trust me, if I'd known I'd never have gone through with it. No matter how drunk I was.' For most people these days, marriage was kind of disposable. Especially one undertaken under the influence at the last minute in Vegas.

But Toby wasn't from her world, far more than she'd even realised last night. For British aristocracy, she was pretty sure that a marriage wasn't something a person could just brush off as if it had never happened.

Toby sighed with relief and his shoulders slumped a little. 'Okay. Well, of course I'll make sure you're settled. Financially, I mean. So you don't lose out by this little... unfortunateness.'

'You'll pay me off so I don't go to the papers, you mean.' Oh, now her temper was rising again. She thought they'd established that she wasn't some gold-digger, but here he was, offering her money not to make a scene. Not to disturb his perfectly ordered life. Two heirs down, one to go, and now it was Toby's turn at the title and he wasn't going to let anything disrupt that, was he? However much he might pretend he didn't want to go back to his fancy estate and his giant pile of cash.

'You lost your job because of me,' Toby said, his voice even and calm. 'Since I was unable to procure you another one—besides the unsatisfactory role of being my wife—it stands to reason I should compensate you for that circumstance.'

She could almost see the stick up his ass getting straighter with every highfaluting word he spoke.

'Because obviously I'm incapable of looking after myself, right?'

'Well, you did marry the first guy who came along,' Toby shot back, irritation colouring his tone.

Oh, that was the last straw.

'Because you looked like you might fall apart without me!' He had, she remembered suddenly. He'd looked so lost—not in Vegas, but in life. In himself. *That* was why she'd done it. Because he'd looked, in that moment when he'd proposed, like he needed saving. And with her inhibitions lowered, she couldn't help but say yes.

She shuddered. So stupid of her. Hadn't she promised herself she wouldn't be responsible for another person that way ever again?

It was just as well he was turning out to be such a donkey's behind. That made walking out and finding her own future, alone, much easier.

But not before she told him a few home truths.

'You obviously don't realise it, but I am *not* going to fall apart without *you*.' She stood up as she spoke, towering over him from atop the four-poster bed as she shook a finger at him the way her grandmother would have done. Although Grandma definitely wouldn't have been wearing nothing but a bathrobe and last night's make-up. Autumn suspected the whole thing would have been much more effective if she wasn't wobbling slightly on the too-soft mattress.

'I didn't say—' Toby started, his back ramrod-straight again, but Autumn cut him off.

'I know your type. You think women are weak, helpless, in need of saving. Well, maybe the ones you meet at your garden parties at the Palace or whatever need you to save them, but not me. I can save myself. I've been doing it for long enough. I've been on my own in this world for years, and responsible for myself and others since long before I turned eighteen and, trust me, I've made the best of it. I've worked on cruise ships and plantations, I've organised weddings at a palace and fundraisers in museums, I've dealt blackjack as often as I've tended bar, I've sung backup for the Danish Eurovision entry—I've even worked as a mermaid!' She was on a roll now, righteous anger coursing through her veins, and she knew Toby was pinned to his seat by her words. Time to really drive her point home. 'I've done jobs you don't even know exist, and I've kept myself afloat doing it. And do you know how? Because I know one thing that you never will—how to get along with people. In fact, I'll give you a tip for free. Step one: don't offer them money instead of talking to them like a human.'

It would have been the perfect time to flounce out, if she'd been fully clothed. As it was, she could do nothing but stand on the bed, her breath coming too fast, watching him watch her.

His eyes narrowed. 'You're right,' he said, and she almost fell over with surprise.

'I'm right.'

'Of course you are.' He pushed himself up to standing, wincing at the effort. She suspected her rant hadn't helped his hangover much either.

Good. I'm not here to help him.

'Come on, let's go and get some real breakfast, and we can talk. Like humans.'

The hotel obviously served an extensive breakfast buffet, but it was also the first place Finn would look for him when he got back from wherever he'd run off to that morning, so Toby avoided it. Instead, once they'd both showered and dressed—and he'd persuaded the front desk to let him hang on to the room for a little longer, for a price—he let Autumn lead him away from the main Strip and to a breakfast diner called Bagel-Bagel which, counter-intuitively, seemed mostly to serve pancakes.

As she perused the menu, he studied her instead. He'd known her less than a day, and had been blackout drunk for most of that, but still he felt as if he understood her already. As if he could see deeper into who she was than he usually managed with people.

Most of the people in his life had either always been there—the family friends, the old school and university mates—or were business acquaintances he'd met since he'd set out on his own, where all he needed to really know about them was whether or not they were likely to invest in the company he'd founded with Finn when they'd left university.

The other group were the residents on the estate that his family had owned for generation after generation, many of whom knew his own family history better than he did himself.

Still, it wasn't like he was bad with people, whatever Autumn thought. He was generally thought of as a fairly amiable chap. The fun younger Blythe brother. He knew how to deal with people.

He just didn't know how to deal with *her*.

She, of course, had no such problem. She happily chatted with their server, debating the merits of various pancakey offerings with him before plumping for something so sweet it made Toby's teeth ache just reading the description.

He ordered more coffee and a bagel, because really, the place was *called* Bagel-Bagel. Then he put his menu aside and found Autumn watching him, much as he'd been watching her.

'So,' she said, after a pause that stretched out into awkwardness. 'You wanted to talk.'

It seemed to Toby that they'd been doing nothing *but* talking since they'd woken up and realised the mess they were in. It just hadn't got them anywhere. It was time to take action, to make decisions, all the sort of thing a viscount had to do, from what he remembered from the lessons his father had taught Barnaby. As a younger son, the lessons had never been for him, but he'd tagged along often enough to get the gist.

Do the right thing. Be bold but sensible. Keep the status quo.

Give everything you've got to your duty, even if it kills you.

That sort of thing.

And as he'd watched her lecturing him on his many flaws, and telling him how capable and likeable she was, an obvious solution to both his problems had occurred to him. One he was almost sure wasn't totally influenced by how magnificent she'd looked, angry in a bathrobe.

His father and his brother had both *loved* Wishcliffe in a way he'd never managed to quite feel, but they'd both also freely admitted that the responsibility, as much as the actual management of the estate, was a lot. But neither of them had tried to do it alone.

His father had his mother by his side. Barnaby had Victoria.

Maybe that was what Toby needed too. Someone at his side as he took on this new challenge.

'Come on, Tobes.' In his head, Barnaby sounded about twelve again. *'There's nothing to be scared of if we're together, right? Safety in numbers.'*

Back then, his brother had probably been talking about exploring the caves in the cliffs or running through the neighbouring farmer's fields. But the point still held.

There was safety in numbers. And Toby was alone.

Or he had been, until he'd woken up married.

Still, now the time came to actually put his plan to her, the words seemed stuck in his throat. Was this crazy? Probably. But it was still the only plan he had.

'I've been thinking.' In between the pounding hangover and the being shouted at. 'About this marriage thing. I know it might not have been exactly planned on either side, but you *are* my wife.' The marriage certificate had shown up in the pocket of the trousers he'd been wearing the night before, already creased and crumpled.

'If this is you about to offer me money again—'

'It's not,' Toby said quickly. Now he'd had some more coffee, he could see the flaws in that plan. He'd never paid for sex—he wasn't about to start paying for marriage. Not to mention the scandal it would cause if it came out. His father would be revolving slowly in his grave already, but if anyone else found out what had actually happened here he'd probably go into a full-on spin.

'Then what?' Autumn asked impatiently. 'I've got to go and clear out my room after this. And, you know, find another job.' She waved her phone at him too fast for him to make out anything more than the vague impression of a text message. 'My roommate says the boss is about to throw my stuff out into the street if I don't go and collect it. I mean, I travel lighter than most, but I'd still like to not lose *everything* I possess, if you don't mind?'

'I think we should stay married.' The words flew out unbidden, sending Autumn's eyes wide and her mouth clamped shut. 'I meant to build up to that a bit more,' he admitted, rubbing a hand across his aching brow. 'Explain my reasons and such. But, in essence, I think we should stay married and you should come to Wishcliffe with me. For a time.'

'For a time,' Autumn echoed, letting out a breath. 'So this isn't a happy-ever-after thing? You don't think you've suddenly fallen in love with me because I shouted at you or anything? I mean, I know you high class Brits have some issues—'

He couldn't help but laugh at that, which seemed to reassure Autumn. Her shoulders relaxed back down from up by her ears and she smiled cautiously as she awaited his response.

'I assure you, this is purely a convenience, for both of us.'

'Moving to the other side of the world is convenient for me?' Autumn reached for her coffee cup, her eyebrows raised sceptically.

'Having a roof over your head and a job that pays a decent salary would be convenient for you, I imagine.' He'd never really been in a position where he'd been without either, but Toby couldn't believe it was very comfortable.

'So being married to you is a job now, is it?' She tilted her head to the side as she blinked at him.

Toby thought of his mother, who'd slipped peacefully away three years after his father, as if she'd simply run out of reasons to stay alive. The moment she was no longer the lady of the manor, the moment Barnaby became the Viscount, she'd had no purpose. She'd haunted Wishcliffe like a ghost those last few years, as much as Victoria had tried to involve her in the work on the estate.

His mother had made Wishcliffe, and his father, her life's work. And while there was plenty she could have done with her life after his death, being Lady Wishcliffe had seemed to be the pinnacle of everything she'd wanted.

He worried that Victoria would feel the same way. That was why he'd given her the year, when she'd asked. But now…they'd stayed in touch over the last twelve months, and she'd slowly involved him more and more in discussions and decisions about the estate. But she hadn't talked about herself, how she was coping with such unimaginable losses. How she could still look out over the cliffs behind the house at the sea that had taken her husband and son every day.

Those were things to ask when he returned. But he couldn't ask Victoria to give any more to Wishcliffe.

And he wasn't asking Autumn to give her whole life over to the estate. He only needed six months from her. He wasn't staying any longer than that.

'It is, the way I see it,' he confirmed. 'I told you I'm going back to Wishcliffe to take over the reins as Viscount. But it's not what I see myself doing for the rest of my life.' Not least because he wanted the rest of his life to last a little longer than the last two Viscounts' had.

'I'm not sure a hereditary title is something you can just give up.'

Watch me.

'Various members of the aristocracy and at least one ex-King would beg to differ. Besides, it's not the title I object to particularly. It's the estate itself. My family have fought for years to try and keep it viable, to keep everyone employed, to keep the local village going. But it's a losing battle.'

'You're planning to sell the estate?' Her eyes widened again as he nodded to confirm her guess was correct. 'Then what on earth do you need a wife for?'

'These things take time.' Despite Victoria's updates, until he got there and looked things over himself, Toby had no real idea of the condition of the estate or the accounts. He trusted his sister-in-law, and the people she'd got working for her, but selling was different to maintaining the estate. He needed to get a handle on what he was selling before he could name a price. And even then, finding the right buyer could take a fair while. He might not want to be Viscount himself, but that didn't mean he was willing to throw the people of Wishcliffe to the wolves. He'd only sell to someone who would do right by the estate. 'And I don't want any fuss.'

Autumn rolled her eyes at that. 'You Brits never do.' Then her eyes narrowed. 'I assume you mean that you don't want any of the people dependent on the estate to get wind of what you're doing until you've got a deal sewn up?'

She really was a lot more perceptive than he'd given her credit for. That, or his hangover was making him even less subtle than usual. He tipped his coffee cup to acknowledge her point.

'Okay, so you want to go back to Wishcliffe with a little wife in tow to convince people that everything is just hunky-dory, or whatever it is you people say, then in a year's time—'

'Six months.'

'Fine, six months, we…what? Just disappear into the sunset and never see each other again?'

'Basically. I haven't really thought through *all* the details.'

She tapped her short nails against the side of her coffee cup. 'I don't see why having a wife is integral to this plan.'

'It isn't,' Toby admitted with a shrug. 'But since I find myself in possession of one, it seems to make sense to use the advantage.'

Her beautiful face scrunched up into a scowl. 'I don't like being referred to as a possession.'

'I wasn't—' Toby sighed and started again. 'What I mean is, I could do this alone—that was my plan. But, thinking about it on the walk over here, I saw what drunk me meant last night, about solving both our problems.'

'So we're trusting the version of you that got married to a woman whose last name you didn't know to plan our future. Good to know.'

'You didn't know mine either,' he pointed out. How had she imagined today going? Not like this; that much was clear. But she must have had some idea. He'd ask her maybe, later. If she came to Wishcliffe with him. 'The point is, having a wife—a Lady Blythe—has certain advantages.'

'Which are?' Autumn asked. 'I mean, if I'm applying for the job, I'd at least like to hear the job description.'

It was easy enough to think back and list all the things he remembered his mother doing. And there were a few other chores that had occurred to him on the walk over that Toby was happy to add.

'A lot of it is running the household, although you'll have a staff to help with that. I imagine I'll be expected to throw some sort of social gatherings upon my return—you said you planned weddings at one point?' She gave a short nod. 'Great, so that shouldn't be a problem. Um… another big part is basically being charming and liked. Which apparently you're much better at than me anyway.'

'True,' she said without a shred of modesty. 'But won't my being an American be an issue?'

He shrugged. 'I'd like to think we've moved on, so hopefully not. Besides, if everyone takes against you, that could work too.'

'You mean they'll be glad to see the back of us when you sell?'

'Precisely.' Toby paused, uncertain whether to add his final reason. One beyond just not wanting to do this alone. But Autumn called him on it before he could decide.

'What else?' she asked, pinning him with that direct green gaze. 'I can tell there's another reason.'

'I need a shield.' It sounded so weak, but it was true. He remembered Barnaby and Harry's funerals, the assessing gazes of the society women—and Julia's more direct proposition—and shuddered.

'A shield?' Understanding dawned in her bright eyes and Autumn's lips curved up into a wide smile. 'To protect you from all the gold-digging ladies, right? Boy, you really do have a complex. You truly think they're going to be throwing themselves at your feet just because you have a title?'

Toby glowered at her, as darkly as his hangover would permit. 'Maybe not all of them. But my ex—'

'Ah! Say no more. I know about terrible exes.' Sitting back in her chair, Autumn surveyed him across the table, and he knew she was weighing every aspect of his proposal. Probably figuring out how much to ask for to perform the role for six months. 'So, let's be sure I've got this right. You want to pay me to play lady of the manor for you for six months, protect you from money-grabbing exes, distract the locals from the fact you're selling up, then divorce you and go our separate ways at the end of it. Right?'

'Right.' He wondered how much she'd ask for. Toby had a figure in mind, but he could be flexible. After all, he was getting a good deal either way. And he *had* got her fired last night.

She needed this job.

Which was why her response blindsided him so completely.

CHAPTER THREE

'No.'

He blinked at her as if he'd never heard the word before. 'Excuse me?'

'No, thank you?' she tried.

'I don't understand.'

Clearly he didn't. Maybe he really *hadn't* ever been told no before. He was a viscount, after all. Even if that was a fairly recent development, the odds were that his life before that had been pretty charmed too.

Well, hers hadn't. And she knew better than to believe any offer that sounded too good to be true.

He hadn't even named a salary, presumably waiting for her to ask for what she thought it was worth. Or hoping he could get away with paying less than he would have offered outright, if she undervalued herself.

He was offering her a life of luxury as lady of the manor, all the way over in Britain, and all she had to do in return was throw a few parties and smile at people who weren't his ex?

Yeah, no. There was *definitely* a catch here.

She might believe in seeking out new experiences and fun, in taking chances and hoping for the best, but this… this was making her nervous.

'Look, whatever it is you're planning, whatever

scheme or con you're running, I'm out. I mean, actually marrying me was one heck of a move, but I'm still not buying it, okay?' The guy had surely committed to whatever the hell this ploy was, but a marriage certificate didn't really have to *mean* anything these days, did it? Not if she didn't want it to.

'I am no conman,' Toby said, his words clipped and sharp. 'And since we *are* married, whether you like it or not, and without a prenup, that gives you certain rights over my estates and finances. Ones I would like to reconcile fairly *before* I sell Wishcliffe.'

That gave her pause. She wasn't exactly up on marriage law on this side of the pond or the other. But if he was thinking she was likely to sue for alimony in any divorce, he really hadn't been paying attention to who she was at all.

'So this is all just another attempt to pay me off and sign away my rights?' She laughed. 'Toby, I'm not even sure I believe you're an actual lord or a viscount or whatever. I'm hardly likely to divorce you for half your estates.'

'You really think I'm trying to scam you?' He crossed his arms over his chest and raised an eyebrow. 'Because this seems like an awful lot of trouble to go to when it seems to me you don't have much worth scamming you for.'

This was true. The text from her roommate had only reminded her of that; Cindy had already packed Autumn's meagre belongings into her single suitcase and small backpack. But that was because Autumn liked to travel light, not because the things she owned weren't valuable.

To her, anyway. She was pretty sure Toby wouldn't get anything much for her grandma's bible on the open market. Hell, he'd lost more than her overall net worth at the card table the night before.

But money wasn't the only thing worth conning people for. She'd lost money before, believing the wrong person. But she'd lost more than that too. She'd lost trust. Faith. In the world and in herself.

Lost control over her own life for a time, and not even seen it until it was almost too late.

That was the last time she'd dared to think of something longer term than 'just fun for now'. With Robbie. He was the only time she'd let herself believe in happy ever after—only to be reminded, once again, that nothing good lasted, and people weren't always what they seemed.

She'd escaped that situation—run away, giving up the money she'd arrived with in return for her freedom. Robbie had spent most of it by then, anyway—all the proceeds of the sale of her grandparents' house. The bank balance that had seemed unimaginably huge straight after the sale had trickled away fast enough as soon as Robbie had his hands on her bank card.

So maybe Toby wasn't after her money. Maybe he hadn't been as drunk as he'd seemed last night. Maybe he was just trying to trap her into a controlling marriage where she lost everything about herself that mattered. She'd only met him last night, after all. He could be lying about everything.

Even though her heart said he wasn't. Her heart told her he was exactly what he appeared to be. A rich, gorgeous British guy who'd suffered a lot of loss and was now obviously going through some sort of crisis of confidence. One he seemed to think she could help solve.

But maybe her heart wasn't the best thing for her to be listening to. It had led her astray before, after all.

Autumn pulled a few notes from the pocket of her jacket and tossed them onto the table to cover her share of the bill.

'Maybe this is legit, maybe not. Maybe you really are a viscount. But I'm out.'

She turned away from the table before Toby could tempt her to stay—with his words, or even another one of those heart-stopping smiles—and walked straight into the broad chest of another guy.

'He really is a viscount, you know.' The guy stepped back and smiled gently down at her. 'And in thirty years of being his best friend, and ten of running a business with him, I've never known him do something that wasn't "legit".' He looked between her and Toby and took the seat opposite his friend, motioning for Autumn to take the one beside him.

She wavered for a moment. She should leave. She was already leaving.

But she kind of wanted to see how Toby was going to explain his way out of this one. And at some point they were going to have to sort out that divorce thing, so it wasn't like she could completely walk out of his life for ever in one dramatic move, anyway.

She sat down.

Toby's friend grinned. 'So, what's going on, guys? And why wasn't I invited to breakfast?'

'How did you even know where we were?' Toby asked, his head starting to pound again as Finn motioned to the waitress for a menu.

'I set up the tracker on your phone.' Finn reached across, stole Toby's black Americano and took a gulp. 'Before I left you last night. Just in case.'

'Well, you're a few hours too late tracking it,' Autumn

drawled from her seat beside Finn. 'I mean, if you were hoping to keep the Viscount here out of trouble.'

Finn shot him a surprised look. Toby didn't usually advertise his title if he could help it, and his best friend knew that. Of course Autumn read the look as confirmation that the Viscount thing was rubbish—he could tell by the way her eyebrows shot up and an *I knew it!* smile appeared on her list.

'She doesn't believe I'm a viscount,' Toby said tiredly.

'Neither do I, most days.' Finn grinned. 'But it is sadly true. Hang on, I'll show you.' Phone still in hand, he swiped the screen a few times then held it up to Autumn. 'See? The Wishcliffe estate website, with our Toby's photo front and centre.'

Toby groaned. He'd objected to that website update but been comprehensively overruled.

'And if that's not enough…' Finn whipped the phone away, swiped a few more times, then pushed it back towards Autumn. 'News reports of his brother's death and Toby's ascension to the title. Ooh, look! There's a nice bit about the business in here too…'

Autumn glanced at the screen, then looked away. 'Fine. So he's a viscount. And he has a business…' She squinted at the text again. 'Helping companies embrace the remote revolution, whatever that is. That doesn't mean I have to stay married to him.'

Under any other circumstances, Toby would have enjoyed the sight of Finn being rendered speechless for once. He was damn sure it hadn't happened at any other time in their friendship.

Even now, it didn't last for very long.

Finn blinked several times, fast, and looked between them, his mouth open.

'I left you alone for a couple of hours and you got *married*?'

Toby sighed and nodded.

'In fairness, you left him alone *drunk* in *Vegas*,' Autumn pointed out. 'It's not like this is totally unprecedented.'

'I assume you were also alcoholically impaired?' Finn asked.

'Well, he'd just got me fired and lost me my home, so when he offered to buy me drinks I didn't say no.'

The waitress returned with Finn's coffee and he took it with a flirtatious smile and a thank you, before turning back to them, his face stern. 'Tell me everything.'

So they did.

Well, not *quite* everything. There were huge chunks that Toby couldn't fully remember, and Autumn didn't seem any more inclined than he would have been to fill in the part that covered spending their wedding night together. Other than a pink flush to her cheeks when she said the word 'consummated', he wouldn't have known that she was remembering it at all.

It was enough to send Finn into uproarious laughter anyway. 'Oh, this is priceless. I mean, really. Toby. This beats the time you swapped rooms with that Russian guy on the Belize trip and ended up accosted by the doctor in stockings and suspenders.'

A story a good friend would never let die, of course.

'This is not making me feel any more confident about his plan,' Autumn said flatly.

'And what exactly *is* his plan?' Finn turned to her with a curious grin.

'He wants me to go to England with him as his wife for six months, play lady of the manor and get paid for it, then disappear as soon as the divorce is sorted.' She didn't mention him selling the estate, and Toby couldn't quite tell if that was because she knew it was a secret, even from Finn, or because it was the least important part of the situation to her. Either way, he was grateful.

'Sounds like a good gig to me,' Finn said with a shrug, as if just picking up a wife for six months was perfectly normal. Given the way Finn was approaching his own life lately, maybe it was. Toby would be more worried about his friend if he didn't have his own mess to deal with. 'Assuming it's all business rather than pleasure?'

'Of course!' Toby straightened in his chair at the implication. Then he looked at Autumn. Had *she* been thinking he was suggesting setting her up as his mistress for six months? Because that might explain things.

But she just rolled her eyes. 'No, this was very much a business proposal. Don't worry, I'm not going to get him arrested for soliciting or anything.'

Toby put his head in his hands so he couldn't see Finn's patronising head shake.

'I really shouldn't let you out without a minder, should I?' his best friend asked.

'I don't know why I thought you'd make this harder,' Toby muttered. 'Really, you're a huge help.'

He'd considered, for a moment, taking Finn into his confidence about his fears for the estate, and why he had to sell it. Finn was his oldest friend, his business partner, and he'd trust him with almost everything.

But Finn had spent his whole adult life trying to regain his own family estate, his heritage, after his father sold it purely to spite him. Of all the people in the world, he knew Finn *couldn't* understand this.

Maybe that was why Toby's inebriated mind had latched onto Autumn for support instead.

Finn turned back to Autumn. 'So, now you know he's the real deal, are you going to go along with his plan?'

'Do you think I should?' she asked.

'Great. So you trust his opinion—the man you just met—more than mine. The man you actually married.' The insult stung, no matter how ridiculous the situation.

'I've known you for maybe twelve hours longer. Fifteen at the most.' Her tone was dismissive but, as she met his gaze, Toby saw something else there.

She *did* know him better. She knew his body. She knew how he kissed. How he felt inside her.

And she, damn her, could remember all that, even if he couldn't.

But hell, he wanted to. Badly.

This isn't a sex proposition. This is strictly business, he reminded himself sternly. Not that his libido seemed to be listening.

Finn looked as if he was seriously considering her question, which didn't make anything feel better. Toby tried not to squirm in his chair like a schoolboy as he waited for his friend's answer.

'I think that Wishcliffe is an excellent place. I think Toby is one of the finest men I've ever met, and you can trust his integrity on any deal you strike. I think it could be a fun opportunity to visit Britain, stay in a stately home and make a little cash along the way. And obviously Toby here thinks that having someone else along for the ride will make his homecoming easier, for some reason.' Finn leant closer to Autumn, his expression more serious than Toby was used to seeing. 'But, mostly, I think it has to be your decision.'

She was wavering. He could see the indecision in the way her gaze darted between him and Finn.

She was going to say yes. He wasn't going to have to return to Wishcliffe and face all those memories alone.

The thought caught him off-guard. Was that truly what this was about? It seemed he'd been thinking with his heart more than his head ever since he'd sat down at that card table last night.

That or you just really want to get in her knickers again.

The voice in his head, as ever, was Barnaby's. His elder brother offering advice from beyond the grave—even if Toby knew that in reality it was only his own guess at what his brother would say.

Barnaby couldn't help him now.

He mentally shushed the voice as Autumn opened her mouth to speak.

'I'll think about it,' she said.

And then she walked out of the diner, leaving Toby alone with his very amused best friend and a marriage certificate.

Autumn sucked in the thick air of the Vegas side street as she stepped outside the diner. She didn't dare look back, walking quickly in the direction of the main Strip. She couldn't look at those men again. She needed to think.

Was she really considering moving to England to play house with a guy she'd only met the night before?

Yes.

She shouldn't be. It was a crazy idea. Damnably stupid. Her grandparents would be horrified at the very idea.

Well. Grandma would probably like the viscount part, and Granddad would just assume she'd *'got into trouble like your mother'*, since he was apparently unaware of things like birth control pills. And even in the heat of the wedding night, she and Toby had managed to remember to use a condom. *That* wasn't what she was worried about.

What *was* she worried about? She'd taken jobs on far less information, travelled the world without a moment's hesitation when someone asked, moved in with people she only knew from an advert in the paper.

Her whole adult life had been spent taking chances and seeking new experiences.

But not since Robbie.

Robbie was what had changed—he'd changed her. She'd not left Vegas since she'd arrived, racing away from him and a bad situation. He hadn't followed—he'd had her money, which was all he'd really cared about, she supposed. He'd probably moved onto the next susceptible young woman with ready cash who would fall for his charm. Probably never given her a second thought.

But he was still living rent-free in her head.

When she'd sold her grandparents' house she'd made herself a promise—that after so many years of living up to their expectations, and then of nursing them through their final illnesses, she'd never get tied down again. She'd go wherever the wind blew, take every chance, seize every opportunity to live life to the fullest.

And she had. Right up until she'd found Robbie, and lost herself. Until she'd forgotten that nothing good ever lasted, and it was always better to get out while things were still fun.

Her mother had taught her that, in a way, as much as her grandparents had. Her mom's life had been nothing but fun, until she had Autumn. Then, when things had got really bad, she'd left Autumn with her grandparents and gone on to find new adventures again, only coming back for occasional visits where she told her about all the amazing things out there in the world waiting for her, when she grew up.

Her grandparents, of course, had a rather different view of what Autumn's life should be like. And she'd tried, really she had, to live up to what they'd wanted for her. But then they'd got sick, and she'd felt the wind calling, just like her mom had said it would, before her visits had stopped altogether.

Shaking her head, Autumn ducked down a side street towards Harry's Casino and Bar, where, until last night, she'd been an employee. Whatever she decided, she needed to get her stuff together before Harry tossed it in the nearest dumpster.

Slipping around the back, she climbed the metal fire escape to her door and let herself in. Cindy must be downstairs working, as the place was empty—although her suitcase was leaning against her un-slept-in bed.

Autumn took a moment to look around and remember the place. Her room above the casino wasn't much, but it had been home for the last year. She wasn't exactly sorry to say goodbye to it, but it had been another stepping stone on her route through life. She liked to keep track of where she'd been, as much as where she was going.

With that in mind, she grabbed the flyer for Harry's Casino and Bar that lay on the table by the window and tucked it inside her rucksack. Then she turned around and walked out, locking the door behind her and slipping the key through the letterbox.

Another part of her life she was done with. Time to move on.

She just had to decide where to.

As she passed the front door to the bar, it flew open and Cindy came rushing out, her blonde curls angelic around her heart-shaped face.

'You're leaving. Do you have somewhere to go?' She bit down on her lower lip, her eyes wide with concern.

Autumn shrugged. 'I have some options. Don't worry about me.' Cindy had never become a really close friend—they didn't have enough in common for that—but she'd been a decent roommate and work colleague. Autumn was *almost* sad to say goodbye to her, except she'd promised herself years ago that, for her, goodbyes would only ever mean new opportunities, not sadness about what she was leaving behind.

'I just hate to think of you being on your own.' What Cindy actually meant, Autumn was sure, was, *I'd hate to be on my own, so you must too.*

People always thought that. People were wrong.

She laughed lightly, to try and reduce Cindy's concern. 'Honestly, it's fine! I've spent plenty of time on my own before, and I really don't mind it.' She'd say she preferred it, but she didn't want to hurt Cindy's feelings.

Cindy's smile turned sly and knowing. 'What about the guy you left here with last night? Not thinking of running away with him, perhaps?'

It would make Cindy worry less if she thought Autumn was leaving to be with some guy. Which was ridiculous, since in Autumn's experience that was a far riskier proposition than going anywhere on her own.

Still. She didn't want her friend to worry.

'He has offered to take me back to Britain for a few months, for a visit,' she confided.

'You should go!' Cindy's eyes widened to cartoon proportions. 'How often are you going to get *that* kind of opportunity?' Her smile turned dreamy. 'Maybe he'll turn out to be a lord or something, or live in a castle. Maybe you'll meet the Queen!'

Autumn laughed. 'I don't think so. But…you think I should go?'

Cindy's gaze turned serious. 'Autumn. I've spent a whole year listening to you tell stories of all the adventures you used to have, the places you've seen, the people you've met—the crazy parties you've gate-crashed and the weird jobs you've done. Be honest. This is probably the longest you've stayed in one place since you left home. Isn't it?'

'I guess.' Even with Robbie she'd only managed eleven months. Over a year was a definite record. Had it really been so long since she'd arrived in Vegas, broke and desperate? She supposed it had. Which was weird, because it was only ever meant to be a stopgap. Somewhere to get back on her feet again.

'Well, aren't you ready for a change?' Cindy asked.

Autumn nodded slowly. She'd found her feet, then lost them again last night. She'd taken her first step onto her next crazy adventure by marrying Toby in the first place—a drunken glimpse of the girl she'd been before Robbie stole that from her. Was she really going to stop there? Say no to adventure and go back to hiding from a guy who'd probably not even thought about her twice since she'd left?

No. She was not.

And besides, this wasn't like it had been with Robbie. Toby *needed* her as his wife. She didn't need or love him. Which meant she had all the power. She could walk away at any time.

She'd stay for the fun and leave before it could go bad. Just like she always had before Robbie.

She'd be *herself* again.

'You're right.' She grabbed the handle of her suitcase tight. 'I'm going to go.'

Cindy beamed. 'Good.' Then she glanced over her shoulder and her smile fell. 'But…uh…you might want to go fast. Harry's heading over and he's still pretty pissed about last night.'

'Got it.' Leaning in, Autumn gave her friend a quick hug, then grabbed her bags. 'I'll see you.'

'Let me know you get there safe!' Cindy called after her.

Autumn waved to show she'd heard, but she didn't turn around.

She wasn't going backwards. She was moving on.

But she was going to do it on *her* terms—not Toby's.

CHAPTER FOUR

THE TINTED WINDOWS of the limousine Finn had called to take them to the airport mercifully blocked out the worst of the early afternoon sun, but it wasn't enough to stop Toby's head from pounding.

He'd waited back at the hotel room until the last possible minute, but there was no sign of Autumn. Which meant he was going back to Wishcliffe alone, and he'd still have to find a way to get in touch with her once he was there to organise the divorce.

As if he hadn't been dreading returning home enough in the first place.

He groaned as he realised he was going to have to tell the family lawyer what he'd done, and get his help to resolve it. Old Mr Stevens had been the Blythes' lawyer since long before Toby was born and, since he appeared to be basically immortal at this point, he'd probably still be the family lawyer long after he was dead too. He *had* to have seen worse than this in his career, right? Still, a viscount getting drunk and married to a barmaid in Vegas…that wasn't exactly the sort of thing that was going to bring honour and respect to the title or the estate. Especially in the absence of any prenuptial agreement protecting his finances.

They'd just have to keep it very, very quiet and hope

that the papers never caught wind of it. Autumn didn't seem like the type to kiss and tell, but Toby knew from friends' experiences that a person could never be totally sure of that. If she needed the money…

I offered her money, he thought irritably.

He'd offered her more than money.

And she'd turned him down.

Toby wasn't used to being turned down. Turned out he didn't like it very much.

In fairness, she'd said that she'd think about it, but Toby knew what that meant. It was something a person said when they didn't want the hassle of saying 'no' right then.

The door to the limo opened, letting in a shaft of blindingly bright light. Toby winced and covered his eyes.

'Jesus, Finn, shut the door, will you?'

There was a shuffle and suddenly a scent Toby half recognised. Not Finn's aftershave, for sure. Something softer, not sweeter. Something that made his body tighten reflexively.

'I'll sit up front and let you two talk,' Finn said as he slammed the door shut, the vibrations making Toby grit his teeth.

Then, once he was sure the car was dark again, he opened his eyes.

Autumn sat opposite him, her auburn hair curling around her shoulders, her green eyes bright, looking far better than anyone who'd got drunk enough to marry a stranger the night before had any right to look.

'I've thought about it,' she said. As if that was really what she'd meant when she'd said she would. Huh. Who'd have thought?

'And?' Toby asked. With anyone else, he'd take the fact that she was in his limo to the airport with a suitcase as a sign of a done deal. But this was Autumn. She could just be scamming a ride before she got on a plane to anywhere but where Toby was. He wouldn't be surprised.

'I have conditions,' she said with a warning tone in her voice.

'Of course you do.' She had all the power here—the future of his estate and finances in her slender fingers. But conditions meant she was considering it. Planning on going with him to Wishcliffe, even, as long as he agreed.

Conditions he could work with.

'First, I'll sign up for three months, not six,' she said. 'After that, I want to be off on a new adventure, okay?'

Three months. That gave him until, what, early December? He could work with that. If need be he could always claim she'd gone home to her family in the States for the holidays. He'd need to work fast on selling the estate, but it was doable. And maybe he'd be able to talk her into another week or two if he really needed it, for a price.

'Okay. What else?'

'Money.'

Naturally. 'How much do you want?'

She shook her head. 'It's not about that—well, I mean, it is, of course. This is a job. But, whatever we decide on as a salary, I want it all in writing. A formal contract—one that makes it clear I'm not after anything from you in the divorce either. I want everything upfront and official.'

'That sounds like one of my conditions, not yours.'

She gave him a lopsided grin. 'I just don't want anyone to be able to say I did this to scam you out of anything.'

'Your motives are pure.'

'Absolutely. I'm only doing this because of how pathetically hungover you look right now.'

Toby winced. 'You know that wives are supposed to bolster a man's ego, not tear it down, right?'

'Wives are supposed to be honest with their husbands,' Autumn said, straightening her shoulders and looking down her nose at him. Then she dropped the superior act with a grin. 'Or so I've heard, anyway. I've never actually been married before.'

Toby started as the limo jolted forward, but it wasn't the movement of the car that had startled him, he realised. It was Autumn. He'd had no idea if she'd ever been married before. He knew nothing about her—and he was inviting her into his home.

Suddenly, he wondered if this really was the best idea he'd ever had.

But it was too late now; she was already listing her conditions. At least the financial paperwork one worked for him.

'Is that it?' he asked, and she shook her head.

'One more.'

'Name it.'

He could see her chest rising as she sucked in a deep breath and he knew that, whatever it was, he wasn't going to like it.

'No sex,' she said, and he blinked.

'Isn't it a little late for that? I mean, granted, I don't remember *everything*—'

'You don't remember anything,' Finn yelled from the front seat, ruining the illusion that they had any privacy at all. 'Because you are terrible when you're drunk.'

'But we definitely woke up naked,' Toby finished.

'No sex *from now on*,' Autumn ground out through gritted teeth.

Toby considered her words. It wasn't as if he'd actually imagined they *would* be having sex—this was a business proposition, after all, not a real marriage. But now she'd explicitly ruled it out…

He wished he could remember. Wished he at least had the memory of her body under his, around his. Of her lips against his own. Of her kiss, her touch…her everything.

Except maybe that would be worse. Because then he'd know exactly what he was saying goodbye to here. More than just the memory of her bare skin covered by thin bedsheets, or that gaping bathrobe.

'Goes without saying,' he said as casually as he could manage now he had the image of Autumn in that bathrobe, bouncing on his hotel bed, stuck in his brain. 'This is business, not pleasure, after all. But it's always good to have the specifics spelled out. Means less confusion, right?'

'Exactly.' Autumn gave a sharp nod. 'So you agree?'

'I do,' he said, only realising a moment too late, as a loud chuckle came from Finn in the front of the car, exactly what he'd said.

'You already said that last night, mate.' Finn pulled open the screen dividing the driver's area from the luxurious back seat of the limo. 'But glad you two have got all that sorted out. Now, let's see how long it lasts, eh?'

It would last the agreed three months at least, Toby knew, as he held his new wife's gaze. Because he'd do whatever it took to make sure he didn't have to face being at Wishcliffe alone.

They spent the rest of the ride to the airport in awkward silence. Autumn had expected long queues and annoying waits like every other time she'd taken a plane anywhere, but it turned out that travelling with Toby and Finn was a whole new experience.

First, there was the way that the limo swept them right up to the entrance, without any parking garages or shuttle drop-offs miles from the right terminal. Then they bypassed all the queues and got shown directly to a private lounge, where Toby promptly collapsed into an armchair and fell asleep, while Finn pulled out his laptop to work. Autumn distracted Toby's friend with questions for a little while, until he had to take a call and Autumn was left to, well, think.

She stared out of the window, watching planes take off and land, and wondered how she'd got there. And then, somewhere mid thought, she must have fallen asleep too, because the next thing she knew, Toby was shaking her arm gently to wake her and she was being shown into the most opulent first-class compartment she'd ever imagined could exist.

'Wow.' It wasn't just the seats that turned into actual beds, with real mattresses, or the privacy screens and the TVs and the clatter of real crockery. It was the smiles of the staff, the deferential looks, as if she had to be someone who *mattered* to be there.

She supposed she was, in a way.

She was Viscountess Wishcliffe. Kind of.

'You're lucky he didn't insist on hiring a private plane,' Finn murmured as he passed her, claiming his own sleep pod and putting earbuds in, clearly ready to ignore the world for the ten or so hours it would take them to get to London.

'We're over here.' Toby guided her to her seat, next to his but separate enough for her not to feel crowded. Geez, this was a long way from her usual economy class seat, crammed between two other people in the middle row.

She'd expected Toby to sleep through the flight like he'd slept through the wait, or at least to ignore her in favour of the in-flight entertainment. But instead, as the plane climbed to reach its cruising altitude, he turned to her, a small frown line between his brows. They hadn't pulled the screen shut between them, but he still had to lean forward a little to talk to her.

'Can I ask you something?'

'Of course.' They were husband and wife now, after all, as well as boss and employee. She supposed he deserved to ask her a few interview questions.

'Why the no sex rule?'

Except that was no interview question.

Before she could respond, Toby ploughed on, his frown deepening. 'I don't mean… I mean, I understand that you might… Well, what I mean is…'

'Toby?'

He stuttered to a stop. 'Yes?'

'Take a breath and start again.'

With a grateful smile, he did just that. 'What I was trying to say was, I'm not questioning your reasons for not wanting to sleep with me. I can absolutely see why you might want that boundary in place, especially now we're working together, so to speak.'

'So what's the question?'

Looking up, he met her gaze with his own, and she was surprised to find genuine concern there. 'Why did you feel the need to state it? Because if I did anything to make you feel like it was necessary, or—'

'Toby, no.' Autumn smiled reassuringly at him.

He was sweet. She hadn't really expected him to be sweet. Up until now he'd mostly been grouchy, controlling and difficult.

Apparently all he needed to be a decent human being was a catnap in the first-class lounge.

'I was just thinking, when I was dozing at the airport. And I was worried that you thought I might have other ideas about what I was expecting to employ you for, despite what you said at breakfast.'

'That wasn't what I was thinking,' she assured him, hoping that would be the end of it.

It wasn't. 'Then what *were* you thinking?'

The arrival of a flight attendant with glasses of champagne bought her a little time to consider her answer. Toby turned slightly green at the sight of the alcohol, and he declined. Autumn wanted to accept hers—after all, how often was she likely to be served complimentary champagne on a flight?—but the cocktails from last night were still churning in her stomach too and, besides, she needed her wits about her for this conversation. Regretfully, she shook her head.

'So?' Toby pressed, killing all hope that he'd forgotten what they were talking about.

Autumn sighed. 'I was thinking… I guess I was thinking that sex muddies the waters. It fosters connection, closeness.'

'And those are bad things?'

'They're bad when they lead to obligation. I'm working for you, Toby. I don't want to feel obliged to stay in a job I'm ready to leave because I'm also sleeping with you.'

He nodded slowly. 'Although I'm guessing that would make a lot more sense if we weren't already married.'

'Probably.' Shifting in her seat, she tucked her legs up under her as she turned towards him. 'It's not that I don't trust you. Well, as far as our contractual obligations will go, anyway. It's just… I've been in situations before where a romantic relationship made me feel I owed someone a lot more than I did.' And then he'd taken everything anyway.

'What happened?' Toby's expression was suddenly very serious, and Autumn flinched.

'It doesn't matter now.'

'It does to me.' Reaching across the divide between them, he placed a hand lightly on her arm. When she looked up there was a soft, friendly smile on his lips. 'You're my wife, after all.'

She rolled her eyes at that. 'My ex, Robbie. I thought he loved me, and I made certain sacrifices because of that.'

'Like what?' God, he was relentless. Autumn was slightly worried that, with a ten-hour flight ahead of them, he might have ferreted out all her secrets before they landed in London. Because it was hard to shut down a person sitting so close and looking so genuinely concerned for her.

'Settled down. Stopped travelling. Got a proper job.' She shrugged. 'Gave him access to my bank account.'

Toby winced. 'Ah. Well, at least you know I'm not marrying you for your money.'

'Because I haven't got any,' she shot back. 'Right.' Because that made her feel loads better.

'You will have, though.' Grabbing her hand, he looked earnestly into her eyes. 'I promise you, Autumn, whatever happens between us at Wishcliffe, you'll leave this situation in a better position than we started it.'

'Hungover, naked, unemployed and broke? I damn well hope so.'

That made him laugh, which was exactly what she'd been hoping for. Toby was far too easy to talk to, she was finding, and that made her nervous.

That was why she'd made her no sex rule. She wasn't here to get close to her husband. She wasn't about to risk falling in love with him and feeling tied down and obliged to him and his world. Maybe Toby didn't want her money, but she was under no illusions that he wouldn't take her time, her energy and her attention if they served him well.

She knew herself well enough to realise that if she went too far, too fast and all in with Toby—like she had with most things in her adult life—she could end up deeper than she wanted to be. She needed to remember that this was just a temporary contract. A stopgap between adventures.

She wasn't looking for connection. She was looking to get the old Autumn back. The one who craved new experiences and fun, and never stayed anywhere long enough to see things turn bad.

Three months, and she'd move on. That was the deal.

She pulled her hand away, gave Toby a friendly smile, then settled back into her seat, reaching for her headphones. If this was her only chance to ever fly firstclass, she intended to enjoy it. Then they'd be in England and it would be time to get to work.

She'd do a fantastic job as Viscountess Wishcliffe. But she wasn't staying any longer than her three months. And nothing Toby could do to tempt her would make any difference.

Finn left them at Heathrow, claiming a meeting in the City that he definitely hadn't told Toby about. He disappeared with one last knowing smirk and a shake of the head at Toby, who pointedly ignored him. He might be his best friend, but Finn was also hands-down one of the most irritating and meddling men on the planet—when it came to Toby's love-life, at least—and Toby was glad to be rid of him.

Because he needed the drive to Wishcliffe to talk to Autumn, without any hilarious interruptions from Finn.

It felt strange, being back on English soil. It wasn't as if he'd been away for years, but he had travelled a lot—both before his brother's death and after. Running a business that encouraged other businesses around the world to embrace remote working—through new systems, new technology, as well as providing and maintaining ad hoc meeting and office spaces—meant being in other companies' buildings more than his own. He'd seen more of hotel rooms than his flat in London, and more of airports than the sprawling manor house at Wishcliffe.

He'd stayed away on purpose—he could admit that to himself. With Barnaby and Victoria in charge of the estate, there hadn't been a place for him there. He'd always known that, as a younger son, he'd need to find his own place in the world—even if that had turned out to be more of a nomadic existence than he'd dreamed was possible.

Now, going home…well. It didn't quite feel like going home, not when he wasn't planning on staying any longer than was necessary to sell the place.

But he needed to prepare Autumn for what was waiting for them there. Which meant remembering himself.

His car was waiting for him outside the terminal, having been brought around from long stay parking by a valet. Autumn yawned as he took the keys and tipped the valet, before lifting their bags into the small boot.

'Tired?' he asked, and she nodded.

Toby had slept for most of the flight after their illuminating conversation on her no sex rule, but he suspected that Autumn had stayed awake to enjoy the experience of flying first-class. It wasn't something he really thought about but, from her wide eyes as they'd boarded, he suspected it had been a novelty for her.

Well. If first-class had impressed her, Wishcliffe might blow her mind.

Which was why he needed to prepare her.

He decided to wait until they were out of the airport

complex and safely on the motorway before raising the subject, but by the time he'd escaped the airport traffic and joined the supposedly open road Autumn had fallen asleep, her head lolling in what looked like a very uncomfortable position against the seatbelt.

He smiled to himself as he stole glances at her in between concentrating on the road. If she hadn't slept much on the flight, no wonder she was exhausted. It had been a hell of a couple of days, for both of them.

Toby mused on the events of the last forty-eight hours as he navigated the familiar roads that took him away from the capital and towards the southern coastline of England. They seemed even more inconceivable here, back on familiar turf. If it weren't for Autumn, dozing in the seat beside him, he wouldn't believe they'd happened at all.

But they had.

Thank goodness she'd agreed to come with him. Whatever it cost him in the end, it would be worth it to not have to walk into Wishcliffe House alone.

He hadn't listed that in his reasons for offering her the job, but in some ways it might be the most important.

He really didn't want to do this alone.

Alone, all the focus would be on him. All the people who'd known his father, known his brother, watched them both run the estate effectively and traditionally and seen that it still hadn't been enough. All the people who'd watched Toby grow up and knew that he'd never been meant for this role. That he wouldn't—couldn't do it as well as the men who'd come before him.

Knew he wasn't good enough.

At least with Autumn at his side there was something else for them to focus on. A distraction—and a delicious one at that. The new Viscount showing up with a new

American bride would feed the gossip mill in the villages on the estate for weeks, if not months.

Three months, hopefully. Because that was all the time he had now to get this sorted.

They were far from the city and wending their way along the coast road towards Wishcliffe when Autumn let out a loud snore then jerked awake, blinking at the scenery outside the car window as she came to.

'Ah, you're awake,' Toby said, not taking his gaze from the road as it wound treacherously close to the cliff edge. 'Good.' He'd been starting to worry that she wouldn't wake up until they reached the estate, and then it would be too late to prepare her for any of it.

'Where are we?' She reached for the water bottle tucked into the outside pocket of her bag by her feet and took a long gulp.

'Not far away now. About another fifteen minutes to Wishcliffe village.'

'I can't believe I missed London, and all the scenery on the way.'

'You don't see any of central London flying into Heathrow, anyway. Have you been to England before?'

Autumn shook her head.

She'd never been to England. How had he not asked that before now? He knew that she'd travelled, but if this was her first time in his home country, he felt an added obligation to sell it to her.

'I've done some of Europe,' she said, still staring out over the cliffs. 'But never the UK somehow. It'll be exciting to live here for a few months.'

Which was a great opening for everything he needed to say, but still Toby wasn't sure quite where to start.

'Uh…do you have any questions?' He swerved around another bend in the path and wished they'd been able to do this when they were stuck in traffic on the M25. 'About Wishcliffe, I mean.'

He risked a quick glance across at her and found Autumn looking at him, eyebrows raised, the view out over the English Channel apparently forgotten.

'Other than *everything*? Toby, you've told me practically nothing about the place.'

'Right. Well, I mean, you'll be seeing it soon. But, uh, I could give you the basics?'

'That would be good.' And then she sat there watching him, waiting to hear all the nitty-gritty details of his family estate.

Toby took another swerve around another bend and wished he hadn't started this conversation.

'Well, I mean, it's a few years since I've spent any real time there…'

'Toby.'

'Right. Um, the main house was built in the seventeenth century, but it has been added to over the years. It's a working estate—with farms, orchards and such, as well as more modern additions, like the holiday cottages and the retreats we offer for companies and the like.' That had been Barnaby's idea, Toby remembered. It had taken him years to convince their father to branch out into anything new at all, but in the end the finances had demanded it.

'Sounds busy.'

'It is.' Something else he remembered from his youth. His father was always busy, the estate demanding more and more of his time, his energy, his life. Those lines in his forehead getting deeper and deeper, his shoulders more stooped with the weight of responsibility. Until he'd handed the whole damn thing over to Barnaby when he'd died.

'What else?'

Toby tried to refocus. This wasn't about the past. It was about the present—here and now—with Autumn. And the estate hadn't killed Barnaby or Harry, not really. Toby knew that in his head. Even if his heart felt differently about it. Because even if their deaths had been at sea, not on the estate, Toby knew from Victoria it was *because* of Wishcliffe. Because Barnaby had been looking for another way to bring in visitors, to make more money, offering sailing opportunities along the nearby coastline.

Barnaby had been an accomplished sailor. What had been different about that day? Toby supposed he'd never know. But he'd never stop wondering either.

Still, the estate wouldn't kill Toby. Because he wasn't staying around long enough to let that happen.

Three months. That's all. I can do this for three months.

He didn't want to. But he could.

Having Autumn there would help. And because she didn't love him, he didn't have to worry about her getting the same haunted look in her eyes that he saw in Victoria's on every video call, if the worst *did* happen. He wouldn't lumber her with the estate either. When they drew up the paperwork, he'd figure something out.

But for now Autumn was still waiting to hear about the place where she would be the lady of the manor.

'There's two different villages either side of the estate lands.' The map of Wishcliffe House, the village of Wishcliffe and the second village of Wells-on-Water was burned into his brain. He could see it from above, like a seagull flying over and studying the lie of the land, from all the times he'd studied the maps with Barnaby and his father. As a child, he'd used to creep into his father's office to trace the lines of rivers and streams and hedgerows and lanes on the large map that hung over his desk. 'Centuries ago, they'd have been tied to the land, and the people who lived there the responsibility of the lord of the manor. These days, the villages are their own places—apart from the cottages on the actual estate, no one has to pay us rent or anything. But a lot of the people who live there still work for the estate businesses. There's not a massive amount of industry around here besides tourism, so we're all interlinked really.'

'All one big happy family?'

'Something like that.'

'And what about the house itself?' Autumn asked.

'Hang on a moment and you'll see it for yourself.' They were so close now, only a mile or so away from Wishcliffe village. Two more bends and they'd find themselves at the perfect viewing spot: at the end of the long avenue of trees that led from the house all the way to the edge of the estate by the cliffs. It gave the occupants of the house a perfect view of the sea, and passing travellers a perfect view of the house—even if there were still another couple of miles of curving roads to reach the driveway and the house itself.

One bend. Two. And— 'There. Do you see it?'

The trees lined up along the avenue and suddenly Wishcliffe House was visible, its pale stone glowing in the early September sunlight and the glass of its many, many windows glinting like the crests of the waves on the sea below. Majestic, imposing but serene. Part of his landscape.

'Pull over,' Autumn said suddenly.

Toby, who'd slowed the car anyway to give her a better look, checked his mirrors and swung into the lay-by off the side of the road. He wasn't surprised she wanted to linger here and look a little longer.

'Impressive, isn't it?' he said, turning to her with a smile.

But Autumn wasn't listening. Because she'd already fumbled the door open and was throwing up on the edge of the cliff.

CHAPTER FIVE

She couldn't do this. There was absolutely no way she could do this.

Pressing the back of her hand to her mouth, Autumn looked up at the imposing sight of Wishcliffe House. It had to be a mile or more away down the avenue of trees, and it still loomed immense over the cliff road.

That was not the small manor house Toby had led her to expect. *That* was basically a palace.

Growing up in her grandparents' large home in New England had been enough of an adjustment after the tiny flat she'd shared with her mum. Her grandparents' home had grounds, a terrace and a gated driveway—plus a full-time housekeeper and cook, and occasional staff for the parties Grandma liked to throw. When she'd sold it, Autumn had been pretty sure she'd never live anywhere so palatial again.

Seemed she'd been wrong.

She thought fleetingly of her grandmother's bible, sitting in her suitcase in the back of Toby's flashy silver car. Not an *actual* bible, although Grandma had gone to church and feigned religion as well as all her neighbours. No, this was the book she'd really lived by. The one she'd bequeathed to Autumn long before her death, as soon as it became clear that she couldn't do everything by herself any longer.

'This book will tell you everything you need to know, Autumn.'

'About what?' she'd asked, running her fingers across the scarred and battered leather cover.

'About how to manage your home, your life, your marriage. About what to say when there are no words. About how to deal with people who you'd rather not bother with. About how to live. This book has all the rules you need.'

It had seemed a big ask of just one book. But as Autumn had flicked through the yellowing pages she'd realised what her grandmother meant.

The book wasn't a printed book—or rather it had been once, but its purpose had been well and truly taken over. In between the printed pages of recipes, and over most of them, had been pasted other things. Notes on etiquette. How much food to serve for a finger buffet for seventy. Checklists for planning a party, or a wedding, or a funeral. Ideas for conversation starters and tips on introducing people who might get on. Napkin folding arrangements. A secret recipe for stuffing. A page on tricks to keep a husband happy in the bedroom that Autumn had blushed to even look at with her grandma beside her.

This book was her grandmother's brain on paper—everything she'd learned about entertaining, running a home and life, over her eighty-five years of life. She'd still been adding to it right until the end, dictating new notes to paste in from her prone position on the sofa, unwilling to take to the grave anything that Autumn might need to live a successful life.

She'd followed her grandmother's rules religiously when organising the funerals, and even found a note on preparing a house for sale that was useful.

And then she'd packed it away in her bag and not looked at it again.

Because she'd lived by her grandparents' rules her whole life, it seemed—at least since she'd moved in with them at eight. But it had always been clear to all three of them that those same rules that made Grandma and Granddad feel safe and certain only chafed at Autumn's edges. They hemmed her in, made her less than she wanted to be.

'You're too like your mother,' Grandma would say. *'You just can't be happy in one place, can't be satisfied with one life. You want to live them all at once.'*

But Autumn had put all those possible lives, those potential futures, on hold to look after them when they were sick, and she knew her grandparents appreciated that. They might not have understood each other but they had *loved* each other, and that had been enough. It had also been another reminder that nothing lasted—good or bad. Now was always a good time to move on.

So after the funerals Autumn had sold the house and turned nomad, and the bible had been no use to her on Thailand's beaches or in the rainforests of South America. It hadn't had any tips about appearing on stage at the Eurovision Song Contest. And the wedding planning company she'd worked for had their own checklists.

But still, she'd carted it around the world with her, the one constant in her slimline suitcase. And now, here, at Wishcliffe House, it looked as if she might need it after all.

A bottle of water appeared in her vision, and she blinked to find Toby holding it and looking at her with concern in his eyes.

'Was it the twisty road, last night's cocktails or the house?' he asked as she took the bottle and unscrewed the cap. The water tasted fresh and chill going down and Autumn closed her eyes to focus on that, instead of the immense bulk of Wishcliffe House.

'Probably the roads,' she lied. She'd travelled in the most rickety of buses across India, taking bends so fast they'd ended up on two wheels and never had a moment's queasiness, but a little travel sickness had to be less embarrassing than terror at the sight of a house, right?

'Of course,' Toby said, obviously not believing her.

Autumn drank some more water to avoid looking at him. Or his house.

'It really will be all right,' he said.

'Of course it will.' Smiling brightly, Autumn poured water over the evidence of her illness—not much, thankfully—and then recapped the bottle and climbed back into the car.

'You're sure you want to do this?' Toby asked as he settled into the driver's seat. 'I could take you back to the airport if you wanted. Buy you a ticket to anywhere and give you enough money to get started. I'd just need your contact details for the, well, you know.'

'The divorce.' One more thing her grandma's bible *hadn't* covered was how to get divorced from a man you'd just met and married on a stupid drunken whim. But it had been very clear on the matter of agreements between equals, and the importance of keeping promises. So, as much as she wanted to run, she shook her head. 'No. We made a deal, and I don't back out on those. Three months. You're stuck with me for the next three months, just like we agreed.' As long as she stuck to her own rules, her own beliefs, she'd be fine. And by Christmas she'd be on her way to her next adventure. Another possible future to explore.

'Okay, then. Let's go.' He pulled out of the lay-by and back onto the twisting cliffside road.

Autumn took one last look up the avenue towards Wishcliffe House. She really wished her grandma was still around to help her with this.

Autumn was mostly silent for the rest of the drive to Wishcliffe House, which suited Toby just fine. He wasn't much in the mood to talk anyway.

With every landmark they passed, every familiar bend in the road, Toby felt the weight of home settling heavier on his shoulders—and with it came the fear of what he was letting himself in for.

There was the cliff path he and Finn had climbed in a storm one winter, and almost been swept away to sea. There was the farm that neighboured Wishcliffe, with the farmer's daughter who had seduced him one New Year's Eve when he was sixteen and she eighteen. The small stone circle that had fascinated him since he was tiny, that no one seemed to know anything much about.

The road bent in another improbably angled direction, away from the sea and inland, and they passed Finn's father's old estate, the third side of a triangle between Wishcliffe, Orchard Farm and the sea, the house and land sold years ago now and his father residing in London, estranged from his only son.

And as they grew closer still, there was the village of Wishcliffe, so exactly as Toby remembered it from his childhood that his chest ached to see it again. The stone marker with the 'Welcome to Wishcliffe' sign perched above it. The King's Arms—the pub where he'd drunk his first legal pint and sneaked plenty of illegal ones under the cover of darkness in the small beer garden at the back.

Past the rows of terraced cottages, painted the colours of the sunrise over the waves beyond. Past the small Norman stone church, and past the other pub—the pub he didn't go to. Well, not any more anyway.

Autumn, staring out of the side window, murmured, 'The village is lovely. Just as I always imagined an English village would look.'

Toby hummed his agreement, but made no further comment. He was too lost inside himself for words.

And then they were out of the village and onto the familiar road that continued all the way to Wishcliffe House. He wanted to slow down, to crawl the last quarter of a mile home. But he was already driving below the speed limit, and the road disappeared fast beneath his wheels.

'Here we are.' He took the last turn onto the driveway, the gravel crunching under his tyres as he pulled to a stop in front of the house. Risking a glance across at Autumn, he saw her eyes were wider even than when she'd woken up and realised she'd married him. Her cheeks were also tinged with a little green. God, he hoped she didn't throw up again in front of the staff. That would not be the most auspicious start to this whole experiment. 'Ready?'

'As I'll ever be.' She opened her door and he followed suit, rushing around to her side to hold it open and help her out before his father's old butler, Andrews, could do it.

'Then come and meet the household.'

They were all lined up on the steps to the house, and Toby suddenly realised how archaic and period drama this must really look to an outsider. But Autumn simply straightened her back under his palm as he guided her towards the house, a bright and happy smile pasted on her face.

A newlywed smile. As if this really had been the plan all along.

He wondered how that would feel—returning to Wishcliffe with a bride he loved on his arm, taking up a role he'd waited his whole life for. In another universe, where he'd been the eldest son, the heir, groomed for the viscountcy. Where he'd risked his heart and had his love returned. A universe where he might be planning a family, a happy ever after of his own.

A world where he hadn't lost his brother and his nephew in a tragic accident.

A world where he wanted this.

A world where the woman beside him was there for love, not money.

But there was no point spending too much time wondering because this wasn't that world. Not even that universe.

And if he'd needed any reminder of that, seeing Victoria appear through the open front door in her dark charcoal skirt suit would have knocked some reality into him. She looked tired, he realised, behind her tentative smile. The kind of weariness that came from carrying the world on her shoulders, along with all that grief.

At least he could take some of that away from her now. He should have stayed last year, he knew. The guilt at not staying had been gnawing away at him for months. But she'd been so determined to stay, so sure that this was the best thing for both of them…

He was here now. He could fix things. And he wasn't alone. That would make a difference.

Of course, it was only when he felt Autumn suck in a surprised breath that he thought to wonder if he'd remembered to tell his new wife that his sister-in-law was still in residence at their new home…

* * *

The woman standing at the top of the steps by the front door of Wishcliffe House was poised, elegant and graceful in her charcoal-grey suit, her dark hair swept up into one of those chic chignons Autumn had never managed to force her hair into. She was also frowning. A lot.

God, she hoped this wasn't going to turn out to be some weird revenge bigamy thing. Or even a bitter ex-wife who wouldn't leave. Or something worse she was too tired to imagine.

Wait. Hadn't he said something about a sister-in-law?

Without even looking at Toby, Autumn murmured out of the corner of her mouth, 'Anything you forgot to mention?'

'Not just to you,' he muttered back, which made no sense at all.

It was just as well she wasn't *actually* a besotted newlywed or she'd be worried she was stepping into a horror movie waiting to happen.

As it was, she wasn't feeling entirely confident about the whole setup. She almost wished that Finn had come with them from Heathrow, and that was saying something.

'Victoria,' he called, and the woman started down the stone stairs towards them. 'Come and meet my new bride.'

Victoria's steps faltered and for a moment Autumn was afraid she might stumble and fall. But with a grace Autumn knew *she* wouldn't have possessed in the same circumstances, she caught herself and continued descending at a stately pace, as if it were what she'd intended all along.

'If you got married and didn't invite me, Toby Blythe, you're going to be in rather a lot of trouble.' Her voice rang like Grandma's crystal glasses, bright and sharp as cut glass, but her smile at least was warm.

As she reached them, Toby removed his hand from the small of Autumn's back long enough to reach out and hug the other woman. A proper hug. One you'd give someone you actually liked rather than someone you had to pretend you loved because they were family.

'Victoria, this is Autumn,' he said, still smiling, but there was concern in his eyes as he looked at Victoria. Now she was closer, Autumn could see the lines at the corners of her eyes and the dark shadows under them. 'Autumn—' He didn't know her second name. Why hadn't they shared at least basic information like that before they'd arrived? 'Autumn Blythe,' he finished with a laugh, as if it were what he'd meant to say all along.

'You really got married?' Victoria's eyes were sad, and Toby shifted uncomfortably from one foot to the other as he avoided her gaze. Such a man.

'It was rather spur-of-the-moment, I'm afraid,' Autumn said, reaching out a hand to Victoria. 'I mean, he was coming home and, well, we just couldn't bear the idea of not being together.'

Something like that, anyway.

Victoria took her hand and smiled warmly, which went a long way towards releasing the knot of tension in Autumn's chest.

'Sweetheart, this is my sister-in-law Victoria.' Toby wrapped an arm around her shoulder and pulled Autumn to his side, as if he couldn't bear to be physically separated from her for a moment longer.

Sister-in-law. His dead brother's wife. Okay. She could work with that.

'It's lovely to meet you,' Autumn said. This was probably where she should add, *Toby's told me all about you*, but since he hadn't, she didn't.

'Victoria has been looking after the estate for me while I've been tying up my business concerns, like I told you,' Toby went on. From the look that passed between them, Autumn couldn't quite tell whose idea that had been.

'And I am more than ready to pass it all on to you, now you're back. Time for me to get back out in the real world and find my own path again.' Victoria's smile was sad, and Autumn couldn't help but wonder how mixed her feelings must be right now. She'd married a viscount, had a family and probably expected to grow old here at Wishcliffe House and pass it all onto her son in the end.

Instead, Toby had showed up with some random American and was kicking her out of the house. Even if she said she wanted to go… Autumn gazed up at the rows of windows and chimneys and tried to imagine how it must feel to give up such a place.

She couldn't.

'And I don't even have to worry about you getting overwhelmed, since you've brought help with you,' Victoria went on, that brittle smile directed at Autumn again. 'I'm sure everyone on the estate will be excited to have a new lady of the manor running things.'

'But you'll stay a while, won't you?' Autumn blurted out, before she could think it through. Probably this kind of invitation was something she should have discussed with her husband first—she was sure Grandma's bible would say so. But since he'd forgotten to tell her that Victoria would be here at Wishcliffe in the first place, she figured it was a fair question.

And, luckily, it seemed he did too. 'Autumn's right,' Toby said. 'There's no reason for you to rush off just because we're back. Stay a while, help us get settled in.'

Victoria's gaze darted between them and she bit down on her lower lip, obviously considering her options.

'Besides, I'll need someone to show me the ropes, right?' Autumn added as an extra push, and Victoria smiled.

'I suppose I could stay another couple of weeks,' she said. 'The cottage I've bought needs some work doing anyway. It would be nice not to be living in it while that happens.'

'Then it's settled.' Toby offered his arm to Autumn, and his other to Victoria. 'Now, how about we go show my wife her new home?'

'Don't you want to carry her over the threshold?' Victoria teased.

Toby shot Autumn a look, and she knew he was remembering her throwing up on the side of the road and figuring the odds of it happening again if he picked her up and jostled her too much.

'Let's save that for the bedroom later, honey,' she said, patting his arm.

It was only as they reached the front door that she realised what she'd said.

Bedroom. Singular.

Oh, hell.

Maybe there were more parts of this plan they hadn't discussed than sisters-in-law and surnames.

CHAPTER SIX

IT WAS, TOBY REFLECTED, very strange.

Not just being back in the main dining hall at Wishcliffe House, although he'd avoided the place so thoroughly in the past five or so years that, in itself, that felt odd.

But sitting at the head of the table with his wife at his side…

That was beyond odd. That was slipped-into-another-reality strange.

But the housekeeper, Mrs Heath, and Cook had insisted on a formal dinner for his first night in residence as the Viscount, so here they were.

Victoria sat opposite Autumn—the Dowager Viscountess opposite the new. Conversation between the three of them was a little stilted, but since they kept being interrupted by new plates of food—how many courses had Cook prepared?—it wasn't too awkward. There was always a new delicious morsel to discuss, and Autumn—to Toby's amusement or relief, he wasn't quite sure—showed no hesitation about knowing exactly which set of cutlery went with which course. He wondered idly where she'd picked that up. As far as he was aware, Americans usually used their cutlery the other way around, but Autumn seemed to stick to the usual British way without thinking.

Perhaps she had British parents. She'd said she hadn't visited England before, but that didn't necessarily mean anything. Which way round did they use cutlery in Australia? He didn't know.

He didn't know very much at all about Autumn's history, he realised, just as Victoria decided to start quizzing him on it.

Including the all-important history of the their relationship.

'So, how did you two meet and fall in love?' Victoria asked between mouthfuls.

Toby froze, his fork halfway to his mouth. Another thing they should have discussed on the journey here—they needed to get their stories straight, or someone would out them as frauds in no time flat. Gossips in Wishcliffe knew their business and Victoria, much as she'd deny it, was one of the worst.

With a small secret smile, Autumn glanced adoringly over at him and Toby tried not to do a double-take at the sight.

'Do you want to tell the story, honey, or shall I?' Her voice was sweet, tinged with excitement, for all the world as if she really were sharing a true love story with a new relative. Had she included 'actress' in her vast and varied résumé? He couldn't remember now. But if she hadn't, she should have.

'Oh, go ahead.' Toby settled back in his chair to listen. 'I know how much you love telling it.'

'Finn already had to listen to it all on the flight over,' Autumn admitted.

'Finn was with you?' Was it his imagination, or had Victoria stiffened slightly at his best friend's name?

'He met us in Vegas,' Toby said shortly. 'But missed the wedding. Don't worry, *everybody* is cross with me about that.' Or they would be, if this really had been his one proper, true love wedding. As it was, he imagined people would get over it when he and Autumn split in three months.

Plus, they'd all have much more to be cross with him about by then.

Making a mental note to tell Finn whatever story Autumn decided on, Toby motioned for Autumn to continue. Putting down her fork, she leaned forward and started storytelling. With gusto.

It was an incredible performance. If Toby hadn't been there for what had actually happened—although, given how impaired his memory of events was, he might as well not have been—he would absolutely have believed her. She spoke with such enthusiasm, throwing in all the little details that made it feel real, it was hard to believe that none of it had actually happened.

The most impressive part, Toby decided, was the way she wove the truth in between the lies.

They'd still met in a bar, and he'd still stepped in to save her when a patron got too drunk, angry and handsy. But in Autumn's version this had happened several weeks ago—apparently he'd been in Vegas for business on and off for a month, a fact she'd shot him a quick look to clarify before confirming. She hadn't lost her job, but he'd kept coming back to the bar whenever he was in town, and they'd struck up a fast friendship that had quickly become something more.

'I know it must seem very sudden,' Autumn said, shyly reaching for Toby's hand over the table. 'I mean, it felt pretty sudden to us too! But you know how it is. When you know, you know. And I knew that if I let Toby leave when his business was done, with a chance that I'd never see him again… Well. I'd just kick myself for ever.'

'I'm sure,' Victoria said, non-committal. Toby tried to look suitably besotted to help sell the story.

Autumn flashed him a cheeky grin. 'Of course, he didn't tell me he owned this place—or that he was an actual *viscount*, of all things—until *after* we were married.' Another truth, if only by accident. Toby could see what she was doing, though. Making sure that Victoria knew she hadn't married him for his money or status. 'If I'd known that taking on Toby meant taking on this place, well… I'd have had to think a bit harder before saying yes, that's for sure.'

'You would?' Victoria asked, curiosity clear in her voice. 'Why?'

With a light shrug, Autumn's smile faded to a shadow of its former self. 'Houses—estates—like this… Well, they come with an awful lot of responsibility, I reckon. Not just to the family, but to the land, and to everyone who relies on it for their livelihood. If you have this kind of privilege, you just *have* to do right by the people that don't, right? I mean, I don't know much about this place yet—although I'm keen to learn. But I can't imagine it runs itself. You must have taken on a lot of work, and a lot of responsibility, while Toby's been gone this last year. And I don't think it would be right to jump at the chance to marry that kind of obligation without a good bit of thinking first.'

Toby could see in his sister-in-law's face the moment that Autumn won her over. It wasn't the stories she spun about romance or love. It was the way she talked about responsibility.

Because it sounded the same as the way *Victoria* talked about responsibility. Autumn couldn't know, but her words almost echoed the same things Victoria had said the day after the funeral, when she'd suggested she stay on at Wishcliffe for a year while he tied up his own business obligations. At the time, he'd assumed she was asking for *her*. But now, looking at her tired and knowing eyes, he wondered. Had his sister-in-law just been giving him the space he'd needed to come to terms with his new responsibilities so he could do them the right way?

And in turn, of course, Victoria echoed Barnaby's words about the responsibility of being the Viscount. And he'd got it from their father, who'd had it from *his* father, and back through the centuries.

Until the Wishcliffe line of succession had reached him. The Viscount who wasn't willing to give his life, his health, his everything to a piece of land that never gave anything back. The heir who should never have inherited, the one who could never live up to the men who'd gone before him.

He wasn't born for this, for this responsibility. His father had made that clear, and so had his brother, albeit in a more teasing, loving way. And even if they hadn't, events since then certainly had.

He'd made a career out of not having to stay in one place—something he and Autumn actually had in common, he supposed. He'd found his own life away from Wishcliffe. His business came with its own responsibilities, of course, but on *his* terms, and with Finn there to always back him up. His choices, his love life, they'd never affected everyone around him until now.

But it seemed that somehow, against the odds, he'd made the right choice of bride, regardless. Victoria's approving smile told him that she knew Autumn would fit in just wonderfully, despite the surprise of their marriage.

He just shuddered to think what she'd say when she realised he was planning on selling his legacy of responsibility to the highest bidder.

* * *

'So. That went well.' Toby's satisfied smile went a long way to calming Autumn's nerves.

Her sister-in-law-in-law—how did that work?—frankly terrified her, but at least she didn't seem about to cause any ructions about Autumn arriving to take her place.

After Autumn had told her the fake story of her love affair with Toby, Victoria had seemed to relax enough to chat more easily through the next four courses and coffee. She had plans, it seemed, to get back out into the world and start again. Her own cottage, a new job in her former career—antiques and art history, apparently. A life away from Wishcliffe.

'Now I can leave the place in safe hands, of course,' she'd said, smiling meaningfully at Toby and Autumn as she'd left the table after dessert, to retire to her new rooms in the East Wing.

Autumn had very carefully not looked at Toby as she'd said it. Obviously Victoria had no idea of his plans to sell, and she couldn't imagine that she'd approve.

'She bought the love story, at least,' Autumn replied now she and Toby were alone again. 'That's a start.'

'It wasn't just the…er…reimagining of our courtship,' Toby said, making her snigger at his choice of words. Courtship? That was definitely a stretch for what they'd shared. 'It was the way you talked about this place. About responsibility. That was definitely the right track to take with Victoria. Clever of you to spot that.'

But it hadn't been clever—or, if it had, it had been unintentional cleverness. She'd just spoken about Wishcliffe as she saw it. As anyone would see it, surely?

Even Toby, who planned to sell the place as soon as he could, was doing so because he didn't want the responsibility of looking after it. At least, she had thought that was why, until they'd arrived here. Now she wasn't so sure.

Maybe they needed to talk about that a bit more.

But, before she could ask him anything, Toby swallowed the last of the wine in his glass, slammed the glass down on the table and stood up. 'Come on,' he said. 'There's got to be somewhere more comfortable than this for an after-dinner chat. I think there's quite a lot we need to talk about, don't you?'

Since she'd been thinking the same thing not long before, Autumn could hardly disagree. Finishing her own drink, she followed him out of the dining room, down a shadowy corridor, turned right at a staircase, and knew that, despite the comprehensive tour she'd been given on arrival that afternoon, she was going to be horribly lost for most of the next three months.

Eventually she gave up even trying to remember their route or guess where they were going.

Toby pushed open a heavy wooden door that looked like all the others, peeked inside the room, then turned back to her with a grin. 'Just as I thought. The staff here are total creatures of habit.'

The door swung all the way open to reveal a comfortable book-lined room with a dark wood desk, a roaring fire and two comfortable-looking armchairs.

'This was my father's study,' Toby explained. 'And then it was Barnaby's, I suppose, although I never really saw him use it. Mostly because I tried not to be here. But my father used to retire here every evening after supper, and the staff would always have the fire lit for him, except in the hottest summer spells. The old house gets cold, you see.'

Autumn *did* see. After summer in Nevada, September in England was already proving mighty chilly, and she knew she definitely didn't own enough sweaters to cope with winter. She was going to have to go shopping. Online, probably, since Wishcliffe village didn't look exactly packed with clothing stores.

Maybe her next stop after England would be somewhere really exotic. From the price she and Toby had agreed on the plane for her three months here, she'd have enough to take an actual holiday too, before she found her next employment. That could be nice. Lying on a beach with drinks with little umbrellas, doing nothing at all…

Oh, who was she kidding? She'd never been good at doing nothing. But at least she didn't need to worry about how much her next adventure paid. That was something.

Toby ran a hand across the surface of the desk before motioning for her to take a seat in one of the armchairs.

'I guess this is your study now,' she said as she sank into the cushions.

'I suppose it is.'

And how do you feel about that? she wanted to ask, but she wasn't sure they were there just yet. Besides, Toby looked so lost in thought, staring at his father's desk, she wasn't sure he'd even hear her.

So she waited. And, after a few long moments where the only sounds were the crackle and pop of the fire, he looked up and gave her a tight smile.

'You wanted to talk,' she reminded him, and he nodded. 'What about?'

Moving to take the armchair on the other side of the fire, Toby looked as though he was choosing his words carefully.

'The story you told Victoria at dinner…'

'You said it went well,' Autumn interrupted. 'You said she liked me.'

'I think she does,' Toby replied. 'But that only means she's going to have *more* questions. About you, and about us. And if she wants to be friends—or even if she's just going to be showing you the ropes around here—she's going to expect you to know certain things about me too.'

'The relationship basics,' Autumn agreed with a nod. 'All the stuff you usually get out of the way in the first few dates.'

'Except we didn't have those. Which is why I think we should do it now.'

He looked as if he'd swallowed something unpleasant, Autumn realised. As if the prospect of hearing about her personal particulars was abhorrent to him.

Unless it was his own particulars—his past, for instance—he didn't want to talk about. That made more sense.

'You could start by telling me what it was like growing up here at Wishcliffe,' she suggested. 'What were your favourite things about living here?'

That earned a small smile, at least. Looked like his past wasn't *all* bad, then.

'I suppose my favourite times were spent with Barnaby, before he went away to school—before I did too. Or the summers when we were home together.'

'You went to boarding school? Did you like it there?' Autumn had read so many books about English boarding schools, from the bookcase in her room at her grandparents' house, but she had no idea if they were at all accurate. Besides, they were all about girls' schools back in the first half of the twentieth century. She couldn't imagine they bore much resemblance to Toby's experience.

He shrugged. 'It was okay. I didn't hate it, like some of the boys there. But I wasn't a king of the school either. Finn was there with me, so that made a lot of things bearable. And Barnaby was only a couple of years above, if I had any problems.'

So. Okay childhood, okay school experience, loved his brother. Autumn still wasn't seeing the trauma.

'So it was your parents and you, growing up?' He hadn't mentioned his mother yet, she realised suddenly. And if anyone knew the emotional trauma mothers could cause, it was Autumn. Maybe that was it.

Toby nodded. 'Yes. My father died seven years ago, when I was twenty-four. My mother died three years later, almost to the day.'

'You were young to lose them both.' But at least he'd had them to start with.

Another shrug. 'They were older when they married, when they had my brother and me. Mother had been in bad health for a few years, so it wasn't really a surprise. And our father…he had a massive heart attack. Brought on from the stress of running this place.'

He cast a scowl around the study then shook it away, but not before a hundred questions welled up inside Autumn's brain.

'And your brother? You said he and your nephew died last year. Can I ask…?'

'It was a sailing accident. At sea. Barnaby was…he wanted to start some sailing holidays and lessons here at the estate, to become another income stream. He and Harry went out to try out a new boat, but something went wrong. There was an inquest but…' He shook his head. 'Death by misadventure.'

'I'm so sorry.' She thought of Victoria's sad eyes and wondered how Toby's sister-in-law was still getting up every morning.

'Nothing good lasts, and nothing bad lasts. You just have to keep on moving, baby.'

Her mother's voice was still as clear in Autumn's head as the day she'd said it, waving goodbye as Autumn stood on the porch with her grandma's arm around her. She hadn't believed her to start with. But life with her mom had been good, until it wasn't. And then life with her grandparents had been good until she'd hit her teenage years and it turned out there was more of her mom in her than any of them would like.

Then they'd got sick, and things had been worse. That was when she'd started to believe that maybe her mom had a point after all.

She wondered if Toby felt the same. Finn had told her a bit about the business they ran together when they were at the airport, and it seemed to her that it was mostly about letting people still clock in for their jobs from wherever they were in the world. No ties, no need to stay in one place or worry about a daily commute.

Being Viscount tied him to Wishcliffe. A place that he thought had killed his father and possibly his brother, although he hadn't said as much. No wonder he wanted to sell.

Victoria's face came back to her again, her loss etched in every line. Was that why he'd wanted a bride he didn't know or love? Maybe this hadn't been his plan, exactly, but he'd leapt on the opportunity when it had presented itself. Was it because he knew the same things about the world that she did—that if you stayed in one place too long you got hurt, one way or another?

'Toby. I—'

He turned his sharp blue gaze firmly on her, speaking before she could even articulate the thought. 'What about you? I take it you're not a Las Vegas native?'

So, they were done talking about him, then. The walls behind his eyes were high and thick.

'Not even slightly.' He didn't respond, just waited for her to keep talking. Which, she supposed, she had to do.

He was right. People would get suspicious if he didn't know *anything* about her past.

She could make up a history, she supposed. Reinvent her whole life the way she wished it had been, rather than the way it was. But what was the point? This was who she was, and it wasn't like she was going to be sticking around long enough to care if people whispered and gossiped about her past behind her back when they found out.

Besides, the truth was always easier to remember than a lie.

'I was born in California, but I grew up in a small town in upstate New York with my grandparents.' Of course, that was the kind of statement that invited more questions. Toby didn't ask them, though. He just waited some more.

'My dad…well, whoever he was, he didn't stick around. For the first few years it was just me and my mom. We managed well enough, most of the time.' Some of the time. Autumn remembered good days, but she also remembered when there became more bad days than good. When the only good days were unexpected, rainbows on cloudy days. When her mom wasn't high, or dumped again, or just crying and unable to get out of bed. 'But when I was eight she decided it was time for a new life. She took me to my grandparents' house and left me there.'

Eight was old enough to remember. She'd often wondered why her mom hadn't dumped her sooner. Before she remembered what life was like, just the two of them. So she wouldn't remember that terrifying bus ride across the whole country that seemed to go on for months. Wouldn't remember standing on the doorstep of that grand and imposing house in a whole new state, waiting for someone to answer the door, hoping they liked her even though she'd spilt chocolate milk over her best dress and it hadn't all come out in the bus station rest room.

'She didn't stay with you?' Toby's voice was soft, his blue eyes warmed by the light of the fire.

Autumn shook her head. 'She and Grandma…they could never get along. It was why Mom left home in the first place when she was only sixteen. She said it was just for a visit, though. Then she went away and…well, for the first few years she came back to see me now and then. And then she stopped. It took me almost two years to realise that she really was never coming back.' And by that point she hadn't even wanted her to.

Life with her grandparents had been rigid, structured, and the expectations they placed on her were high. But it had been predictable, and Autumn had craved that to start with. She'd liked knowing exactly what would happen, when. She'd tried so hard to be just like them. To enjoy the comfort of following the rules. To luxuriate in the order and the calm.

But her mother's genes had kicked in fully during her teen years, and she'd known that she could never really live that way. Still, she'd tried, for their sakes. It was only later, after she'd nursed both of her grandparents through the last days of their lives, that the urge for freedom, for adventure, had become irresistible. That was when she'd followed in her mother's footsteps and escaped that huge house in New York State.

'Were you happy there?' Toby asked.

'I was. Mostly.' Autumn glanced around the room so she wouldn't have to face the pity in Toby's eyes any longer. 'This room reminds me of my grandfather's study, actually. Their house…it wasn't anything like this place, of course. But it was bigger than I'd ever imagined a house being, when I arrived. My grandparents…they were important in local society. You know the sort. There were lots of garden parties and dinner parties and bridge socials and so on. Grandma used to get me to help organise them all, so I'd know what to do when *I* was a wife and a mother.' Autumn laughed, surprised to find it sounded watery. She hadn't cried over her grandparents in years; by the end, it had been a relief for them both to go, and Autumn had known better than to try and hold onto them.

Nothing lasts. Good or bad.

She'd been sad, of course, but she'd made her peace with their deaths.

Now, though, she wished more than anything she had her grandma there to guide her through this. If anyone knew what to do when one had accidentally married a viscount, it would be Grandma.

'Sounds like the perfect training for this place,' Toby said, ignoring her tears. He was a man, after all—an English aristocrat, at that. Everything she'd ever seen on TV told her he'd be uncomfortable with feelings.

Except then he gave her an incredibly kind smile and murmured, 'You must miss them a lot. I'm so sorry that you lost them so young.' And she thought that maybe he wasn't that bad with feelings after all.

Especially when he slipped from his chair, kneeled in front of her and opened his arms to offer her a hug.

She leaned into his embrace and, with his arms tight around her, for the first time since she'd arrived at Wishcliffe, she felt like maybe it could be a home. Something she'd forgotten how to even want until now.

CHAPTER SEVEN

TOBY WAS PRETTY sure he hadn't imagined the warmth in Autumn's eyes as they'd talked and hugged in the study. Which was good because if they were going to be married, even just for a few months, it helped if they liked each other.

But he also couldn't ignore the stiffness in her shoulders as they reached their bedroom door.

'I suppose it's too much to hope for that married aristocracy sleep in different bedrooms?' she said softly as he turned the handle.

'I'm sure some do,' he acknowledged. 'But my parents never did, and neither did Barnaby and Victoria. I suspect the gossips would have something to say if I didn't share a bed with my new bride.'

He'd assumed the no sex rule would be an easy one to follow. Yes, Autumn was gorgeous, and yes, the image of her naked in his bed but for a thin cotton sheet would stay with him for a very long time, but they had an agreement and he had no intention of going back on that.

All the same, the idea of lying next to her in their marriage bed every night for three months and never touching her seemed like a curious punishment for his impulsive wedding.

The door swung open and they both stared at the large,

opulent bed that occupied the centre of the room. It had been a long time since Toby had been in the master suite at Wishcliffe, and it seemed that his brother had done some redecorating in his absence. Victoria had moved out of the room months ago, to one of the guest rooms on the far side of the house, but the housekeeping staff had certainly made the suite ready for the newlyweds, right down to the red roses on the dressing table and the candles burning softly along the windowsill.

Toby drew in a breath. 'There's a sofa. I can sleep on that.'

'Are you sure?' Autumn asked. 'We could…um…take it in turns?'

That hardly seemed chivalrous, although Toby had to admit his back would probably appreciate it.

'It's late, we've both had a day that has been going on so long it feels like a week, and we've got three months of this to get through.' Shutting the door firmly behind them, he crossed to the sofa under the window and dropped onto it. It seemed comfortable enough. 'I could probably sleep anywhere tonight, so let's just…get some rest and we'll figure it out in the morning.'

Autumn's grateful smile assured him that was the right move.

Their bags had already been unpacked and it didn't take either of them long to prepare for bed—a cautious dance taken behind the locked door of the en-suite bathroom. Toby made sure he was settled on the sofa before Autumn came back into the room, so there could be no more debate. Her smile as she sank onto the mattress made the dip between the cushions, right at the base of his spine, more or less bearable.

'Goodnight, husband,' Autumn murmured as she switched off the bedside light.

There was amusement in her voice that made him smile as he replied, 'Goodnight, wife.'

He hadn't really imagined he'd be able to sleep much on the too short and very uncomfortable sofa, whatever he'd told Autumn. Still, it had been a long couple of days, and as a result he managed to fall into the sort of exhausted, blackout sleep that even dreams couldn't disturb.

He woke, jet-lagged and nauseous, to an early morning knock on his bedroom door.

'Toby? Are you up yet?' Victoria. Making up for some big-sister-like tormenting she'd never got to do in her childhood, he imagined.

He pulled the pillow over his head and something in his back twinged. 'No.'

'Well, get up then!'

'Can't. I'm asleep.' He rolled over to try and block out her voice, and promptly fell onto the floor with a crash.

Right. Sofa. He'd forgotten that part. It would explain the pain in his back, anyway. Which probably wasn't helped by the falling off bit either.

Still, his rapid descent to the floor managed what Victoria's yelling hadn't, and woke Autumn, who sat bolt upright in bed, her eyes wide with alarm.

'What's going on?' Her hair had puffed up all around her head like a halo, shining strawberry blonde in the sunlight coming through the curtains they'd forgotten to close.

'Victoria is trying to make my life a misery.' And if she gave up knocking and walked in to find him on the sofa she was going to have a hell of a lot more questions.

Tossing his pillow onto the bed beside Autumn, he stashed the blankets he'd used under the sofa and jumped onto the bed beside her. She blinked at him a few times then settled back down against her pillow, muttering something that sounded like, 'I am too tired to care about this.'

Toby threw some duvet across his lap and tried to look as if he'd been there all night.

'I am *not* trying to make your life a misery.' The door opened and Victoria strolled in—without his permission.

Clearly being Viscount Wishcliffe meant nothing these days.

'Excuse me. Newlyweds here.' Toby waved a hand between him and Autumn, who lay with the blankets tucked up under her chin and her eyes closed. 'We could have been up to *anything* in here that you wouldn't have wanted to walk in on.'

Victoria rolled her eyes. 'That never stopped you when Barnaby and I… Anyway. I knocked. I gave you plenty of warning.' Her gaze moved to where Autumn lay, eyes closed, apparently asleep again. 'I wanted to show you some of the improvements we've made to the estate over the last few years. And now is the best time to see it all at work.'

'Now being?' Toby squinted out of the window at the sun, still low in the sky, but he'd never been any good at telling the time by it.

'Seven o'clock.'

'In the *morning*? You realise that's like…' he did some quick calculations '…eleven o'clock at night in Vegas?'

'Well, that's fine then,' Victoria said, too cheerily. 'You never go to bed before midnight anyway. Come on!'

Beside him, Autumn gave a small delicate snore. Victoria folded her arms over her chest and tapped her foot.

Toby sighed. He wasn't getting out of this.

'Give me twenty minutes.'

'Ten,' she said sharply. 'I'll meet you downstairs.' Her

footsteps faded away then, just when he thought she was gone, she called out, 'And Toby? If you're not there I'll be back to rip that duvet away and drag you down there myself.' She slammed the door shut hard enough to make even the solid ancient walls of Wishcliffe House think about rattling. Autumn didn't stir.

Toby groaned, and then he got up.

Three hours later, he'd seen every single inch of the Wishcliffe estate, including some parts he wasn't even sure he'd ever known existed before now. Victoria's reports had been informative and complete, but somehow he just hadn't grasped the full scale of what she and Barnaby had been doing here until he saw it with his own eyes.

'So?' Victoria asked as they paused outside the last of really quite a number of barns. 'What do you think?'

He looked down at his brother's widow and finally realised something he'd managed to miss all morning.

She was nervous.

Victoria Blythe, the Dowager Viscountess Wishcliffe, force of nature and love of his brother's life, was nervous. He'd never have imagined it if he hadn't seen it with his own eyes, but it was all there—the way one cheek was slightly drawn in as if she was chewing on the inside, the tension in her shoulders, how she looked as if she might bolt at any moment.

She'd been taking care of the estate alone for a whole year now, and before that Toby knew she'd been closely involved with everything Barnaby had planned for the place. And since he'd been gone she'd had nobody to tell her she was doing a good job, or that she'd made the right decisions, or even just that she wasn't screwing up.

Because he'd just left her to it and run away, not ready

to face up to any of the responsibilities that were never meant to be his. He'd checked in and he'd read reports but he hadn't been *there.* He'd left things to her judgement because she was the one on the ground.

His concern from the night before returned, a feeling of guilt gnawing at his insides. Those responsibilities weren't meant to be hers to carry alone either. Barnaby would have been furious with him for what he'd done to Victoria—and rightly so, he realised now, a whole year too late.

'Tell me something,' he said. 'When you suggested that you run this place for a year while I tied up my business commitments… Was that for your benefit or mine?'

'You know you're eleven months later asking that than your best friend?' Victoria replied, with a small smile.

'*Finn* asked?'

She shrugged. 'He's your business partner. I guess he was hoping I'd have some inside track on how you becoming Viscount was going to affect your business.'

'Maybe.' But he'd never mentioned it. That was unlike Finn. Normally he talked about *everything*, all the time, until Toby had to beg him to stop. 'You didn't answer my question.'

With a sigh, Victoria hopped up to sit on the fence beside them. 'Honestly? I think it was a bit of both. I… You looked so thrown by it all, and everything had happened so fast and I knew you weren't ready. You'd never… None of us ever thought you'd have to do this. It wasn't fair to expect you to just drop all the plans you'd made for your whole life and take over here. Especially when there was so much still to be done.'

'So you did it for me.'

'Not just for you,' she admitted. 'I wasn't ready to say goodbye either.'

'And you are now?' Because she wasn't just talking about Wishcliffe, Toby knew. She'd lost her whole future in a heartbeat too. The love of her life. Her *child*.

Victoria stared out beyond the boundaries of the Wishcliffe estate. Not out to sea, where she'd lost her husband and son, but inland. Toby rather thought she might be looking towards the future.

'It's time,' she said eventually. 'I need… I need to start again. Find whatever happens next. God, I'm only thirty-three. There has to be more life out there for me. Doesn't there?'

It wasn't a rhetorical question; he could hear the pleading in her voice.

Tell me there's more, Toby.

'Definitely,' he said firmly. 'As long as you know you always have a home here at Wishcliffe too.'

He took her hand and she smiled. Together, they looked out over the land in silence for a long moment, until Victoria squeezed his hand and dropped it.

'You know you didn't answer my questions either,' she said. 'What do you think of what Barnaby and I did with Wishcliffe?'

At least that was a question that was easy to answer. 'It's amazing. Honestly, Vic, I can't believe how much you've done here. Not just how well the farm and the orchard are doing, but all the side businesses too. The farm shop and café, the events areas, even the holiday cottages. It's fantastic.'

It wasn't enough, though. They both knew that. It would take more to pull Wishcliffe out of the red and turn it into a growing concern. But it was a solid start. One he could sell to an interested buyer, he was sure. If Barnaby had lived, maybe he'd have saved the place for good after all.

The thought made something twist in his stomach, especially as Victoria's cheeks turned pink at his praise.

'I tried to. Well, mostly I just tried to follow what I knew Barnaby would have wanted for the place, and hoped that you'd want the same thing when you came back.'

Maybe that was true, but Toby had definitely seen some hints of Victoria herself in every part of the estate. From the range of herbal teas in the café to the displays in the orchard, the educational boards around the farm for visitors and the decoration of the cottages. Toby had loved his brother more than anyone in the world, but he knew Barnaby wouldn't have come up with the plans for those.

And the money. He'd looked over the most recent accounts when they'd stopped back at the house for morning coffee, and the estate was in a better financial position than it'd been when he'd inherited even, which in turn was better than when *Barnaby* had inherited. His brother had possessed the grand vision for what the estate could be, but Victoria was the one who'd wrangled the numbers to make it happen. Barnaby had always given her the credit for that—loudly, and to anyone who'd listen to his proud pronouncements.

'You've done an incredible job,' Toby said now, making sure to put the emphasis on *you.* 'I can't thank you enough for everything you've done here. I trusted you to keep things going while I sorted myself out, and you've done so much more than that.'

Victoria looked at the ground, her smile fading a little. 'Well, it was my last duty as Viscountess. I wanted to do it right.'

Now Wishcliffe had a new Viscountess. For the next three months, at least.

'I wasn't just saying it. You really can stay, you know,'

he said, even though he knew it was a promise he wouldn't be able to keep for long. 'As long as I own Wishcliffe—or any home, really—there'll always be a place for you there.'

'Thank you.' She looked up and he saw the sadness that always lurked behind her eyes these days. Sometimes she hid it better than others, he'd noticed. But it was front and centre now. 'But, honestly, it's time for me to move on. Do you know, I've *never* lived alone? I moved straight from my university shared flat into Wishcliffe with Barnaby—which was quite the upgrade, I can tell you. And then, even when he and Harry were gone… You're never alone at Wishcliffe, you know that. And I think I'd like to try being on my own. Just for a little while. I'll stay the two weeks I promised Autumn, but then I'll be leaving.'

'Well, if you're sure.' Toby tried not to let the relief show in his face or his voice. Keeping this charade going would be all the harder under Victoria's scrutiny.

His phone buzzed in his pocket and he pulled it out quickly to answer it.

Then he checked the screen and saw the name of the agency he'd contacted about preparing to put the estate on the market. Something else he really didn't want Victoria asking questions about.

'Excuse me. I need to take this.'

Victoria nodded and said, 'I need to be getting back to the house anyway. I'll see you at dinner.'

She turned and walked away. But he still waited until she was all the way across the yard before he pressed 'answer'.

While she'd had a perfunctory tour of the house with Toby and Victoria on her arrival, Autumn knew that the tour she was heading on now was the one that really mattered. This was the tour that would teach her everything she needed to know about running a house like Wishcliffe—and, more than that, it was her best chance to make friends with the people who really mattered around here.

Never mind the family; she needed to get in with the staff.

A house as big as Wishcliffe didn't just keep going by itself. And while the staff these days might be a lot smaller than the ones in her grandma's beloved period dramas, they still had more influence over what actually got done around the place than anyone else.

She started with the housekeeper, of course. Mrs Heath was at her desk in her small office, just off the kitchens, when Autumn appeared, dressed in jeans and a blouse that she hoped looked neat but casual. It was hard to know what sort of sartorial elegance was really expected from her here, in her home, but she had to work with what was in her suitcase anyway, so she didn't have a lot of choice.

'Can I help you, ma'am?' Mrs Heath got to her feet as soon as she spotted Autumn, which was kind of embarrassing.

'Oh, I hope so. You see… Toby and Victoria gave me a lovely tour of the house last night, and I must say I've never seen a more beautiful home. You must have all worked so hard to keep it this way.'

'It's an honour to be in charge of such an historical property's upkeep,' Mrs Heath said stiffly.

'I'm sure,' Autumn agreed. 'But the thing is, what they *didn't* show me was how this house actually *works*. All the effort you and your team put in every day to keep the place running smoothly for them. And all the secret nooks and crannies they wouldn't even think about but would be fascinating to an outsider like me—you know… all the house's secrets.'

Mrs Heath still wasn't looking convinced. 'I'm not sure—'

'Oh!' Grandma had taught her never to interrupt, but sometimes it was necessary. 'And I haven't even *seen* the gardens at all. I'm sure they must be *wonderful*.'

Mrs Heath's gaze shifted, just as Autumn's had, to the well-tended window box just outside her office window.

'Well, yes, the gardens really are quite splendid,' she admitted.

The first yes. That was always the key to getting someone on your side—you got them to agree with you about something, anything. It was much easier to keep them saying yes after that, Grandma had always said.

Granddad had just laughed and said that was how conmen operated, but Grandma had shrugged and said, 'Whatever works.'

'I suppose I do have a little time this morning to show you around.' She gave Autumn an assessing look. 'And you'll have to meet Old Gareth, our groundskeeper, eventually. Might as well be today.'

The staff they met with on their tour of the house were clearly unsure about this unexpected new lady of the manor—and not even a British one at that—but Autumn set about charming them the way her grandma had always taught her, and it seemed to work well enough to be getting on with, anyway.

The house was far larger than her quick tour of the public rooms would have led her to believe. She itched to try out the huge kitchen, rolling out dough for her grandma's famous apple pie crust, but knew that would have to wait until she'd properly won the trust of the staff.

Which will probably be around the time I'm ready to leave.

From one of the guest bedrooms' windows Mrs Heath pointed out all the other areas of the estate—the money-making ones that Victoria was apparently showing Toby around that morning. The holiday cottages, the farm and shop, the café, the orchards…

'You grow your own apples here?' Her mouth was already salivating at the idea of apple pie with fruit fresh from the tree, just like she'd made back home with her grandparents.

'Of course. How else would we make the Wishcliffe Estate cider?' Mrs Heath gave her something that almost resembled a fond smile. 'Come on. We'll tour the gardens next.'

The gardens were every bit as wonderful as Autumn had been hoping for. The dahlias were still in bloom in their walled garden, and the trees a few weeks off turning for good, although she spotted the odd yellow leaf amongst the green. She trailed behind Mrs Heath along winding paths through the formal gardens, through arched doorways in high stone walls and past statues and sundials.

'I'm going to need to spend weeks exploring these gardens before I can be sure I've found every beautiful thing,' she declared, not minding the challenge at all.

'As long as you're not planning on trying to *change* things.' The gruff, disapproving voice came from over a lowish wall. Autumn stepped onto a raised stone ledge, then stretched up on her tiptoes to rest her arms along the top of the wall and smiled at the bearded, scowling man leaning on a garden fork on the other side. Behind him stood a veritable orchard of trees all starting to grow heavy with fruit.

'Gareth, I presume?' She smiled her best, most charming smile.

Gareth's scowl deepened. 'And you'll be the new lady muck.'

'That's me! Ready to muck in and help out.'

Now he looked positively offended. 'You think I need your help?'

'No!' Autumn made sure to sound scandalised at the very suggestion. 'Quite the opposite. You see, my grandfather taught me all he could about gardens, and the small orchard he looked after. But he died before I could hope to learn enough to look after *these* gardens, and these beautiful apple trees. And do you know? I don't think I've ever even *tried* cider.' She shook her head sadly, quietly amused at his scandalised expression. 'No, I'm afraid you're the one who will have to educate me, Mr Gareth, in all the things I need to know to make sure my husband and I don't suggest any foolish changes to your gardens in the future.'

'You want to learn about the gardens?' There was disbelief in Old Gareth's voice, but a hint of hope too. If Autumn had gauged him right, talking about his gardens was probably one of his favourite hobbies, the same way it had been one of her Granddad's. And, just like Granddad, there was probably nobody else interested in listening.

She nodded. 'I hope you can bear the extra burden.'

'I suppose I'll manage,' he grumbled contently. 'I usually do.'

Autumn beamed. 'Then I'll come and find you for my first lesson tomorrow!'

Without giving him a chance to object, she hopped

down from the stone ledge and turned back to Mrs Heath. 'Where next?'

Mrs Heath gave her another one of those assessing looks, but this time Autumn rather thought the assessment might be more favourable. 'We'll go and look at the holiday cottages,' she said. She waited until they were well out of earshot of the orchard before adding, 'Well, you certainly knew how to handle Old Gareth.'

Autumn shrugged. 'He reminded me of my grandfather.'

'Hmm.' Mrs Heath's close-lipped reply didn't indicate whether she thought that was a good thing or a bad thing.

Autumn smiled to herself all the same. She'd won over Old Gareth, she was sure.

She glanced across at Mrs Heath. One down, many more to go.

Maybe she'd go back to her room and spend some time with Grandma's bible after her tour. She had the feeling she was going to need all the help she could get.

Dinner that night was a more relaxed affair than the one before, but bedtime proved rather more tension-inducing.

'I can take the sofa tonight,' Autumn said, so soon after the bedroom door closed behind them that Toby knew she must have been thinking it all the way up the stairs.

'I don't mind it,' he lied. 'It's comfortable.'

'No, it isn't. I sat on it earlier and almost put my back out,' Autumn replied. 'Nobody should have to sleep on that thing two nights in a row.'

'Nobody should have to sleep on that thing at all,' Toby muttered under his breath.

They both stared at the sofa for a long moment.

Then Autumn said, 'You know, this bed is pretty big.

We could put a row of pillows down the middle of it or something. If you wanted.'

What he really wanted was to curl up in that bed with Autumn in his arms and revisit the wedding night he couldn't remember but, since that wasn't on the menu, Toby said, 'That could work.'

The bed, even with its dividing line of cushions gathered from various furniture around the suite, was certainly more comfortable than the sofa had been. But as Toby lay there, staring at the ceiling, listening to Autumn breathing on the other side of the pillow wall, he knew he wasn't going to be able to sleep.

Last night he'd had the advantage of bone-deep exhaustion, jet lag and a still-lingering hangover. His body had taken over and shut down for the night. Tonight, his brain was in control. And it was far too busy thinking to bother with anything like sleep.

He'd expected to be kept awake by worries about the estate, about Victoria, about selling Wishcliffe—or even regrets about the fact that he couldn't quite remember the last thing his brother had ever said to him, or not playing a game of football with Harry in the garden the last time he'd visited. He'd fully expected Wishcliffe as a whole to keep him awake and stressed out every night he had to stay there until it was sold.

He *hadn't* expected to be lying awake listening to his wife breathe and wondering what she was thinking.

'If you sigh one more time *just* as I'm about to fall asleep I'm going to dismantle the pillow wall and beat you with it,' Autumn said, which at least answered his wondering.

'Sorry,' he said, and then sighed again. Mostly on purpose.

As he'd half expected, Autumn's face appeared over

the pillow wall. 'What are you sighing about anyway? Missing your torture device of a sofa already?'

'No. I was just…thinking.'

'Sounds like it was painful. I'm so sorry.'

He rolled his eyes at her, before realising she probably couldn't see that in the half-light of the moon through the window. 'I was thinking how weird it was that you remember more of our relationship than I do. It gives you an advantage over me.'

Autumn flopped back onto her side of the mattress. He thought she might ignore his comments entirely, until she said, 'I've already told you what I remember.'

'Not all of it.'

'How we met, how you lost my job, how we ended up getting married… What did I miss out?'

'What happened after that.' Toby swallowed. 'You remember our wedding night, and I don't.'

The silence from the other side of the pillow wall was oppressive. Was she remembering it now? Or just preparing to beat him with cushions?

'I don't remember *everything*,' she said after a long pause.

'Still more than me.'

The covers rustled and Autumn's face appeared above the pillow wall again. 'What do you want to hear? That you were good in bed, even blind drunk?'

Toby grinned. 'If it's true, then hell, yes.'

'Typical man,' Autumn muttered with a roll of her eyes. 'Fine. It was good sex. For a drunken one-night stand.'

It was too dark to tell if her cheeks were red but, from the way she quickly dropped back out of sight after her words, Toby suspected they might be.

He couldn't resist. 'Just "good"?' He laughed as a pillow landed on his face.

'Go to sleep, Toby.' Like that was going to happen now.

'Good night, Autumn,' he said anyway and turned on his side, away from her.

But he still heard her, moments later, as she said very softly, 'Better than good.' And when he did finally fall asleep he was still smiling.

CHAPTER EIGHT

AUTUMN AWOKE TO find the pillow wall destroyed, and Toby thrashing around on the mattress next to her like the minions of hell were after him. She blinked, trying to make sense of what was happening.

'Barnaby!'

A nightmare. He was having a nightmare about his brother. His dead brother.

Well. Their second night in a bed together was definitely a change in pace from their first.

Autumn shivered at the anguish in his voice. Gently, she reached for him, shaking his shoulder to try and bring him out of it.

'Toby. Toby, it's okay. I'm here.' She kept talking, nonsense mostly, just trying to sound soothing as he slowly calmed under her hands. 'It's okay,' she repeated as his eyes fluttered open at last. 'I'm here.'

'Autumn?' His voice broke on her name, and she felt her heart crack in her chest at the sound.

'I'm here.' It was all she could say. All she could offer.

Lurching forward, Toby wrapped his arms around her, clutching her tight to his chest. Heat radiated off him, heat and fear, seeping out of him and into her skin as he held her.

Then he pulled back, just enough to look into her eyes

with his own unfocused ones. 'You're here,' he whispered.

And then he kissed her.

At first she was too stunned to react. And once her brain caught up with her lips…it was too late. It already felt so good and she wanted him so much, even like this, desperate and needy and still half lost in a nightmare. His mouth felt so damn good on hers, his arms so safe around her. Autumn sank into the kiss and let the feel of him surround her, consume her.

Until he pulled away.

'Oh, God,' Toby gasped, suddenly half a bed away. Autumn shivered at the loss of his heat. 'I'm so sorry. I shouldn't have done that.'

'It's…it's okay.' Autumn forced the words out as she pushed down the lust that had risen through her body at his touch. 'You were upset. I understand.'

He hadn't meant it. Of course he hadn't meant it. She'd just been there. And from the look on his face, he was *horrified* that he'd crossed that line they'd so carefully drawn. Probably didn't want her getting any ideas that the ring on her finger *meant* anything.

'Still, I'm sorry.' He seemed calmer now, his breathing starting to even out until she could hardly hear it. 'It was just…a nightmare.'

Autumn shifted to rest against the headboard, pulling the covers up over her pyjamas to ward off the chill of the night air. 'Do you want to talk about it?'

'Not really.' Of course he didn't. He probably wanted to get all British and stiff upper lip about it all. But that didn't mean he didn't *need* to talk to someone about what had him screaming in his sleep.

And it wasn't as if there was anyone else here in the bed for him to talk to.

'You were calling for Barnaby,' she said softly. 'You were dreaming about him?'

There was silence from the other side of the bed, then a long exhale before Toby moved to sit against the headboard too. The pillow wall was history, but he left more than a cushion's width between them anyway, probably to stop her from getting the wrong idea again.

'I have… I guess you'd call it a recurring dream. I've had it at least once a week for the last year,' he admitted.

'What happens in it? Can you tell me?'

Another long pause. 'In it… I'm there, on the cliffs above the beach, the day he and Harry died. And I'm watching—even though I couldn't possibly have seen them from that position if I'd been there. But I'm watching as it happens. As the boat rolls on a wave and Harry goes over. As Barnaby follows to save him and hits his head on the hull. As Harry disappears under the waves. As they both—'

He broke off, but Autumn heard the words he didn't say all the same.

As they both die. Jesus, he's watching his brother and nephew die in his sleep every week.

'And then the cliff starts to crumble, down into the waves, taking me with it. And the house, and the orchard…it all just falls into the sea and I can't stop any of it.' He shook his head as if he were trying to shake away the memory. 'It's ridiculous, I know. I mean, I wasn't even in the country when they died. And there's so much land between the house and the cliff anyway.'

'Dreams aren't meant to be real,' Autumn pointed out. But she couldn't help but think there was a good dose of reality in his dream all the same—the reality in his head anyway.

'I just hate that it…it *feels* so real when I'm in it.' Toby ran his hands through his hair and, even in the dark, she could tell he was still shaking a little.

'You're scared to be back here, aren't you?' Grandma had always been on at her to try and use tact, but Autumn found that the blunt truth got her places faster most of the time.

'Wouldn't you be?' Toby shot back. 'It killed my father, my brother and my nephew.'

'Do you really think that?'

He sighed. 'No. I suppose not. I mean, logically I know that it wasn't this *house* that killed them. Dad had a weak heart, and Barnaby and Harry…that was a terrible accident. But sometimes… I wonder if I could have stopped it if I was here.'

'You know you couldn't have,' she said. 'You can't blame yourself for it, Toby.'

'I know. I just…'

'Do.'

'Yeah.'

And she didn't know how to convince him otherwise. As he said, this wasn't logic. This was emotion. And that was far harder to argue with.

'Maybe being here at Wishcliffe will help,' she tried.

'Perhaps.' Toby didn't sound convinced. The bed dipped for a moment, and she watched the shadow of him in the dark as he stood up and gathered one of the spare blankets they'd found. 'You should go back to sleep.'

'Where are you going?'

'Downstairs. To the study. If I'm not going to sleep, I might as well get some work done.'

He was gone before she could convince him to stay, leaving her with nothing but the memory of his kiss and an aching sadness for him in her chest.

* * *

Time seemed to move differently at Wishcliffe.

Toby couldn't quite explain it, but it seemed all at once as if he'd only arrived home yesterday, but at the same time that he'd been there for ever.

'It's probably just the routine of it all,' Autumn said when he mentioned the phenomena. 'I mean, you're working hard but you're doing the same sort of things every day, right? Makes it feel endless but new.'

He wasn't sure that made any sense at all outside of Autumn's own brain, but he had to admit she was right about the routine they'd fallen into over the past few weeks.

He spent his mornings learning more about the estate—either working on the business in his father's study, or out on the farm or land. There was always plenty to do, it seemed, and plenty of people waiting to tell him what it was they needed from him.

He always tried to make it back to the house for lunch, though, because that was the only time he and Autumn ever seemed to have alone together when they were both awake. She'd meet him in his study with two loaded plates and chat through their lunch break about everything *she'd* been doing that morning, before asking about his work.

Then she'd pick up their plates and disappear again, and his world would go silent.

He used to like silence. He wasn't sure what had happened that he now missed that chatter when he was alone, staring at all the paperwork that went with trying to sell an estate the size of Wishcliffe.

Because his afternoons were all about the sale. He told Victoria, and anyone else who asked, that he was catching up on paperwork, or even his own business interests.

But mostly he was organising surveys and answering questions from the agent he'd employed to help him sell.

Dinner was always a formal affair in the dining room, and Victoria usually joined them. Her cottage in Wishcliffe village still needed more work, so for now she remained resident at the house. Which meant Toby and Autumn had to keep up their charade.

He was pretty sure that should have been harder than it was.

But their lunches together had helped to build a friendship Toby already knew he'd miss when it was over. Adding in a few touches—a kiss against her hair, an arm around her waist as she passed him—weren't exactly difficult. In fact, it was remembering *not* to do it when others weren't watching that Toby was finding trickiest.

Especially when they still had to retire to the same bed every night.

They'd both been extra vigilant about the line of pillows down the middle of the bed since that first night, however ridiculous it felt. He'd also discovered that if he worked hard enough—out on the estate as well as in his office—and late enough, he passed out quickly and deeply enough when his head hit the pillow that there were no more nightmares. Which he had to assume was a relief for both of them.

It was a routine, for sure, but one that was working for them. And if some nights it felt harder and harder to say goodnight and turn his back on Autumn and the pillow wall at the end of it, well. That was only natural too, right? They were pretending to be in love. That kind of thing had an effect.

He just had to remember that it was all a business arrangement. One with a very strict no sex clause.

Except all the work in the world couldn't stop him imagining. Wondering. Wishing.

'I think the worst part is that I can't even remember what it actually felt like in the first place,' he complained to Finn, almost a month into his marriage contract with Autumn.

'Sleeping with your wife?' Finn barked a laugh. 'You won't be the first husband to say that.'

'Yeah. But I mean it *literally.*' He looked around them at the London pub they were drinking in, and admitted to himself, for the first time since he'd left Wishcliffe for the city that morning, why exactly he'd come.

Yes, there was the meeting with the agent, but that could have been done over video call easily enough. And yes, he needed to catch up with his best friend and business partner, and Finn appeared to be avoiding Wishcliffe like the plague recently. And of course his penthouse flat in London could do with checking in on, but he could have asked the housekeeping service he paid to do that. Or he could have brought Autumn with him, showed her the bright lights of London. Victoria particularly had seemed surprised that he hadn't done that.

But bringing Autumn would have defeated the real objective of his trip—the one he was only admitting to himself here, now, after three pints.

He was avoiding his wife. Or, more precisely, he was avoiding temptation.

'Your Vegas wedding night memories still eluding you, then?' Finn's eyes were faintly mocking over the rim of his pint glass. Still his first pint glass, Toby knew, and likely to be his last too.

'Sadly so.' Even worse, now he had just the scraps of memory that Autumn had shared with him, the first night they'd slept in the same bed at Wishcliffe. His mind felt obliged to fill in the blanks for him, and he was starting to wish he'd never asked. It was just so…distracting, not knowing if his imagination lived up to reality.

Finn shrugged. 'So seduce her again then. Find out what you've been missing. I mean, you're *married*, Toby. Not only is it not against the rules, it's positively allowed! Why the hell the two of you haven't been making the most of this situation for the last few weeks I have no idea.'

'Because we agreed no sex. Weren't you listening in the limo to the airport?'

'Well, yeah. But I just assumed that was the hangover talking. Like saying "I'm never drinking again" after a heavy night.'

'Not just the hangover. There's actual paperwork confirming it.' Locked away in the bottom drawer of his father's desk, an actual contract stating that he and his legal wife would not actually have sex, even though they'd already consummated the marriage by the time they'd signed it, so it wasn't as if an annulment would have held water even if they hadn't been living together for weeks.

Finn winced on his behalf. 'Ouch.'

'Yeah.'

'So she really doesn't want to sleep with you then.'

'Apparently not. Except…' Sometimes, some days, he was sure he saw the same longing in her eyes. The same want. The same desire he felt coursing through his body every time he looked at her now.

He remembered meeting her in that bar in Vegas. He remembered thinking she was pretty, that she had the kind of curves he adored. He might not remember the sequence of events that had led to them falling into bed—and a chapel—together, but he remembered the attraction.

And it was nothing like he felt now, almost a month later.

Now, he felt as if he might lose his mind if he couldn't kiss her. Now, his hand burned when he touched the small of her back to guide her towards the stairs at night. Now, her smile over his desk at lunchtime heated his blood, and the way she licked her lips made him have to swallow a groan.

And it was worse than that. Now, he found himself watching the clock on his father's desk, counting down the seconds until she'd join him for lunch. Now, he spent dinnertime coming up with new questions to ask her before bed, to cause her to linger with him just a little longer before she turned away.

'Except?' Finn repeated, his voice amused. Clearly Toby had forgotten to keep talking.

He shook his head. 'It doesn't matter.'

'If you're here with me instead of there with her it obviously does.'

His friend had a point. Toby sighed. 'Sometimes I think she wants the same thing I do. But she won't let herself have it, and I don't know why.'

'Well, that's what you need to find out then.' Finn drained the last dregs of his pint and banged his glass on the bar. 'Because you've only got, what? Another couple of months married to her. If you want to change the terms of the agreement you need to find out why she *doesn't*.'

'And if I don't like those reasons?'

'Then you respect them anyway.' Finn clapped him on the shoulder. 'Not that I think you'd do anything else, honourable bastard that you are.'

Toby managed a smile at that. Finn was right. He'd respect whatever Autumn's reasons were, but he knew he couldn't be imagining the connection between them. The way her eyes softened and warmed during those private conversations at the bedroom door. The way she leaned into his touch as he guided her up the stairs.

He needed to know why she wouldn't give into this, in case there was a new deal to be struck. He'd leave the decision in her hands, but he needed to know.

Because, damn it, he wanted to know everything there was to know about Autumn Blythe. Not because she was his wife but because she fascinated him more every day.

'Go home to Wishcliffe, Toby,' Finn said, and he nodded.

Time to go home. Again.

Toby had gone to London. Without her.

Ostensibly, Autumn was annoyed about this because she would have liked to see London, and because the staff kept giving her pitying looks as if she were an actual abandoned wife. She'd heard one of them murmur, 'Honeymoon must be over then,' when they thought she couldn't hear.

So, yeah. She had every right to be annoyed that Toby wasn't holding up his end of the charade.

But the worst part was that, even if she wouldn't admit it to anyone else, the *real* reason she was annoyed was that she *missed* him.

That was definitely not part of their plan.

Missing Toby when he wasn't there was something else to add to her list of things that weren't going to plan, actually. She hadn't planned for their lunches together to be the highlight of her day. And she definitely hadn't planned for the way her heart lurched every night when he said goodnight. Or the way he invaded her dreams even with the wall of pillows between them…

Anyway. He was gone, which meant she *definitely* shouldn't be thinking about him. He hadn't even come back last night, and she'd had dinner with Victoria—avoiding concerned looks from her sort-of sister-in-law—then headed to bed. Alone.

And she was so sick of that.

It was ridiculous. Before the single night with Toby following her marriage she'd been alone since she'd moved to Vegas. She'd been *relieved* not to have to share her bed, share her life with anyone, after Robbie.

But now…she was already sharing her life, her days, with Toby. Usually. They were even sharing the bed—just not in the way her body and her memories kept reminding her they *could* be sharing it.

It was getting harder to remember why that was. Just for the couple of months they had left together. Why *not* enjoy this time to the fullest of their ability?

Because it wouldn't be enough. You'd go all in, fall too hard, want more. Just like always. And you don't want that, because it'll end and it'll break your heart. Besides, Toby doesn't want you falling for him either. This is purely business.

He wanted *her* though, she was pretty sure. In fact, if she had to guess, she'd say he was struggling with exactly the same fantasies she was. At least, if the accidental kiss they'd shared after his nightmare was anything to go by…

Autumn shook her head to banish the memory. It didn't matter. Couldn't matter today. Because he wasn't even *there*.

Deciding to put her husband out of her head for the rest of the day, Autumn headed out to her favourite place on the Wishcliffe estate—the orchard.

Old Gareth was already there, a basket against his hip as he collected low-hanging apples.

'Planning on making your own cider?' she called as she clambered over the wall from the gardens. It was so much faster than walking all the way around to the official orchard gate.

'Not me. These are for the missus. She wants to make apple pie.'

'I love apple pie,' Autumn said, aware as she was saying it just how classically American she must sound.

'Help me pick some more apples and maybe you'll get one then.'

Smiling, Autumn hopped down from the top of the wall. She was perfectly capable of making her own apple pie but, since she still wasn't allowed in the kitchen, she'd have to rely on the kindness of Gareth's wife.

'Say no more.' Scrambling up the nearest tree with the help of the rickety wooden ladder that Gareth had leaned against it, she swung herself up into the branches, testing their strength until she could find a safe perch to pick apples from.

They picked apples in companionable silence for a while, Autumn tossing them down for Gareth to catch in his basket. A cool October breeze rustled the leaves and branches around her, but the sky was blue and puffy white clouds still sped across it, and for a short time Autumn was able to forget entirely about her sort-of husband and his trip away.

So entirely, that when Old Gareth suddenly said, 'Ah, good morning, my lord,' she promptly fell out of her tree.

The ladder clattered to the ground, dislodged by her abrupt unbalancing, and she heard Gareth shout as he jumped out of its way, but by then she was falling and she couldn't focus on anything except the wind whooshing in her ears, her blood pumping too hard, and the fact that she might be about to die.

With a sharp scream, she grabbed hold of the branch she'd been sitting on as she sailed past it and hung there, her feet not *quite* able to touch the ground.

'Autumn?' She couldn't quite tell if that was concern or despair behind the astonishment in her husband's voice. But then his arms reached up to wrap around her legs and she decided it was probably concern after all. 'You can let go. I've got you.'

And he did. As she reluctantly uncurled her fingers from the branch, she felt his grip shift, lowering her down into his arms until her throbbing head was resting against his sturdy chest and her feet were on solid ground again. He didn't let go, though. His arms remained firmly around her, as if holding on was the only way he could be sure she wouldn't keep falling, even though there was no longer any further for her to fall.

Except maybe to the ground. She pulled away, just slightly, and her legs wobbled so violently that Toby grabbed her again and held her even tighter.

'You okay?' he whispered into her ear.

She shook her head against his shirt. 'But I will be. I just need to get my breath back.'

But then she looked up at him and the breath she'd fought to get into her lungs disappeared again. The fear in his eyes, starting to fade now she was safe on the ground, looked just like the fear she'd seen in the moonlight as she'd woken him from his nightmare.

'I thought…' His hold tightened for a second, bringing her even closer to him. Except now, instead of her lips being pressed against his shirt, they were tantalisingly close to his own. If she just stretched up on her toes a little, they'd be kissing.

Just like that night. When Toby had pulled away from her in horror.

He didn't want this. He might want her body now, but he didn't want her in his life, not once he'd sold Wishcliffe. So she couldn't give into her natural tendencies here. No falling too far or too fast.

Nothing lasts, remember?

But heartbreak and grief lasted a hell of a lot longer than love or pleasure, in her experience.

And she was starting to think that Toby might be a

man she could love, so she couldn't risk getting close enough to him to find out.

Autumn rocked back on her heels, putting his lips out of reach, and Toby's arms around her loosened. His throat moved as he swallowed, and she saw his gaze dart to the side and land on the basket of apples on the ground.

'You do realise that we pay people to pick all these apples, right?' He made a good effort to sound amused, rather than affected by their closeness. Unless Autumn really had been reading him wrong. 'I mean, to make the cider. It's sort of a business thing. Unless you were scrumping for apples…'

Old Gareth gave an awkward cough, and for the first time Autumn wondered whose permission he had to take apples from the orchard for his wife's apple pies.

Well, hers, she supposed. As Viscountess Wishcliffe. Lucky for him.

'I told Gareth it would be okay for him to take a few apples for his wife to make apple pies.'

She turned her face from Toby's chest and saw his eyes light up. 'For the Fire Festival?'

'Well, of course, sir.' Old Gareth sounded faintly defensive. 'She always makes the pies for the festival, as you well know.'

'Fire Festival?' Autumn frowned up at Toby. 'What's the Fire Festival?'

'The Fire Festival is the best thing about Wishcliffe.' Toby let her go, just long enough to wrap one arm around her waist so they stood side by side instead of front to front. 'Come on. I'll tell you all about it on the way back to the house. That's enough scrumping for you for one day.'

CHAPTER NINE

EVER SINCE HE was a child, the Wishcliffe Fire Festival had been Toby's favourite day of the whole year. Better than Christmas, when he was required to dress up in stiff, uncomfortable clothes and go to church. Even better than his birthday, since people only ever seemed interested in that for the first couple of hours, and then it was just like any other day.

But not the Fire Festival. The excitement that went along with that was felt for weeks.

This year, even more than usual. As soon as he'd explained to Autumn about the estate's slightly pagan autumnal celebration, she'd embraced the concept and insisted on being deeply involved. Victoria was thrilled to have a co-conspirator to help with the planning, and for the last two weeks the house had been filled with the scent of apples and cinnamon, and an almost tangible excitement that something big was about to happen.

Personally, Toby had been glad of the distraction. He'd hoped his night away in London would help him move past his infatuation with his wife, but instead it seemed to have had the opposite effect. Watching her slip from that branch of the apple tree had almost stopped his heart; holding her to him, safe and close, had set it beating again. And now that heartbeat had taken over his every waking moment, like a part of Autumn inside his chest, distracting him.

Try as he might, he couldn't banish the memory of that midnight kiss. Or forget how close he'd come to kissing her again under the apple tree, without the excuse of being half asleep and lost in a nightmare.

He just wanted to kiss her. Repeatedly.

Toby sighed. He needed to talk to her about what was between them, and whether she felt it as strongly as he did. He didn't know where it might lead them, but he knew it was a conversation they needed to have.

But he was putting it off, all the same. And having Autumn distracted by the Fire Festival was definitely helping with that.

Even better, it was distracting Victoria enough that she hadn't noticed the surveyor visiting the property the other week, or the photographer snapping shots of the house and the estate for the sales website.

And *that* was why he was putting off the conversation with Autumn. Because, even if it went as well as he hoped, they still only had another six weeks of this pretend marriage ahead of them. And if it went badly, well, they still had another six whole weeks to keep pretending.

It felt kind of lose-lose. Not that this strange limbo was any better.

Feeling restless and a little lost, Toby looked out of his study window at the activity in the fields to the left of the formal gardens. Tonight was the Fire Festival. His favourite night of the year. And he wasn't going to waste it mooning around after the wife he couldn't touch. He needed to distract *himself* for a while, and the Fire Festival was the perfect way to do that. He'd head out there soon. Just a few more emails to finish up…

His attention strayed out of the window again, and he closed his laptop with a sigh.

Out on the field, wooden stalls were already set up ready to serve hot food—and warm cider, of course, from last year's supply. This year's apple harvest was in and the cider-making process could now begin. That was what had started the festival, really—although Toby suspected it had much older, more pagan roots within the community.

The modern version, as instigated by his grandfather, was a celebration for the whole community, bringing together all the people who'd worked to pick the apples to make the cider for the following year. These days, they mostly hired seasonal workers, but it used to be the estate families and workers who pitched in to pick the fruit, and this party was their extra reward, on top of their daily pay.

In the centre of the field, far away from the distant trees that lined the estate, stood the bonfire—tall and wide and stuffed with sticks and wood and leaves and other flammable things. Toby wasn't sure *exactly* what Old Gareth used to make sure the pile went up with such a dramatic whoosh of fire, but he'd decided it was probably best not to ask. The important thing was, when the time came, the bonfire would be ready.

'Are you ready?' Autumn poked her head around his study door, a green bobble hat perched adorably on her russet curls. 'The band are just warming up, and the first cider is being poured. People will start arriving soon.'

'Right. Coming now.' He glanced down at his desk to ensure that any papers to do with the sale were hidden and, when he looked up again, Autumn was entirely inside the room, this time holding out a padded coat and a bright red bobble hat to match her own green one. 'It's really not that cold out there,' he said, blinking.

She shook the hat at him, bobble waggling wildly. 'It's fall, Toby. In England. You need a hat.'

'Doesn't it bother you that you're named after a season that isn't even a thing in your country?' he asked.

She rolled her eyes and shook the hat again. 'Doesn't it bother you that you have five middle names and one of them is Felix?'

He knew he shouldn't have let her see the marriage certificate. Although, to be honest, he was pretty impressed he'd managed to *remember* all his names in the moment, given how drunk he'd been when he'd stepped into the chapel. 'I'll be standing right next to a bloody great fire, Autumn. And I grew up here, remember? Trust me, if you think this is cold, you're going to *hate* January.'

Except she wouldn't be there in January, would she? Their three months would be up before then, and she'd be long gone, home to wherever she decided that was going to be next.

His good mood soured, Toby grabbed the hat and jammed it onto his head. 'Happy?'

Giving him a lopsided grin, she stepped closer and reached up to adjust his hat. As her fingers brushed against his temple, Toby found himself holding his breath. Not daring to breathe in, knowing that just the scent of her would make him want to kiss her and never stop.

'You're ready.' She stepped back and gave him a nod and a grin, but he was sure he wasn't imagining the tension in her smile. Did she feel it too?

Before he could ask, she'd already stepped back outside the study door, leading the way to the Fire Festival celebrations, and all Toby could do was try to keep up.

But one thing he was sure about. He couldn't put this

off any longer. Distractions weren't enough now. It was time to face this thing between them head-on.

He wasn't letting her out of his sight tonight. Not until they'd talked, finally.

And maybe even more…

The festival atmosphere hit Autumn the moment she stepped out of the side door of Wishcliffe House. The early evening air buzzed with excitement as the sun slipped behind the trees and twilight fell.

This was the magic time. The crisp chill of the fall air, the crackle of the fires in the braziers by the food stalls, the crunch of the leaves underfoot. Stars were popping out all over the night sky and the air smelled of apples and cinnamon and the changing seasons.

And, beside her, Toby was wearing the most adorable woolly hat. No wonder she'd almost kissed him right there in the study. The combination of the festival atmosphere and his general kissability had almost defeated all her better impulses.

Although, really, would kissing him really be all that bad…?

Yes, Autumn, she told herself sternly. *It would be.*

It was just getting harder to remember why.

It was the pagan associations of the whole thing that were confusing her, she decided, as Toby fetched her a cup of Wishcliffe cider from the first stall they passed. Victoria had told her *all* about this festival, and how it came about. Maybe Toby thought it had to do with the apple harvest, but everyone else knew better.

They were past the Autumnal Equinox already—*her* equinox, if she wanted to be particular about it—and heading into Samhain, the end of the harvest and the start of winter.

In centuries gone by, this time of year would have been the last chance for people to visit family and friends in other villages, before the winter snows set in. Fires would have been lit to guide people home, and to celebrate. They were moving into the time where the veil between the living and the dead thinned, where the world became uncanny—especially in places with as much history as this.

But it was also the end of the old Celtic year and the start of the new, she'd learned. A chance to let go of old ways and old beliefs and start new ones. A time, perhaps, to take a chance and try something new…

She'd always been good at that.

Toby returned, elbowing his way through the growing crowd, to hand her a cup of cider.

'What do you think?' He grinned as he looked around at the gathering. There had to be hundreds of people here, Autumn thought, all locals, all part of his land, his estate. His family, in a way.

'I think it's incredible. And I'm so glad I got to be here for it.'

'Me too.' From the intense way he looked down at her, his eyes sparkling in the firelight, she knew he wasn't talking about himself. He was glad she was there.

Maybe he was even glad he'd married her. And not just because she distracted everyone from his plans to sell the estate.

God, he was still selling the estate. Would there even *be* a Fire Festival next year? Could this *really* be the last one?

It was hard to imagine it in this moment. With Toby smiling down at her, bobble hat bright against the darkening sky, his eyes alight with promise of the evening ahead. Hard to imagine anything past tonight.

Nothing lasts. Not even this moment.

She swallowed, her whole body feeling too warm suddenly.

'When is Gareth lighting the bonfire?' Her words broke the moment and Toby glanced away, towards the giant pile of wood and sticks that Gareth had spent weeks building.

'As soon as it's properly dark,' he replied. Then he grabbed her arm. 'Come on. Let's go explore.'

Autumn had been involved in the planning of the festival, so she knew all the stalls and activities that were planned for it. She'd assumed Toby would know the same—from previous years, at least, if not this one—but he appeared amazed and entranced by every new thing they stumbled across as they toured the field.

There was the folk band, playing impossibly fast with harmonising tunes that would put even the best bluegrass players she knew to shame. There was the small circle of wooden toadstool seats, filled with young kids, and the wizard with a pointy hat reading them stories. Toby gasped at the scale of the fireworks that had been set up in the next field, all orchestrated by computer.

'I used to be my dad's assistant, darting out there to light them all one by one,' he explained as they turned away towards the next thing. 'He'd definitely think this was an improvement.'

There were stalls of local produce, as well as the hot food and drinks being served. One whole stall had been given over to sweets, and most of the kids who weren't listening to the wizard, or carving pumpkins, or making fairy wands in the craft area, were queuing up for candy.

Finally, they refilled their cider cups and grabbed a pork and apple roll from the hog roast stall, then perched upon one of the benches set back from the fire to watch the main event, joining in to chant the countdown as Gareth took slow, measured steps towards the pile of wood, a flaming torch held alight over his head.

As the crowd reached a shouted 'One!' Gareth placed the torch to the pile then jumped back, his satisfied smile illuminated by the rush of flames that flew up the side, engulfing the whole stack in seconds flat.

'Now *that* is a bonfire,' Toby murmured in Autumn's ear, and she shivered. 'One day I'm going to get him to tell me how he does it.'

And Autumn didn't point out that he wouldn't be here to ask Gareth next year. That maybe *Gareth* wouldn't be here either, depending on who bought the estate.

This, she decided, was one of those perfect moments in life. No point ruining it with reality, even if it couldn't last.

Another one of her mother's life mottos floated through her head, unbidden.

'You have to grab your perfect moments when they come, because they might not come again.'

She was leaving in six weeks, and none of this would even exist for much longer.

Which was why, when she turned to Toby and saw the want in his eyes, the desire in the curve of his lips, Autumn grabbed her perfect moment and leaned in to kiss him.

He was kissing his wife.

Finally.

Toby swallowed a moan as he reached out to hold her closer to him, wrapping a hand in those gorgeous auburn curls and dislodging her bobble hat as he deepened the kiss. A proper, conscious, non-nightmare-induced kiss. One he didn't have to wrench himself away from with the knowledge that she didn't want this, because this time *she'd* kissed *him.*

How could he have forgotten how this felt? No amount of alcohol could have taken away this perfect feeling, surely?

Except maybe it hadn't felt like this that first night, because he hadn't *known* her then. Not like he did now. And now...oh, he never wanted to stop kissing her.

'Well, isn't this romantic? Newlyweds kissing by the fire. Practically picture postcard.'

Never mind that the things he wanted to do to Autumn were *not* suitable for sending by Royal Mail, he *recognised* that voice. He just hadn't expected to hear it again, especially here and now.

Reluctantly, he pulled away from Autumn—who was already retreating from him—and looked up. 'Julia. What the hell are you doing here?'

'Now, is that any way to greet an old friend?' Bumping him out of the way with her hip, she sat down beside them on a bench that was clearly only made for two. Toby grabbed for Autumn and held her onto the seat with an arm around her shoulders. 'Aren't you going to introduce me?'

He really didn't want to. He didn't want these two parts of his life to intersect in any way at all. But what choice did he have? They were surrounded by the people from the estate—some of the biggest gossips in the country, his father had always said, with a vested interest in his love life. And some of them would probably remember Julia from her past visits...not necessarily fondly.

Toby sighed. 'Autumn, this is Julia. Julia, this is my wife, Autumn.'

Julia schooled her face into an interested but astonished look. Toby, having seen her practice such looks in the mirror, wasn't particularly impressed by it, but Autumn shuffled uncomfortably under his arm.

'I have to say, I didn't believe it when I heard the news. Toby Blythe, married? And to an *American?* I told them they must have it wrong. *Toby's* not the marrying kind. But here we are!' Her high, tinkling laugh grated in his ears now, Toby realised, when once he'd found it charming.

Before he'd really known her.

'Here we are indeed,' Toby replied. He couldn't say any more. If he even opened his mouth again, he knew it would all come out.

I offered to marry you! he'd say. *I wanted to marry you and have our baby together, but you said no. That I wasn't the sort of man you married...just the sort you had fun with before you found your perfect husband.*

Of course, that had been before he'd become Viscount. If her pregnancy scare had occurred *after* Barnaby's death, Toby suspected her answer might have been rather different. Which just made everything a whole lot worse.

'I always say that nobody is really the marrying kind, until they find the right person to marry.' Autumn's voice was bright and happy, as if she'd missed all the undertones in the conversation. But Toby knew her better than that. Knew she'd probably read the situation *perfectly* and was now employing the tactic that would annoy Julia the most and get rid of her the quickest.

That kind of social brilliance was why he'd married her. Well, it wasn't, but it was why he was damn glad he had.

That and the kissing, of course. He really wished they could get back to the kissing.

'Take me, for instance,' Autumn went on, her American accent thicker than it usually was. 'I mean, no one ever expected *me* to get married. Too much of a free spirit, always going my own way, never sticking to nothing. My grandmama used to despair of me!' She was veering into Scarlett O'Hara territory now, but Julia was still buying every bit of it. '"Autumn," she'd say. "What man is *ever* going to want to marry you if you insist on doing things your own way all the time? That's not what a man wants! He wants someone who will stay home and make apple pie and pop out kids for him. That's all!"'

'Did she really say that?' Toby asked in a whisper, and Autumn gave him a scathing look. Probably not then.

'Lucky for me,' Autumn went on, her voice back to its normal, familiar accent again, 'Toby just fell in love with me, and wanted to marry me for myself. Isn't that wonderful?' And, with that, she grabbed him around the shoulders and kissed him again, deep and hard and meaningful.

It was enough to make Toby forget that Julia had ever existed in the first place.

'Well. I'll just leave you two lovebirds to it then,' Julia said as an approving whoop went up from the crowd around them at the kiss. Toby tried to raise a hand to wave, but his fingers seemed reluctant to leave the tangle of Autumn's hair, so he didn't bother.

When they finally came up for air, Julia was gone and the watching crowd had obviously got bored of their antics and moved on too. It was just them, the fire and the strains of the fiddles and a song from the stage on the other side. Some people were dancing, Toby realised, and wondered if he should ask Autumn to dance too. But it was so comfortable, just sitting together, he didn't want it to end. Not unless it was going to lead them somewhere even better.

Autumn leant her head against his shoulder and gave a satisfied sigh. Toby decided to take that as a good sign.

Then, after a long moment of just watching the flames together, she said, 'My ex stole all my money.'

Toby blinked, and tried to keep up with her thoughts. 'The one you told me about on the plane?'

'Yeah. I told you I made sacrifices for him, right?' She looked up at him and Toby nodded. 'The truth was, I didn't think they *were* sacrifices. I thought we were building a future together, so I saw them as investments in that future. Something that was going to *last.* But it turned out he wasn't really interested in a future with me at all. He just wanted to get his hands on the money and run.'

Toby swore, and held her closer as she continued talking.

'I should have known better. My mom always told me that nothing lasts. But I didn't just hand over my cards, you know. I wanted to take things slow. And when we started out I was so sure he loved me...but then it got more and more about what he wanted. About what he thought was right. And maybe getting the money was taking too long, or maybe he realised it wasn't going to be enough. Or maybe he just liked having me under his control. Every aspect of my life...' She shook her head and Toby's chest tightened with the sort of rage he hadn't felt since the day he'd got the call about the boating accident that killed his brother and nephew.

'He hurt you.'

'Mostly he just scared me. In the end... I left the money, I left my stuff, I left everything and I ran. And that's when I knew that it was the money he'd wanted most—the money from the sale of my grandparents' house and then, when that was gone, the money I brought in from work. Because he never even looked for me after that. Which…it was a relief. I knew how lucky I was to get away without any reprisals. But also…' She gave a small shrug and let her words trail off.

Toby could hear them clear enough, though.

'Why tell me this now?' Toby asked, because it felt like the only safe thing he could say. If he asked for more information there was a solid chance he'd be on the next plane back to the States looking for the guy to ruin his life.

'Julia…she's your ex, right?' Autumn flashed him a small, soft smile. 'I guess I figured that if I was going to ask you what the story was there, I should at least tell you all of mine first. You don't seem to like to talk about your past much.'

He didn't tell her it wasn't just the talking. Most days, he didn't like *thinking* about his past. It just reminded him how much he had to live up to, and how inadequate he was to the task.

'She's my ex, yes.' Leaning back against the wood of the bench, he pulled Autumn more securely into his arms, wrapping his arms around her middle as he tried to think of the best way to tell the story. 'We met when I was working in London for a spell, setting up the business. Finn and I were hunting for investors, so we went places where people had a lot of money. She liked me because I had the right family background, and I liked her because she helped me meet the people I needed to meet, I guess. Neither of them great reasons to be together. I don't think it was love, not for either of us. More convenience.'

'So what happened between you? I mean, if it wasn't true love, then she came a long way tonight to be sure you really were married.'

'She fell pregnant,' Toby said bluntly. 'Or she thought

she had. I proposed because I thought that was the right thing to do under the circumstances. And she…'

'She said no?' Autumn guessed when he went silent.

'Worse. She laughed in my face.' Even now the memory stung, but he knew it was his pride and not his heart that had been wounded. 'She said I wasn't the sort of guy girls like her married. That it had been fun, but she wasn't going to settle for someone like me. She said… she said she'd rather get rid of the baby than spend her life shackled to me.'

Autumn's face paled even in the firelight, her eyes huge and round. 'She *said* that?'

Toby shrugged. 'It was certainly implied, if not said. Then it turned out she wasn't pregnant after all, but obviously things were over between us then.'

'Of course they were!' Toby took a small amount of pleasure in how horrified she was on his behalf. The same way he'd been angry on hers, he supposed.

Barnaby and Victoria had already been happily married for almost a decade by then, running the estate, teaching Harry about his heritage. At the time he'd taken it as further evidence that this was something else he couldn't do, couldn't manage. He would only ever be the inferior younger son, never living up to the ideal that Barnaby and his father had set.

He'd thrown himself into the business with Finn, travelling more and more as they grew, became more successful. Staying away from Wishcliffe as much as he could. Until the day he'd got the worst phone call of his life and came running back, too late.

'I didn't see her again until the funerals,' he went on. 'I was still too much in shock from Barnaby and Harry's deaths to really process any extra at seeing her, and she pretended that last conversation never happened. I heard her telling Finn that we'd just grown apart, or realised we needed different things, but obviously she wanted to be there to support me at such a terrible time.'

Autumn shouted a laugh. 'I hope Finn told her where to go. Because of course you'd told him the truth?'

Toby shook his head. He'd never told anyone else of the argument that had ended his relationship with Julia. It had cut too deep to discuss. He wondered now if he should have.

Autumn reached out and took his free hand in her own and held it tight. 'She was right. You're not the kind of guy girls like her marry, because you're far, far better than that. You deserve so much more than her.'

'It was a lucky escape.' He brought their joined hands up to her chin, raising it slightly so she looked him in the eye. 'Because if I'd married her I could never have met you. And that would have been unthinkable.'

Just a couple of months ago, he'd never have imagined being married. Even when he'd arrived home at Wishcliffe with a wife he hadn't dreamt that she could matter so much to him.

But she did. And he really wanted to kiss her again.

Autumn's pink tongue darted out to wet her lips, and he could almost see a stream of thoughts and emotions racing behind her eyes—but not well enough to read them. 'You know, you never did carry me over the threshold of our bedroom.'

He swallowed, trying to control the lust surging through his body at her words. 'Then I think it's time we remedied that. Don't you?'

CHAPTER TEN

BLOOD POUNDED IN Autumn's ears as they raced up across the fields towards the house with the kind of urgency that made it clear to everyone who saw them that they were reacting to an emergency.

A sex emergency in this case, but Autumn figured that still counted.

After all, she'd been married for *months* now, almost, and still hadn't had sex since her wedding night. Also, she really didn't want to give herself time or space to change her mind.

'Are you sure about this?' Toby asked, panting a little, as they reached the front door.

'That I want you to carry me across the threshold?' Autumn raised her eyebrows as she purposely raked her gaze across his arms, torso, then down to his legs. 'Are you worried about my weight?'

'I'm worried you're going to change your mind again by tomorrow morning.'

The first flicker of doubt fluttered through her head, and she batted it aside. 'This isn't about tomorrow. It's about tonight. *Just* tonight.'

Toby started to frown, which wasn't okay at all, so she reached up on her tiptoes and placed a kiss right between his eyebrows. Then she dropped down to press against his lips, coaxing them open with her own until he gave in.

Making a low, almost growling sound in the back of his throat, Toby yanked her flush against him, his arms tight around her hips. Then, without warning, he hoisted her up into his arms, laughing when she yelped with surprise.

'You wanted to be carried over the threshold, Lady Blythe.'

'So carry me,' Autumn said, although, really, she was more concerned with just getting to the bedroom as fast as possible.

Luckily, it seemed that Toby had the same idea because, once they were inside, he kicked the door closed behind them and set off at a steady stride for the stairs.

'Put me down,' she ordered as they reached the first step. When he raised an eyebrow at her request, she added, 'I'll race you to our bed.'

He dropped her so fast she almost lost her footing, but she still managed to beat him to the bedroom, even with her seemingly desperate need to keep touching him at all times. Like if her fingers weren't caressing his skin, he might disappear back out of her life as quickly as he'd appeared.

Toby seemed to be having the same problem, if the way he kept tugging her closer to kiss her again every few steps was any indication. As they reached the bedroom he pressed her up against the door, every inch of his body touching hers, the heavy heat of his arousal hard against her belly. His forehead resting on hers, he whispered, 'Still sure?'

'Very,' she replied, kissing him again. He turned the door handle and they both fell through into the room they'd been sharing for weeks—just not like this.

She faltered for a second when she saw the careful line of pillows they'd erected down the centre of the bed, and remembered why they were there. But then Toby was behind her, kissing his way down her neck, and she reached out to toss those pillows aside.

Tomorrow. I'll think about it all tomorrow.

Tonight, she just wanted to enjoy the moment.

And her husband.

He couldn't get enough of kissing her. Touching her.

Every sensation sparked as if he was feeling it for the first time. Toby stripped her clothes away, then ran his hands down across her skin, hardly daring to believe he got to have this for real.

No more wondering about the night he'd missed. No more relying on his imagination to tell him how incredible they could be together.

'Lie down,' he told her, the words husky in his throat. She did as he asked, but he saw the question in her eyes.

Swallowing at the sight of her, bare in the moonlight from the window, Toby crawled across the bed until he covered her, holding himself up over her.

'Aren't you still wearing a few too many clothes?' He could hear her breath in the still air, hard and fast as the heat between them grew.

He shook his head. 'Not for what I'm planning.'

'And what are you planning?' she asked, her eyes darkening.

'I'm going to commit you to memory,' he told her. 'Starting here.' He placed a kiss at the pulse point on her throat, then began to work his way down towards her collarbone, smiling against her skin as she writhed against him, desperate for more touch.

'Not yet,' he told her, right before taking the rosy

peak of her left nipple in his mouth. 'I'm not taking any chances with forgetting this night.'

Later, much later, after he'd tasted and touched and kissed every inch of her body until she screamed, he made love to her. Pressing inside her, her hands entwined with his against the pillow, he looked into her eyes and knew that he was exactly where he was meant to be.

He was home.

Then she urged him on with her hips and they moved together in the darkness, while outside the sky exploded with fireworks.

'What are you thinking?' Autumn asked him afterwards, as they lay sweaty but sated in the bed, surrounded by the remnants of the unneeded pillow wall.

'I don't think I've regained the ability to think yet,' Toby replied.

'Liar. You have your thinking face on.' She yawned then rolled onto her side, smiling up at him, her hands folded neatly under her cheek. 'Tell me.'

He mirrored her, moving onto his side to face her. 'I suppose… I was thinking that I'm glad now, that I don't remember our wedding night.'

Her brow crumpled into a frown. 'You are? Why?'

'Because this, tonight, was perfect. Whatever happened that night couldn't possibly live up to how I feel here and now, in this moment. How incredible this felt now I *know* you, rather than when we first met. I like that this is my first memory of us together.'

The frown faded and she smiled, even as her eyes began to flutter closed. 'That's sweet,' she said, her words slurred by encroaching sleep. 'You're sweet.'

Smiling, Toby kissed that spot right between her eyebrows where she held all her frowns and whispered, 'Sleep tight, sweetheart.'

Because he knew he would. There'd be no nightmares tonight.

And tomorrow would be better still. Because he had Autumn in his bed, in his life. And maybe in his heart too.

Autumn awoke the next morning to sun streaming through the open curtains, a heavy arm across her waist and a thrum of satisfaction humming through her body.

Then reality set in.

She'd broken her own rules. Hell, she hadn't just broken them. She'd thrown them on Old Gareth's fire and burnt them.

'You always jump right in without thinking about any of the consequences.'

Her grandmother's words, spoken so many times over the years, rolled through her head. Was she remembering them from the time Grandma had to shave Autumn's head after an unfortunate experiment with home-made hair dye? Or from the time she'd signed up for three after-school activities at once, without thinking about how she could be in three different places at the same time? Or the time she'd brought home the pregnant feral cat? Or so many other times?

She'd wanted to sleep with Toby, so she had. And this time it wasn't even as if she hadn't thought about the consequences. She'd thought about nothing else ever since she'd come to Wishcliffe.

She just hadn't cared enough about them in that moment to pull away from that first blinding kiss.

She'd wanted him—this…them—too much.

She could blame the firelight or the cider or even his ex-girlfriend, or just the festival atmosphere. But what it came down to was, she wanted Toby. She wanted her husband a lot more than she should, when they were only going to be married for another month and a half.

'You go too far, too fast,' Grandma had said.

'Don't forget that nothing lasts. Keep looking for the next adventure,' her mom had whispered as she'd left her.

Wishcliffe had been her next adventure, and she'd known from the start it couldn't last. And still she'd gone too far.

Because Toby couldn't be a casual fling, not when he was also her husband. Not when he was good and kind and someone she could really fall for, if she let her guard down.

Not when he was selling up and moving on to *his* next adventure, without her, soon.

She shouldn't have slept with him again. Shouldn't have put her heart at risk that way, knowing herself the way she did, knowing how easy it would be for her to fall.

And yet...and yet lying there beside him in the early morning sunlight, she still couldn't *entirely* regret it.

'You're awake then,' Toby murmured as she sat bolt upright in bed, grasping for the sheets to keep her body covered. 'Seems to me we've been here before. Except this time I have a much better recollection of what brought us here.'

Grinning up at her, he waggled his eyebrows suggestively, a ridiculous move that still made her want to drop back to the mattress beside him and kiss that smile.

Which she was definitely not going to do, she told herself sternly. She might not regret last night, but that didn't mean she wanted to repeat the same mistakes. She'd done enough of that in her past already.

'We shouldn't have done that. Last night, I mean.' She'd been carried away, that was all. By the firelight and the music. Or the conversation, hearing how Julia had treated him…she'd wanted to show him that he didn't deserve that. And maybe she'd needed him to show her the same about her ex.

Whatever, it had been a mistake, brought about by circumstance. And now they needed to get back to their regularly scheduled marriage of convenience.

Because she really wanted to kiss him far too much.

'Why not?' Toby propped himself up on his elbow as he looked up at her. 'We are *married* after all. I carried you over the threshold and everything.'

He had too. Autumn's cheeks warmed at the memory: his arms tight around her, his chest hard against her cheek, her squeals of laughter when she'd thought he might drop her trying to open the door. And then…

Oh, then. Everything that had followed. Every kiss, every touch, every miracle of discovery between them. Every gap in her memory of their first night together had been filled. No, more than that. Their first night together had been completely erased, overwritten by what they'd shared last night.

'I'm glad now, that I don't remember our wedding night,' Toby had said, and she'd understood, deep in her bones, exactly what he meant.

The night they'd married they'd been strangers. Now they were…what? Friends? More than that. Lovers, she supposed.

Now she knew him, and he knew her. Now he could tease her, make her laugh, and she could return the favour. Now…now, there was something building between them that she'd tried so hard to avoid.

Something she couldn't risk tumbling any further into.

'I'm not trying to tie you down, if that's what you're worried about,' he went on. 'I'm just saying, why not enjoy a little no-strings fun while we can?'

'We're married, Toby. The strings are already there.'

'Even more reason to make the most of them then.' His broad grin showed he was certain this was a winning argument. But she knew she had to disappoint him.

'We signed a contract,' she said. 'We agreed. No sex.'

Toby nodded slowly, as if he was only just realising she was serious about this. 'We did. But Autumn, that was an agreement between you and me—just us. Which means we can change it if we want. And last night…' He trailed off with a frown.

'Last night I wanted to. Very much.' She had to admit that much to herself, and to him. 'But I think I was carried away—by the Fire Festival, our conversation, the music…'

'All those pagan fires. Thank God it wasn't Beltane, I suppose. Who knows what we'd have got up to if it was?'

He was trying to lighten the mood, she knew. Trying to show he was okay with this. But his stiff shoulders as he sat up against the headboard, and the tightness of his jaw, told her otherwise. When had she got so good at reading him, anyway?

'I just think that, since I'll be leaving so soon anyway, it doesn't make sense for us to get involved in anything more than we agreed to in Vegas. A contractual marriage only.' That sounded calm, reasoned, didn't it? Probably he couldn't hear the panic that was racing around inside her, behind her words.

The fear that if she let herself get any closer, for any longer, she'd fall too hard for him. She'd *care* for him, more than she already did. More than she could afford to risk.

She'd thought she loved Robbie, and look where that had got her. Trapped in a relationship that, for him, was only ever about getting what he needed from her—

money, control, fear. Whatever made him feel more of a man. And it had broken her heart, and maybe something more inside her too. The part that let her trust herself, her instincts.

Oh, she *knew* Toby wasn't the same kind of man as Robbie. Of course she knew that.

But she was still the same woman. And she knew herself.

She knew Toby too. Knew his plans for the future didn't involve their relationship being any more than a bit of fun before he sold up and moved on. That was what they'd both agreed to, after all.

If she fell he'd break her heart just as completely as Robbie had, as losing her grandparents had, and she wasn't sure she could take that again.

Nothing good lasts... You just have to keep on moving...

That was what she needed to remember.

'A contractual marriage,' Toby repeated as she scampered around the room in a sheet, trying to find all her clothes. *Surely* she'd had underwear last night?

'That's right.'

He was silent so long she risked a glance up at him as she shimmied back into her jeans, just to check he was still there.

'If that's what you really want,' he said finally.

'It is.'

It isn't.

But it was what was safe for her to have.

'Then I guess I'd better work on forgetting about last night too then.' Toby heaved himself out of bed and, grabbing his trousers, slammed through the connecting door into the bathroom.

Autumn sighed and finished dressing quickly. She really wanted to be gone before he came out.

Because, as much as she was doing the right thing for both of them, she didn't want to hang around until Toby figured *that* out for himself.

The next week was miserable. Not just for Toby, but he suspected for everyone else he came into contact with too.

'God, I'm glad I moved out,' Victoria said, visiting one morning for coffee. 'This place feels like a library that just got a really, really strict new librarian who is in a really bad mood all the time. Nobody dares whisper a word.'

Since Toby suspected he was meant to be the librarian in that analogy, he just glared and didn't respond, which only made her laugh and say, 'Poor Autumn.'

Except *Autumn* seemed perfectly happy with the whole state of affairs. They weren't sleeping together, which had been her number one wish in the whole world. The pillow wall was firmly back in effect and he didn't think that anything would entice her to take it down again—not even another one of his nightmares.

Worse, they weren't even having lunch together, or talking and joking the way they used to. Dinners were silent, and he'd taken to going back to his study to continue working afterwards, until he could be sure that she'd be asleep on her side of the bed when he joined her.

He'd have assumed that spending the night together after the Fire Festival had simply worked all of the tension between them out of their systems—in fact, if it hadn't been for one late night incident, he'd have been sure that Autumn had no more interest in him at all. But then, long after midnight one night, when he'd been leaving his study and heading to bed, he'd bumped into her—quite literally—at the top of the stairs.

She hadn't seen him either; that was clear from the shriek she let out as they collided. Mindful of their location, he'd grabbed her fast to ensure she didn't take a tumble down the stairs, and suddenly found himself pressing her against the banister at the top for safety. She'd been wearing nothing but a thin pair of pyjamas, and he'd been able to feel her whole body against him. How fast her breath had come, puffs of air against his cheek. How wide her eyes had been as she'd stared up at him, her lips parted and so damn kissable. And how her nipples had tightened under her thin T-shirt in a way he'd bet money had nothing to do with the chilly late October air…

God, he'd wanted to kiss her. And he was damn sure she'd wanted it too. But they'd made a deal.

So he'd stepped back, apologised. She'd stammered something about getting a glass of water, then fled back to the bedroom drinkless.

And he'd spent the whole night tormented by dreams of her, while she'd slept soundly on the other side of the pillow wall.

Now, a whole week after the Fire Festival and their night together, things seemed to be getting worse, not better. He'd returned to Wishcliffe with a desire to sell up and find someone else to take over the responsibility of running the estate, sure it was the last place he wanted to spend his days. It seemed cruelly ironic that the Wishcliffe estate was now providing him with an escape from the unbearable tension of his marriage, as he threw himself into managing the place to put more distance between himself and Autumn.

The only thing he wanted to run away from now was his growing and unreciprocated feelings for his bloody wife.

But the following Monday morning the phone rang

with a call from the agent he'd instructed to find a buyer for Wishcliffe. And suddenly his larger escape plan felt possible again.

'You've found someone? Really?' For all that the estate was a great investment for the right person, there weren't really that many people in the world for whom that was the case, especially given the caveats on the sale that Toby had put in place to protect the current workers and residents of Wishcliffe and the surrounding villages.

He'd been hopeful that they'd find someone before his three months with Autumn was up, but as the weeks had gone on he hadn't been optimistic. Now it seemed a miracle had come through for him after all.

The agent droned on about the details, including a long list of documentation the buyer's solicitors wanted to see pronto, which Toby told him to email over because he knew he wasn't going to remember it all.

He was too busy thinking.

He'd achieved exactly what he'd set out to do. He'd found a buyer for the estate without anyone even noticing he was planning on selling, thanks in large part to the false security and distraction brought by his marriage to Autumn.

Shouldn't he be excited? Thrilled, even?

Why did he feel so…conflicted?

He *wanted* to sell. He didn't want to be Viscount, and he didn't want the responsibility of running the Wishcliffe estate that had killed his father and Barnaby in a way. He didn't want the life that should have been his brother's, when he knew he couldn't live up to his memory.

Except…he'd enjoyed it. He'd *liked* getting to know the estate and its people, even if it felt like stepping into his dead brother's boots to do it. He'd *liked* doing the work he'd always avoided even learning about. He'd even liked being the one responsible for it, to his utter surprise and shock.

But a lot of that, he knew, was because of the situation here. To start with, he'd had Victoria guiding him, and she'd moved on already. More than that, he'd had Autumn…

Autumn to have lunch with every day and talk through how things were going on the estate. Autumn to report back to him on what the staff and the tenants were saying about how things were going, because she'd managed to make friends with *everybody,* even Old Gareth. Autumn to sit by the fire with in the evening and make plans for the future. Autumn in his arms, in his bed, for one precious night.

She was the reason he'd liked this life—and the reason he'd been so miserable in it for the last week. In another month, she'd be gone. Would he really want Wishcliffe without her?

'Right,' he said in response to whatever the agent's latest question had been. 'Send me the list and I'll get all that information over to you. I want us to move fast on this.'

Done and dusted before Autumn left him, for preference.

Then he'd get back to his normal life. Travelling the world, working from anywhere, free to go wherever he wanted. Without her.

Hanging up the phone, Toby refreshed his email inbox obsessively until the list from the agent landed. Opening it, he scanned the text and sighed. Everything he'd needed so far had been digitised and easily available, thanks to Barnaby and Victoria's careful management of the estate. But the stuff they wanted now was older, more obscure, which meant it could only be stored in the wooden filing cabinet where his father had kept all the important estate documents. Spinning his chair around, he pulled open the first drawer and began compiling what he needed.

He was only on the second file when he found the envelope, addressed to him and Barnaby in his father's handwriting, and a sense of dread started to fill his heart.

CHAPTER ELEVEN

TOBY HAD BEEN like a bear with a sore head for over a week. Autumn knew that, even though she'd been carefully staying out of his way, because almost everyone else who'd had to deal with him had told her so. Some of them had even gone out of their way to hunt her down and impart the information, just in case she hadn't noticed that her husband was miserable.

Most seemed sympathetic to her plight, although a few gave her accusing looks as if to remind her that this was all her fault and she could fix it if she wanted.

She ignored those people.

Not least because that was what she wanted to do most.

She knew he was mad because he was confused. But hell, so was she!

What scared her most, though, was the way she wanted to go to him and soothe him, to save him, to look after him. Because that told her that it was time to go, before it became impossible to do anything but stay.

She'd been here before. Not just with Robbie—who'd been needy and loving in the beginning, in a way it seemed she was genetically predisposed to respond to—but with her grandparents.

They'd wanted her to go away to college, had *told* her to go, that they'd get someone in to help them out around the house, or with any medical needs that cropped up. But then Granddad had his first heart attack and she'd known she couldn't leave them. Whatever their differences over the years, they were family. And underneath all the arguments ran a current of love, so strong and deep she couldn't ignore it. She'd loved them too much and knew she'd never forgive herself if she didn't stay and look after them.

So she had. She'd nursed them through their final few years, through the hard times and the worse times. And she didn't regret it, because it had probably been the most important thing she'd do in her life. The only way she had to pay them back for taking her in when no one else had wanted her.

But she also couldn't forget how it had felt, trapped in that house, unable to reach for any dreams outside those four walls. Fighting her true nature, the part of her that was her mother's daughter above all and wanted to be out there seeking new adventures.

If she let herself fall any further for Toby, she'd want to stay. And she'd promised herself for too long now that she wouldn't let herself tie herself down that way again. She'd broken that promise for Robbie, and it had been the biggest mistake she'd ever made. Because she'd forgotten the other important lesson that her mother had taught her—nothing lasted. Especially not love.

Maybe Toby wouldn't be a mistake. Or maybe he'd be an even bigger one. Because if she gave him her heart, her everything, and all he wanted was her name on the marriage certificate for a few more months, and her in his bed at night…she wasn't sure how she could come back from that.

And, on the other hand, if he fell as hard and as fast as she did—well, that could be even worse, couldn't it?

Because he wasn't staying at Wishcliffe, with this happy life she'd come to enjoy. He was leaving. And even if he wanted her to go with him, she'd be chasing *his* adventures, not hers.

She'd be stuck, following him around, resenting him in the end. And the love wouldn't last.

So she couldn't sleep with Toby again. Couldn't risk letting herself fall in love. There was too much at risk—not just her heart but her freedom too.

She'd earned that freedom. She wasn't giving it up for something as fickle and demanding as love.

And she'd probably better start making plans for leaving, sooner rather than later. She hated to back down on a deal, but maybe she could convince Toby that it would be better for both of them if she got out early. He could use her desertion as a reason to want to sell the place he thought they'd been happy together, or something.

It wasn't what they'd agreed, but she wasn't sure she could give that to him. Couldn't give him any of the things it seemed he wanted most.

But she *could* take him a cup of warm cider and one of the apple and cinnamon muffins she'd stolen into the kitchen to bake that afternoon. Because, really, cheering him up was basically a public service at this point.

It was well past dinner—which Toby had missed completely—but the light was still burning in his study. Juggling her plate and hot mug, she pushed the door open with her hip and let herself in without knocking.

Toby didn't even look up. Irritation prickled up across her chest, until she realised he wasn't ignoring her. He hadn't even noticed she was there.

He was completely focused on the piece of paper in his hand. A letter, by the look of things. Handwritten.

'Toby?' she said softly. 'I brought you a drink. And a muffin.'

He looked up, blinking in the inadequate lamplight. 'You… Did I miss dinner?'

'Hours ago.' Autumn placed the muffin and cider on the desk and looked at him with concern. 'What's happened?'

Dropping the letter face down on the desk, he rubbed a hand across his weary-looking eyes, then reached for the cider. 'I had a call from the agent. There's been an offer to buy Wishcliffe.'

Autumn sank into the visitor's chair opposite. She hadn't expected the tug in her gut at that news—was it regret? Loss? How could she miss something that had never really been hers? But the idea of Wishcliffe belonging to someone other than Toby, of all the people she'd met and come to like here being passed onto the highest bidder…suddenly it turned her stomach.

'That's good, isn't it?' she asked, realising that Toby didn't look so sure either. Maybe he was having second thoughts. Maybe he wanted to stay too. And if he stayed…

But he gave a sharp nod. 'It is. I was starting to worry we wouldn't get it done in time. But they needed some documentation to send over to the solicitors, and when I went looking for it… I found this.' His hand hesitated for a second as he reached for the letter, then his lips tightened into a line and he grabbed it and handed it to her, seemingly before he could change his mind.

Oh, she had a very bad feeling about this.

But her grandma had always taught her the value of facing bad news head-on. So she turned the paper over and started to read, scanning the text quickly before reading it again to make sure she hadn't got it wrong.

She hadn't.

My sons,
This letter is the hardest thing I've ever had to write, because I hate the thought of destroying any respect you held for me when I confess.

But, once I am gone, someone needs to know the truth, and to do what is right. So I'm placing that responsibility in your hands, and I am sorry for it.

You need to know...

'You have another brother.' No point sugar-coating the reality.

'An illegitimate one. A brother he cheated on my mother to conceive. A brother that proves my father wasn't the man I thought he was. A brother nobody but me knows exists.'

'And him, I assume,' Autumn said, and Toby glared at her. 'I mean, the letter asks you to contact him. Suggests he'll know who you are if you did.'

A grunt of agreement was all she got at that.

'Did Barnaby know?' she asked, trying again.

'I don't think so. The letter was still sealed. And anyway…' He trailed off.

'Anyway?' she prompted, before he could get so lost in thought he forgot she was there at all.

'He'd have told Victoria if he knew. They told each other everything. And she'd have told me when I inherited, I'm sure of it.' Husbands and wives, sharing everything. He almost sounded jealous at the idea.

She wondered if he realised he was doing the exact same thing now, with her.

'What are you going to do about it?' Another heir, illegitimate or not…surely that had to affect the sale. There was a request in his father's letter to 'do what is right' in the way that he, himself, had clearly been unable to. And Autumn had no doubt that Toby *would* do the right thing; that was just who he was.

What she didn't know was what the right thing *was*.

And neither, it seemed, did Toby.

He turned to her with wide, lost eyes and said, 'I have no idea.'

Autumn swallowed, and reached across the table to grab his hand and squeeze it reassuringly.

'I keep asking myself what Barnaby would have done. What Father would want. But I feel like I have no idea who my father was, all of a sudden. And Barnaby…'

'Is not here,' Autumn finished for him. 'They're both trusting you to make the right choice for them.'

Toby gave a hollow laugh and looked away. 'They… they wouldn't have, if they were alive. I was never the responsible one, the one who stayed home and took care of things. That was Barnaby. I was the son who cared more about exploring the world and having a good time.'

From the way he said the words, Autumn had no doubt he was quoting someone. If it wasn't for the English accent, it could have been her grandma, talking about her.

'Toby, you run your own business—a very successful one, according to Finn. You're hardly a layabout letdown.' Which was how Grandma had always described Autumn's mother. How she'd probably have described her life over the last few years, if she'd been alive to see it.

Toby shook his head. 'It didn't matter. In their heads I was always the fifteen-year-old getting into trouble with the neighbours, or the drunken university student getting kicked out of the pub. Even the business. I think they just thought it was Finn and me finding excuses to bum around the world. Because all they understood was Wishcliffe and the responsibilities they had here. Everything else just…mattered less.'

Including him, from the bitterness in his voice. Autumn wanted to tell him how much he mattered to her, but the words got stuck in her throat.

'They loved me, and I loved them,' Toby went on. 'And I miss them every day. But we were just so different…'

Autumn couldn't help but smile at that. 'I know that feeling, trust me. It was just the same with my grandparents. We never saw the world the same way, but that didn't mean we didn't love each other.'

He caught her gaze. 'What would *you* do? I mean, if you suddenly discovered you had another sibling you never knew existed before?'

It wasn't impossible that she did, Autumn knew. Her mother had dropped out of her life so comprehensively, and Autumn had never gone looking for her. She'd thought about it from time to time, as she'd drifted around the world. But she wasn't sure she wanted to know. Either the worst had happened, or else…or else her mom had settled down, perhaps. Given up her nomadic lifestyle. Found a new family. New children even.

But Autumn had known instinctively that, if that were the case, there'd be no place for her there.

'I don't know,' she said finally. 'I mean, I always wanted a brother or a sister when I was a kid. But you already had one, growing up. Maybe it's different for you.'

'No,' he said slowly. 'I don't think it is. But I'm not a child any more. Maybe this new brother of mine will want nothing to do with me.'

Autumn gave him a half smile. 'I guess you'll never know unless you ask.'

* * *

After a week of discreet enquiries, of delicately putting off the agent and the buyer's solicitors with a series of increasingly implausible excuses for the missing paperwork, and of late-night debates with himself about what to do, Toby was no closer to solving his brother problem.

Max. His Max problem, to be precise.

The son of his father and a local barmaid, as far as he could tell from his research. Only two years younger than Barnaby, and two years older than Toby himself.

His father's letter had contained nothing but the basic information that this man existed, that he was his son and that he wanted his *other* sons to do the right thing. Whatever that was.

Toby wished beyond anything else that his brother was still alive to help him decide what to do. It felt… wrong that he was the only one left, dealing with this. This was a family matter, one that they should have faced together, as siblings.

But Barnaby was gone, and the issue had fallen squarely into Toby's lap. However much a part of him wished he hadn't found the letter until after the sale had gone through and there was nothing to be done about it, the fact was that he *had* found the letter. And he wasn't the sort of person who could ignore that or pretend otherwise.

He knew the right thing to do. He was almost sure. Knew, at least, what he would want if the situation were reversed, and he were the brother out in the cold.

But so many certainties he'd thought he knew—that he only had one brother, that his father had been an upstanding, honest and faithful man, that his family had no dark secrets beyond the dwindling accounts and the hole in the roof—had fallen away since he'd found that letter, he was doubting himself.

Not to mention the fact that it could upend all his plans for selling the estate, and everything else, in just one conversation.

So, yeah. He wished Barnaby was there to share the load. Or at least tell him he was doing the right thing.

In the absence of his brother, he'd done the next best thing and spoken to Victoria, who had gone very quiet and then said, 'I know you'll do the right thing, just as Barnaby would have,' then hung up before he could ask exactly what the sainted Barnaby would have done.

He'd tried Finn next, who'd been shocked, amused, sympathetic, but ultimately unhelpful. 'I'm afraid, mate, this is one of those things you need to figure out for yourself. But when you do decide what to do, I'll be here to back you up. Whatever it is.'

In the end, though, there was only one person he really wanted to discuss the matter of his unexpected brother with. Autumn.

She'd been more friendly, more present, since the night he'd found the letter, although he still felt the distance she'd imposed between them. It still hurt, every time she shifted away from him, or smiled that smile that didn't quite reach her eyes. He wanted to feel her really *with* him, not mentally halfway across the Atlantic already, as her departure date grew ever closer.

She hadn't mentioned it, but he could tell she was already counting the days until her contractually obliged three months were up. Then she'd be gone, even if the estate hadn't sold, and even if Toby *still* hadn't decided what to do about his brother. Which would be easier if a lot of the mental space he should be using to settle the issue wasn't being clogged up daydreaming about Autumn.

Daydreaming. Honestly, it was as if he'd regressed to a schoolboy crush again.

No. It was time to stop dithering and make progress on *all* his problems.

He knew the right thing to do; he just wanted to make sure he did it right.

And so he reached for his phone and dialled the King's Arms in the village and booked a table for that evening. Then he reached into his drawer for the notepad where he'd jotted down another phone number, one he'd never dialled before, and did the right thing.

'I can't believe I've been living here for two whole months and never tasted this before.' Autumn's eyes fluttered closed as she chewed another mouthful of her goat's cheese, walnut and beetroot tartlet starter.

Toby smiled, and congratulated himself on a good idea well executed. 'I'm glad you like it. And I'm sorry I didn't bring you here before now. You know, most of the meat, vegetables and cheeses on the menu come from the Wishcliffe estate.'

'So the menu tells me,' she teased. Then, as she pushed her empty plate away, her face turned more serious. 'But you didn't bring me here because of the food. Did you?'

'No. I suppose I didn't.'

Tilting his chair back a little, Toby surveyed the pub. He'd had his first legal pint there, years before—and a few illegal ones before that. Back then, the place had been more of a local dive than the gastropub it had morphed into in the years since he'd left Wishcliffe.

It had also been the place where his half-brother's mother had worked.

He'd googled Max as soon as he'd found out about his existence, of course. What he'd found out had been oddly reassuring, in a way. Max was a successful businessman, who'd left Wishcliffe for the city years ago. By all accounts, he didn't need whatever share of the family estate he was entitled to, and he'd probably understand Toby's reasons for selling it well enough.

But that didn't mean he didn't deserve to have a say in the future of the family land, business and money. Barnaby would never have sold Wishcliffe without discussing it with Toby first—well, Barnaby would never have considered selling Wishcliffe, full stop. But the point still stood. He and Max were the only Blythes left now, and he couldn't make such a fundamental decision without discussing it with his half-brother.

First, he just needed to let that half-brother know that he knew he existed.

'You're going to talk to Max,' Autumn said, watching him.

'How did you know that?'

She shrugged, and flashed him a smile. 'I know you. And it's the right thing to do, you know.'

'I hope so.' Max could cause trouble. He could hold up the sale for months, years, if he wanted to. He had the money, power and influence to take it all the way through the courts. Legally, Toby's solicitors assured him, he was on safe ground. But that wasn't the point. In the face of a lengthy court battle, would any buyer really want to see it through? Already his current interested party was complaining about the delay in paperwork.

He sighed. It *was* the right thing, and he'd do it.

'I called him this afternoon. Left a message asking if we could meet in London some time soon.' He hesitated for a moment before asking the real question he'd brought her here for. The one he'd known he wanted to ask since he'd decided to call. 'Will you come with me?'

'To London?'

'To meet Max.'

Autumn's eyes widened. 'As your wife?'

'I guess so.' It seemed strange to realise it, considering their whole relationship was based on a business arrangement. But he wanted her there as his partner in life. The other half of the Wishcliffe whole. The person he couldn't imagine doing this without.

And given that she'd be leaving him in just a few weeks, Toby really didn't want to think too hard about what that might mean.

Neither did Autumn, if the way she shifted in her seat and started eyeing the door was anything to go by. 'I'll come as your friend,' she said finally. 'If I'm still here by then.'

'Of course.' Toby forced a smile as the waitress came and cleared their starters, ready for their main courses. 'If you're still here.'

Autumn stared at herself in the mirror in the pub bathroom. Her eyes looked too wild and too wide, her face pale, her curls ruffled as if Toby had already been running his hands through them.

Already. As if it was inevitable.

Was it? Had she already given in, inside?

No. She couldn't.

But it was a darn close thing.

She slumped against the sink, refusing to look herself in the eye any longer, and thought back to the moment things had changed.

It was that damn letter, of course. His father, appearing from beyond the grave with one last secret…and Toby had looked just like he had the night she'd married him. Lost, and in need of someone to take care of him. And she'd known she couldn't walk away from him when he needed her.

So she hadn't talked about leaving sooner. Had put off making any plans for where she might go next. She'd thrown on another jumper and tried not to think of catching a flight to somewhere sunny. And she'd ignored the part of her that was relieved that she didn't have to give all this up just yet.

She'd believed it was only a matter of time. That once Toby had dealt with this latest blow he'd be okay again and she could move on. Because, as much as it *felt* like he needed her, she knew he didn't really. Not for long.

But now she couldn't shake the nagging feeling that she was getting in too deep.

When had *that* happened? Earlier that day perhaps, when Toby had appeared, beaming, in the second drawing room, where she was having a meeting with Victoria about the Wishcliffe social calendar for the next few months, and announced that he was taking her out for dinner. Even though she'd known it would be something to do with Max, or the sale of Wishcliffe—something he didn't want to discuss at the house—she'd still felt that warm feeling spreading through her at the idea of a night out with him, like a real couple.

Or maybe it was the meeting with Victoria itself, as they'd discussed plans for the holiday season. The Christmas carol service at the church, the advent wreath the estate always presented to the vicar at the start of December, the fete that would be held in the old stable yard with local craftspeople selling Christmas presents. The decorations that would be needed for Wishcliffe House itself, and where they were stored, or where the fresh greenery could be sourced from.

Victoria had a whole binder full of notes on the subject—checklists and contacts and reminders. Just like Grandma's bible. Autumn had recoiled at the sight of it and Victoria had laughed, assuming she was overwhelmed by the idea of so much work.

'Honestly, it practically runs itself these days. Everyone here knows what needs doing,' she'd assured her.

But that wasn't the problem. Autumn knew she could learn what to do, knew she could do it competently. She just also knew that, if she did, she'd be doing it every year for the rest of her life.

Because if Toby asked her to stay for Christmas, she would. And then it would be Valentines, or Easter, or the Beltane fire festival he'd mentioned. There would always be something else to be involved in here in Wishcliffe, if Toby didn't sell up soon.

And if he didn't, if he kept hold of the estate and asked her to stay, would she have the strength to leave?

Or would she stay and take care of things, while Toby went back to his life running around the globe? Would she stay until he fell in love with someone else and wanted to get married for real, and she got kicked out? Or until he decided to sell after all, or maybe until Max came in and took over the estate instead?

Even the best-case scenario she could think of was a horror show. She stayed, let herself fall in love with Toby, and discovered he loved her back—until she went stir-crazy stuck in one place and ran away again and broke his heart.

There were so many 'if's in her head, she couldn't keep them straight any more.

Just focus on now. This moment.

Toby wanted to take her to London, as his wife, to meet his mysterious half-brother. And she'd said yes, because how could she say no?

But she already knew she couldn't do it. Yes, Toby needed her. And she *liked* being needed. But she loved her freedom more. It was always a push and pull between the two, in her life—the legacies of the two opposing women in her life, the one who'd given birth to her and the one who'd brought her up.

But, in the end, they were both saying the same thing. For once, their voices were in perfect agreement in her head.

'Nothing lasts, baby. You have to keep moving.'

'You never could stick with one thing, Autumn. You're always jumping onto the next one.'

She'd promised herself she wouldn't get tied down again like this. Which meant she needed to cut the strings holding her, before too many more were added.

She needed to leave. Now, ideally.

But… Autumn turned and met her eyes one more time in the mirror over the sink and saw the truth there.

She loved him too much to go without at least one more night in his arms. She could give herself—and him—that much. Couldn't she?

Bargain struck with her own reflection, she nodded and headed back out into the pub dining room to seduce her husband.

For the last time.

CHAPTER TWELVE

THIS, TOBY REALISED, was how every morning should start.

The late autumn sun—or was it early winter by now?—eased weakly through the curtains, and the woman in his arms snuggled closer for warmth.

Toby wasn't entirely sure what had changed her mind but, whatever it was, he was wholeheartedly grateful for it. Autumn had returned to their table in the pub, smiled a smile that tugged at his memory—not from the night of the Fire Festival but earlier, the night of their marriage, before his memory gave way completely. But that smile… he knew that smile, and he knew what it meant, and he'd thanked every lucky star he had because he'd been on the edge of insanity with wanting her again.

Still, he'd taken things slowly—finishing their meal, talking some more about Max and about the village and growing up there, the conversation turning more flirtatious as they'd progressed to pudding.

She'd leaned into him on the walk home, his arm around her waist. Then, as they'd approached the gates of the house, she'd reached up and kissed him, his back against the stone pillars that held the wrought iron gates.

'Are you sure?' he'd asked, remembering how he'd said the same the night of the Fire Festival. The last time she'd given in to the thing that burned between them.

'Very,' she'd replied, and he'd thought how much more certain she sounded this time around.

And now it was the next morning, and she was still in his arms and, as her green eyes fluttered open, he didn't see the panic he'd seen every other time they'd woken up together. In fact, her gaze seemed…calm. Sure.

Toby's heart rate settled again as she smiled at him.

'Good morning,' he murmured against her lips and she returned his kiss, so soft and sweet it made his chest ache.

'Hi there,' she replied as he pulled back.

'So, what do you want to do today?' It was Saturday, technically a day of leisure for them both, and Toby had very clear ideas on how *he'd* spend the day, given the choice. But he wanted to hear her ideas too. Maybe she'd like a romantic if chilly walk in the orchard. Or they could go into the nearest city for lunch. And *then* come back and spend the rest of the day in bed.

Her smile froze just a little, just for a second. But it was enough for Toby to know he wasn't going to like what came next.

'Autumn—'

'It's time for me to go.' Her words were soft but firm and they felt like an arrow in his heart.

'No.' Not after last night. Not when she made him feel like…like he really *had* come home, in a way he'd never expected to feel at Wishcliffe.

Not when he thought he might be falling in love with her.

'Toby, it's time.' There was no room for argument in her tone, but Toby was going to argue like hell anyway.

'We had a contract. You said three months. Those three months aren't up yet.' He just needed more time. Time to figure out what the hell was going on in his life. With the estate, with Max, with his future—with his heart.

Three months would never have been enough to work all of that out, but if it was what he had then he'd work with it. But not if she walked out on their deal now.

'They're nearly up,' she pointed out gently. 'Toby, you knew I was going to leave at the end of this. Nothing lasts for ever, right?'

'Yes, but—'

'But what? That was the deal we made.' She shrugged her bare shoulders, as if this was nothing at all to her. As if *leaving* him was easy.

Maybe it was. For her.

He just couldn't believe he was deciding his future naked in bed with her. Again.

His wedding ring felt heavy on his hand, a reminder of how they'd ended up in this mess in the first place. Seemed like nothing in his life had made sense since that night in Vegas.

'So what was last night?' he asked, desperately trying to understand it all.

'I guess it was goodbye.' Her eyes were apologetic, and the meaning of her words sank in slowly, chilling him.

She'd known last night she'd be leaving—she just hadn't told him. She'd flirted with him, kissed him, taken him to bed, all the while knowing it was the last time.

No. He wouldn't—couldn't—accept that. They couldn't have gone through this whole charade together for her to just walk out. Not after last night.

'You said you'd come and meet my brother with me.' He was guilt tripping her now and he knew it. He'd feel worse but from the way she looked down at the sheets, her lower lip trapped between her teeth, it looked like it might be working.

He was desperate. He'd try anything.

No. That wasn't true.

If she truly wanted to go, he'd let her. But last night… it hadn't felt like goodbye to him.

It had felt like the start of something.

Like possibility.

And if she was just running because she was scared of that…well, that was a whole different story.

'I did say that,' she admitted, still looking down. 'And I'm sorry I can't keep that promise. But I think it's for the best. After all, if I showed up there with you, he'd be expecting us to be a real couple, right? But we'd both know I'd be leaving soon. You don't want to start off your relationship with your brother with another lie.'

'You mean as opposed to the lie I've been living with everyone at Wishcliffe?' Except it hadn't *felt* like a lie. That was the part that Toby was finding the hardest to make sense of.

He'd come here expecting to lie and leave. Instead, his time at Wishcliffe, his marriage with Autumn, had felt more real than anything else in his life for a very long time.

'I'm sorry,' she said again, but the words fell empty on the bed, meaningless.

'Do you hate it here so much?' He ducked his head to see her eyes as he asked. Those bright green eyes never really managed to hide anything from him, as far as he could tell. However much she bound herself up in rules and contracts and lies, Autumn's eyes always gave her away.

This morning they just looked sad.

'The opposite, actually,' she whispered. 'That's why I have to go.'

Toby shook his head. 'You know that makes no sense, right?'

'It does to me.'

'Then explain it. Please.' He needed to understand. If he was going to figure out his next steps without her, then he at least needed that understanding.

'Being here, with you, at Wishcliffe…' She sucked in a deep breath and looked him in the eyes, and what he saw there astonished him. 'It's felt like being home.'

'Then why—?'

'But it's *your* home, not mine. I'm not looking for another home. And that's why I can't stay.'

The confusion on Toby's face hurt her heart, but she didn't know any other way to explain it. Pulling the blanket from the end of the bed around her toga-style, Autumn paced to the window as she tried to find the right words to make him understand.

'I had a home with my grandparents. And before that I didn't—not really. My mom and I moved around the place all the time. So I've done both, right?'

'You're telling me you preferred moving around the country all the time with the mother who abandoned you to having a loving home with your grandparents?' Toby's raised eyebrows were disbelieving.

Autumn recoiled from the idea, turning to stare out of the window at the turning leaves dancing in the wind. 'That's not what I'm saying.'

'Then what *are* you saying, Autumn? Because I swear this doesn't make any sense to me. I'm falling in—'

'Don't!' She spun round and stared at him, her eyes so wide they hurt. '*Don't* say that.'

If he said it she'd never leave. How could she?

They stared at each other in silence for a long moment,

the tension so tight between them that it almost hummed. Finally, Toby looked away, reaching down to the side of the bed for his pants and pulling them on.

Clearly this was no longer a conversation to have naked.

'I'm saying… I learned lessons from both of them. From my mom and my grandma, okay?'

She tried to imagine a page in Grandma's bible on the subject of leaving your fake husband and failed. But that was because this lesson didn't need a page. It was ingrained in her soul.

'My grandma taught me that I needed to be true to myself, and to understand who that person was. She knew that I'll always be my mother's daughter, always want all or nothing, always be seeking the next adventure.'

'And your mother? What did she teach you?' There was a bitterness in Toby's voice she couldn't ignore.

'That nothing lasts,' she said softly. 'The world turns and things change. I could stay here at Wishcliffe, but for how long? You'll sell up and leave, or I'll want to go back to travelling the world, and then what?' She shrugged. 'Better to end it now, when it's still fun, than wait for something else to end it for us.'

'Like it did for Barnaby and Victoria. Like it did for my parents.' He'd got it now, she hoped. He understood. He'd realise in time that it wasn't just death that soured things and ended them. He'd realise she'd made the right decision for them.

'You know, I promised myself, after my grandparents died, that I'd live by my own rules. That I'd keep moving, that I'd be true to my nomadic nature, like my mother was. That I'd enjoy all the experiences life has to offer but keep moving on, because there was always another adventure around the corner. And that's what

I'm doing now.' She took a deep breath. 'There's more to life outside Wishcliffe than in it, and I don't want to stay here for ever.'

I'm scared I will *want to stay here for ever. And it'll break my heart when it ends. I can't take that again.*

She'd lost her mother when she'd left her behind, her grandparents when they'd died, and even Robbie when he'd turned out to not be the man she'd believed him to be, the man she'd loved.

She couldn't lose Toby too, not if she opened her heart to him and it still wasn't enough.

Toby turned to face her again, his face white and pinched. 'So that's the truth of it. You're bored of Wishcliffe, bored of me, so you're moving on. Even if I need you.' Toby's voice was totally flat, emotionless, in a way she hadn't heard from him before. 'Then I guess you're right. You should go.'

She couldn't leave it like this, even if he was giving her the perfect out. Not when it was clearly causing him such pain.

He almost told me he loved me.

And she knew now, watching his hunched shoulders as he sat on the far side of the bed, that she loved him too—more than she'd thought possible. The truth of it had been creeping up for days, and every time she thought she understood the magnitude of it.

But it was only now, as she saw his pain, that she realised how deep it ran. Almost too deep.

She needed to go. She needed to *run.* As far and as fast as she could, or it would be too late. She needed to fill her life with fresh experiences again, new adventures, unexpected opportunities and surprise delights.

Everything her impromptu marriage had turned out to be, it seemed.

'Toby—'

'Don't,' he snapped.

'I was just—'

'You were about to try and make me feel better. To mollify me with some kind words on your way out the door. But there's no point, Autumn. You see, I know you're wrong.'

He turned to look at her and she saw, for the first time, the anger burning in his eyes.

'You're not leaving because I'm in love with you. You're leaving because you're too scared to love me.'

She swallowed a gasp, trying to shake her head, but it didn't make any difference. Toby kept talking.

'I know scared, Autumn. I know terrified of what's being asked of you in this world. I've lived it. Hell, I got plastered and married in Vegas to try and avoid it. To avoid the responsibility of loving this place, these people, my legacy.'

'And you're still selling it,' Autumn pointed out sharply. 'You're still running away from that responsibility.'

'Am I?' His smile was twisted. 'And you just admitted you're running away from us.'

'No. I—' She had. She was. But that didn't change anything. Did it? And what did he mean, 'Am I'?

'You're running away. Because you're scared the same way I was scared. You're scared of wanting too much, of not being good enough, of being hurt by how much you feel, of being mistaken in that feeling. But that's because you're looking at it all the wrong way.'

'Oh, I am, am I?' Folding her arms across her chest, she raised an eyebrow. 'Please, mansplain my feelings to me.'

He shook his head. 'Not your feelings. Mine. And maybe I'm wrong and you don't feel the same way. But *you* changed the way I feel about things—marrying you, falling for you. And I can't let you leave without at least trying to do the same for you.'

'Then say what you need to say,' she told him. 'Because I've got a plane to catch.'

Toby sprung to his feet, covering the distance between them in a few long strides, and grabbed her hands in his own, staring earnestly into her eyes as he spoke.

'I was scared to come home. Scared to step into my brother's shoes, to try and be the man no one ever expected me to be. This wasn't supposed to be my role—and believe me when I tell you that *everyone* was glad of that. Barnaby was the Viscount. I was just the unreliable youngest son. I revelled in that for a while, but even then I found my own niche. My own way to live and succeed and find fulfilment. I travelled the world and had no plans at all to settle down in one place. Until my brother died.'

She wanted to say something—to take away just a little of his pain. But she forced herself to stay silent. She'd promised she'd listen, after all.

'The responsibility scared me. Not, I realise now, because I didn't want it. But because I thought I couldn't be good enough at it.'

This was his life, not hers, Autumn reminded herself. It had nothing to do with her. There was no reason any of it should resonate with her at all.

So why was she thinking of the day her grandmother had died, and she'd realised she couldn't stay in that house a moment longer? Couldn't be the person they'd hoped for without them there?

Why was she thinking of Robbie, and the realisation that, no matter how hard she tried, how much she obeyed his rules, he was never going to love her the way she wanted?

She knew now that Robbie simply hadn't been capable of it. But that didn't change the tiny fear, deep in her heart, that it was *her* who hadn't been good enough.

'You showed me different,' Toby went on, the conviction in his voice startling her. 'You arrived here without knowing *anything* about this place, and yet you fitted in like you belonged. And because you did… I started to see that I could too. That things didn't have to be done the exact way they always had been when my father was alive. That I could make this *my* place too.'

Autumn couldn't help herself. 'So you're staying at Wishcliffe?'

'I don't know. It depends.'

'On what?'

'On you.'

Anger surged up inside her, hot and fierce like the Nevada summer sun. '*This* is why I can't stay! You're putting all your happiness on me! You're making *me* responsible for your future, and I don't want that! Don't you get it? *Nothing lasts!* If I stay and it doesn't work out, what then? You'll sell up after all? I don't want to know that you'll only stay if I stay—that if I leave you'll make the wrong decision. That's not fair, Toby!'

'That's not what I meant.'

'Yes, it is.' Autumn pushed the anger down inside her until it became a simmering, constant heat. A reminder of why she didn't want love. Of why she was leaving. She was going to need that fire over the next few days, or weeks. Just until she found her own life again. 'Because that's what marriage is, isn't it? It's holding another person to you, even after they should have left. Clinging on long past when the fun stops. You just want to hold me here until *you're* ready for this to be over.'

'Is that really what you think of me?' Toby's face was

ashen. 'Because, if so, maybe it really is best that you leave.'

'I don't need your blessing,' she reminded him. 'I don't even need your damn money. I'll make my own. All I need from you is a signature on the divorce documents.'

'Then you'll have it,' he promised, his voice dull as he got to his feet.

'Good.'

Toby headed for the door, pausing only for a second as he spoke softly. 'But Autumn? If you really think that nothing can last, maybe sometimes it's because *you* leave before it has the chance.'

Then the door clicked shut behind him and she couldn't hear him any more.

Which was when she finally let her tears fall, hot and angry and confused, against her skin.

CHAPTER THIRTEEN

'THANKS FOR COMING with me today,' Toby said as they approached the glass and concrete office building in Central London.

Finn shrugged. 'I know I wasn't your first choice, but…'

'Don't.'

'Have you spoken to her yet?'

'I said, don't.' Which was a better answer than, *No, because she didn't even have the decency to leave a forwarding address.*

Finn sighed. 'If nothing else, you're going to have to talk to her to sort out the divorce, you realise.'

'Can we just… I don't know. Focus on one major life crisis at a time, here? Starting with my mysterious half-brother?' He jerked his head towards the office building, where the revolving door was waiting for them, along with an annoyed-looking security guard.

'I suppose. But we're revisiting this over a pint later.'

'Along with why you haven't been to visit Wishcliffe in months? Not even for the Fire Festival?'

'By all accounts it's just as well I wasn't there.' Finn stepped into the revolving doors. 'Look how badly you screwed things up on your own. I'd have only made things worse.'

The door had turned before Toby could reply, and he decided to save whatever Finn's problem was for later. He had his own to fix.

They didn't have to wait long before being herded to the elevator and delivered to a top floor office with a view out across the Thames and the South Bank.

The man behind the desk stood as they entered, his eyes wary but his handshake firm. He was taller than him, Toby realised, his hair darker and his eyes brown not blue. But he could see his father in the shape of his nose, the set of his shoulders, even his wryly amused smile.

'So,' Max Blythe said. 'You're my brother.'

'Apparently so.'

'Then I guess we'd better talk about why you're here.' He motioned to the chair opposite his desk. 'Take a seat.'

'I'll wait…over there.' Finn waved a hand out of the doorway and disappeared. Which was no help at all.

Autumn would have stayed.

Toby pushed the thought away as soon as it surfaced, especially since Autumn *hadn't* stayed. Not at all.

'My father left me a letter,' he explained. 'Well, left it for me and my older brother, Barnaby, to find, in an old filing cabinet that it seems Barnaby never had cause to look in, because I only found it after his death.'

'I'm sorry for your loss.' The words were automatic, Toby knew, but the feeling behind them seemed real.

'Your loss too, really,' he pointed out. 'Anyway. That letter was the first I knew of your existence. In it, our father asked that we meet you and, in his words, "make amends". I'm assuming this meant that *he* had known about you for at least most of your life and failed to act responsibly in the matter.'

He'd spent a lot of long nights wrestling with that idea,

trying to reconcile it with the man he'd known. He wasn't sure he'd managed it yet.

'That's about the sum of it,' Max murmured.

Toby looked down at the file in his hands. Strange to think that he'd been so afraid of not living up to the responsibility his father and brother had left, only to find that his father hadn't either.

Well, maybe this was something he *could* do right.

'In the interests of full disclosure,' Toby went on, 'I should tell you that I only found this letter because I was looking for documents to aid me in the sale of the estate.'

Max's eyebrows shot up at that. 'You're selling Wishcliffe?'

'I was looking into it,' Toby corrected. 'I changed my mind.'

'I see.'

'Would you…would you have wanted to buy it, if I had sold?' Toby asked.

Max shook his head. 'I don't think so. I have my own business interests, as you can see. As do you, I understood?' At Toby's look of surprise, he added, 'Just because my father never acknowledged me in life doesn't mean I didn't know where I came from, or that I didn't keep an eye on the family.'

Toby wasn't sure why he was so surprised by that. He'd have done the same thing, he imagined, in Max's shoes. But how difficult it must have been, to always be looking in.

'If you're familiar with the estate these days, then you know we have a lot of holdings. More than we can fully make use of.' Despite their best efforts to make every square inch of the estate pay its own way, they had to focus the time and money they had on things that would make the most difference.

Toby passed the file in his hand across the table and continued. 'This is the manor house across the way from Wishcliffe, outside the village of Wells-on-Water. It used to be the home of the first son and heir to the estate, and it comes with a courtesy title to boot. Barnaby pressed me to take it when he became Viscount, but I refused. But since any heir I may have in the future will be a long way off needing their own home, I would like you to have it. If you want.'

Max flipped the file open and stared at the contents. 'You must realise that if I wanted a manor house I have the means to buy my own.'

'I do.' But that wasn't what Toby was offering him, and he knew that Max must know that too. He was offering acceptance. Legitimacy. A family, even if that only really consisted of him these days.

Max closed the file. 'I'll think about it.'

'Good.' Toby nodded. It was too much to hope for a happy ending to this story just yet, he supposed. He stood to leave, then paused. 'But, whatever you decide, I hope that now we've found each other we can stay connected. I've already lost one brother recently. It would be rather nice to hang onto the only one I have left.'

'I think we can manage that,' Max replied.

They shook hands again, and Toby took his leave. But when he reached the door Max called him back. Toby turned and paused, waiting to hear what his brother needed to say.

'Can I ask… What was it that changed your mind? About selling the estate, I mean.'

Autumn.

Except it wasn't just her. Yes, she'd helped him see all the things he loved about Wishcliffe, helped him imagine a future there. But in his head that future had always included her.

The day she'd left he'd immediately planned to go through with his plans to sell the place, unable to imagine staying there without her. But then he'd calmed down, started thinking more rationally. And he'd realised that the words he'd spoken to her were true.

He'd been scared to take on the responsibility of the estate, afraid he couldn't live up to the men his father and brother had been. Discovering that his father *hadn't* been the peerless, honourable, faultless man he'd imagined him to be had gone a way to helping Toby move past that fear of imperfection.

He'd been scared too, that Wishcliffe would take more than he had to give. That it might even drive him to an early grave the way his father and brother had been.

But he knew now that being scared wasn't enough of a reason not to do something. Not when it was something that mattered.

Autumn had left because she was scared. Autumn *always* left, because she was afraid of *being* left, if she didn't get there first.

It had taken him a lot of sleepless nights to realise that.

'I think I finally realised that responsibility doesn't have to be all one-way. I was apprehensive about taking on the weight of the estate and the village and everything that goes with it. I thought it would be a sacrifice, giving up the life I'd built for myself away from Wishcliffe, I guess. But then I came home. And I saw that everything I gave to Wishcliffe, it gave me back tenfold. And I realised that it wasn't just my responsibility, or my duty, the way our father had always told Barnaby it would be his. It's my home, and it's my honour. I don't want to give that up.' He shrugged, pleased to have found an answer that didn't mention Autumn at all. 'Maybe I just grew up.'

Max nodded slowly. 'I see. Thank you. I'll be in touch soon with my own answer.'

Outside the office door, Toby found Finn flirting with one of Max's co-workers, and dragged him away towards the pub. Over a pint, he recounted the meeting with Max.

'So, overall, I think it went as well as could be expected.'

'Good.' Finn gave him an assessing look. 'So. You've decided to keep your estate—thanks for not even telling me you were planning on selling, by the way.'

'You'd have told Victoria,' Toby pointed out. 'I couldn't tell you.'

Finn flinched at that, which was odd, but carried on all the same. 'You're keeping Wishcliffe. You've made amends with your long-lost brother. What are you going to do for your hat-trick?'

It was funny how little thought the biggest decisions of his life took sometimes, Toby realised. Like marrying Autumn in Vegas.

She leaves because she's scared of being left.

Well. He hadn't left Wishcliffe. He hadn't left Max out in the cold.

He'd be damned if he'd leave Autumn without offering her everything he had to give. Without at least trying to make her believe he meant it when he said he wanted them to have forever.

'I'm going to go and win back my wife,' he said. And he smiled.

Las Vegas was pretty much as Autumn had left it.

The sun was still shining, despite the lateness of the year, and the jumpers she'd bought online in England were instantly consigned to the back of her wardrobe. Harry had mostly forgotten about why she'd left, and completely remembered why he'd hired her in the first place—something to do with his dislike of most people and being able to tolerate her, from his mumblings—so she had her old job back. There hadn't even been a discussion about it. He'd just tossed her a branded polo shirt as she'd walked in the door and told her she had the late shift.

Her bed in her shared room with Cindy was still free, so she'd dumped her case on it and sat down beside it, wondering why she didn't feel more at home.

Well, not wondering. Not really. She knew exactly why.

Toby wasn't there.

Toby would never be there again.

But she'd done her crying—all the way from Wishcliffe to the airport in the taxi, to be precise—and she wasn't going to waste any more time on it now. She'd moved on. And when she'd checked the back account she'd given Toby when she'd signed the contract, she'd found all the money he'd promised her in there, even though she hadn't stayed the full three months. So obviously he was ready to put the whole sorry marriage thing behind them too.

Eventually, there would be the divorce to sort. But she wasn't thinking about that just yet.

She wasn't thinking about anything except getting through her day-to-day. And she *definitely* wasn't thinking about the last things Toby had said to her, and how right she was afraid he was.

Except for in the middle of the night, with Cindy snoring lightly in the next bed, when those words were *all* she could think of.

But even during her shifts she wasn't completely free of Toby's memory. She'd be serving a table and think she'd glimpsed him over at the bar. Or she'd pass the spot where they'd met and almost *feel* him in the room.

It was very distracting.

Lunch times were the worst, though. It seemed she'd forgotten how to eat lunch without sitting opposite him, making him laugh as she told him about her day.

'You're mooning again,' Cindy said one evening as they passed by the bar. It was a quiet night for once, which meant Autumn had far too much time for thinking.

'I'm not mooning,' she lied.

Cindy rolled her eyes and sighed dramatically, drawing attention from the guys at the nearest table as her ample chest rose and fell again.

'You are the textbook definition of a mooning person.' Cindy leant across the bar towards her. 'What I don't get is why you don't just catch the next plane back to England and say sorry and live happily ever after. I mean, that's *obviously* why he sent you the money, isn't it? He's waiting for you to come back.'

'I don't think so. I'm pretty sure the money was a goodbye.' He'd given her the freedom to leave, even though she knew it wasn't what he wanted. She'd accused him of trying to tie her to him, but actually he'd done the opposite. She wasn't sure what to think about that.

Cindy shook her head. 'You really have no idea, do you? He didn't want you to go in the first place, right? So, if you're this miserable without him, how do you think that poor bastard is feeling?'

'It doesn't matter.' Autumn pushed away from the bar and picked up a cloth and tray to clear a table that probably didn't need clearing, just for something to do. 'I decided to come back here for good reasons, and I stick by them.'

'Because you wanted to be free to find your bliss or whatever, right?' Cindy said dismissively. 'Hun, d'ya ever think that your bliss might be right where you left it? In some mansion in England with your prince of the realm, or whatever he was.'

'Viscount,' Autumn corrected absently. 'He's a viscount.'

He was everything she'd never thought she wanted. Marriage, commitment, responsibility, certainty. Tradition rather than spontaneity. He might have said he wanted to leave Wishcliffe, to sell it and carry on travelling the world, but she'd seen the truth in his eyes every time she'd walked the land with him.

He belonged there. And, for a time, so had she.

But that time had passed.

Hadn't it?

Or had it only gone because she'd left? If she'd stayed…

She'd left because she was scared, she could admit that. Scared of her own feelings and scared that none of it could last.

But even if wanting the freedom to explore the world again had only been part of the reason, an excuse maybe, she *had* thought that getting back out on her own, moving on, would help with getting over it. But, if anything, it had made it worse. She hadn't even looked at new opportunities and adventures; she'd just slotted right back into her Las Vegas life again. Moping.

It was the worst of all possible worlds.

'At least call him,' Cindy yelled after her as she crossed the room. 'It's time for your break, anyhow.'

Dropping her tray onto the bar, Autumn let Harry

know she was getting some air on her break and left. Outside, the Vegas nightlife was only just starting to hot up. Groups of people laughed and hollered as they made their way along the Strip, some dressed up to the nines, some much more casual—and more than one or two in wedding dresses.

Autumn blinked the sight away, walking without seeing anything much at all beyond the blur of the lights, until she realised where her feet had carried her to.

The chapel where she'd married Toby.

She hesitated outside, hearing the sounds of a wedding in progress from within.

Was Toby right? Was her fear of being left what had made her leave him? He was the first thing that she'd wanted to really stay for in so, so long…

And was Cindy right? Had she really left all she'd ever wanted behind, in search of some greener grass that didn't exist? A freedom that didn't *feel* free at all.

Here she was, living the same old life she'd had before. No new adventures yet and, honestly, she wasn't sure she had the energy for them if they did show up.

Wishcliffe had been an adventure. Marriage to Toby had been an adventure.

Maybe the biggest one she'd ever get to live.

A burst of music, a cheer and plenty of laughter, and the happy couple were leaving the chapel. Autumn stepped back out of their way—and promptly stood on someone's foot. She turned to apologise and— 'Toby?'

CHAPTER FOURTEEN

AUTUMN STUMBLED BACKWARDS and Toby reached out to keep her upright. The last thing he wanted to do was fly all this way just to give her concussion.

No, the last thing he wanted to do was fly here and screw up what might be his last chance to fix his life. But the concussion thing would be pretty bad too.

'What are you doing here?' She shook herself free of his grasp and he stepped back, out of her personal space. If she needed to run again, he wouldn't stop her.

'I'm not here to guilt you into coming back, if that's what you're worried about.' He'd practised this on the plane, thankful for the almost empty first-class compartment. By the time they'd reached the halfway point over the Atlantic, though, he had most of the cabin crew weighing in on what words would be most effective, or what phrasing would express his feelings most accurately.

It had helped. Helped him see what not to say this time, if nothing else, and to pinpoint exactly where he'd gone wrong before.

If she didn't love him, and didn't want to be with him, Toby knew he'd live. But if she *did,* and his lack of communication skills meant it didn't happen, he'd never get over *that.*

More likely, though, it would be her fear that stopped

them. Fear was a powerful force. He knew that well. He just had to have faith that love could overcome it.

'Then why? Why come all this way to have the same conversation we had before we left?' She sounded more curious than defensive, which Toby took as a good sign.

Outside the chapel, the newlyweds were trying to take photos so Toby guided Autumn inside, surprised to find the place looked vaguely familiar to him. He still had no memory of the wedding itself, and had only found the place thanks to the logo on the business card attached to the marriage certificate, but all the same he had a strange sense of…something.

'I didn't want to leave things the way we did,' he started.

Autumn instantly folded her arms across her chest. 'You're here about the divorce.'

'Quite the opposite.' Toby smiled and tried to remember the perfect words he'd found in mid-air. 'I wanted to tell you that I'm keeping Wishcliffe, whatever. It's my home, and my duty, and I want to usher it into its next stage. I couldn't bear to watch anyone else do that.'

'I knew that before you did,' Autumn said, her smile wry. 'It was obvious from the moment we arrived.'

'Yeah, well, sometimes I'm a bit slow on the uptake.' Like with realising he was in love with his own wife. That had happened too late. Or maybe not, he hoped. 'I spoke with Finn—a lot, because you know Finn. We've agreed a way to keep taking the company forward but delegating more of the travel so we can both be in England more. But I'll still have plenty of opportunities to get away if I get itchy feet.'

He gave her a meaningful look that he hoped conveyed the idea that *she* would have that opportunity too, if she came home. He never wanted her to feel as if he was tying her down. As much as he could tell she loved Wishcliffe, she wasn't the sort of person to only stay in one place, any more than he was.

'That's good,' she said noncommittally, and he figured he had a way to go yet.

'I met with Max too. He's…well, I don't really know yet. But I hope to find out. He's agreed to take on the manor house out at Wells-on-Water, although it needs some patching up, so I'm hoping we'll be seeing a lot of each other.'

'That's… Toby, that's fantastic. You have a brother again!' Her excitement was infectious, even though Toby knew there was still a long way to go with Max. He'd never replace the brother he'd lost, but the idea of finding a family again, after so long, was appealing. As was the thought of making up for his father's mistakes.

'I hope so,' he said. 'So, the point is, things are fine at Wishcliffe. Better than fine. They're good.'

'Without me there, you mean?' She framed it as a joke, but he could see the pain behind her eyes.

He hated to cause her that pain but, at the same time, it gave him just a bit of hope about what came next.

He took her hand in his own and hoped to heaven that he could get this next bit right. 'Without you, everything is fine. And if you choose to stay here, or wherever you want to be, we'll carry on being fine. But I know that if you were at Wishcliffe with me, things could be so much better than good or fine. They'd be incredible.'

Her eyes widened, her lips parted just a tiny bit, but she stayed silent. Which was unusual enough for Autumn that Toby figured he'd better take advantage of it.

Never letting go of her hand, he dropped to one knee and smiled up at her.

'I love you, Autumn. So much more than I ever imagined I could when we last stood in this place.'

'You were so drunk you couldn't imagine anything, Toby. Not a great example.'

So the stunned-into-silence Autumn was gone. Good. He'd missed her voice.

He rolled his eyes and continued. 'Fine. More than I thought I could when I suggested you come home to Wishcliffe with me. I thought we could just manage a convenient marriage that would give us both what we wanted. But it just showed me how much *more* I wanted from life. *You* showed me that.'

'So what *do* you want from life?' Was that a hint of nerves in her voice? God, he hoped he could say what she wanted to hear. That she would want the same things.

But all he could do was be honest with her.

'I want to spend my life with you, loving you, trying to make your days the happiest they can be, and always being at your side. That's the first and most important thing.' He glanced up and her smile encouraged him to continue. 'I want to have adventures with you, experience new things, go to new places—but I want to have a home too. I want to come home to Wishcliffe and know that we belong there, together. Because I know I can be what the estate needs now, because of you. I was terrified of going back there alone, but with you at my side I faced my fears. You showed me—you made me believe that I could be the person Wishcliffe needs—and I know I'll always be the best version of myself when you are with me.'

'Toby—'

'I'm almost done,' he promised. This was the most important part, after all. The part that he and three cabin crew members had workshopped for over an hour before landing. 'You helped me to see that responsibility and love aren't a burden at all. They're a gift and an honour. I don't want to tie you down. I don't want to limit your opportunities. I want to experience them with you.'

He took a breath and plunged on.

'I know you're afraid that what we have can't last, that nothing that feels so right can be forever.' She looked away at his words, and he knew he'd hit a nerve. 'I understand you've been left before. I know that the good things in your life have soured. So I know I'm asking a lot of you here. I'm asking you to face that fear and give us a chance. To trust that our love is stronger than fear. I'm asking, Autumn, will you marry me again? Will you come to Wishcliffe and be the lady of the manor for real this time?'

Her heart stopped beating. Just for a moment. Then it kicked into gear again, stronger and more powerful than ever before.

This love, Toby's love, it wasn't the sort she'd built up in her head as the enemy. It wasn't the kind that locked you up and took away your choices. It wasn't the sort that changed and went away and hurt and scared you.

It wasn't the sort that disappeared when you walked away.

Because, even if love meant risking the pain of loss, she knew now that the pain of being away from the other half of her heart wasn't any better. She didn't want to live like that any longer.

Maybe it wouldn't last for ever. But, for once, she knew the chance that it *could* was worth risking heartbreak. It was worth risking *everything.*

'I promised myself when my grandparents died—'

'Autumn—'

'Just listen,' she scolded, and he did. 'I promised myself that I wouldn't let life or love limit me. But, instead, I let fear do that even more. I was so scared of caring too much, or of hurting when it was over, that I hurt *myself*, and you, by walking away. So scared of losing my choices, I couldn't choose the one thing that would make me happiest. That would make my life feel full. Love.'

Still on his knees, Toby was smiling now, and she knew that she was getting it right at last.

'Leaving you, coming back here, it showed me the truth,' she went on. 'Love doesn't end when you leave. If I'd truly loved Robbie, then leaving him wouldn't have stopped that. And when my grandparents died… I still loved them, even though they were gone. I wouldn't give up those last years with them for anything. And if I *had* left when they were sick, I'd still have loved them then too, and it would have been just as hard in another way.'

Toby squeezed her hand, and it felt as if it gave her the strength to carry on, despite the tears pooling in the corner of her eyes.

'I was scared of losing things, of being left behind like I was as a child, so I always left first. You were right about that. But I was scared of love too. Of how much it asks of you, how much you have to give it. I just didn't realise until I walked away from it—away from you—how much it gives you in return.'

Toby surged up and kissed her, holding her close against him as their lips met, as if he was pouring all his love into one kiss—and she could feel it flowing from him into her. Filling her up.

Her whole world was expanding, beyond that tiny circle of fear she'd kept herself balled up in. As she opened herself up to love, she saw at last all the real opportunities and excitement the world had to offer.

Love, she realised, would be her biggest adventure yet. And, best of all, she got to take it with the man she loved more than anyone in the world. The man who made her laugh, who made her feel, who comforted her, who challenged her, and who made her think.

Her husband.

'Excuse me?' They separated to find a tall guy in a suit, holding a clipboard, approaching. 'Are you here to get married? Only we're booked up for the next little while, and the next party are waiting outside…'

Toby and Autumn shared a glance and laughed.

'Don't worry,' Toby told him. 'We're already married.'

'And besides,' Autumn added, 'it's time for us to head home.'

Holding hands, they strolled out of the chapel and into the fading Nevada evening, ready to face whatever adventures life, Wishcliffe and love had in store for them.

EPILOGUE

WISHCLIFFE WAS FILLED with flowers.

The house, the driveway of the estate, the village itself—and most especially the little chapel that sat between the village and Wishcliffe House—all bloomed with tulips, daffodils, hyacinths and every other spring flower the locals had been able to pull up and tie a ribbon around.

'I hope none of the guests have hay fever,' Finn muttered as they waited outside the chapel to greet people when they arrived for the service.

Toby shoved an elbow in his best man's ribs. 'I think they're lovely. They're a sign of how happy everyone is that Autumn and I are getting married.'

'Again.'

'Properly, this time,' Toby corrected. 'With everyone here to see.'

Since they'd returned to Wishcliffe in the winter, they'd told only the people closest to them the truth about their marriage. But they had stated their intention to hold a proper wedding for the whole estate in the hearing of Old Gareth, who had told his wife, who had told everyone else in a five-mile radius.

The vicar had called on them the next day, and now here they were.

Getting married. Again.

And this time Toby intended to remember every single moment of it.

The vicar poked his head out through the heavy wooden doors of the chapel. 'It's time, gentlemen.'

Toby took deep breaths as he walked down the aisle, smiling to the guests as he passed their pews. But then the pollen started to make his nose tickle, so he reverted to more normal-size breaths instead.

He remembered standing in this chapel, right where Finn was, as Barnaby's best man. Remembered standing up as Harry's godfather. Remembered Christmas carol services and Easter egg hunts around the gravestones outside. Tried not to remember the funerals out there. Not today.

Today was a fresh start—for him and Autumn, and for Wishcliffe too.

And he couldn't wait for any of it.

'Stop scowling,' he told Finn as the organist switched from the gentle background music to something more commanding, transitioning into the familiar notes of the Wedding March.

The wooden doors began to creak open again, and Toby held his breath as the whole congregation stood and started to turn. To help keep his cool, Toby picked out familiar faces. Mrs Heath, Old Gareth and his wife, Lena, from the local pub. And there, right at the back, stood Max, looking wildly uncomfortable, but there all the same.

Then the doors were fully open and all he could see was Autumn, draped in a creamy white lace dress, her russet curls tumbling down her back and her smile radiant.

'God, she's beautiful,' he murmured, mostly to himself.

'Green's not her colour,' Finn replied. Which made

no sense at all until Toby spotted Victoria, walking beside Autumn's friend Cindy, as they held her train, both in pastel green bridesmaids' dresses.

Interesting. But not something he was going to worry about today.

Autumn took the last few steps on her own, beaming up at him as she took his arm.

'Ready?' he asked softly.

She nodded, then flashed him an impish grin. 'Think you'll be able to remember this one?'

'I'm pretty sure today will be one I'll never forget,' Toby replied.

Because, since that first morning he'd woken up beside her, every moment with Autumn was scorched into his memory.

'I can't wait to see what new memories we can make together,' he said.

Autumn sniffed. 'Don't make me cry. We've got the whole service to get through.'

'Just blame it on the flowers,' Toby replied. 'That's what Finn is going to do when he gets tearful.'

He could just feel Finn rolling his eyes beside him. But then the vicar was speaking and it was really happening, and Toby concentrated on paying attention to every little detail of his wedding day.

Because this time around he wasn't going to miss a thing.

* * * * *

[illegible] a very short while.

SNOWBOUND WITH THE PRINCE

CARA COLTER

MILLS & BOON

To all those kindred spirits who have found sanctuary and salvation through imagination.

CHAPTER ONE

VALENTINE'S DAY TOMORROW.

Was there a worse day to be single? Particularly newly single? Somehow, Erin O'Rourke had thought Valentine's Day, this year, was going to be extra special.

After the disappointment of no ring at Christmas, she thought Paul had decided on the much more romantic Valentine's Day to spring the question.

Erin had pictured wine. Roses. And maybe, just maybe, a ring, small diamonds sparkling, tucked into the red velvet petals of one of those roses.

But she couldn't have been more wrong. How could she have missed all the signals? How could she have interpreted a situation so incorrectly?

Two weeks ago, Paul had announced, *It just isn't working.*

Erin had been stunned. It wasn't?

While she was indulging a fantasy of commitment—wedded bliss; a little house; someday soon, a baby—her boyfriend of two years, Paul, had been moving in the opposite direction. How to get out of it. How to escape the traditional values—the ones she had adored—of the family he had been raised in.

So, instead of celebrating her new engagement, here

Erin was on the eve of Valentine's Day. Free. Well, basically free. There was always, thank goodness, Harvey.

She patted the bulge of precious cargo at her tummy, pulled her toque down even lower over her brow and her ears, her hair all tucked beneath it.

She had just gotten off the Lonesome Lookout chairlift, the highest chair at Touch-the-Clouds ski resort. Her grandfather had started the Rocky Mountain resort more than fifty years ago.

The resort had come a long way from its humble beginnings. It had once had a single chairlift and a T-bar, a simple, cavernous lodge heated by a stove made from a salvaged oil barrel.

But Touch-the-Clouds had some of the best deep powder in the world and, over the years, it was a secret that had gotten out. It had grown in popularity, particularly with the rich and famous. Finally, it had grown beyond her grandfather's capacity to keep up.

It now consisted of an entire village with bars and hotels, shops, restaurants and condos. It offered a dozen different chairlifts and hundreds of runs. While it was still the preferred ski retreat of the rich and famous, everything depended on snow. They'd had a bad few years.

And a bad review in *Snow Lust* magazine. The resort had been called "tired and overrated."

Although it was owned by a big corporation now—as were most high-end ski resorts that wanted to be viable—Erin was employed in the accounting department, and she knew the resort had spent several years in the red. How long could they keep that up? She lived at an apartment provided for her in the ski village complex, and she still had exclusive use of her grandfather's original cabin, Snow Daze, but for how long? The cabin was well off the beaten track, and the snowy trail to it could only be accessed from this chairlift.

She had decided that Snow Daze was where she would spend Valentine's Day, taking the day off tucked away in the rustic cabin. She hoped the intense quiet of deep snow outside and the crackle of a fire inside, and a cat on her lap, would soothe something in her, as they always had.

That way, tomorrow, she would not be on the receiving end of sympathetic looks from her coworker, Kelly, as she acted surprised and gleeful over the delivery of flowers and a gooey card from her husband.

Erin had, so far, managed to keep her humiliating breakup to herself.

See? There was a good side to Paul never producing a ring. A suddenly naked ring finger was like sending out an announcement card.

However, so was *nothing* arriving for her at the office on February fourteenth. It would be the equivalent of posting a group email around the office, its message the opposite of a valentine. *I'm a failure at love. It didn't work. I'm single.*

Erin regarded the mountain in the waning light of a cold winter day. She knew it as few people did, and the snow was now coming so thick and fast that she could no longer see the peaks of the mountains that surrounded this bowl.

She had caught the chair as the old attendant, Ricky, was turning everyone else away for the day.

"You're cutting it close," he'd warned her. "I sent the ski patrol up twenty minutes ago to sweep the mountain for stragglers. You're only about thirty minutes from full dark. I don't think you can make it all the way down in that time."

"I'm not going all the way down. I'm heading to the

cabin," she'd said. "Lots of time for that." She'd patted her front pocket. "I've got a satellite device. I'll let the patrol know when I get there."

He'd cast a look at the thickly falling flakes of snow. "Okay, but be careful."

She had actually laughed. "Going to that cabin for me is as routine as an afternoon commute for most people."

"I know," he'd said. "I helped your grandpa build that place. I know you're as at home here as anywhere else. But it's still a mountain, and Mother Nature can still surprise you. That looks like one doozy of a storm building. I don't think we could mount a rescue in it."

"You won't be rescuing me," she had assured him.

His concern for her had been a comfort.

On the chair, she put a hand on the warmth radiating from her belly and said out loud, "*This* is our family. Touch-the-Clouds is our home."

And that, Erin was determined, would be enough.

Now, at the top of the run, in absolute solitude, Erin pulled her hood up as extra protection from the heavily falling snow, and slid her goggles over her eyes. She used her poles to shove off and heard the wonderful hiss of her ski edges cutting into the new powder.

She crouched, picked up momentum and speed, and felt her heartaches blow away as she became fully immersed in the exhilaration of the moment.

Snow, wind, the skis beneath her. Since she was a child, those things had filled her heart with a euphoria that nothing else had ever replicated.

Including her love for Paul, she realized.

She had also been going to Snow Daze since she was a baby. Her memories of the cabin were of multigenerational family gatherings. She had grown up to ducking through strings of clothes drying by the fire, wet from sledding and building snowmen. Her memories were hot-chocolate scented, rambunctious card games won and lost around a beat-up wooden table, books devoured in a rump-sprung easy chair, waxing skis on the kitchen counter.

Still, realistically, hadn't those moments been few and far between? Her father's pro racing, and then his coaching career, had sent him all over the world. Her mother, exhausted from his inability to say no to anyone who was charmed by the combination of fame and extraordinarily good looks, had finally left him when Erin was eleven.

The remainder of her childhood had been spent between their two households, with their ever-changing international backdrops. And partners.

She had longed for the things other people's families stood for and that they seemed to take for granted.

Stability. Connection. Loyalty. Love.

Those were the things she had hoped for when she'd started dating Paul… Erin shook it off. The entrance to the trail that led to the cabin was difficult to find at the best of times. Part of the healing power of the mountain was that it forced you to stay focused.

There was no room up here for daydreaming. There were consequences for errors. It would be too easy in these conditions, even for someone as familiar with the mountain as she was, to swoop by the trailhead and have to do the arduous, sidestepping climb to backtrack up to it in the growing dark and the thickening storm.

She skidded to a halt, loving the wave of snow that shot out from her skis, the familiar ache of muscles used hard. Between wind gusts, it was deeply silent. Even the rumbling hum of the chairlift was gone, shut off for the day.

Still, the snowfall, she realized, was developing a different quality, becoming shardlike. She squinted through ice-crusted goggles up the hill and then slid them onto her forehead. She caught a single glimpse of the sky. It was taking on the ominous purplish tint that said, to those who knew the mountain, a storm was coming.

A doozy of a storm, just as Ricky had predicted.

She might end up at the cabin for more than a day, but that suited her. The cabin was always well stocked, plus she had, in her backpack, a special Valentine's feast for one. She could check in with the resort by her sat device to let them know her plans.

Paul, not much of a skier, had never been to the cabin, so there was nothing there to remind her of him.

Had she deliberately saved it? Thinking it would be the most delightful place in the world for a honeymoon? Thinking, if they had a summer wedding, they could hike into that secluded place, untouched by modern technologies, and have a few blissful days all to themselves?

No phones. No computers. No interruptions.

Paul and his phone: the constant checking, tapping away, shutting out the world, shutting out her...

Again, she shook off her sudden awareness of the insult of it. Instead, Erin looked toward the tree line. Barely visible was the tiny opening that marked a secret trail. Nailed above it was a small sign, faded, nearly covered with snow, that said Private. No Entrance. It was a largely unnecessary warning since only someone looking for this narrow gap in the wall of silent, snow-covered fir could find it.

She slid the goggles back down, tightened her hood, and pointed her skis toward the opening. She was just about to plant her poles when a voice stopped her. Was it a voice? Or just the storm announcing it was intensifying with the odd howling wind gust?

She had thought she was alone on the mountain. She

turned and squinted up into the driving snow. She saw nothing.

But then she heard the voice, louder than before. Definitely not the wind.

"Alisha, wait." The voice was deep and masculine.

Alisha? Did that mean there were two people still out on the slopes in the storm? She couldn't see anyone, the snow was so thick. Erin noticed it was beginning to blow sideways rather than drift straight down.

Then the veil of snow lifted and she saw him, making his way down the mountain toward her. It was a steep section and the visibility had gone extraordinarily flat, but he was a good skier, very technical, and she could see a natural athleticism in the aggressive way he tackled the challenging slope and traversed the ground between them.

He swooshed to a stop in front of her, covering her in a cascading wave of snow as powdery as icing sugar. As she shook it off, she was irritated, not because he had covered her with snow, but because he was still on the mountain after it had been swept.

Still, her annoyance abated somewhat as she became aware of his sheer physical presence. The storm seemed to pause around them. The wind and snow stopped abruptly. Was it possible it was going to blow over? Not likely.

He was much taller than she was and for some reason she noted that, probably because for two years she had been trying to shrink, as if her being taller than him was some sort of slight to Paul.

The athleticism she had seen in the way this man navigated the hill was even more apparent at close range. His shoulders were broad under a very expensive ski jacket and he wore the tight, flexible pant of a ski racer. Those pants molded the large muscles of powerful thighs. He carried himself with such sheer confidence that the reprimand she wanted to give him—what the heck was he still doing on the mountain—died before she spoke it.

It felt as if he, not she, had been born to this mountain, as if he owned not just it, but all the earth.

His eyes were covered by mirrored goggles. Below those goggles, he had chosen to be unprotected from the conditions by not pulling his neck gaiter up over his face. Was there something vaguely familiar about him? Probably. She had likely seen him around the resort village. He was the kind of man you would notice—and then quickly *not* notice—if you had recently been devastated by a long-term relationship exploding in your face.

Or fizzling, as the case might be.

She had to ground herself. She could not let the lull in the storm distract her from the seriousness of his situation, or that of his still missing companion, Alisha.

But instead of feeling grounded, Erin felt compelled to look at him again. A renegade tingle went up and down her spine.

It was just the wild unpredictability of the winter weather, Erin assured herself. It was increasing the intensity of her awareness of everything, including the stranger who had come out of its understated prelude.

Coming storms did this, infused the air and the earth with a humming current, both powerful and mystic. The awareness she was feeling because of the storm was transferring to him, it wasn't *because* of him.

If she thought about it, she was also aware of the feeling of each snowflake falling on her face, the deep, muffled quiet, the scent that always rode in with strong weather. Indefinable. Pure. Untamed.

"Alisha," he said. "I thought I had lost you."

Any illusion Erin had that the intensity of her awareness was caused by the mountain preparing to unleash its savagery around them evaporated.

His voice was like warm honey. It was deeply and deliciously exotic. He had the faintest accent that carried her far away from the storm, to sun-drenched places that smelled of spice and flowers.

She wished she was Alisha.

Slowly, with a sigh, she lifted her hand, flipped down her hood and then raised her goggles off her eyes.

CHAPTER TWO

PRINCE VALENTINO DE OSCARO STARED, shocked, into the greenest eyes he had ever seen. The shock was intensified because he thought he had finally, in this lull in the snowstorm that was in equal parts terrifying and exhilarating, been reunited with his head of security.

"You're not Alisha," he said.

It was stating the obvious. The ski jackets, the height—unusually tall for a woman—were similar enough that he had made the initial error of thinking it was Alisha, particularly since that was who he had been looking for. What were the chances, after all, of two women of similar appearance being out in this storm?

But his head of security, Colonel Alisha Del Rento, was the antithesis of this woman: her life experiences honed into her face, unapologetically tough and weathered. The colonel was as dark as this woman was pale.

The prince realized the word *pale* did not do justice to the woman in front of him. *Fair* might be better. There was the wholesome glow of the outdoors dusted on her skin, giving her a look most women would want but that could never be attained out of a makeup bottle.

These observations were peripheral. Where was Alisha? Though she took pride in the fact that she could handle anything that life threw at her, neither she nor the other two members of his security team were familiar with this mountain.

They had, he knew, trained for winter conditions, but still he felt concerned. This was on him. He had insisted, despite the worsening weather and against his security team's wishes, on one more run, the new snow making the powder too exquisite to resist.

The woman might not physically resemble the colonel in any way, but that tight-lipped look of disapproval was familiar.

"What on earth are you doing out here?" the woman asked.

Valentino was unaccustomed to sharpness of tone and, despite his worry for his team, he felt oddly delighted by it.

Just as he felt oddly delighted by the storm. It was so real. A man and a mountain, pitting his strength, his abilities, his intelligence, against the elements.

Of course, he had two women, now, who were really annoyed at him. The one before him, whose green eyes were sparking with an intriguing inner light, and his head of security, who had strongly advised, given the weather, they not make this final run.

But he had insisted, *loving* the challenge of it.

Only one of those women would feel free to express her chagrin, and that was the one in front of him.

He felt himself rising to the challenge of her, too. He answered her question by repeating it.

"What on earth are *you* doing out here?" he shot back.

Her look of disapproval intensified. Who, besides his mother, had ever dared be disapproving of him?

"I live here."

He glanced around. "Where? Under one of the trees?"

She failed, apparently, to see the humor. "I also work here. You shouldn't be on the mountain in this storm."

"But you should?" he asked mildly. "Besides, it seems to be letting up."

"I thought so, too, but don't underestimate mountain weather. It's possible it has barely hit yet."

Could that be true? The snow had paused but was coming again, though lighter than it had been before. The wind had died down almost completely.

Glaring at him, as if he was a horrible inconvenience to her, she planted her poles and pulled off her gloves. He was not sure why he noticed her fingers were ringless. She unzipped an outer pocket of her jacket. He noticed a slight bump at her waistline and something in him went cold.

Was she pregnant?

Valentino felt suddenly and astonishingly protective of her—and also in way over his head. As he looked at her, the bulge in her stomach area *moved.*

Good grief, was she going to have a baby? Out here in a storm that, according to her, had barely hit yet? With him, of all people? He wasn't wholly loving the challenge of the mountain—and of her—quite so much now.

Thankfully, she produced a cumbersome item that looked like some kind of phone, and he felt the relief sigh within him. Signals on his own cell phone had been intermittent since arriving at the resort.

She held her apparatus up to the sky and shifted her glare from him to it. She took a few sidesteps up the mountain, and he recognized, despite her condition, how at ease she was on the skis.

She held up the device again.

"What are you doing?" he asked.

"Searching for a signal. It's a satellite device," she

said without looking at him. Her face brightened. She quickly lowered the device, punched in numbers, and put it to her ear.

"What's your name?"

Valentino simply was not accustomed to being snapped at like this: as if he were some sort of nuisance, causing aggravation to someone. Despite the fact that he was somewhat lost, with a storm apparently nowhere near over, with a woman who was pregnant, he contemplated how what should have been an insult instead felt oddly refreshing.

Had he ever, in his entire life, had someone have absolutely no idea of who he was?

And so, he didn't want her to know. Not just yet. He would enjoy this anonymity for a little while longer by just giving his first name. Of course, once she got someone on the other end of that phone, she was bound to find out the Crown Prince of the Kingdom of Lorenzo del Toro was missing.

"Valentino," he said. He wanted to say something more North American. Like Fred. Or Joe. But there was the security team to consider. They would be frantic with worry for him, wherever they were. So, as delightful as it would be to remain anonymous, his duty to others came first. As always.

"Seriously?" Her green eyes narrowed skeptically on him, as if he *had* given her a pseudonym.

"Excuse me?"

"Your name is Valentino?"

"It is," he said.

"What are the chances?" she muttered.

"Excuse me?" he said again.

She sighed heavily. "What are the chances that I would

find a man named Valentino on the mountain on the eve of Valentine's Day?"

"It had completely slipped my mind that tomorrow is Valentine's Day," he told her. Then, before he could ask her name in return—and if she shouldn't be with her husband to have her baby on Valentine's Day—she moved on, snapping another question at him.

"And your companion? Alisha? When's the last time you saw her?"

"We were on the chair together. There were actually four of us total."

"Four?" she said, and her green eyes widened in alarm. Now was probably not the time to notice how thick her lashes were, the snowflakes—the snow *was* deepening again—crusting on them like tiny diamonds.

It might reduce her alarm to tell her his team were all specialists in a number of areas that would likely more than prepare them for the challenges of the mountain. But then, he was concerned about them himself, and admitting to being accompanied by a "team" of specialists of any kind would certainly give clues that she had not run into just an ordinary joe on the mountain.

The prince was not yet ready to give up his taste of anonymity.

"Yes, we were skiing together. They're very accomplished."

Her look of skepticism was not reduced. Again, it was novel to have someone doubt him.

"To be honest," he offered, "I don't know how we were separated. It seems impossible."

Given his team's absolute devotion to his protection and safety, it really did seem astonishing that somehow they had lost each other. One moment he had been swooping down the mountain, elated, and the next he had been aware of the deepening of the storm and that he was alone.

"The mountains love to make fun of what people think is possible and impossible," she said and then turned her attention to the phone.

"Hi, Stacy. This is Erin."

Erin. He contemplated that name and how well it suited her. In his world, women had feminine names, so this added to his sense of being let loose in a different time and place.

Erin's voice drifted to him. For all that her name wasn't particularly feminine, her voice was.

"I've come across a guy up here on the Lonesome runs. Valentino."

He was irrationally glad he hadn't told her he was Joe or Fred, because he liked the way his name sounded coming off her lips.

"Four total in his party," she said then raised her voice. "Four."

She listened and then pulled the phone away from her ear. Even with a bit of distance between them, he could hear a hissing and crackling on the line. She waited, patiently, until it subsided, and put the device back up to her ear.

He expected his moment of anonymity was about to be lost. She would be told she was with a member of the royal family from a small Mediterranean island kingdom. Everything would change. She would look at him with deference, a new respect, but it would be because of his title, not because of who he was. He felt unreasonably deflated by that.

She was squinting at her device, disgruntled. She held it up, sighed, then shoved it back in her pocket.

"The signal evaporated," she said with a shrug, none

the wiser to who he was. "Which is not so surprising in this weather. But I understand that the rest of your party is accounted for, thank goodness."

His sense of relief was instant. Despite the fact the soldiers of his personal guard were experts who had trained in survival from the Italian Alps to the Arctic Ocean, he still had known it was because of him they'd been out in the storm. If anything had happened…

"Good," he said. "I'll meet them down there."

She looked pensively at the weather, took in a deep breath of the air, as if it gave her clues.

"We aren't going down," she decreed.

We? And who had placed *her* in charge of *him*? He raised an eyebrow. In his world, that was all it took.

But she knew nothing of his world.

"I think it's too close to dark," she stated. "We can't make it all the way down to the village, especially if the storm gets worse, which I think it is going to."

"Do we have an option?" he asked. He did not want to be trapped on a mountain, in a storm, with a woman who looked like she might be about to have a baby. His gaze drifted to the terrifying bump at her belly. He thought he detected a slight motion again. A baby at any moment!

Again, she considered the weather. "I don't think so."

"What exactly does that mean?" Valentino asked. "That we have to shelter up here?" He had kidded her about living under one of the trees, but now it didn't seem funny.

She was silent and preoccupied, pulling the goggles back over her eyes, fastening her hood tight around her toque.

"We can build an igloo," he proposed. He couldn't have predicted that this morning. That he would be building a shelter, a storm raging, a baby coming. His life rarely handed him surprises. But he didn't feel trepidation about the challenge.

Instead, he felt ready. Protective. And fierce, as if a warrior spirit he had not known he'd possessed had stepped up to do battle with these elements.

He felt the huge weight of the responsibility to get her through this, but he also felt ready to test himself against the mountain, to not be pampered and protected. But instead to be the protector. He felt astonishingly alive, vibrating with urgency.

"An igloo?"

He frowned at her. The one who claimed to live here didn't seem to be getting the peril they were in since she had decided they couldn't make it back to the village. It was probably a form of protective denial. Because of the baby.

"Yes, you know," he said, keeping his voice calm, patient, reassuring. "We'll have to find some crusted snow. And cut blocks from it. It will protect us from the elements until morning."

"I know what an igloo is." For the first time, a smile tickled her lips. He noticed they were unglossed and generous. And gorgeous.

What kind of man made that kind of note about a pregnant woman's lips? It seemed like something you might have to admit to in the confessional!

Besides, he had to keep the priorities straight, since she was obviously not going to. How could she not know how dangerous this all could become in the blink of an eye?

Still, that smile changed everything about her. The sternness left her face and she looked very youthful and wholesome, not to mention extraordinarily beautiful.

And then she laughed.

He might have enjoyed the sound of that more if he hadn't had the annoying sense she was not just making light of their predicament, but laughing *at* him. Not *with him*—because he was not laughing.

This was an extraordinarily novel experience. Not at all enjoyable, like his anonymity had been.

"An igloo," she snorted between chortles.

He frowned at her. Was she mocking him? A frown from him had always been enough to bring instant respect. She, however, did not take the frown as a reprimand, as he had intended. Not at all.

"And you know how to make one?" she asked, the music of her laughter still tinging her voice. "An igloo? Or do you think I know how to make one? A mandatory part of being Canadian?"

She was continuing to be amused at his expense! The novelty of her not knowing who he was, was thinning rapidly.

"I'm sure I can figure it out," he informed her stiffly. "I saw it on a documentary once."

She managed to contain, finally, her awful chortling, though her lips still twitched. "Well, that would certainly make you an expert," she said. Her tone was not sarcastic, but soothing, which made it twice as insulting, as if she were speaking to a child who had told her he knew how to build a rocket ship to the moon.

"I could, in a pinch, put together a rudimentary shelter from the elements."

"Yes, of course, you could." There was the patronizing tone again. "But we aren't going to need your igloo expertise."

As much as the prince wanted to be mistaken for a normal person, he didn't want this stranger on the mountain thinking she was going to patronize him, and worse, be in charge of things. She seemed to think she was going to protect him, not the other way around. The insult of it was grating.

"We need to think about the baby," he informed her sternly.

She looked astonished. And then she glanced down at the bulge under her jacket, as if she had forgotten her delicate condition. That annoying *amused* smile deepened. Thankfully, it was not accompanied by the chortle, though she looked as if she might be biting it back.

"I have a cabin up here. That's where I was heading. We're ten minutes from there. Let's move."

She had a cabin? A young woman alone on the mountain? A young woman who was about to have a baby? Because of the gathering twilight and the intensity of the snow, the light was growing stranger around them by the moment.

Between that, and the prince standing on the unfamiliar ground of being both unprotected and with someone who had no idea who he was, this whole incident was beginning to have the faint, hazy texture of a dream.

Or a fairy tale.

And then, before his very eyes, the baby bulge her jacket was stretched across moved quite violently!

If that baby decided to arrive, the dream could turn into a nightmare very quickly!

CHAPTER THREE

As Valentino grappled with all of that, Erin set her poles.

"Follow me," she ordered, all business, borderline bossy. "We have to make time. We're losing the light. Try to keep up."

There was that hint of an insult again, both at being given an order and at her instructing him to keep up.

But when he looked down the slope, he was a little shocked by how conditions had diminished suddenly. The snow had thickened to nearly zero visibility, as if the two of them existed alone after being dropped into a milk bottle.

Apparently, she had been right about the storm barely hitting before. Now, it descended on them with its full force. The wind suddenly screamed into the silence, stopped, then screamed again.

He had to raise his voice to be heard above it. "Let's go."

Valentino had been taught by some of the best instructors in the world since he was a small boy. He had skied some of the most exotic places in the world, including the alps of Italy and Switzerland. Skiing to him was like riding. Both activities came as naturally to him as breathing.

He thought Erin should probably be worried about keeping up with him! Particularly in her delicate condition. She would need to protect herself.

But she did not seem to have those concerns. And she quickly proved him wrong about who would be keeping up with whom. She found an almost invisible trail through some trees. Valentino knew he skied well, and maybe extraordinarily so.

But she skied differently than anyone he had ever seen before. Despite the fact she was carrying quite a large pack on her back—and a baby on her front—her movement was both powerful and seemingly effortless. She wasn't conquering the slope of the mountain, she was melding with it, dancing with it, celebrating it.

It was an extraordinary thing to witness, at the same time he was terrified of her falling! He would have shouted at her to slow down, but he never got close enough to make his voice heard above the storm that howled and pulsated around them.

It was also humiliatingly hard to keep up to her. Between the speed she was traveling and the heavily blowing snow creating a blanket between them, it took all his considerable skill to keep her in his sights.

As their passing disturbed them, heavy snow dropped in clumps off the needled branches of the trees. It was like being in a war zone: a sense of life-and-death urgency coupled with the relentless whistling of the wind, snow now dropping from branches like bombs on both sides of the trail.

And then it was over.

Not the storm.

But the sense of urgency and peril. The trail abruptly ended in a small clearing. They had beaten the storm.

Barely visible through the driving snow and ebbing light was a structure. With towering trees at its back, a tiny cabin faced the clearing. It was like something off a Christmas card, the kind of place he thought probably only existed as nostalgia, a figment of imagination, a longing for simplicity and sanctuary in a busy, complex world.

With one last huge effort, he launched himself toward the cabin's promise. They had arrived at safety.

As Valentino stopped at the steps to the cabin, Erin was already stepping out of her bindings and tossing her skis over her shoulder. He felt like a man who had crossed the desert in search of water and could not be certain that what he was seeing was not a mirage. He took it all in.

Constructed of logs, long since weathered to gray, the cabin was anchored on one side by a sturdy chimney made of round, smooth river rocks in varying shades ranging from gold to mauve. In the shadow of a large porch that wrapped around the entire structure, a brightly painted red door welcomed. There were red shutters around the square-paned glass of the windows. The snow, stacked up on the roof, was at least two feet deep.

Valentino was a man who had been raised in grandeur and opulence. The palace of his family was often compared to the Palazzo Brancaccio in Rome, though, as his mother liked to point out to anyone who was interested, it predated that structure by several hundred years. Their house, Palazzo de Oscaro, was arguably the most photographed palace in the Mediterranean.

He followed Erin's suit and kicked off his skis, and then tumbled, grateful, through the door of the cottage. He had to put his shoulder against it to close it. It was as if the storm was an intruder, demanding to come in with them.

With the storm closed out—howling as if angry at its exclusion—Valentino became aware of a feeling he'd never had before when, at this moment, he felt it for the very first time.

As he leaned his back against the door, he was enveloped in a sense of warmth, a sensation of arriving, finally, after a long, long journey, at the place called home.

But then, sharing the small entryway with him, Erin yanked off her toque and a cascade of hair tumbled out as golden as ripened wheat. She ran her hands through it, tossed it over her shoulder with a shake of her head. He could smell some heady scent.

His sense of having found a safe place, a place called home, evaporated. As someone who had grown up royal, he had had it drummed into him from the first small hop of a hormone: do not *ever* put yourself—and therefore your family—in a compromising position.

In a world that was always under a microscope and always under control, he had never encountered a situation quite like this one.

He was going to be snowed in, alone and entirely unchaperoned, with a woman. A very beautiful woman.

A strange sense of danger, every bit as intense as what he had felt on the mountain and from the storm enveloped him.

A very pregnant woman, Valentino reminded himself. *Thank the gods.*

Valentino on Valentine's Day, Erin thought as she yanked off her toque and ran her hands through her hair, contemplating the option that someone was punking her.

She glanced over her shoulder at the stranger to see if he was amused. An igloo? It had to be a trick of some sort.

But the man looked only relieved to be inside. Besides, who could have put such an elaborate trick in play? It would mean someone had known about Paul breaking off with her. It was possible, given that it had happened two weeks ago, that he was slowly letting people know, even if she was not.

But really? She didn't know anyone in their circle of friends, thank goodness, who was cruel enough to make a joke out of that.

Besides, the whole premise rested on a chance encounter on the mountain. And Valentino seemed to genuinely think she was pregnant. So, no, it had to be the universe having a snicker at her expense.

Well, at least she'd managed to punk back a little bit by letting him believe she was pregnant. And by besting him at skiing. He had skied beautifully, but Erin allowed herself a small snippet of satisfaction that, even so, he couldn't keep up to her.

She patted the bump under her jacket, just to get a reaction from him, but it backfired. The reaction was hers.

Because Valentino lifted his goggles from his eyes.

Any brief satisfaction she had felt by besting him at skiing evaporated like mist before the sun. His eyes were utterly astonishing. A deep, deep brown flecked with gold.

Now that she wasn't, well, taken, and now that they had found sanctuary and safety from the storm, it gave her permission to really look at him as he leaned over and released the buckles on his boots.

She fought the temptation to look at him longer. Instead, she took out the satellite device and tried for a connection. No go. She typed in a quick text to let people know they had arrived safely. Generally, it would send the next time the device found a signal.

She accidentally jostled him as she bent over her own boot buckles.

"Oh, sorry," she said, annoyed that she was blushing as he regained his balance and kicked off the boots.

"I'll set those outside," she said.

He passed the boots to her and his hand brushed hers. She still had her gloves on; he did not. It was impossible that she felt the heat of his touch, wasn't it?

She was so close to him. In the fading light, his golden-toned skin seemed to glow. She could not help but notice his nose: perfect, strong and straight. He had high, commanding cheekbones. He was clean-shaven, which accentuated a faint cleft in his chin, a feature Erin had not realized she found attractive until this very second.

A hint of a dark shadow on his cheeks—added to that exotic skin tone—suggested he might have dark hair beneath the custom-painted ski helmet that complimented the rich navy of his jacket and pants.

For some reason, once her eyes found them, she could not look away from his lips, which were firm and wide. The bottom one was enticingly puffy, the faintest line dividing it in two. What form of madness was this?

Aside from the fact they were going to be stranded together for at least one night, she was freshly heartbroken! This jolt of pure awareness his lips were causing in her seemed entirely inappropriate.

It felt as if, given the circumstances, she should be ashamed of her awareness of the sensual fullness of his lower lip. She tried to muster that feeling.

Instead, Erin was aware of feeling free, like someone who had been inside a house too long suddenly being let out to breathe fresh air.

It felt liberating, and exhilaratingly so, to just look at a man and appreciate him. It felt good to *not* be taken, spoken for, committed.

Erin was shocked at herself and a new and niggling awareness of how superficial she was capable of being. She turned quickly away from him and put the sets of heavy ski boots outside the door. Snow blew in, right up under the porch. When she stepped back in the door, Valentino had not moved, but was studying the interior of the cabin.

The look on his face was extraordinary. It was as if he was lit from within. Her eyes moved to the puffiness of that lower lip again.

Then he threw back his head and laughed. Was it because he had noticed her fixation on his lips?

"Encantado," he declared softly, his accent unconsciously seductive. And then his eyes came to rest on her. He had spoken in Spanish, so he translated. "I'm enchanted."

She felt as if her breath stopped.

Was he referring to her? To her gazing at his lips? She quickly looked away, over the broadness of his shoulders, and tried to quiet the fluttering of her heart.

All her life she had lived with her father's unending appeal to women, and her mother's bitterness over it. But until this moment, she had not experienced a pull toward someone that felt so compelling. She was shocked to feel something primitive and powerful stir within her.

She had not felt this before—a naked animal awareness of a member of the opposite sex—and it shook her. After all, she knew nothing about this man who was looking so intently at her with a gaze that set fire in her blood.

Wanting.

Wanting what? Erin asked herself primly. She just wasn't the kind of girl who went around lusting after strangers on the ski hill.

Erin did not like weakness. And she particularly did not like *that* weakness. She sighed inwardly. The universe had not only provided her with a Valentino for Valentine's

Day, but one that was going to challenge everything she believed about herself.

For instance, that she was not in the least impulsive.

She did not believe people had instincts they could not control.

She certainly did not believe in love at first sight.

He took off his jacket and reached to hang it on a peg behind her. He was very close, in fact, and his presence was so electrical that some of her hair reached out and attached to the sleeve of his white, long-sleeved undershirt.

When she reached out to yank her errant hair back, she realized the undershirt was not wool, but something finer, like alpaca or cashmere. The texture of it made her want to sink her fingers in to it. Or maybe that was the scent that tickled her nostrils, every bit as invigorating as the scent of the coming storm she had detected earlier.

It was faintly spicy, faintly cold, faintly pure man.

Then Valentino removed his ski helmet and reached by her again to put it on a peg. Despite ordering herself not to, Erin could not help but stare at him.

A cascade of damp curls, as black and as shiny as the wings of a raven, had been released from underneath that helmet.

He shook them and then ran a hand through the tangled mop of his hair. He was so gorgeous, it felt as if her heart would stop.

She suddenly was not so sure she did not believe in love at first sight.

That was a thought that had to be resisted wholeheartedly!

"When's the baby due?" he asked, a certain tender protectiveness in his tone that could melt a susceptible person's heart. She was determined she would not be that person.

"I'm not pregnant."

Valentino looked quizzically at her stomach. And then a blush changed the tone of his golden skin. He thought he'd *insulted* her.

Harvey, no doubt recognizing they were home, wanted out. Valentino's eyes widened at the violent wave of motion under her jacket.

She stepped by Valentino into the main room and unzipped her coat to reveal the rounded hump of baby carrier underneath it.

"You skied with a *real* baby?" he breathed, aghast, apparently not familiar enough with baby paraphernalia to realize a head should have been visible if she was, indeed, carrying a real baby.

"Well, my baby."

"But that's not safe!"

"This is the same baby carrier my father used to put me in to come here when I was just a baby," she said. "My family skis as easily as most people walk."

"Still," he said, appalled, "you could have fallen. On your baby."

"Think of it like people in Europe riding bikes with babies in the carriers."

"It's not the same—"

At that moment, Harvey decided he'd had enough. His paws emerged first, over the lip of the carrier. And then he hefted himself up, poking his gray furry head out of the carrier He eyed the stranger in his domain balefully through slitted amber eyes.

Valentino took a startled step back. "That is not a baby!"

"Really?" She looked down at Harvey with pretended astonishment. "Where did he come from?"

Valentino eyed her with such annoyance, a shiver went

up and down her spine. He had that look of a man far too certain of himself, a man that people did not cross.

"You're not pregnant," he said, something edgy in his voice.

"Is there any reason you would sound disappointed by that news?"

"You let me believe it. You let me think I might be delivering a baby in an igloo."

"I'm in no way responsible for other people's absurd conclusions!"

"You're skiing with a cat and you call me absurd?" he shot back.

"I don't think I would have been out here skiing by myself if I was that close to having a baby. What do you take me for? An idiot?"

"I feel as if I've been the one played for the idiot," he said stiffly. "You could have told me right away. Plus, you could have seriously injured your animal."

"Not just an idiot! An irresponsible idiot! Believe me, if I had fallen on Harvey, I would have come out of it in worse shape than him."

Valentino looked at her with narrowed eyes. She could feel a spark in the air between them. She didn't like sparks between people! She liked calm.

But look where that liking had gotten her. Paul had told her, in his little breakup speech, that their relationship was boring. It reminded him of his mother and father's relationship. It was obvious—look at her relationship with Harvey—that she wanted children. Soon.

He wasn't ready. Kids and family felt like jail to him.

Erin's focus moved again to the intrigue of that puffy split in Valentino's bottom lip. She contemplated the feeling that rippled through her. Whatever it was, it was not boring.

She was annoyed with him. He was aggravated with her. And still, underneath that ran a current of…something. Something she could not encourage, or investigate, given their circumstances.

Not that she would want to under any circumstances. That kind of spark was dangerous! It could burn a whole forest down before you even blinked.

They were about to be snowed in here, together, for who knew how long. There was no room in that equation for *wanting.*

CHAPTER FOUR

THERE WAS NO room for wanting, Erin told herself sternly, no matter how delectable Valentino's lips were. Part of her, to her own disgust, sighed. *What would one little taste hurt?*

There would be no such thing as a *little* taste of those lips. It would be like trying to have only one little bite of fantastic chocolate.

And there was no room for attractions or sparky arguments, either, even if it did make her feel faintly invigorated.

"Let's call a truce," she suggested. *And not look at each other's lips.* "I'm sorry I let you believe I might be pregnant."

"For your own amusement," he said.

"You obviously did not get the script," she told him with elaborate and sarcastic patience. "This is the part where you say, 'I'm sorry I insinuated you were an irresponsible idiot.'"

Valentino was silent. He looked stern. Almost forbidding. A man who rarely had to give an inch to anyone and who didn't plan to now.

"I have food," she told him. "And wine. And I'm not above bribing you for a truce."

"I'm bigger than you. I could just take them." But finally the stern line around his mouth softened.

"But you wouldn't," she said.

He cocked his head at her.

"I can tell by looking at you. And since we're stuck here together for a while, it would probably be better if we made an attempt to be civil. So, truce?"

He considered. He nodded. "Truce."

Having won that reluctant concession from Valentino, Erin released the cat from the carrier and set him on the floor. Harvey would have normally headed straight to his dish and complained loudly at finding it empty. Instead, he marched over, tail high, and wound himself around Valentino's legs.

Despite her call for a truce, she couldn't believe her cat.

Traitor.

She could usually count on Harvey to be an equal opportunities hater. He had held Paul in utter contempt for the entire length of their relationship.

Valentino squatted and scratched under the scruffy cat's chin. "You look like an old warrior," he said.

She was suddenly not so sure how wise calling a truce had been. Valentino's deep voice, roughened with affection, sent a tingle up and down her spine. If she was not mistaken, her cranky cat was reacting about the same way. He rounded his back as Valentino's hands moved from his chin to his tail.

Erin stared at his hands. They were not the hands of a working man, but rather beautifully shaped and manicured while still being entirely masculine. He must be an executive. Actually, given that take-charge, brook-no-nonsense demeanor, she was willing to bet he owned and ran a very successful company.

He was doing something with those hands—caressing—

that made that *wanting* leap to the fore more powerfully than when she had first fought it back.

The cat preened under his touch.

"How old is he?" Valentino asked, not the least bit aware, thank goodness, that she had become entranced with his hands.

"I've had him since I was eleven," she said. "And he wasn't a kitten, then, so he's at least fifteen, maybe older."

"And you travel with him?"

Was she eager to let him know she was not some eccentric single woman who could not be separated from her cat? It would seem so. But, wait a second, wasn't she the one who had decided to embrace the single life?

Looking at Valentino's hands on that cat, she was embarrassingly aware she didn't want to be perceived as a career single person and a crazy cat lady!

"He's going slowly blind," Erin explained. "And deaf. He's nervous when I'm not around, so I've increasingly found ways to keep him close to me. He sleeps most of the time now, so it's no problem to have him under my desk at work. I'm in accounting at the resort."

"Accounting?"

Was she relieved at the surprise in his voice? When had she started being a person who didn't want to look like she was in accounting?

About half an hour ago!

"Yes, accounting. Harvey is kind of the office mascot, even though he has a nasty streak."

"A nasty streak?" Valentino said, giving Harvey's chin another scratch before straightening. "I don't believe it."

Harvey cast her a look that clearly said he'd been *seen*.

"That's an unusual amount of dedication to a pet on your part," he said.

Paul had thought it was distinctly weird, not admirable.

"I owe him one," Erin said. She went over to the kitchen counter and removed some long matches from a jar.

"That's interesting. How can you owe a cat something? I would think it might be the other way around. You provide for him. Food. Shelter. Tummy rubs."

"No, it's definitely me that owes him." She began to move around the room, opening the valves on the wall lamps and lighting them, one by one, until the room took on a soft glow. It was full dark outside now and the lights made the cabin seem like a cozy nest in the middle of the storm that raged right outside the windows.

"What can I do?"

"Could you feed Harvey? His food is in the top drawer over there and his dish is beside the fridge."

Valentino crossed the room, telepathic cat on his heels, and Erin could not help but notice the grace and athleticism she had seen on the mountain was still very evident in the way he moved. He carried himself with supreme confidence. He found the one-serve cat food and broke one open.

Harvey, at the sound of the package opening, yowled as if he hadn't been fed for a week. Valentino, somehow at home, rummaged around in another drawer until he found a spoon, leaned over the dish and scraped the food into it.

Harvey, impatient, kept pushing his hand out of the way, until Valentino laughed.

Erin retrieved her backpack and began taking its contents out. She left the bakery box with the heart-shaped cake in the pack. She had bought a candle for it that was shaped like the number one. She had planned a defiant celebration of finding herself single by having a Valentine's Day feast for one. Now, she didn't know what was going to happen. If the storm abated overnight, in the morning she would be taking Valentino down the slopes. Would she come back up? Somehow, celebrating being single on Valentine's Day had lost its appeal.

And if he was still there, she was not sure a Valentine's Day feast would be appropriate.

It occurred to Erin that it had been a long time since she had shifted a plan spontaneously. A long time since things had gone out of control in her world.

She told herself she liked it that way, the plans and predictability. That's why she worked in accounting. The world of numbers was safe and regulated. You applied formulas and got expected outcomes.

And yet, if she were honest, wasn't she rather enjoying this scenario?

Of not knowing what would happen next? Of things being slightly out of her control? Wasn't life suddenly and unexpectedly infused with a sense of adventure? Didn't it feel oddly and wonderfully exhilarating to be ensconced inside the cabin—stranded—with a gorgeous stranger?

Maybe that had been missing from her life.

Maybe Paul was correct when he had declared it all a little too dull and predictable, too boring. Maybe they had been—she had been—too young for that, to be acting like his parents.

"Steak it is," she muttered. Some of the items needed to go in the fridge and again she found herself in close quarters with Valentino.

The problem was, was her sanctuary ever going to feel the same after this? Or would his substantial presence—his laughter—leave a mark here, like a shadow?

He watched, grinning, as the cat gulped down the food. "There's no possible way you owe him," he decided.

"I do."

"Like he saved you from a burning building or something like that?"

"Something very like that," she said. "I've heard that you do not choose a cat, a cat chooses you."

Because of Paul's almost instant animosity to the cat, Erin had never told him that part, never trusted him with her vulnerability around the cat. Harvey wasn't just her pet. He was her family.

She moved quickly out of the kitchen, adjusted the thermostat in the living room and heard the comforting chuff of the propane-powered furnace kicking over. She finally shrugged off her coat and removed the carrier.

"Electric heat," he said, his surprise evident in his voice. But when she glanced at him, he didn't seem that interested in the furnace.

His eyes rested for a moment on her and she was glad for her choice of this sweater—white angora—this morning. It flattered her, a sweater that said—if sweaters could say such things—*Is this the sweater of a woman who has just been thrown over by her boyfriend?*

"Propane, but it does the trick. It's quite a modern igloo," she told him, annoyed at herself for being glad about the sweater. "We even have an indoor bathroom."

"Okay," he said, holding up his hands, cowboy surrender. "I think we've moved on from the igloo stuff. It's in the terms of the truce."

"I'll have to see a written copy."

His laugh, again, was so delightful. Warm. It filled the space with its richness and vibrancy.

"Anyway, I get it," he continued. "All the modern conveniences. No igloo stereotype. It actually seems more like something out of a fairy tale than an igloo."

Valentino was looking around with very real interest, and Erin followed his gaze, trying to see the familiar space through the eyes of a stranger.

"You mustn't be much of an expert on fairy tales," she told him, trying for a light tone. "Don't they usually take place in castles?"

With a prince, she reminded herself. It was embarrassingly easy to envision him, with his very evident confidence and composure, and with that exotic lovely accent, as the kind of prince who rode through the pages of fairy tales rescuing damsels in distress.

That, given her recent breakup, she might qualify as.

"Ah, castles," Valentino said with a shake of his head, pretending to be a man weary of such things. It was her turn to laugh.

He grinned back at her.

"This seems much preferable. The gingerbread cottage that Hansel and Gretel found in the woods," he elaborated.

She was sure her place on the mountain was just like thousands of other Canadian cottages, and yet she loved this space so much. A big stone fireplace dominated the room, the rough-hewn timber mantel littered with dusty ski trophies. Cozy furniture, covered in carelessly tossed plaid throws, circled around it, and stuffed bookshelves flagged both sides. An L-shaped kitchen with knotty-pine lower cabinets and open-shelving uppers took up one corner of the not very big space.

The main living area of the cabin was all one room, but this expanse inside the door had a large square of tile that could handle snow melting off clothes better than wood. On the wall behind the door was an abundance of pegs to hang wet clothing.

Still, the kitchen space suddenly seemed very tight. Erin was aware, again, of his size. Not just that he was taller than she, but that the sizzling masculine energy of him made her feel almost small and decidedly feminine. Small was something she had rarely felt! She had been five foot nine inches by the time she was fourteen.

His gaze fell on her and he smiled. “Minus the wicked child-eating witch, of course.”

“Don’t underestimate Harvey.”

Just like that, they were laughing together, the soft light from the lanterns illuminating his skin tone, his mouth, his hair.

The man was absolutely, stunningly, gorgeous.

Gorgeous, and yet Erin was aware of that feeling again, that she had seen him before. She must have caught a glimpse of him in the village, though that didn’t feel quite right. He did not seem like the kind of man a person—even one who’d had her dreams of a ring for Valentine’s Day dashed—would forget seeing.

“What?” he asked her softly, and she realized, embarrassed, she was not just staring but being very obvious about it. She looked away quickly.

“I’m not sure. You look familiar,” Erin admitted, glancing back at him.

“Do I?” he asked. Did the faintest of shutters lower over those amazing eyes? Was he being deliberately unforthcoming, as if he was accustomed to being recognized?

She realized he might be a model: that’s how gorgeous he was. Maybe she had seen him in a glossy magazine, in one of those supersexy ads for men’s cologne or out-of-reach holidays on tropical beaches.

Except his sexiness was threaded through with a distinct dignity she was fairly certain was not for sale.

A film star, then? No, that wasn’t quite right, either. Though he definitely had a star quality, a presence, he simply did not seem, in their short acquaintance, like a man who could pretend to be someone else for a living.

"You're probably mistaking me for Sebastian Avio," he said, naming a famous Mediterranean opera singer. His tone teasing, he said, "Lots of people do."

Only if Sebastian were thirty years younger than Valentino was, Erin thought.

"You should take off your pants," she said, trying to shift her awareness of him and seeing they were shedding a puddle on the floor.

"I bet you only say that to guys who remind you of Sebastian Avio," he said, his tone still teasing.

She could feel heat moving up her cheeks. Surely, she could have thought of another way to word that? She didn't have to act as if she was a gauche schoolgirl in the presence of her secret crush.

"I'll expect you to serenade me later," she said, hoping to hide her discomfort with a bit of banter.

She didn't think she'd succeeded. He seemed faintly amused by her lack of composure and though he dropped the suspenders off his shoulders—making her even more aware of the broadness of them—he made no move to take off his ski pants. She realized, the heat growing in her cheeks, that if he only had an undershirt on under the jacket, that might be all he had on under the pants, too.

She turned away from him, vacating that tight-shared square of space as if she were in danger of catching fire. And it felt like she was!

"Go in to that second bedroom over there." She gestured at one of the doors off the main room. "There should be some clothes that will fit you in the closet."

"Thank you," he said.

"I'll just get the fire going," she said. "It will help warm it up more quickly in here and save on propane."

Not that she felt chilly. Embarrassingly warm, actually.

She busied herself with that, not looking at him as he moved by her, concentrating on preparing the paper and the kindling as if her life depended on it.

Something tingled at the back of her neck and Erin was aware that Valentino had not gone through to the back bedroom.

"'Enrique O'Rourke,'" he read off the trophies. "Wow."

"You know him?" she asked carefully.

"Of him. Who doesn't? A legend."

"My father," she admitted. "My grandfather started this resort."

"That explains it."

"Explains what?"

"Being allowed to keep a cat under your desk, for one. Your access to this Hansel and Gretel cabin in the middle of nowhere, for another. But more than that, how you ski. To be honest, when you first told me to try and keep up, I almost laughed out loud."

She turned to look at him and allowed herself a small smile. "I know. I could tell."

"Then that must have made it extra delightful for you to leave me eating your snow all the way here."

"It did," she said. And then they both laughed. The shared laughter, again, should have eased some tension she was feeling but it did not. It made her more aware of him, how easy and natural it felt to laugh with him. "You made me work at it, though. Leaving you eating my snow."

"I can swallow my pride for Enrique O'Rourke's daughter. I've never seen anybody ski like you. Except maybe him, now that I think about it."

"Thanks," she said. "He taught me, so our styles should be similar."

"It's as if you're folding yourself into the mountain somehow. Not on top of it, but part of it."

Was it his accent that made the words feel like pure poetry? Whatever it was, it was lovely to be admired.

She felt hungry for it. Almost pathetically so. Her father had been stingy with compliments. And so had Paul.

She frowned. Was there a connection there?

"My father really never forgave me when I didn't want a career in skiing," she said then wondered what on earth had made her say that. It seemed way too personal.

But she glanced over her shoulder at Valentino again. He seemed to be contemplating her words gravely.

"I think maybe it is the nature of growing up to want different things than our parents," he said. "Be grateful you had a choice."

And then he, too, looked regretful, as if he had said too much or revealed too much.

Valentino left the room quickly. But no matter how she tried to concentrate on the fire in front of her, it felt as if another fire was starting.

Deep inside her.

Ridiculous, she told herself. She would not be so weak and facile as to drown her sorrows over her recently shattered dreams in the deep and inviting sea of a stranger's charm.

She would not see it as a gift from the universe that she was stranded on the eve of Valentine's Day with someone named Valentino.

No. More like a test.

A challenge.

A trial of her strength of character.

One that she was resolved to pass.

CHAPTER FIVE

VALENTINO MADE HIS way down the hall to the bedroom. He was glad to be leaving the room that Erin was in. He was so *aware* of her. Her scent, the melody of her voice, the way that spun-with-gold hair tumbled over her shoulders, the sweet cling of that sweater.

But perhaps that awareness served as a distraction, because he was dealing with extremely weighty issues. He had escaped to Canada, to the Touch-the-Clouds resort, to make a decision.

In two weeks, his engagement to Angelica, princess of the neighboring island kingdom of Sorrento, was to be declared. The engagement event would be huge: a dinner where the formal announcement would be made, followed by a ball.

The palace had been in a frenzy of preparation for a month. And the people of Lorenzo knew it was coming. Never had there been a people so eager to celebrate life, and this would be their day, as well as his and Angelica's. Families would be picnicking on the palace grounds in anticipation of the balcony door opening, the king and queen stepping out onto it, he and Angelica following… They would cry for that first kiss, and their applause and cheers when it happened would be like a tidal wave of sound.

Angelica and Valentino had known each other since they were children. Their union was expected—it had been negotiated at her birth. He was now twenty-seven; she was twenty-two. The pressure had been building for two years. It was *time.*

He liked Angelica, and she liked him, in that comfortable way of old friends who had common ground and much of it. With her massive dark curls and her ready smile, she was beautiful, she was smart, and she was funny.

As far as arranged marriages went, Valentino was aware he had hit the jackpot.

And yet…he was chafing against this choice being made for him. Still, he had been raised with a sense of duty and service. The needs of his island kingdom came before his own, and the alliance with Sorrento was imperative.

So why was he here? Why had he run away for a break in Canada? What good could it do? His fate was cast.

Valentino knew he would have accepted that. It was Angelica who had made him need to get away from it all. To clear his head. To gain perspective. To make a decision.

Their encounters, since they had hit puberty, had been closely chaperoned, and that day a week ago had been no different. Angelica had suggested a ride so that they could speak privately, the chaperone trailing behind them on a forest path.

Angelica loved to ride. She rode well and aggressively, but that day she had been subdued. He could tell Angelica's spark was being snuffed. She was *so* unhappy.

He had probed the unhappiness and, casting a guarded glance back, she had admitted she didn't feel ready to get married. She didn't feel ready to surrender to the expectations, which would be to produce a royal heir as soon as humanly possible.

"Don't take it personally," she had pleaded with him. "I love you, Valentino, but like a brother. I want to *feel* things. I want to feel so in love that it's as if I can't breathe when I'm not with that other person. I want to feel passion so hot, I become the flame, consumed by the heat of another person's touch."

It was his turn to cast a wary glance back at the chaperone. Because it was evident to him that Angelica already had met someone who made her feel exactly those things.

If she was already acting on them—and because of the flush in her cheeks and the smoldering in her dark eyes, of that he was fairly certain—she was going to do something rash.

If he called off the engagement before it was announced, could he protect her, a least a little bit, from the outrage and disappointment such a breakup would bring on the instigator? Would such a move actually free her or would her parents make new arrangements for her immediately?

Where did the good of his own kingdom fit into all of this? He was an only child. He knew—and was reminded constantly—the royal legacy fell on him.

He sighed, rolled his shoulders, trying to relieve the weight on them. He opened the closet door and looked at the clothing offerings, which seemed to lean toward plaid shirts and blue jeans.

A few minutes later, feeling as if he was in the most ridiculous costume, he went back out to the main room.

Erin, who had pinned her hair up into a loose bun, was in the kitchen. She glanced at him and grinned. He had the renegade thought that he wanted to free her hair, to pull those pins from it, one by one.

Valentino had always prided himself on his intense discipline, and so the wayward thought took him aback.

“You look very Canadian! You could pass yourself off as a lumberjack.”

“My greatest ambition,” he said, his tone deliberately dry with no hint of *I want to pull the pins from your hair* in it. “I thought we were going to avoid Canadian stereotypes?”

She seemed to think about it. “Hmm. Is it in the agreement? Because, at the moment, you actually look like someone who could make an igloo.”

He frowned at her. “I thought we had decided to leave that behind us?”

“I still haven’t seen a written version,” she teased him.

He contemplated that. Being teased. He decided he liked it, even as it made keeping a cool distance between them more difficult.

She glanced at him. “Okay, Val, come and make yourself useful.”

Val? Make yourself useful? Again, Valentino was not sure he had ever been addressed quite like that in his life.

“How can I assist?” he asked.

“You can open the wine, and then I’ve got ingredients for a Mediterranean salad. You look like you’d be an expert on both those things.”

Valentino was not sure what would make him look like an expert on such things. The truth was, he had never opened a bottle of wine himself and he had certainly never made a salad. Mediterranean or otherwise. He was aware of a strange tension at the back of his neck, as if this were a test he needed to pass.

He went over to where the bottle of wine was on the

kitchen table, trying to appear casual, like this was a workaday event for him. He regarded the bottle. It felt like the enemy.

He picked it up, trying to buy some time, studying the label. “A white,” he said. “Sauvignon.”

“It’s a Canadian wine. From a British Columbian vineyard. I try to buy local. And I avoid screw caps.”

All the more shame, he thought as he tentatively peeled away a silver-foil seal that revealed a cork firmly embedded in the neck of the bottle.

“The corkscrew is in the drawer over there.” Erin gestured with her head.

The drawer was on the other side. He moved by her. Her scent tickled his nostrils. She was seasoning a steak. Thank goodness, it looked as if one of them knew what they were doing.

He opened the drawer she had pointed to. It was full of items he didn’t recognize, most of which looked like they had been designed to compel confessions in the torture chamber. The corkscrew, thankfully, was easily recognizable as the instrument used by the palace sommelier to open wine at the table.

Valentino grabbed it and went back to the bottle. He’d seen wine opened a zillion times, even if he had never done it himself. Confident now, he jammed the sharp tip into the cork. Then, putting a bit of weight on it, he twisted. Instead of coming out, the cork seemed to recede deeper beneath the lip and down the neck of the bottle. He must not have made sure the corkscrew was seated firmly enough. He pressed harder. The cork moved in the wrong direction.

The last time he’d opened a bottle of wine, it had been to smash it across the hull of a ship he had been invited to christen.

He had, on several official occasions, seen champagne uncorked with a sword. Valentino slid Erin a look. She wasn't paying the least bit of attention to him.

He bet uncorking a champagne bottle with a sword would impress her.

Did he *want* to impress her?

What man didn't want to impress a beautiful woman? And maybe, in that realization, he had already made up his mind about Angelica and what he needed to do. Because his entire life, he had been *taken,* and so had not felt awareness of women the way he now felt it about Erin.

Was it because of their circumstances? Escaping the storm, followed by the intense solitude of the situation he found himself in with a woman who was a stranger to him?

Or was it because, somewhere along the line—maybe from the moment he had stepped on the royal plane headed for Canada—he had already known what he'd needed to do.

"How's that coming?"

He put more weight into the corkscrew. The cork groaned down the neck of the bottle, letting loose suddenly and splashing into the wine, where it floated, baleful evidence of his failure.

"Um…done," he said, turning to her, blocking her view of the bottle with his body.

"Great. Can you start the salad? I'm just going to run out and turn on the grill. Unless you'd rather do that and I'll do the salad?"

He looked at the heap of ingredients on the kitchen counter at her elbow: colorful peppers, cucumbers, tiny tomatoes, olives, a block of white Feta cheese.

Everything was whole. He wasn't sure where to even

begin tackling the vegetables. On the other hand, a grill? It sounded like a good way to blow them both up.

"I'm fine with the salad," he lied.

"Knives are in the block there."

She picked up the steak and opened the side door to a small porch. Wind tossed snow in before she quickly stepped out then nudged the door shut again with her hip.

He went over to the block and took out a knife. It was a huge, heavy thing that looked as if it might be good for a beheading. A pepper? Not so much. One by one, Valentino took out the knives and studied them. Finally, in the interest of self-preservation, he chose the least lethal-looking one.

Carefully, he cut the pepper in two and was astonished to find *stuff* inside it. He'd been unaware peppers contained *contents.*

Were the contents—tiny seeds and feltlike bits—part of the salad? He didn't recall ever seeing anything that looked like that in a salad before. He tested a seed and pared off some of the felty substance. He sampled that, too. It tasted just like a pepper to him. Was it possible he hadn't seen it in a salad before because of some form of *snobbery*? Surely common people ate everything that tasted good? Having revealed his own privilege to himself, he carefully chopped up the remainder of the pepper, including all its parts, and tossed it in the bowl Erin had provided.

The wind shook the cabin. He wished she would come in out of it. He should have volunteered to do the grilling. He didn't like it that she was out there and he was in here.

He abandoned the salad and went to the door. The wind pulled it out of his hands.

"Can I help you?" he asked her. "We could switch, if you're cold."

"No, almost done," she said, apparently unbothered by the wind and snow whistling around her. Delectable smells drifted to him. "How's the salad?"

"Great," he said, "I could probably have my own cooking show."

Wouldn't that give his mother conniptions? Still, Erin laughed, and he liked that.

He returned to the kitchen and focused on the block of Feta cheese. He was feeling quite pleased with how easy it all was when his knife hand slipped. He stared down at the cutting board in a kind of paralyzed horror.

Unless he was mistaken, that was a tiny tip of his finger sitting there among the crumbled cheese and red-pepper juices. He looked at his finger.

Blood was gushing from it.

The door opened. "Steak is done," she sang.

He turned to her, slowly, holding up his hand.

"I seem to have had a small mishap. It doesn't bode well for my cooking show," he said.

She dropped the platter holding the steak. It landed on the floor with a clatter, and she rushed to him. She took his hand in her own.

He considered how all he should have felt was pain. But the pain had not set in yet and what he felt was her touch. Cool. Comforting.

"Let's just get that up," she said, guiding his hand to a more elevated position. Then she led him over to the couch. "Sit down. I'll get the first-aid kit. I think it's in the medicine cabinet. Don't worry. It's nothing."

He didn't feel worried at all, but he heard something shrill in her voice.

Erin tossed a dish towel at him. "It's clean," she said, "wrap it around your finger."

She looked pale and shaky as she disappeared down

the hallway. Meanwhile, the cat had launched himself on the steak that had fallen to the floor and greedily had his face buried in it.

He got up and rescued the steak from the cat, who was clearly furious to have his prize taken from him. Valentino set the steak on the counter.

"Here it is," she said, coming back, waving a white, tin first-aid kit triumphantly. "What are you doing? You need to be sitting down." The shrillness in her voice had increased.

"It's just a scratch," he told her mildly.

"It's not!" she said. "Sit!"

He sat. She knelt at his feet and placed the kit on a hassock. She rummaged through it. He studied the top of her head, the sun-threaded gold of her hair. One of those pins that was holding that bun together was loose. Just the tiniest nudge with his finger…

"There," she said. She had items laid out on the hassock like a field doctor preparing to do surgery. She closed her eyes, inhaled a deep breath, and opened them again.

She took his hand in hers. She was trembling as she peeked inside the dish towel. He was the one who was hurt!

The towel had become quite saturated with blood in a very short time and, if it were possible, Erin paled even more.

"Are you afraid of blood?" he asked.

"I'm afraid you're going to bleed to death," she said, but the denial was weak.

"You're afraid of blood."

"I don't think *afraid* is the right word," she said, not denying it this time. Well, how could she? Her face was as white as that snow outside and she was trembling. "But—"

She took another deep, fortifying breath and finished unwrapping the dish towel from his hand. Blood spurted out the end of his finger. She hastily wrapped it again.

"I can do it myself," he said.

"No! I'll do it." She took off the towel again. This time she had a wipe ready and quickly cleaned the wound. It looked as if he had managed to remove the entire pad from the tip of his finger.

"Hey," he said, "that'll be handy if I commit a crime. No fingerprints."

She did not seem amused at his attempt to distract. Her face determined, her tongue caught between her teeth, she began to wind gauze tightly around his entire finger, crisscrossing the tip. His finger was beginning to look like a marshmallow, but she was being so brave—for him—that he said nothing.

Finally, she reached for her carefully laid-out medical tape, leaned close and began to wind it around his finger. He couldn't help it… He reached for that errant pin, felt the silk of her hair under his fingertips.

Pulling that pin was like pulling one card from a shaky house of them. Her hair tumbled down.

Much better, he thought.

She glanced up at him, wide-eyed, her eyes as green as a piece of perfect jade catching the light.

"It was falling out," he lied.

He immediately felt contrite. She looked even worse than before, shaky as an olive tree leaf in a faint breeze. Of course she would look like that! A strange man removing pins from her hair. It was a terrible faux pas.

"Here," he said, getting up, crouching beside her, putting his shoulder under her. "Your turn to sit. Let me look after dinner."

"You're the injured one," she protested, though her protest lacked vehemence.

He held out his gigantic white-wrapped finger to her. "All fixed. I'll take it from here. You relax. Thank you for doing that. Especially since you are afraid of blood."

"Since I was a child," she admitted.

Thank goodness! Her current state of wooziness seemed to have nothing to do with his fingers, acting separately from his brain, reaching for her hair.

Given the intensity of the circumstances, he had to make sure he didn't do anything so inappropriate again.

Valentino spun away from Erin, eager to put a bit of distance between them while he regained his sanity.

CHAPTER SIX

ERIN WATCHED AS Valentino moved away to the humble kitchen. She should protest his offering to get dinner, especially now that he was handicapped with a giant, white-wrapped finger. Maybe she had gotten a little carried away with the first aid—but she hadn't wanted any blood to leak through that bandage. She felt woozy enough already.

Embarrassingly, she had been dizzy even before he had touched her hair. Good grief, she had gone from faintly light-headed to full swoon in the blink of an eye.

Harvey stalked him into the kitchen and waited, hopefully, under the counter for a drop. There was something endearing about watching Valentino in the kitchen. For a man with such grace and athleticism on the ski hill, he now looked like a duck out of water, completely unsure of himself.

After contemplating his options for a moment, he started with the steak, which he inspected. He rinsed it under the tap and then blotted it. She remembered it had fallen on the floor.

"You were planning this meal for yourself only," he noted, cutting the steak, which was not large, in two. "Thank you for sharing your supper with me."

"Of course!" she said. She was glad the heart-shaped

cake with its embarrassing *"1"* candle was still hidden in her pack. "The dressing for the salad is in the fridge."

As she watched, he finished up the salad and then plated the food and poured them each a glass of wine. He found a metal tray and put everything on it. Balancing it carefully, he brought it over to her. He shoved aside her first-aid supplies on the hassock, set the tray down and settled on the couch.

The couch wasn't large—more like a love seat—and his thigh touched hers. An electrical current of awareness jolted through her.

"M'lady," he said. He leaned over and took a wineglass off the tray with the hand that was not bandaged. He awkwardly handed it to her. He took the other one.

"A toast," he said.

She lifted her glass.

"To surprises."

"To surprises," she agreed.

They clinked glasses and she took a sip, as did he.

"This is really a nice wine," he said. "It's dry but fruity. I almost get an overtone of lime in it."

He seemed to know quite a bit more about wine than she did. To her distress, Erin felt something chunky in her mouth. She tried to figure out what it was and what to do. She had an awful decision to make. Spit it out or swallow it?

"Ah, there was a little problem with the cork," he said, noticing her expression just as she made a decision to swallow.

"It happens," she said, setting down the glass. He handed her a plate and some utensils. She regarded his offer solemnly, took her fork and poked through the pepper part of the salad. It seemed, like the wine, to have foreign components in it.

He was watching her, eager for her to sample it.

"Oh, sorry, I was just wondering—"

"Yes?"

"What exactly is this?"

He regarded the item she was holding on her fork. "Pepper insides." He blinked at her with elaborate innocence. "Don't you use them?"

"Not generally."

"We do. In my country."

She felt her lips twitch at so obvious a lie. "Don't take up poker," she suggested.

"I happen to be an excellent poker player!"

"Have you ever made a salad before?"

"I have not," he admitted. His lips twitched, too.

"Or cut vegetables?"

"No."

"It's a good thing I didn't ask you to chop wood," she decided. "You probably would have lost a hand."

"Except for the fact that's true, I'd be insulted," he said.

"What exactly were you planning on doing if I had a baby?"

"Boil water!"

And then they were both laughing.

The steak, despite his running it under the tap, had grit in it, The wine had the odd piece of cork, and the seed-ridden salad was possibly the chunkiest she had ever eaten.

But with the storm deepening and howling outside, and the warmth and the wine inside, it felt so good. As good as anything in Erin's life had felt for a long, long time.

Valentino took away their plates and fetched the rest of the wine. He refilled their glasses.

"Tell me about where you're from," she invited. A

voice inside her added, *And what you do, and who you love. Valentino, tell me every little intriguing thing about you.*

"I come from a small island in the Mediterranean, Lorenzo del Toro. Have you heard of it?"

Had she? She thought so, but the wine and the warmth of the fire, her stomach full, his gaze touching her face, made her not very sure of anything about the world. "I'm not sure."

"Ah, well, let me take you there." And just like that, his voice swept her from the little cottage and the storm that raged outside the door.

They were in a sun-drenched land of olive groves and vineyards, ancient buildings and quaint stone cottages and cobbled streets. The flowers were so colorful and so abundant that the air was perfumed by them. Donkeys pulling carts and shepherds herding sheep blocked narrow country roads.

"And what do you do there?"

"I'm in the family business," he said. Did she hear a note of caution in his voice?

"And what is your family business?"

Again, did she sense hesitation?

Valentino took a sip of wine. He refilled her glass. He looked at the fire. "We manage a number of enterprises," he finally said. "The business is hundreds of years old."

"Do you like it?"

He thought about that for a minute. "I'm not sure I've ever thought of it in terms of liking or not liking. It is what I was born into."

"That's what you meant when you said to be grateful I had a choice about whether or not to follow in my father's footsteps? That you did not? That you were expected to go into the family business?"

"Yes," he said. "That's what I meant. But enough about me now. Tell me about you. About growing up with a father like yours."

Maybe it was because of the wine. Or maybe it was because their experience was a little like being trapped with a stranger on an elevator given the relentless storm outside, but there was a kind of instant intimacy developing between them. However, there was a time limit on this.

He lived around the world in a place she was never likely to go. After the storm abated, she was probably never going to see him again.

Why did that feel, already, like a sadness?

Still, Erin found herself confiding in him about growing up in the crazy world of professional skiing with a very famous father.

"I had skis on practically as soon as I could walk. And I loved to ski—and still do. It's my place where I feel one hundred percent engaged. Present. Alive.

"But, to my father's great disappointment, I wasn't interested in putting my natural ability, which I had inherited from him and my grandfather before him, to work for me. I'd raced since I was tiny. When you're small and everyone gets a trophy, it was fine, and fun.

"But I grew to hate it," she said softly. "There was too much pressure on me because I was the great Enrique's daughter.

"Remember when Sebastian Avio's daughter wanted a career in music? And everyone kept comparing her to him? It was like that. I mean… I was just a kid and I was being interviewed on the evening news after a race.

"Plus, even at the junior levels—we're talking under ten—racing brought out this horrible competitive side in my dad. He became my mentor and my coach. I could do nothing right. If I won a race, he started dissecting how

I could have done better immediately. If I lost, he'd be furious, pouting and sulking.

"It took what I loved the most and changed it into something I could barely recognize. So, at age eleven, I stood firm and told him I was leaving my career as a ski racer behind me. I quit. Nothing was ever the same between us after that, as if he couldn't handle it that my life didn't belong to him.

"In retrospect, with everything going on in the family, I think ski racing had become just one more pressure. One I was ill-prepared to handle."

"What was going on in your family?"

Erin thought she had really said quite enough. And yet there was something about the way he was looking at her and listening to her that felt like an elixir: if she drank of this cup, she would feel better.

That was astonishing because she hadn't been aware she *wasn't* feeling okay. Harvey jumped on her lap and she scratched his ears. Valentino reached over and scratched his ears, too.

It was such a nice moment. It had a lovely intimacy to it. Their total isolation from the whole world made her feel as if she could tell him anything.

Not just as if she could tell him anything, but as if she had carried a burden too long by herself and this stranger had come along and unexpectedly offered to share it.

During the tumultuous years of her childhood, and just before they'd called it quits for good, her parents' relationship had been more volatile than ever.

"My mother," she said softly, "had just discovered my father had yet another love interest. The days were filled with the sounds of slammed doors and shouted arguments. So many accusations and so much pain. Love that had burned too hot had finally consumed everything in its flame, destroying everything around it."

Erin cast a look at Valentino. That's where mooning over someone's lips got you. That was where passion led.

"That's why I said I owed the cat," she confessed. "Harvey chose me. He showed up on our doorstep and became my shadow, just when I needed him most. Even back then, when he was young and handsome, silky-furred and svelte, Harvey hated absolutely everyone. Except me.

"This silly old guy reserved his absolute devotion for me, at the time in my life when I could do nothing right in my father's eyes and our family unit was exploding around me. Maybe some people—maybe most people—would see my loyalty to the cat as odd, but he gave me hope when the world seemed utterly hopeless.

"The cat was my constant as I moved between my parents' ever-shifting households, partners, locations.

"I fell asleep at night, in whichever house I was in, often with my pillow soaked in tears. But the cat curled in close to me, his purr reassuring and solid."

Solid. Stable.

She cast a glance at Valentino. His hand had gone still on the cat's fur. He was frowning at the fire.

She had said *way* too much.

But when he looked away from the fire and at her, his dark eyes were even darker, shadowed with sadness, as if he had, indeed, taken some of her burden as his own. Erin felt something she had not felt for so long.

A trust in this man beside her unfurled within her.

"And tell me," he said softly, "what all this has to do with you and your cat bringing a feast up here to have Valentine's Day alone."

She wasn't sure if she hated it or loved it. That he saw,

immediately, how her tumultuous childhood and being alone right now were linked.

"Naturally, after all that excitement and chaos growing up, I longed for what other people seemed to have. Family as a place of refuge. Calm.

"I thought I was going to build that with my boyfriend, Paul, because his family was the polar opposite of mine. A mother and father who never seemed to say a cross word after thirty years together. Who had roast chicken on Sunday nights. Who belonged to the bowling league.

"What I didn't realize was that while I'd been enchanted with all of that, Paul had felt oppressed by it, as if his family's solid life was a trap he was being walked into. By me."

Her voice dropped to almost a whisper. "His parting words to me were that it was all just too boring."

Valentino stiffened beside her. "Boring?" he said, his voice soft and deliciously incredulous. And then indignant. "Boring?"

"Which I inferred meant *I* was boring. He certainly acted like it. I mean, near the end, he would barely look up from his phone."

Valentino snorted with an outrage on her behalf that Erin found quite sumptuous. "He wouldn't look up from his phone and he thought *you* were boring?"

"Well, I mean I know I'm not exactly a barrel of excitement. Look at me, a career accountant."

"Look at how you ski!"

"He wasn't a skier."

"You were with somebody who didn't share that passion with you? It *is* you."

It would be easy to just lap up his defense of her, but she felt driven to prove Paul might have had a point.

"I do have a kind of unusual attachment to my cat."

"He didn't like your Harvey," Valentino intoned with a sad shake of his head. "How could he not love the cat who saved you?"

Erin realized she had never shared Harvey's role in her life with Paul. A few hours in, this man already knew more about her secrets than Paul had in the entire length of their relationship.

Wasn't that telling her something?

As was the look on Valentino's face as he gazed at her. It felt as if she was being *seen* and, whatever Valentino saw, he did not seem to think it was boring. His hand left the cat's fur. It cupped her chin. His thumb scraped across her cheek. His eyes held hers.

"A man who could be bored with you is not even a man," he said firmly, his soft, accented voice as sensual as the touch of lips on the back of her neck.

She laughed a little nervously. Despite the snowed-in-together confidences, there was a larger truth here they both needed to acknowledge.

"You don't even know me, Valentino."

Still, she didn't try to move away from his hand, and he looked stunned that she would suggest that!

"I do," he said fiercely. "No man could look into your eyes and not know you. And no man could look into your eyes and ever have a moment's boredom. Not unless there was something lacking in him."

"I'm not the kind that inspires great passions," she protested. But she was aware of how suddenly, and dangerously, she *wanted* to be that woman.

Valentino snorted, moved his hand from her cheek, tucked her hair behind her ear.

"Not inspire great passions?" he said, his hand still smoothing her hair. "A painter would die to paint you. The sun in that hair. That look on your face. A man could get lost in your eyes. He could dive into them as if they were a cool pond on a hot summer day. He could let what is in them fold over him, soothe him, hold him, heal the parts of him that are wounded."

Erin stared at him, her heart hammering so hard she thought it would break from her chest. This close, she could see the faint stubble beginning on his chin and cheeks. She was aware of the scent of him, as crisp, as exotic, as she imagined the land he came from would be.

Everything he was saying about her eyes held true for his own. Fringed with an incredible abundance of sooty lash, they were as rich as dark chocolate, melted. They held depth and compassion, and mystery. A mystery a woman could spend her whole life solving…

He dropped his hand from her hair and abruptly created some space between them on the sofa.

"I'm sorry." His voice was a scrape of pure gravel. "That was way too personal. I'm not generally—" he looked genuinely abashed "—given to poetry." Then his eyes found hers again and he sighed with a kind of surrender.

"But that is what your eyes do," he said softly. "They call out to the poet in a man."

Oh, God, something in her was absolutely melting. They'd had too much wine, obviously. Both of them. Too much wine, and the feeling of being safe inside, together, as the storm raged on, was creating a natural affinity between them.

Even knowing those things, even knowing what they were experiencing was akin to being shipwrecked on an island together, it felt as if she was being seen in a way she had not ever been seen before.

And she wanted, suddenly and urgently, to be a person she had never been before.

Not boring.

But the one Valentino had just seen. Fully a woman. A sensual woman who called to the painter in a man, and the poet.

She wanted to embrace the adventure of finding out who she really was, if there were hidden facets of herself that she had never discovered.

It felt as if maybe she never would discover those hidden things if she did not say *yes* to what was right in front of her, in this moment in time. She wanted, not to shrink away from the power he said she had, but to embrace it, to uncover it, to unleash it.

She wanted to get lost in his eyes and say *yes* to whatever hid in their dark, compelling depths. Empowered by what he had said, she reached out and traced that plump split in his lip. At that touch, her heart felt as if it had slumbered.

Not just now, but with Paul, through her entire life, a protective layer around it that fell away like a thin layer of ice tapped with a hammer.

Valentino went very still. His eyes were steady on her face, full of knowing, full of hunger. And then he opened his mouth ever so slightly, just enough to nibble the finger that explored his lip.

A kind of insanity overtook her. A delicious loss of mind. Years of careful control evaporated as if they had been a muddy puddle waiting for the heat of the sun. Years of feeling as if she knew exactly who she was vanished like a mirage in the desert.

This was who she really was.

This was who she was always meant to be.

She leaned into him. And she took his lips with her own. His hands came up and bracketed each side of her head, tangled in her hair. He pulled his mouth away from her and whispered endearments in her ear in another language, his words soft with the poetry of the heart.

Then his mouth found hers again. Urgent. Questing.

And Erin's world was changed for all time. Even as she took his lips, she knew whatever was happening, she could never, ever, go back to the way it had been—and she had been—before this moment.

"Love me," she whispered against his lips. In her tone, things she had never heard before. Urgency. Desperation. Hunger. "Please."

"How could I do anything but?" he whispered back.

CHAPTER SEVEN

VALENTINO PICKED UP ERIN, cradling her against his chest as he strode down the short hallway into the darkness of the bedroom. She wrapped her arms around the beautiful column of his neck. She did not consider herself a small woman, and her ex had consistently made her feel as if she came from the land of the giants.

Yet, in Valentino's arms, in the effortless way in which he had lifted her and now carried her, she felt light as a feather, exquisitely feminine and desirable. She felt cherished. She felt he was like a warrior who had found his way home to the maiden who had waited, her candle lit, believing he would come, even before she had known his name.

If they wanted light, the lamps would have to be lit. But she liked the room as it was, the atmosphere dimly lit and dreamlike.

He set her tenderly into the billowy embrace of a white down comforter. The bed was a beautiful, intricately carved antique that had come with her great-grandparents from Norway in the eighteen hundreds.

It felt right and good. That this bed that had been woven into generations of her family's love stories, was where she would come to know Valentino in every way possible for a woman to know a man.

He stood over her and as her eyes adjusted to the deep shadows, she saw that he was staring down at her with a gaze both tender and fierce. His hand moved to the buttons on his shirt.

He had forgotten his bandaged finger and so had she, and they both laughed, breathless with anticipation and delight, as she scrambled to kneeling and he came to the edge of the bed. She undid the buttons of the shirt one by one, her eyes never leaving his face.

When she was done, she got off the bed to stand before him. She peeled the plaid fabric off him, over his shoulders, caressing the naked skin beneath the shirt as it was revealed to her. Finally, she tugged each arm out of its sleeve. The shirt dropped from her fingers to the ground, leaving her to stare with stunning avarice at what she had unveiled.

Valentino was absolutely perfect. The weak light from the gas lamps in the other room outlined the carved lines of his arms, powerful triceps and biceps, illuminated the broadness of his back, and spilled over the wideness of his shoulders. She had thought, because of his abundance of curls, that he might have a hairy chest, but he did not.

His skin was taut and golden, hair-free, molded to the perfect plain of a deep chest, the pebbles of his nipples, stretched over the slight rise of his ribs and the slender, hard curve of his belly.

She reached out tentatively and laid her hand, splayed, across his heart, and the sensual silk of his warm skin made her mouth go dry. She could feel the steady, strong beating of his heart under her fingertips.

He captured her hand, pulled it to his mouth, anointed the inside of her wrist with his lips and then tugged her yet closer to him.

His hands found the hem of her sweater and he hesitated.

His voice low, he asked, "Are you—?"

The sentence did not need finishing. Was she sure? Was she ready? She had never been more sure or more ready in her life.

Her tongue flicked to lips that suddenly felt dry and his eyes fastened there. She nodded.

There was nothing clumsy now, not even with that bandage on his finger. He peeled the sweater up and over her head, her hair hissing from the static as her head popped free. He tossed the sweater away and smiled, taking in what he had revealed.

Slowly, tenderly, he smoothed her hair with the fingertips of his unbandaged hand, owning her in some way with that possessive gesture that made her mouth even drier, her breath even more ragged, her need even more acute.

Valentino looked at her, a man who could never get his fill, a man with eyes that would paint her. Words spilled from his lips, tender, soft, in a language so universal she did not need to know the words to appreciate their meaning.

He had come to worship at the altar of her femininity.

And she at the altar of his masculinity.

They had entered a dance as ancient and as sacred as the earth itself.

Little by little, slowly, with reverence, the rest of their clothes fell away, until it was just the two of them, at the beginning of time, exploring each other with wonder. With curiosity. With awe. Exploring the miracle and the marvel of a man and a woman.

Together.

Finally, when the urgency would not be denied any

longer, they tumbled together deep into the embrace of the bed. Their bodies met, fused, entwined, melted. They climbed, and climbed, and climbed, exploring the jagged, endless precipices until finally they stood on the edge of a cliff.

And then, unhesitatingly, they leaped off.

Falling into the abyss of pure sensation. Joining the motes of cosmic dust that made up the stars. Joining what had always been; that place that did not acknowledge space or time.

Exhausted, content, they folded their arms around each other and, despite the storm that screamed under the eaves and at the windows, they slept the deep sleep of two people completely satiated.

Erin awoke in the morning to the sound of the storm still raging outside, as if it wanted to pick up the cabin, twirl it in the air and smash it down somewhere else on the mountain.

Her confidence in the sturdiness of the cabin strengthened her sense of contentment, her awareness of how her skin felt under the deep warmth of the down comforter and beneath the heat of Valentino's arm. It felt as if her whole body was tingling; the way it might feel going from a hot shower into a snowbank.

Valentino was on his side, one arm thrown possessively across the nakedness of her midriff, one leg pinning her legs as if, subconsciously, he had wanted to hold her to him, prevent her escape.

But she was a willing captive.

Erin turned her head to study him, aware that a smile amused her lips as she took in the wild corkscrew of messy curls, the stubble on his chin, the flawless perfection of skin that looked perpetually sun-kissed.

She waited for the sense of recrimination to come.

She had, after all, just spent the night—made wild love—to a complete stranger. And yet what she felt as she looked at Valentino was not recrimination. She did not feel that he was a stranger, but that she *knew* him as deeply and as completely as she had ever known another person.

She certainly did not feel any sense of shame. Or guilt.

But freedom.

Tenderness.

Delight.

She was marooned on a desert island with him and she had given herself, completely, to what the moment offered. And she was glad. It was very much like giving herself to the mountain when she skied.

It was a surrender. A great knowing that nature was, always, a more powerful force than you. But the surrender was such a joyous one, it became a dance.

Remembering what had passed between them last night, Erin was aware she felt grateful. She had almost given herself over to a life where this side of her—playful, passionate, curious, sensual—might have gone undiscovered.

Valentino stirred against her. His warm breath tickled her skin. She watched as the dark tangle of those lashes flicked open and revealed the melted-chocolate sensuality of his gaze.

She held her breath. Would he be the one who returned them to sanity? Would he be the one who pointed out that they were strangers? Who questioned if they had gone too fast, too far, too soon? Who asked if they were acting like survivors, exhilarated by the nectar of life, of being alive, without any care for tomorrow?

But when his gaze found her face, the drowsy smile—of welcome, of recognition—lit him from within.

His hands found her neck and tugged her to him, and he wished her good morning with a kiss that held back nothing.

Despite the fact they were in the tiniest of cabins—trapped here, really—with the storm still raging around them, it felt as if the whole world opened to her.

Embraced her.

Sighed for her.

This, then, was how it was meant to be.

Valentino was a man who had collected exhilarating experiences like other men might collect stamps.

He had skied some of the highest and most inaccessible peaks in the world. He had—over the objections of his security team and his family—embraced the sport of skydiving, throwing himself into the endless, vast blue of the sky. He had raced his horse at breakneck speeds over polo fields and along forest paths. He had a powerboat that, at optimum speed, would lift its nose and skim the water as if it were flying.

Valentino had experienced every thrill that being born to his station in life would allow.

And he was aware, now, as he watched Erin move through the kitchen with such grace, that every one of those things had been superficial compared to the exhilaration he felt, trapped by a snowstorm, and just being in the same room with her, sharing the same air as her.

Her hair was in a glorious mess and she had on a man's housecoat that would open every now and then to give him an enticing glimpse of long, long legs. There was a glow about her that could warm a man, as if he had come into a welcoming hearth on a cold day.

Which I have, Valentino told himself. The fire was spitting in the hearth, throwing heat. He had put on only the jeans from yesterday; his chest was bare. It was a kind of freedom to walk around in a state of half dress. And besides, just as he kept sneaking peeks at Erin's legs, she kept sneaking looks at him.

She leaned over and fed Harvey, murmuring to the cat, her fingers caressing his willing ears for a moment before she straightened.

Even that small gesture told Valentino who she was. Gentleness in her. A connection to living things. An ability to immerse herself in the simplicity and gifts of each moment.

And coinciding with those things, the incredible contrast of a passionate fire that burned white-hot within her.

Should I tell her who I am?

It felt as if he should. Right this moment, before it went any further. She needed to know what she was getting herself into. She needed to have a choice.

But it would be the worst kind of distraction. It felt as if she already knew who he was. Better than anyone else, because she did not know about the titles, his position in life, his family. The mantle of royalty. For the first time in his life, Valentino felt *seen.*

He was not aware he had waited his entire life for that.

Until now. Until it happened.

She came and put coffee in front of him. His senses were so heightened that the aroma felt as if it could overwhelm him. But then that sensation receded as her hand found his hair and she combed it with her fingertips, tenderly, possessively. He turned his head and nipped at her hand.

Telling her the truth of who he was faded from his consciousness. It could wait. With the storm continuing outside—the snow so thick when they looked out the windows, they could not see across the clearing this morning—it felt as if there would be plenty of time for everything that needed to be said between them.

She laughed at his playful nip, and that glow intensified. She was alight with life.

"Breakfast," she said. She put a tiny heart-shaped cake down in front of him and sank into the chair beside his.

It was obviously a cake that had been made for Valentine's Day. It had a candle on it, shaped like a number one.

"What does the candle represent?" he asked.

"Me, alone on Valentine's Day," she said. Her laughter deepened, the light flowing out of her to embrace the whole room. And him.

"But now you're not," he teased her, pointing out the obvious. "So, should we throw the candle away?"

"No." She lit it. "It can represent firsts of all kinds. Make a wish before we blow out the candle."

"I wish," he whispered, "that this could last forever."

She was silent for a moment, her brow furrowed.

"What?"

"You're not supposed to tell anyone your wish. Then it doesn't come true."

He was taken aback by this North American superstition, but then realized how deeply he was under a spell. Because, obviously, it could not come true regardless. This could not last forever. Nothing could. The storm that rattled the cabin, that made him a grateful prisoner, would end.

"You make the wish, then," he said.

"I think you're only allowed one wish per cake."

"Too many rules," he decided, and the solemn moment evaporated, replaced by their laughter.

They blew out the candle together, their breaths mingling. She took up a knife she had brought over to the table with her.

Even he, with his inexperience at all things domestic, could see the knife was too large for the task.

"Hey, be careful with that thing," he said.

"Don't worry, I'm not about to trust you with it."

And then, to his surprise, instead of cutting the cake, she lowered that cleaver-like knife as if it were an ax. She chopped the cake into chunks instead of slices.

"I'm taking a lesson from your salad making," she told him.

"But I was going to start a cooking show," he said as he gazed at the mess of chocolate cake and icing on the plate.

She laughed. "Things don't have to be perfect to be… well, perfect."

She proved how true that was. Instead of getting plates and forks, she picked up a chunk of the cake with her fingers and shifted herself onto his lap. He opened his mouth to her then licked the icing off her fingers. The massacred confection tasted of ambrosia, dreams and promises.

Following her lead, he dug his fingers into the rich darkness of the cake and fed it to her. And then he licked the icing off her lips.

Her turn. She took a chunk of that cake and pressed it into the nakedness of his chest.

Valentino groaned as she lowered her head and cleaned it off with her lips.

Soon there was cake everywhere and they were chasing each other around the small cabin, the cat hiding under the couch, miffed.

And then they were in the shower together.

And then back in bed.

He knew he had to tell her. But again, with the storm

unabated outside, it felt as if time would expand endlessly and present him the perfect opportunity.

Obviously now, with the fires stoked in both of them, would be absolutely the wrong time.

Erin woke for the second time that day. She stretched like a cat, feeling luxurious, content, satiated. She was not sure she had ever felt this *full.*

She glanced at Valentino, sleeping on his back, his profile beautiful, his lashes as thick and sooty as a chimney brush, the whiskers darkening yet more on his face. She studied that yummy split in his full bottom lip. How could he seem so familiar already? How could it already seem as if she could not lead a life without him in it?

Crazy thoughts. This kind of thing, whether she wanted to acknowledge it or not, was a fling brought on by the intensity of circumstances, a powerful chemistry between a man and a woman stranded alone.

There was no point in contemplating the future. It would just ruin everything. For once in her life, she was going to give up her need to be in control, to figure out what happened next, to try to make her world safe and predictable.

For once in her life, Erin would do the unthinkable: go with the flow. Just see what happened next. Have no plan. She would immerse herself in the moment.

Her eyes drifted to the window. Still snowing. Still snowing hard. But she detected a difference in the ferocity of the storm, an abatement of the wind. Few people would attempt the mountain on a day like this, but she was so familiar with the slopes, she knew she could find the way down, effortlessly, to the ski village at the bottom of the mountain.

But she did not feel ready to let go. Not just yet.

His wish filled her. *I wish that this could last forever.*

Wrapping herself in the sheet, she got up and gave Valentino's bare skin a smack with her hand.

"Get up, lazybones. We can't sleep all day."

He opened his eyes and looked at her idly. With such frank appreciation, it made her skin tingle.

"I have awoken to a goddess," he murmured and then, pretending he was cranky, added, "Why can't we sleep all day?"

He wagged his eyebrows at her with wicked meaning that had nothing to do with sleep.

"We'll be awake all night if we sleep all day," she said.

He lifted that wicked eyebrow a little higher. "I can think of things to do if we're awake all night."

She smacked his bare skin again and he winced with exaggerated hurt.

"Get up. We should go outside and play. You told me about your island home. It's warm there all the time. How often do you have opportunities to play in the snow? Have you ever built a snowman? Had a snowball fight? Made a snow angel?"

"I have not done any of those things," he admitted.

"Then you must."

Before the spell is broken. Before the reality of nothing lasting forever sets in. Before the storm ends. A voice inside her insisted on reminding her, despite her intentions, of a future that loomed ahead, unknown.

"To tell you the truth, I'd rather—" he waggled his eyebrows at her.

"Stop it." She smacked him again. He held his arm with pretend hurt.

"Okay, okay. A snowman it is," he grumbled. "But this had better be good."

"Oh," she promised, "it will be."

And it was. Erin had never been with someone who had not experienced snow as a matter of course, as a life reality for four or five months of every year.

Valentino had skied, yes, but, just as she had guessed, he had never *played* in snow. They couldn't get a mitten over his bandaged hand, so she had carefully wrapped it in a scarf. And then, laughing, she'd had to unwrap it so he could get his jacket on.

She put Harvey's cushioned basket outside on the covered porch so that he could hear that she was near, and he settled into it contentedly.

The snow was still falling thickly, but the wind had stopped and it had warmed since yesterday. The ground cover was turning from the dry powder that everyone came here to ski, to the heavy, wet snow that was perfect for winter activities.

"First," she said, "Snowman Building 101."

"I think, in the interest of equal opportunities, we should build a snowwoman."

She scowled at him with feigned fierceness. "Are you going to be difficult?"

"Of course!"

"You take a little ball of snow—"

"Snowwomen don't have—"

"Stop it," she warned him, but she was snickering. "You take some snow and you shape it like this."

"That looks like a ball. I thought we had decided—"

"This is serious!" she scolded him. Of course, it was anything but.

She showed him how to put the ball in the snow and push it. Because the snow was so sticky and wet, it stuck to itself and the ball she was making got very large very quickly. She had to get down on her knees and put her shoulder into it.

"A girl who likes big balls," he said approvingly, and she took a rest, scooped up some snow and tossed it at him. It hit him right in the face. He wiped it off with elaborate carefulness. And then he scooped up some snow and stalked toward her.

She got up from her snowball and took off running, aware that nothing was going to go as she'd planned, not even building a snowman. She gave herself over to the simple joy of being open to the moment and to whatever direction the energy between them turned itself in.

Erin did what had been demanded of her since the moment she'd met him. She gave up control.

Screaming with laughter, she tried to put distance between them, but the snow was just too deep. His legs were so much longer and more powerful.

He caught her easily, took her arm, spun her around. He pulled off her toque and smooshed his handful of snow into her hair. Then he tried to put the toque back on over it.

"That wasn't even a proper snowball," she said, wiggling away from him.

"You know, you seem preoccupied with the subject of balls."

She chortled. He threw back his head and laughed. The snowflakes danced around them, shimmering, as if they were the universal manifestation of the rhapsody unfolding between Erin and Valentino.

CHAPTER EIGHT

ERIN SCOOPED UP a handful of snow, smoothing it into a hard sphere with her hands. The cold sank through her mittens, making her fingertips tingle almost as much as they had as they'd explored the heated surface of Valentino's skin.

"Do you know what this is?" she asked him, trying for menace in her tone.

"Um, the item of your preoccupation?" he asked, grinning boyishly. When he smiled like that—carefree, mischievous, charming—it melted her.

"Wrong! Deadly missile."

She let fly. He ducked. The snowball whistled harmlessly by him. He straightened and the boyish expression was put away. He looked at her with pretend sternness—a look at least as sexy as his boyish one—and held up his scarf-wrapped hand.

"Do you think that's fair? Throwing things at a one-armed man?"

"All is fair..." she said, stopping herself just short of finishing the expression. *All is fair in love and war.*

She was certain that Valentino completed the phrase inside his head, just as she did. Because, suddenly, standing there, the snow collecting on their hats and coats and eyelashes, the world became very silent. And very, very still.

It felt as if a huge secret had just whispered itself out of the realm of mystery and into the realm of reality.

She broke the spell. She scooped up another handful of snow, and he took her cue, running, shouting taunts at her in two languages with a smattering of French thrown in for good measure. She let fly with the snowball. It hit him in the middle of his back. He fell as if he had been shot, and Erin dissolved into giggles. Then he rose and turned to her with yet another sexy look. This time, the warrior ready to win the battle.

He caught on to the art of the snowball fight very quickly, soon making deadly snowballs and aiming them at her with accuracy born of natural athleticism. The clearing soon echoed with their shouts, their taunts, their laughter.

They chased each other through the snow until they were breathless, panting for air. Until they could not run one more step.

Erin surrendered first, flopping into the snow on her back. He lay down his snow weapons and collapsed into the deep snow beside her, his shoulder just touching hers. She stuck out her tongue at the sky.

"Try this," she said. "Catch a snowflake."

He stuck out his tongue. She watched a fat snowflake fall on the sensual pink curve of his tongue and melt instantly.

He laughed, low in his throat, delighted. "It's like capturing a single bubble of champagne."

After they had rested for a while, catching snowflakes with their tongues, she rolled away from him then swept her hands up over her head in a wide arc, and then her feet.

"Snow angel," she told Valentino when he looked askance at her. She rose and stepped carefully out of the impression she had made to inspect it. He got up and stood beside her.

"That's quite remarkable."

And then he threw himself to the ground, on his back, and made a snow angel right beside hers, the wings touching. Having caught their breaths, their energy renewed, like children they raced around, throwing themselves in the snow, filling up the entire clearing with a veritable army of snow angels.

Sometime, while they were doing that, it registered with Erin, peripherally, that the snow had stopped. A watery light was trying to pierce the clouds around them.

Done with snow angels, Valentino was executing a new idea. Dragging his feet, he used them to draw a huge line through the snow, around almost the entire clearing, encircling the angels. After a moment, she saw that the line he was pounding out in the snow was taking on a heart shape.

She moved inside the heart and, with her feet, stamped out letters in the snow. Big letters, at least two feet high.

VALENTINO
ERIN

The sun burst through the clouds. The clearing turned into a fairy-tale land of white, the sun's glint making it blindingly bright, as if the snow had been threaded through with millions of sparking blue diamonds.

She could not stop the laughter when she was finished imprinting their names in the snow. With absolutely no planning on her part, the strangest thing had happened.

Erin O'Rourke was having the best Valentine's Day ever.

Valentino stood, his arm thrown around Erin's shoulder, looking at the valentine they had made. With the warmth of the sun on his face, the clearing sparkling with fresh snow, and her at his side, he wasn't sure if he had ever felt so happy.

A sound penetrated his happiness. The clearing was so silent that any noise would have seemed like a violation, but this one seemed particularly intrusive.

At first the sound was at a distance, but then there was no denying that the steady thrum was coming closer and closer.

Erin looked off in the direction the sound was coming from, puzzled.

"That's a helicopter," she said. "They wouldn't usually put it in the air unless there was an emergency." She went very still as she considered that. "I hope someone else wasn't caught in this storm. Shoot. I'm going to go get the sat device and check in. We might have to help with a rescue."

Just like that, she was running toward the cabin.

As she ran, the helicopter broke over the trees and hovered. A sinking feeling overcame Valentino. Not someone else caught in the storm.

Him.

The helicopter—the rescue—was for him.

With desolation in sharp contrast to his happiness of moments ago, he realized, just like that, it was over.

Foolishly, he thought, *I should have never spoken that wish—that this could last forever—out loud.*

His freedom was over.

And suddenly, guiltily, he saw he had enjoyed his freedom at her expense. She had no idea what was about to happen and he had no way to warn her. He watched as Erin froze on her way to the cabin, turned and shielded her eyes as the helicopter began to descend into the clearing.

For a moment, it was a complete whiteout as the wind generated by the blades kicked up a great cloud of white.

And then the cloud settled, the helicopter seesawed down, planted itself in the snow, and the engine was turned off. The blades slowed. Out of the corner of his eye, Valentino could see Erin, puzzled, coming back toward him.

The door of the chopper opened and Colonel Alisha Del Rento stepped out. Though she was not wearing a uniform, she was every inch the colonel in charge of his protection. And close behind her, the rest of his security team. They weren't wearing uniforms, either, but they might as well have been. They looked tense and ready to do battle with whatever they needed to.

"Your Highness," the colonel said just as Erin arrived at his side.

He felt Erin go very still. He turned and looked at her. Her baffled eyes went from him, to the colonel, to the rest of his men, and back again.

At first, she looked bewildered, but then something shuttered in those eyes that had been so open to him.

"'Your Highness'?" she said, her voice flat.

"Erin—"

She cast a glance at Alisha and leaned in close to him. "You lied to me," she said, fury in every clipped syllable she spat out.

His position suddenly felt indefensible, which drove him to want to defend it.

"Isn't finding out an ordinary man is a prince the best of surprises?" he asked her.

"No," she said without a moment's hesitation. "It isn't."

"I was going to tell you."

"Well, you know what they say about the road to hell." She stepped back from him.

"We have much to talk about," he said.

"That's your opinion. I don't feel we have anything to talk about."

Out of the corner of his eye, he registered the shock of Alisha and his security team at the tone Erin had used to address him.

Reasonably, he said, "Let's gather up our things and Harvey, and get on the helicopter. We can talk."

"I'm going to go down exactly the way I came in," she said. "I don't think we have anything to talk about, *Your Highness.*"

He heard something in her tone—particularly in the way she'd said *Your Highness*—that he was not sure he had ever heard before in his life.

Contempt.

The colonel had heard it, too, drawing in her breath with sharp and unmistakable disapproval.

Erin gave her a withering look.

"Don't go yet," she called, turning her back on him. "I have something for you."

Hope fluttered in him. Something for him. A memento. The wax number off the cake. Her phone number. Anything to cling to.

But when she strode out of the cabin moments later, she had two black-plastic bags. When Alisha tried to intercept her, she quelled her with a look.

She handed him the bags.

He peered in the first one. His clothes from yesterday. He looked in the other.

He realized, shocked, she had just handed him the garbage. Then she turned, nose in the air, and marched back to the cabin with as much dignity as the deep snow would allow. She did not look back. She scooped her cat out of his basket by the door, went in and slammed the door behind her with such force that the windows rattled in their panes.

Valentino found himself on the helicopter, lifting in that same cloud of snow. But as the cloud settled, before the nose of the helicopter was pointed downhill toward the resort, he saw it.

Their valentine.

Despite the clearing being so disturbed by the arrival of the helicopter, it was still there, even more spectacular from the air than it had been from the ground.

A lopsided heart encircled all those snow angels. And their names. His and hers, linked together. He cast a look at Alisha. She was staring down at the valentine. She glanced at him and then quickly away, her expression deliberately impenetrable.

But he had not a doubt that she and every other person on the helicopter knew that something had happened when he and Erin had been stranded in that cabin together.

The evidence was right there, printed in the snow.

He had forgotten, put aside, that he was not allowed the whims of ordinary men. He never had been. He had a role to play. An example to set. His was a life guarded against compromising situations. He was on duty all the time. He was not allowed slips. He was not allowed inappropriate liaisons. Not ever.

He waited for regret to come.

And found, in its place, defiance.

Erin stood with her back braced against the cabin door as if she were trying to hold out a band of marauders.

She waited until she could not hear the helicopter anymore before she moved away from the door. She thought she might cry, but she didn't. She was too angry to cry.

She cleaned the cabin with a vengeance, doing dishes, putting bedding in the laundry, stuffing her backpack with her things.

"A prince?" she said to Harvey. "Family business, indeed. No wonder I thought I recognized him. His ugly mug is at the grocery store checkout all the time."

If she was recalling it correctly, the paparazzi *loved* Valentino.

He's not ugly, a voice inside her insisted on protesting.

"Huh," she answered out loud. "Ugly is as ugly does."

Valentino was one of those men—just like her father—skilled in the art of seduction. All of it—the ineptness, the poetry—had probably been an elaborate act to get her into bed. And she had fallen for it! No, not just fallen! Hurled herself into it!

She felt angry, with Valentino and herself, and the anger was much better than feeling sorry for herself. It felt powerful. And passionate.

That passion—and the feeling of practically vibrating with energy—made her realize she was not even the same woman that she had been less than twenty-four hours ago.

Then she had been a *victim,* retreating from the world to lick her wounds, to feel sorry for herself about being dumped so unfairly by a man she had invested two years of her life in.

She didn't feel like that at all right now.

The truth was, she probably had Valentino to thank for this passionate, powerful side of her rising to the surface.

Harvey was hiding under the couch, eyeing her warily, not at all used to this kind of energy crackling off her.

Finally, bedding in the dryer and cottage looking for all the world the way it had always looked—as if nothing exciting or unexpected had happened there—she was ready to go.

She strapped on the baby carrier, stuffed her cat inside it, pulled on her coat, her toque, her gloves, her backpack.

She closed the door behind her.

Was she going to be able to come back here? Or would this place—that had always been her sanctuary—be haunted now?

The ghosts of his smile, his touch, his eyes on her, taking up residence here and never leaving?

She gave herself a shake, turned away, got her skis ready.

The snow wasn't the feathery powder everyone came here for. It was heavy, wet. The kind that was perfect for making the snowman they had not made. Still, even with the snow so challenging, she attacked the downward slope. Threw herself into it.

The passion translated to the way she skied. She could feel it. She embraced the intensity and singleness of focus that mountain required.

Once she got to the village, she made her way to her apartment and dropped off her things. She was stunned that it was only early afternoon. It felt as if years had gone by. In fact, it was still Valentine's Day.

Rather than sit around her apartment sulking, ruminating, going over every detail of the events that had just unfolded, Erin decided to go to work. It was her hidey-hole, after all. She popped Harvey back in his carrier and headed across the resort, enduring the smiles of people who thought she was carrying a baby.

"I thought you weren't coming in today," her office mate, Kelly, said, looking up with surprise when Erin came through the door.

Erin noticed that Kelly's desk sported a vase with at least a dozen red roses.

"I changed my mind," she said, trying to slide through to her office.

"I assumed you and Paul had something romantic planned," Kelly said, shamelessly probing. Her eyes slid to Erin's ring finger, hopefully.

Erin pulled back her shoulders and lifted her chin.

"Paul and I are no longer a couple," she said.

She wondered why she had dreaded this moment. Why she had thought *her* failure would be, humiliatingly, on public display.

Because she didn't feel like that at all.

She felt free. And strong.

She felt like a woman who had heard a man say to her, his tone as touching as a caress, *No man could look into your eyes and not know you. And no man could look into your eyes and ever have a moment's boredom. Not unless there was something lacking in him.*

"I'm so sorry," Kelly said. "Perhaps it's just a spat?"

Erin lifted a shoulder, not prepared to go into the details with her workmate. She found the refuge of her office and shut the door. She took Harvey out of the carrier. He went gratefully under her desk and curled up right on top of her feet.

That was how easy it was to get back to normal. With the cat purring steadily at her feet, soon she was immersed in the world she loved. A world of numbers and formulas. When done correctly, there were no surprises.

Surprises. It triggered a memory of Valentino's voice. In her mind's eye, Erin saw him lift that glass of wine to her and offer a toast.

To surprises.

Is this what her life was to be like now? Was she going to constantly be remembering a man she had spent so little time with?

Oh, but that time!

She shook it off.

Erin had just succeeded at immersing herself in that soothing world of work when her office door suddenly burst open. No knock.

Kelly, nearly lost behind a huge arrangement of flowers, said breathlessly, "See, I told you it was just a spat."

But Erin stared at the flowers, her mouth open, knowing this kind of extravagant arrangement was just not the sort of thing Paul would ever spend money on.

"I think its birds-of-paradise," Kelly said, setting them down and handing her a card. She stepped back to gaze admiringly at them. "And some kind of exotic lily. I don't think I've seen that before."

A tantalizing fragrance tickled Erin's nostrils.

"So beautiful!" Kelly declared, reaching out and touching the white, waxy petal of one of the lilies. She waited for Erin to say something, but Erin was stunned into absolute silence.

"Where do you get flowers like that at this time of year? They aren't from Berkley's Flowers. In fact, there's no tag on them at all. Just that card I handed you. Believe me, I looked! The delivery man wasn't what you'd expect. For some reason, he reminded me of a soldier. He said he'd wait for your reply. He had quite the yummy accent."

"My reply?" Erin managed.

"I think Paul's outdone himself. Open the card!"

If there had been any doubt who the flowers were from, the fact that a man who looked like a soldier and had a yummy accent was waiting in the front office, erased it in Erin's mind. She thought of the men and the woman who had tumbled out of that helicopter ready to rescue their prince.

Definitely soldiers.

Erin remembered his description of his land: the colorful flowers everywhere.

But even he could not have had flowers brought from there this quickly. Still, even without Kelly telling her, Erin knew that the small florist shop in the village could not have produced anything like this bouquet.

Of course, money would be no object for him. He'd probably had some staff member order the flowers and then sent a helicopter to pick them up.

The card was probably a brush-off. *Thanks for a memorable time.* But then, why would the messenger be waiting for a reply?

"Are you going to open the card?" Kelly asked anxiously. She turned and peered out the office door. "Yes, he's still there. I think Paul wants to set up something special. I bet he's going for forgiveness!"

Erin's fingers fumbled with the creamy envelope. She slid out a thick card and stared at it.

Kelly was absolutely correct. On one count, anyway.

She had the message right.

She just had the wrong man.

CHAPTER NINE

ERIN HELD THE creamy-white card. Who on earth had stationery like this on hand, particularly when they were traveling on a vacation? Silly to be seduced by the feel of paper, but it was so thick and rich. Possibly handmade. It was also ever so subtly embossed. The royal crest rose out of the paper and she explored the soft ridges with her fingertips.

That was who had stationery like this. A prince.

The card was handwritten, which made it harder to dismiss. His writing was strong, masculine, spiky.

Please forgive me. Give me an opportunity to explain. Would you come to my suite for dinner tonight?

It was signed *Valentino.*

That newfound sense of herself and her strength faltered. She felt weak with wanting to see him. Just like that, she could imagine his eyes on her eyes, his hands exploring her skin, his lips claiming hers. It made her feel as without strength as a newborn kitten.

But that helpless sense of weakness was just one more reason to say no. What would be the point of seeing him, of hearing his explanation? Where could such a liaison as the one they had shared possibly go?

There was no future in it.

Does everything have to have a future in it? A voice inside her whined. *Does everything have to have a point?*

She thought of the lovely intimacies they had shared: bandaging his finger, eating together, being in his arms, waking up beside him, exploring every inch of him, chasing him through the snow.

She could feel the blood rising in her cheeks. The desire to see him again was unbelievably strong.

She read the final line.

Please bring Harvey.

For some reason that tested her resolve even more than remembering Valentino's lips on hers. He had *heard* her. He understood that she tried to keep the cat with her as much as possible; he understood what Harvey meant to her. Nobody had ever included Harvey before.

Paul had barely tolerated the aging cat and the feeling had been mutual. He had *hated* her attachment to her beloved pet. "Weird," he had cuttingly pronounced it.

But before she gave in to all this temptation, swirling around her like a storm trying to suck her into its vortex, Erin took a black felt marker out of her desk drawer and wrote *NO!!* across the entire invitation.

Under Kelly's horrified eyes, she stuffed it back in the envelope and passed it to her.

"Give this to the man who is waiting."

The great prince couldn't even come himself? Obviously, he had used his resources, and very rapidly, too, to sort out where she worked at the resort.

No. Their worlds were too far apart. If this was that

important to him, he could have come himself. He had lied to her already. She had made love to an imposter.

Not that she had to explain her refusal to herself or to anyone else. *No*, according to a self-help book she was reading, was a complete sentence.

"But—" Kelly said. Her voice drifted away when she saw the look on Erin's face. She turned, reluctantly, and left the office, shutting the door quietly behind her.

Valentino put his phone down and went to the window. From his penthouse suite, he looked out over the Touch-the-Clouds resort. The quaint mountain village was snow-covered, bustling with the after-storm activity of colorful parka-clad skiers. The mountain cradled the resort in its bowl.

And tucked away in those mountains, a secret place, where it felt as if he had left his heart. He had just spoken to Angelica.

She had cried with relief when he'd told her he was not going to ask her to marry him. She had been so grateful but worried, too, knowing the brunt of the breakup would be borne by him.

He sighed and rolled his shoulders. He had told her, truthfully, that he was grateful, and prepared to pay the price. Whatever it might be.

There was no mistaking the sense of freedom. Of shaking off the harness he had worn since the day he was born. He was scheduled to leave tomorrow, and he felt he had to get home as soon as possible. The whole betrothal celebration must be canceled before any more work went into the preparations. Even at this point, it would probably be akin to trying to stop a runaway train. But it had to be done.

Valentino returned his attention to the card his guard had returned to him while he was on the phone.

He took a deep breath and slipped it out of the unsealed envelope.

He stared at it, incredulous.

Erin, in thick, black felt marker, had scrawled *NO* across the surface in two-inch-high letters, adding two exclamation points just to make sure he got it.

The feeling of incredulity died. He was not sure why he was smiling. He should be insulted. But just like that bag of garbage she had handed him, he didn't feel insulted.

Intrigued. A tiny bit tickled. Now that she *knew* who he was, she was not treating him any differently than she would any other guy who had hurt her feelings.

He thought of them in her bed together and admitted to himself that it went a little further than hurt feelings.

Where was it going, then? An apology and a goodbye on good terms?

But why? He was free of the matrimonial expectations that had been placed on him. Why couldn't he—they—see where it all could go?

The truth was, it had been many years since anyone had said no to him. Still, he'd obviously gotten it wrong. You didn't, apparently, beg for forgiveness by way of royal summons.

He had so much to learn.

And he realized he was hoping Erin would be his teacher. But first he had to get her to see him again!

Erin looked at the clock. Time to go home. But why go home? All she would do was think about things she could not change. The only thing that mattered to her—

Harvey—was here with her. She could stay in the office, order supper and keep working.

She could be having dinner with a prince. But, no, she'd be sharing a ham sandwich from the staff cafeteria with Harvey…

A knock came on the door. Kelly, no doubt, to remind her it was quitting time. But Kelly came in, slid the door shut and leaned on it. Was she trembling?

"Kelly?"

Kelly opened her eyes. They were wide with shock. "*He's* out there."

"Who is out there?" Erin asked, trying to keep her voice calm. Of course, she already knew what kind of man would elicit this kind of reaction. Of course, in his world, he would not take no for an answer. Why hadn't she anticipated this and gone into hiding?

"The Prince of—" Kelly glanced at the card she held in shaking hands "—Lorenzo del Toro. I've seen him in magazines. But nothing could prepare me for him in real life." She sighed with so much feeling that Erin feared she might faint.

But then she pulled herself together. "*You* know him." This was said with faint accusation, as if Erin had willingly withheld a secret—that Kelly's survival depended upon—from her.

"Casually," Erin said then felt her cheeks burn. She knew full well why she had not gone into hiding. Because part of her—even with all the evidence that such things were naïve and foolish—hoped.

"He's asked me to announce him," Kelly said and giggled. "I feel as if I should have a trumpet. Toot-doodle-loo! Announcing—"

"Just let him in," Erin interrupted her.

Kelly opened the door wide and called, "You've been

announced," then dissolved into girlish giggles as Valentino brushed by her, giving her an indulgent look.

Erin folded her arms over her chest and did not stand.

Kelly looked from one to the other and, sensing the tension in the room, scuttled out. Valentino closed the door behind her.

"What do you want?"

"I wanted to tell you I'm nearly completely recovered from my injury. See?" He held up a finger. Her first-aid attempts had been replaced with a very neat and tidy—not to mention, small—bandage.

He seemed—adorably—like he didn't quite know what to do now that he found himself there. For a man who commanded a nation, and stood so strongly in himself, it was seductively charming that he was off balance, unsure.

She had to fight an urge to get up and go look at his finger. To take it, and maybe to touch it with her lips… Erin shook off those thoughts, absolutely appalled with herself. She glared at him.

He cleared his throat, dropped his hand into his pocket.

"I wanted to tell you how sorry I am. Since you won't have dinner with me, I have brought the message to you. I should have told you who I was. I never meant for you to be shocked like that."

The very sound of his voice—deep, tender, genuine—weakened her. As did his eyes on her face.

Pleading.

A prince was pleading with her, Erin O'Rourke, for understanding. She felt a lump in her throat. He elicited so much feeling from her. It was dangerous. It was a feebleness.

"All right," she managed to say. "Apology accepted. Your conscience can be clear. You can go now."

A touch of a smile tickled the line of his lips. She ordered herself not to look at that bottom one.

"Is something funny?" she asked.

"It's just no one talks to me like that." He made no move to go. "Please, come have dinner with me tonight. It's my last day here. I fly out tomorrow. I have urgent matters to deal with."

"I get it," she said. "*Princely* duties call you. This will shock you, but I have a life and obligations, too. I can't just drop everything because you have summoned me."

This was so patently untrue that if she was Pinocchio her nose would grow about six feet right now.

"You have a previous engagement," Valentino said. He looked so crestfallen, she felt that dangerous softness for him inside her intensify. If she was not careful, she would be like Kelly, nearly fainting from his nearness.

"But it's been nice meeting you," she said coolly.

"Erin," Valentino said, his voice hoarse, "I just, for once in my life, wanted to be a man like any other. I wanted to be liked for myself and myself alone.

"Whether you forgive me or not, that is the gift you have given me."

She digested that. She felt her position compromised. She hadn't thought of it from his perspective. She hadn't thought how hard it would be to never be sure if someone liked you for you or because you were a member of a royal family.

She had not thought how someone, who had never had it, might long for normal.

"All right," she said, "I accept your apology. And I forgive you. Now, you can go."

He still didn't move. His look of relief was so genuine. "Would you have dinner with me tonight? Please. Perhaps your other engagement can wait, since I'm leaving first thing in the morning? I feel there are things we need to discuss."

"What kind of things?"

"The future."

One thing being an only child of warring parents had taught her was that hope—especially hope that love could win—was the most dangerous thing.

Love?

The intensity of what they had experienced wasn't love. It was a survivor's euphoria of some sort. The isolation, the storm, had led to impulse. A sense of embracing the moment. Infatuation. Passion.

She was going to say no to his dinner invitation. She really was. It would take all of her strength, every single bit of it, and still, the rational part of her knew there was only one answer.

There was no future for an ordinary, common Canadian girl with a prince.

But just as she was forming the word—how could a one-syllable word prove so difficult to get out—Harvey roused himself, stretched and came out from under her desk. He peered around the corner in the direction of Valentino.

The cat was mostly deaf. He was partly blind. He was antisocial.

And yet, somehow—perhaps by that thing called instinct that was so well-honed in the animal kingdom—he knew exactly who was there.

He shot across her office floor with more speed than Erin had seen in him in years. He wound himself around Valentino's legs, "talking" loudly.

Valentino laughed and picked up the cat. He lifted Harvey over his head and then brought him down to his face and planted a kiss on the tip of the cat's nose. He then hugged him into his chest and held him there.

It was the way somebody might handle a baby. She didn't want to think about Valentino with babies.

Babies. That's what she had wanted with Paul. In fact, she had wanted it so badly, it had taken away her discernment, her ability to tell the difference between fantasy and reality. And, of course, there was the fact Valentino was a prince. There would never be any babies with him.

And yet, seeing him with the cat, there it was nonetheless. A longing so powerful it nearly took her breath away.

"Are you going to come for dinner with me tonight, my old warrior?" he asked. He looked to Erin for the answer.

Baby thoughts should have put her defenses up higher. Instead, whatever was left of them crumbled. "Okay," she said, "we'll come."

The fact she was having unexpected longings for babies should provide ample protection against temptation to have another tumble with him. Having a baby was a serious enough business without adding the complication of a prince!

Besides, he was probably surrounded by a veritable army of people at all times. No wonder he had enjoyed his time on the mountain. It seemed to Erin that would be a perfectly awful way to live.

An hour later, standing in front of her mirror in her own apartment, she knew she had been put under a spell and that it was wearing off. Because, really? The dress she had on was terrible. Never mind that she had loved it when she had bought it to attend an awards dinner her father was being honored at. It was the fanciest thing she owned—jade green that matched her eyes, off-the-shoulder, short and sassy. Now, it felt as if she was trying too hard. Way too hard.

She had been in the presidential suite, which the prince and his entourage were inhabiting, only once. The resort had reserved it for a retirement party for the CEO of the company. The suite took up the entire top floor of the Northern Lights Hotel and was posh in a way she hadn't even known existed.

Of course, you wore your best dress for that. To have dinner with a prince.

But then she recalled what he'd said about the gift she had given him of feeling normal.

Gratefully, with a sense of relief, Erin slid off the dress that suddenly made her feel like a child pretending to be a grown-up and threw on a pair of casual stretch jeans and a button-down shirt. She put on a hint of makeup and tucked her hair up into a messy bun.

Then she remembered his fingers taking the pins from that bun—it seemed like a lifetime ago—and the veritable avalanche that had unleashed. She took her hair back down and, before she could overthink it too much, tousled it with her fingers. She pulled on her jacket, picked up Harvey and zipped him inside, and headed out into the Touch-the-Clouds complex.

It was a beautiful star-studded evening and she was aware of it as if the night was alive around her.

But that wasn't quite it.

It wasn't the night that was alive. *She* was alive—tingling with a kind of nervous anticipation—in a way she had not been in a long, long time. If ever.

When she knocked on the door of his suite, she wasn't quite sure what to expect. Staff? What did she say? *I'm here to see the prince. I'm here to play Cinderella to his Prince Charming.*

But Valentino opened the door himself, welcomed her by kissing her, with some formality, on each cheek. The cat popped his head out and Valentino took him from her jacket, good-naturedly kissed both his cheeks, too—just to let her know she wasn't getting special treatment?—and then set him on the floor.

Harvey, blind as he was, ambled across the space and found the most expensive-looking, silk-covered chair in the opulent main living area that was right off the front door. He gathered himself and leaped with surprising prowess into it then curled into a contented ball.

"Apparently he considers himself suited to such a palatial lifestyle," Erin said. The suite was as she remembered; a gorgeous space where you were afraid to touch things. Evidently, Harvey did not share her intimidation.

"May I take your coat?"

She shrugged out of it and was instantly aware that Valentino did not normally take coats, because he stood there not quite knowing what to do with it.

She gently retrieved it from him, opened the coat cupboard and hung it.

"You look lovely," Valentino said.

It made her glad she had not worn the dress. He, too, was dressed casually in pressed jeans and a V-necked sweater over a collared shirt. He looked very much the ordinary guy—except for those luxurious dark curls and a handsomeness that would never allow him to be ordinary!

"Humph," she said, regarding him thoughtfully. "I thought, now that your secret is out, you might have had a prince outfit on."

He glanced down at himself. "What, exactly, would you imagine a *prince outfit* to be?"

"At the very least, a hat with a shiny brim, like army

officers wear. I would think some medals. One of those wide ribbon things across your chest."

He was smiling. She enjoyed making him smile.

"You don't know any more about princes than I know about igloos."

"Or delivering babies," she reminded him. She snapped her fingers. "You should at least have a sword!"

He laughed, as she had hoped he would, and that tension she'd been holding since she had said yes to this invitation dissolved a little bit. This was her Valentino. The one she had chased through a snow-covered meadow.

Shared a bed with.

Not that she wanted to go there. But how was it not going to go there? The tension returned and intensified yet more as he led her through to the dining room. Like the main living area, this room was traditional and opulent. The long, polished, walnut table was set for two with beautiful china, both settings at one end. One at the head and one beside it. Valentino surprised her by holding out the head chair to her. Surely, that was his place at the table?

He took the other chair and reached for the bottle of wine that was sitting in a silver bucket.

"Note, it has already had the cork removed," he said with a grin. "And as an extra precaution, I'm decanting it. According to the sommelier, that lets any sediment drift to the bottom."

The grin, so familiar, tried to ease something in her, but the fact he had a sommelier at his disposal worked against that ease. Now that she was thinking about it, she could hear noises in the kitchen, which, if she recalled from the other time she had been here, was behind that swinging door. Delicious smells were wafting out of it.

Unless she missed her guess, someone was preparing dinner for them.

Well, what had she thought? That he was going to order a pizza?

"I considered impressing you by uncorking it with a sword—"

Valentino, that man whom—in a complete break from her normal buttoned-down personality—Erin had loved shamelessly and spontaneously, was really a prince. And that prince wanted to impress her?

What strange fairy-tale world was this that she found herself in?

CHAPTER TEN

VALENTINO GRINNED AT Erin. It made him, dangerously, *her* Valentino and not a world figure of considerable fame and fortune.

"As I said, I considered uncorking the wine with a sword, but I couldn't find one on such short notice. Someone neglected to pack my ceremonial one."

That, all kidding aside, meant two things: someone packed for him and he actually *had* a ceremonial sword.

"All things considered, that is probably a good thing," she said solemnly and lifted the glass he had poured for her. "I propose a toast."

He lifted his glass.

To surprises, she thought. But out loud she said, "To keeping all your digits."

He wiggled his newly bandaged finger at her. And just like that, the laughter bubbled up between them as effervescent as the wine. Her discomfort eased, but then came back as the swinging door to the kitchen opened and a white-uniformed staff member came through. A royal crest had been tastefully embroidered in gold thread on the breast of his uniform. He was bearing platters of food.

"Your Highness," he said. "Miss."

As he set down the food, did he slide her a look that was ever so faintly disapproving? She shot Valentino a glance to see if he had noticed, but he did not appear to have. Surely, she was being overly sensitive and had imagined it?

"May I bring you anything else, sir?"

"No, Milo, thank you."

Did Milo give her another look before sliding silently from the room?

"I wanted you to have a taste of my country," Valentino said and served them both from the platters.

She took the snowy-white napkin from beside her setting and put it on her lap. She regarded the array of cutlery with a bit of hesitation. Her lifestyle had rarely required she knew which fork to use! In this new setting, the passionate, carefree, confident woman Valentino had coaxed to the surface mere hours ago seemed to be fading with alarming quickness.

Erin watched how Valentino addressed the feast that had been prepared for them, and she did what he did. She was aware that he was as much at home in this world of amazing food, impeccable manners and culinary rituals as she was a foreigner in it.

Her disquiet lessened when he shifted his chair over closer to hers. He plucked a tiny tomato out of a glorious salad with his fork.

He held the fork to her lips. "Try this."

Her lips closed over his fork and flavors exploded in her mouth, possibly made more intense by his closeness, by his fork being in her mouth.

"Delicious?" he asked her.

"Unbelievable." Did that kitchen door squeak open and then shut again? "Somehow I don't think you picked that up at the Snowbound Groceteria."

He laughed. "It was developed by our palace horticulturalist. Its name translates to Tiny Tornado Tomato. We export them around the world now, to upscale markets."

"You travel with your own food?"

"My chef would never chance being able to find the quality or specialty ingredients he likes locally, I'm afraid. When we travel, he brings everything with him. He's snobby that way."

"Isn't it illegal to transport food into another country?" she asked. "My father once got off a plane in New Zealand with an apple they had given him on the flight—and he was charged a fine."

He contemplated that. "I have no idea, but I'm sure we would not do anything illegal. Probably we obtain permits or special permissions."

We. Meaning not him. She realized Valentino simply did not attend to the details of everyday life.

He moved on, making her taste the olives separately. They, too, were a specialty product of his kingdom, developed by the palace horticulturist. Taking great pride in the culinary accomplishments of his island home, Valentino explained each item on the menu to her. Every savory piece of food was evocative of a warm and colorful place.

Still, horticulturalists? Chefs preparing food? Sommeliers? Wait staff? People who quietly looked after permits and entry requirements? Protection staff?

"You must have been laughing when I called that salad at the cabin Mediterranean salad," she said. "Tasting this, it so obviously was not. You must have laughed about quite a bit of that meal. Steak that fell on the floor—"

"Licked by a cat," he told her, his eyes crinkling with merriment.

If she could just look at his eyes, maybe she could believe… "What? You never told me that part!"

"I protected you from it," he said, pleased.

"Oh." A prince protecting her. It stole words really.

"It was one of the best meals I have ever eaten," he said softly. "I would not change one thing about it. Except maybe the cork in the wine."

When the main meal was finished, Milo came out and prepared dessert at the table, two wedges of creamy cheesecake that he spooned a cherry topping onto. And then, with great flourish, he produced a torch, lit it and set it to the cherries. A blue flame danced over them briefly and died.

Milo looked so pleased with himself that Erin almost forgave him the subtle signs of disapproval he was giving off, especially now that Valentino had moved his chair so close to hers.

Valentino waited until Milo had left the room before he took his fork and fed her the stunningly delicious dessert.

She had a sudden memory of eating cake off his chest and felt embarrassed. She would have never done that, if she had known.

She would have probably never done any of it, if she had known.

Valentino seemed to sense her uncertainty. He picked up her hand and turned it, kissing the inside of her wrist.

"Let's talk about the future," he suggested, his voice low and sultry.

The future? Cinderella and Prince Charming belonged in fairy tales. As much as it felt like she had been dropped into one, she had to keep in mind that in real life, worlds that were so different collided, they didn't converge.

"What future?" she asked.

"I want you to come to Lorenzo del Toro. With me. Let me show it to you."

For a moment, she could almost feel the warmth on

her skin, smell the scents. But she had to keep one foot in reality! She had to.

"Obviously, I can't. I can't just drop everything. I have a job."

"Surely, you get holidays?" he said persuasively. "Isn't the ski season nearly over?"

"We have a shoulder season." Not enough of one to bring them out of the red, but still, it kept the resort open and paid basic bills.

His eyes slid to her shoulders in a way that nearly melted her.

"I have a life," she insisted, hoping he would not ask for examples because, at the moment, a life—one without him in it—seemed particularly dreary.

"A cat," she added weakly.

"Harvey can come with you."

He really did not know anything about how real people lived!

"You don't just board a plane with your cat," she told him.

He looked confused, as if that had never occurred to him. But then he laughed. "Oh. Do you think I'm asking you to take a commercial flight?"

"Aren't you?"

"Of course not. We have a private plane. I would send it for you."

Erin was dumbfounded. *He would send a plane for her?* She had grown up with plenty of international traveling, but she had never been on a private jet.

She closed her eyes and let the seduction of the whole thing sweep over her. A vacation in an exotic place. With incredible food. Sunshine. Discovery. A private jet. An intriguing, gorgeous, sexy man.

Milo slid back through the door and stood silently until

Valentino acknowledged him with a look that clearly said *Not now.*

Milo, however, was not to be deterred.

"Your Highness…"

The formal address, the man's deference to Valentino, reminded Erin, again, how far apart their worlds really were. How she didn't really know Valentino at all.

He was not just the playful man who had given himself over to loving her, to playing with her in the snow…

But he was holding out an opportunity for her to get to know him better and on so many different levels. They had shared her world. Now he was inviting her to explore his.

She could feel herself leaning toward it…

Milo spoke. "Sir, the palace has just announced your engagement to Princess Angelica of Sorrento. I wanted to be the first to congratulate you."

Valentino gave the man a stunned look and then dismissed him quickly with an impatient wave of his hand.

Erin froze and let the words sink in. She felt as though she had been slapped. In fact, she fought back the tears rising in her eyes.

Instead of letting him know her distress, she got up slowly, feeling as if she were in a dream. Even knowing better, even having grown up with her father, *still* she had fallen for Valentino's charm. Still, she had believed he'd wanted to show her his world.

"So," she said, tossing down the napkin, "apparently there are two things you neglected to tell me. One, that you're a prince. And two, you're a prince in a committed relationship."

His dark eyes were liquid. He looked at least as distressed as she felt. But she squeezed any sympathy she wanted to feel for him out of her heart. She tilted her chin proudly.

"Let me explain." His voice, his beautiful voice, was low and pleading.

"You had plenty of opportunity to explain," she snapped. "Any time up at the cabin might have been good. Before we were intimate comes to mind."

"Erin—"

"But maybe you don't have to follow the same rules as the rest of the world? Is that it?"

"That's not it. At all. If you would just listen to me—"

"To your explanation? Maybe you'd like to run this by your royal speech writer, but it's pretty hard to explain an engagement to someone else to the woman you have just invited to share time with you." Erin could hear an unnatural and very unflattering shrillness in her voice. She told herself to be quiet. But she couldn't. The words just kept spilling out of her, furious, outraged.

"When were you going to tell me that part? About the princess being your fiancée? Once I was there? When you were hiding me away somewhere like a tawdry little secret?"

Her mother's exact words to her father. *Your tawdry little secrets.*

"How were you going to keep your betrothed, Princess Whatever-Her-Name-Is, from knowing about me? Or is that kind of thing acceptable in your country?"

"Erin, it's not like that. I promise you, it's not like that." He was getting up, easing toward her, gently, like one would ease toward a skittish colt that wanted nothing more than to bolt.

She *wanted* to hear it. She wanted his promises. She wanted his words to smooth it over so that it all made sense.

That's how stupid she was!

"No, I don't want to hear it," she lied, holding up her hand to him in the universal gesture of *Stop right there, buddy.* "I've heard enough explanations, thank you. You can put all the finery around it that you want. You can have your staff and your plane and your exotic food and people who light it on fire for you. It doesn't change the truth."

"The truth?" he asked.

"You, Your Royal Highness, are a complete ass."

Valentino watched, shocked, as Erin stormed from the room. The cat yowled in protest when she picked it up and a moment later the door slammed behind them.

He was tempted to go after her.

Not that he had much experience in these things, but instinct told him there were certain times that you would be taking your life in your hands trying to talk to a woman.

Besides, as he sank back down at the table, he allowed himself to feel the full insult of it. Erin *knew* him. She had to know him. It felt as if she was the only person who had ever truly seen him.

And she was so quick to believe the worst of him.

An *ass*?

No one had ever spoken to him like that before. He had never been called such an insulting name in such a scathing tone.

His indignation faded. Valentino felt a horrible sense of defeat. He resigned himself to the possibility that whatever had happened between them on that mountain was a moment of magic, somehow separate from time and space. It could not, it seemed, be recaptured here on earth.

Perhaps it had served its purpose, giving him the impetus to set Angelica free. For that dazzling moment in time, on the mountain with Erin, he had believed a different life waited for him, but now he was not so sure.

It was obvious to him that someone in his inner circle had reported his involvement with Erin went further than them stranded together in a snowstorm. That valentine stamped in the snow had been a dead giveaway. The delivery of the dinner invitation to Erin's office this afternoon had probably cemented conclusions.

He had been reported, by someone, to his mother, the queen. Possibly, the palace even knew he was entertaining Erin tonight. Probably, Milo had been instructed to make sure that Erin went home and had been given the ammunition to do that.

His family were pulling out all the stops. They were trying to drive him back into the fold, trying to force his hand, with the engagement announcement coming early.

It didn't really matter who had reported him. There was no point chastising them, or Milo, the server who had made the announcement in front of Erin. His staff were loyal to him. But in the end, everyone in the kingdom, including himself, answered the commander in chief, who was his mother. His staff had probably all been ordered to do whatever they could to nip the romance with the Canadian girl in the bud.

Before it had a chance to become an embarrassment.

Or, more important, before it had a chance to persuade him to put his own happiness ahead of his sworn duty.

He had to return to his island immediately. He would announce his breakup with Angelica to his mother personally. There were going to be repercussions, but still, he had to make it clear that certain elements of his life would belong to him alone.

He looked at the remains of the dinner in front of him, his appetite gone. In fact, he felt quite ill.

Milo came through the door. He noticed the empty place and, for just a second, a look of carefully controlled sympathy crossed his face.

"Can I bring you anything else, sir?" he asked.

"No, thank you."

It was everything that Valentino had grown up with: a civil exchange. Emotion was swept under the carpet; the show must go on. Dignity and decorum. The public perception came first and foremost. Always. Control, and discipline, were everything.

He resisted, just barely, an urge to pick up a plate and throw it at the wall.

CHAPTER ELEVEN

ERIN WOKE UP the next morning to the sound of a helicopter lifting in the distance. The steady whomp of the blades slicing the air intensified the pounding in her head. She felt, for all the world, as if she'd had too much to drink, when she was pretty sure she had only had a few sips of that cork-free wine.

She told herself to ignore the noise, but she couldn't. She knew, in her heart, what the sound meant.

Valentino was leaving.

The helicopter would take him to wherever his private jet was parked. Did you park a jet? Was that the proper terminology? Moor it? Who cared? Stupid to waste time wondering about such things.

He was engaged.

Still, if she got up and went to her living room window, she could probably catch a glimpse of the aircraft that carried him. Away from her.

Forever.

Had she really thought, when he'd invited her for dinner, that something could ever come of it? Besides a fling?

She was hardly the kind of girl who inspired grand passions. She was not the kind of girl a prince would choose.

With those thoughts running through her head, Erin refused to let herself run to that window. Her pillow was damp with tears. The hangover she was feeling was an emotional one. Harvey, ever sensitive to her mood, was curled up, purring on the pillow right by her ear. It was reminiscent of the days of the childhood that she had been so determined to leave behind her.

Is that what she had clung to in her relationship with Paul? The fact that emotional turmoil had been happily absent?

But, come to think of it, strong emotion of any sort had been absent. Was that any way to conduct a romance?

Not that what she had experienced with Valentino could qualify as a romance. A tryst, maybe. *A tawdry little secret.*

The prince was engaged.

It was shocking news, never mind that he had seemed as taken aback by Milo's announcement as she herself had been. The fact that Valentino had been romancing Erin—carrying on with her—when he was committed to another woman was despicable. Unforgivable.

It was just like her father. So sure of his charms. Gullible women falling all over themselves to be with him. Probably, women who didn't have a very good sense of themselves in the first place, so wanted to bask in the reflection of his glory.

"Yuck," she said out loud. The sounds of the helicopter had long since faded. She finally got up. As tempting as it was to call in sick, she knew herself too well. Moping helped nothing.

So she scrubbed her face and got herself and Harvey ready to go to work.

An hour later, she was crossing the village square, the snow crunching under her feet. The main floor of the building she worked in housed a minimarket—the one she had teased Valentino about *not* shopping at—and she had to pass right by it to get to her office.

Any hope she had that there was some mistake about Valentino's engagement—that the surprise on his face meant something for the future he had talked about for them—was blown to smithereens.

The tabloids were out on a display rack in front of the building this morning. There were three different ones, but all had a variation of the same front-page headline and story.

Fairytale Romance:
Prince and Princess to Marry!

Someday My Prince Will Come:
Royal Engagement Announced!

Royal Romance:
Prince Valentino Proposes to
Princess Angelica!

Erin was not quite sure how Valentino had managed a proposal since he'd been having dinner with her at the very time his engagement had been announced.

In his world, she thought, miffed, he probably had staff to look after the bothersome little details of an engagement. The Royal Proposer.

Naturally, she hoped Valentino's betrothed was what he deserved, cold and unfeeling. A horrible person. She hoped she had blotchy skin.

But, no, Erin herself was the only one with blotchy skin this morning. The pictures that accompanied the headlines did not show an ugly princess. The furthest thing from it, actually.

Angelica of Sorrento was, naturally—and unfairly—gorgeous, right off the pages of what the heroine of any a fairy tale should look like. She had an abundance of wild, dark curls, an amazing complexion, soft, dark eyes, eyelashes as thick as Valentino's own.

They would make beautiful, curly-headed, golden-complexioned babies together.

In one of the pictures, the happy couple had their heads together, nearly touching, laughing. The caption said it had been taken at a polo match the previous summer.

Of course! A polo match! Erin was surprised the prince wasn't playing in it! Who went to polo matches? Rich people. Sophisticated people. Who had jets.

And who had paramours tucked away in the far corners of the globe.

In another of the pictures, they were both on horses, riding a quiet forest trail, each looking completely comfortable in jodhpurs and riding helmets. Looking completely comfortable with each other. Looking exactly what they were: the most privileged, pampered people on the planet.

The third picture showed Angelica at the top of a curved marble staircase in a gorgeous gown, long gloves, a tasteful tiara. Every inch the princess. Valentino waited at the bottom of the stairs. Look at that! Dressed *exactly* like a prince, including the sword.

Erin, shocked at the level of her own anger, ungraciously hoped he would manage to chop off a finger while uncorking the wedding champagne.

She itched to buy one of the papers—to feed her desire to know everything there was to know about him—

the jerk—but recognized it would do nothing but cause her more pain. So, with difficulty, she refused the urge.

Kelly was already in the office, at her desk. Any hope Erin had that she might have missed the tabloid headlines was lost when she stuffed one of the very papers Erin had just looked at in her desk drawer and gave Erin a look loaded with empathy.

Erin felt, horribly, like the unwanted sympathy might make her burst into tears. Hopefully, she had cried them all out last night. Hopefully, she did not have a single tear left to waste on Prince Valentino!

She hustled into her office, released Harvey from the carrier, and immersed herself in the world that had always been engrossing for her. She wished it brought more comfort. The storm yesterday had come too late. The season was now nearly over. If the snow held, they might have another month. Ticket sales were down nearly twenty-five percent over last year. She had heard several of the concession owners saying they were not having a good year, either.

She had nearly managed to block out everything but the numbers in front of her, when the office door squeaked open.

"Do you want to know the latest?" Kelly asked.

Erin, unfortunately, could not keep her curiosity at bay. She nodded reluctantly.

Kelly came across the floor to her desk and handed Erin her phone. It was open on the web edition of *Rags and Riches,* one of the most notorious of the tabloids.

Erin was stunned to see there was a new headline.

Royal Splitsville:
Prince Calls Off Engagement!

She read the story with an uneasy greediness to know what was going on in Valentino's life.

Only hours after it was announced, Prince Valentino of the island Kingdom of Lorenzo del Toro has called off his engagement to Princess Angelica of the neighboring island of Sorrento.

The prince himself is tight-lipped about the unfolding situation, but the royal family has issued a statement that they have every hope the couple, who have known each other since childhood, will reconcile. They ask for privacy at this time.

Neither the Sorrento royals nor the princess has released a statement, but sources close to her say she is devastated by the stunning callousness the prince has showed in breaking their engagement, which is now, humiliatingly, among the shortest in history.

After that, over the next few days, no matter how hard she tried, Erin couldn't avoid news of him, even if she wanted to.

The headlines had turned nasty. *Happily Never After!* one read.

News turned out to be a loosely applied term because there was really no news, not that that stopped the paparazzi feeding frenzy. Where there was no news, there was no lack of conjecture, no shortage of "sources close to" willing to give statements and expose the depths of heartbreak and misery the princess was experiencing.

Very powerful telephoto lenses, drones and helicopters were capturing pictures of both the prince and princess from a distance and through windows. The criteria for the photos seemed to be to catch Valentino looking grim-faced and cold—villainous and evil—and Angelica looking tear-stained, bewildered and broken—the fragile victim.

If Erin wasn't so angry—*spurned* was probably the correct word—she would have almost felt sorry for Valentino and the hounding he was enduring.

She did feel sorry for Angelica. Was she responsible, in some way, for that stranger's now so very publicly exposed misery? Responsible in the same way that those women her father had taken up with had been responsible for her mother's pain?

In her weaker moments, Erin asked a different question. What if she wasn't just the other woman? Wasn't one of many in a long string? What if Valentino had felt something in the time they had spent together that had made him realize he wanted more—that there could be more?

What if what had happened between them wasn't a sham at all, but was the most real thing that had ever happened to either of them?

What if what he had felt with her at the cabin was the reason for his broken engagement?

But those thoughts would be followed so quickly with *Who are you kidding? Who do you think you are?*

It was so confusing it made her head hurt. Erin felt as if she had a chronic headache. And then the worst possible thing happened.

A week into the tabloid feeding frenzy, Kelly came into her office and closed the curtains that covered the window that overlooked the village square.

"Don't look out there." Kelly passed Erin her phone.

Stunned, Erin saw a fuzzy picture of herself, looking quite frumpy, crossing the very resort square that Kelly had just closed the curtains on.

Under the terrible picture were the words *Prince's Secret Woman?*

Erin was dumbfounded. "How on earth?" she whispered.

"I think any number of people, both here on the mountain, and among his staff, know that the two of you were trapped together overnight. There was plenty of chatter about it in the main office. Then I heard lots of whispers around the resort that you'd had dinner with him. I'm sure that tidbits like these are worth a fortune to these kinds of rags."

She, Erin O'Rourke, girl least likely to create any kind of fuss, ever, was fueling this kind of gossip?

She thought of that toast she had made. *To surprises.* It occurred to her a toast like that required clarification: *Good* surprises.

"They're outside the window, aren't they?"

Kelly went and peeked out the closed curtains. "I'm afraid so. Clamoring, like sharks circling in anticipation of a gut bucket."

Did she have to be that graphic? Erin handed Kelly back her phone. Her coworker swiped to another screen and handed it silently back. There was an even more terrible picture of her, with Harvey creating a bulge under her jacket.

The papers had made the same mistake Valentino had made on their first meeting. The headline blared *Prince's Paramour Pregnant?*

Erin passed Kelly the phone back. "Don't show me any more," she pleaded. Her own phone started to buzz.

"I hope they don't have your number," Kelly said.

But it was Paul's name that came up. Considering, at least before she had met Valentino, that she had longed for this call—and the announcement he had come to his senses, that she was clearly the best thing that had ever happened to him—she looked at it with reluctance. Now? Really?

She hesitated and then, from long habit—she'd always been so thrilled when he'd called her, found time for her—she answered.

"Paul," she said. She heard the total lack of enthusiasm in her own voice. She had been going to marry this man! Why would that make her feel like a loser? She could have had a nice unremarkable life, without any of the current chaos unfolding around her.

She was aware, just like that, she wouldn't take him back, no matter what. Was the current price she was paying worth that realization? She thought it probably was. And then some.

"And I thought you weren't exciting!" Paul said jovially. "A prince?"

He sounded oddly titillated, certainly as interested in her as he had ever been. He obviously was eager to have the inside scoop.

Erin was shocked by what came out of her mouth. "You're an ass, too."

Erin hung up the phone. Kelly giggled, shocked.

Erin's phone started to ring again, almost right away. The number was unknown. She stared at her phone in horror then quickly powered it off.

"Can you get a hold of Ricky for me?" she asked Kelly. "He's probably working the Lonesome lift today. Tell him I need to get up to the cabin, without anyone knowing."

"Done," Kelly said and then looked at her with such grave sympathy. "Oh, Erin, really? You? You are the least likely person to get caught up in something like this."

Almost the exact same message she had just gotten from Paul!

She was getting the same message, over and over, for one simple reason. It was true.

The ache she'd been nursing for days intensified until it felt as if her head were going to explode.

Ricky arrived within the hour and smuggled Erin and Harvey out a back door of her office building and onto a snowmobile. Even the drive up the mountain was good for her head. The further they got away from the chaos, and the more into the quiet sanctuary of high places, the better she felt.

By the time Ricky dropped her off at the cabin, with a sat device, her headache had almost completely cleared.

"Don't use it unless it's an emergency," he said. "We don't know yet who's yakking to the press. But I'll tell you this—I wouldn't want to be them when I find out who it is."

"I wouldn't want to be them, either," Erin said, taking in the menacing look on his craggy old face. He looked very pleased with that assessment and, with a final wave, roared off back the way they had come.

"Family comes in so many different ways, doesn't it, Harvey?"

Just a short while ago, she had resigned herself to this. To her family being the people she worked with. Harvey.

It now, sadly, felt as if it would not be enough to fill the space left in the wake of Valentino.

The sound of the snowmobile engine grew more and more distant, and Erin regarded the cabin and the clearing. She could almost hear her and Valentino's laughter.

She needed to clean the slate, literally. After she deposited Harvey inside the door, she went and kicked snow over where she had stamped their names until the clearing was scrubbed clean. Well, except for the angels. She left the angels. She felt as if she needed all the help she could get.

She entered the cabin with a bit of trepidation. So much had unfolded here! She was going to have days to do nothing but relive memories and be with her tangled thoughts.

The best antidote to the thoughts that haunted her—the main one being *Who do you think you are?*—was to keep busy.

In the daytime, with Harvey happy in his baby carrier, she snowshoed and cross-country skied until she fell into bed at night exhausted.

The ache inside her dulled as she filled moments with busyness that shut off the chatter in her mind. The wood needed to be restocked, kindling always needed replenishing. She found some sandpaper and stripped down the kitchen set, ready for repainting. She had books and she had crossword puzzles.

On her third day in exile, Ricky arrived with groceries and an envelope.

"Are things settling down?" she asked.

"More vultures than ever camped out looking for you," he said.

"They're not letting it go?" It was easy to believe, up here without the internet or TV, papers or radio, that everything could be normal again.

"Um, I think there have been some new developments. I think Kelly put a newspaper in that envelope for you."

"Oh, dear," Erin said without enthusiasm.

"There's been this strange side benefit," Ricky said brightly, "the resort has been rediscovered."

"Rediscovered?"

"We couldn't buy this kind of publicity. The phone is ringing off the hook at the office. The website crashed.

Twice. We're taking bookings for three years away. We've sold more season passes in the last week for next year than we did all this year."

This was what she needed to cling to, Erin thought as Ricky drove away. That there was sometimes a bigger picture. That good could come from bad.

She took her time getting to the envelope. Finally, she opened it.

She was stunned by what she saw.

It was a newspaper, folded in two. The half of the headline she could read.

Happily-Ever-The photo, also folded in two, showed half of a happy couple. The part of the picture Erin could see was of a joyous Princess Angelica.

Her fingers trembled. After all the kerfuffle, the engagement had been foregone. They had gone straight to the wedding. Angelica was an unbelievably beautiful bride. The dress was like something out of a dream. The white handmade lace of the veil against her dark curls was the picture of a perfect fairy-tale ending.

Angelica was the kind of girl who had happy endings. She had been born to them. Erin, the one who was not that kind of girl, couldn't bring herself, not just yet, to unfold that paper to see the other half of the happy couple.

CHAPTER TWELVE

VALENTINO STARED AT the photo of Angelica, radiating joy in her bridal finery. She had sent it to his phone yesterday, before releasing it to the press.

He recognized the groom only vaguely. A member of her protection team, a wholesome-looking young man who clearly would lay down his life for his new wife.

Valentino sighed. He had done his best to protect her. But, no, in the end, she wasn't having it.

She had called beforehand to tell him what she intended to do. He'd tried to talk her out of it and she had laughed.

"Oh, Valentino. I know you mean well, but you're being terribly old-fashioned. I don't need you to carry this burden for me, so that the press can have you as their villain."

"But now they'll make you the villain," he warned her, aching for the misery she was leaving herself open to.

When she'd answered, her voice was strong. "It doesn't matter. I know who I am. It has nothing to do with the stories they tell. You know that. This is my choice to make. It is my right to choose." And then, softly, adding, "Antonio will protect me."

It was someone else's job to protect her. He hadn't realized how seriously he took that self-appointed responsibility until she'd said that, and he'd felt relief wash over him.

One less thing in his world that he was responsible for.

And so, against the express wishes of her parents, and her people, Angelica had run away—taking the beautiful dress and the heirloom veil that was probably intended for her marriage to Valentino—and married the man she'd chosen.

And then she had freed him, Valentino, by publicly releasing a few photos of the event. In those photos, she and her new husband's eyes shone with light, almost blinding, as they looked at each other.

There were going to be repercussions, and many of them, and Angelica and her new husband's faces said that love was worth it. That love made them strong enough for whatever came next.

So far, the paparazzi were indulging the pure romance of a runaway princess bride. But they were clamoring at Valentino's door more than ever. They wanted their story. They wanted to capture him sad and angry and betrayed. They wanted the spurious kind of elements to the story that sold papers.

This was the press: hero to zero and back again, in the blink of an eye.

Of course, his thoughts turned to Erin. He longed for her. Had she seen this? Would it change everything between them? Was there hope? For them? Was there a way, just as there had been a way for Angelica and Antonio?

Could he even, in good conscience, ask her that? He had planned to, that night everything had blown up in his face and she had declared him an *ass*. He had specifically invited her to see if they could discuss the future.

That had been impulsive. He had still been riding the wave of intensity that their time together had created.

Crazy. They barely knew each other. She had made it clear she didn't want to change that. She had made it clear what she thought of him.

Had she seen the news of Angelica's marriage? Surely, it would change her mind? What would he do if it did? If she contacted him?

He would ask her, again, to come here. To see if she could fit into this world, or more important, if she would want to.

But the days went by and there was no word from Erin. Could he blame her? Those horrible pictures that had been printed of her, the headlines, had no doubt given her a taste of the viciousness she might leave herself open to if she chose to pursue a relationship with him.

Valentino fought the urge to be the one to bridge the gap between them. No. If he really cared about her, he would not invite her into this life but protect her from it.

For the next few days, his course chosen, he threw himself into his duties. He did his best to forget her. They had been together in that cottage for less than twenty-four hours. How could he possibly be so changed by that? So obsessed with her? He longed for Erin with an ache that was physical.

He was barely eating and he wasn't sleeping. It might not be the best time to make a decision, but it was in that vulnerable state that he arrived at his conclusion.

This was his truth.

He had been born to power. He was a disciplined man. He had nearly always done what his station required of him.

So he was shocked by this awareness, this unfolding truth, that when it came to Erin, he was powerless. He *had* to see her. If she was not going to come to him, he had to go to her. He could not fight it.

There were pieces to set in place, naturally, so that the press would not be hot on his trail. He and Erin needed privacy. He would arrange a leaked story. Maybe even a decoy to send them in the wrong direction.

While he followed the direction his heart was leading him in.

It was nearly dark when Erin came back through the clearing. She had cut it close, but she was glad. She had snowshoed all day. She was exhausted. Hopefully, that meant tonight she would fall into bed too tired to even think *This is the bed we shared.*

She stopped short and frowned.

There was a light on in the cottage. The golden light from the gas lamps inside spilled out the windows and across the snow, warmly welcoming, like a painting on a Christmas card. She shrugged it off. She must have left them on this morning, but usually she was not careless with the gas lights. On the other hand, nothing about her seemed "usual" right now. Admittedly, she had been distracted.

As she got closer, she realized there was also a faint whiff of woodsmoke in the air. Surely that would not still be there from this morning's fire?

She felt a bit annoyed. Had some skiers or other mountain enthusiasts found her little sanctuary and made themselves at home? These mountain cabins were always left unlocked in case they were needed as emergency shelters, and she didn't begrudge anyone that, but she didn't feel up to company, either.

She had another thought. Maybe it was her father, taking a break from gallivanting around the globe, an aging playboy. Maybe, like the rest of the world, he was curious about her notoriety.

She felt as if she didn't have the energy to deal with him right now, either.

Making as much noise as possible, so much so that Harvey gave a little mewl of reprimand from inside his carrier, she took off the snowshoes, slammed them together and clumped up the steps to the porch. The door opened just as she put her hand to the latch. She braced herself, but nothing could have prepared her for—

Valentino.

"Hello," he said softly. His voice was like a caress. His eyes were like a homecoming. She wanted nothing more than to fly into his arms.

But—

"Aren't you married?" she snapped.

"Married? Me?" He tilted his head at her. "How long have you been hiding up here?"

She didn't like it that he knew she was *hiding.* From the world. From her pain. From the insecurities that had, unfortunately, followed her.

Who do you think you are?

"Someone sent me the paper."

He quirked an eyebrow at her. Something was wrong with his eyebrows. They were white at the tips, and curling, as if he had cleaned a spider web with them. It was distracting.

"Of me? Married?" he asked, innocent, incredulous.

What kind of world was this he lived in? A celebrity world, obviously. One she could never belong in. Wouldn't want to! Engaged one day. Not engaged the next. Married one day…

Did those vows not mean anything to anyone anymore?

She stormed by him.

The paper lay where she had tossed it on the kitchen

table. It was untouched, still folded. She grabbed it and thrust it at him, crossed her arms over her chest, waited for his *explanation.* Oh, how he loved to explain things!

Instead, he looked down at the paper. He looked up at her and had the nerve to smile.

"Sometimes," he said, "you just have to look at the world from a different angle."

He turned the paper over.

She saw the headline completed:

After!

And she saw the photo—the one she had been avoiding but could not quite bring herself to burn—of the groom looking adoringly at his new bride, Princess Angelica.

And that groom was not Valentino.

Her head shot up. She stared at him. Her mouth opened and then closed. She could feel tears filming her eyes.

"Come," he said, helping her out of her jacket, taking Harvey from her. "Sit down. I've made you hot chocolate."

She sat, stunned, while *the prince* brought her hot chocolate, sank beside her on the couch, watched her with that familiar warmth in his eyes. His eyebrows were still distracting.

She was dreaming, naturally. She took a sip of the hot chocolate while she contemplated his eyebrows. Scorched. Surely, in a dream, the hot chocolate would be perfect? And his eyebrows wouldn't look like that.

"Did you have some kind of incident lighting the stove?"

He cocked his head at her and looked a little sheepish. "And the lamps. How do you know that?"

The prince looking sheepish was too adorable to resist. She reached up and touched his eyebrows. "Your eyebrows have turned to ash."

"Better than ass," he said, straight-faced.

She giggled.

"I watched you light the stove and the lamps several times. I might have had the sequence wrong. There was kind of a poof and a flash of fire and light. It was a little more excitement than I anticipated doing such a simple task."

The truth was that everything he did made simple things exciting. But she needed to remember there was a very thin line between excitement and disaster. That *poof* he described was about three seconds away from a cabin burned to the ground.

"Are you ready to let me explain? Ass that I am?"

She nodded. Her heart, that organ she had thought was dead inside her, was living again, thudding a tattoo inside her chest. "Yes, please tell me why you are here. What's going on. Why you didn't marry Angelica."

"Angelica and I have known each other since we were children. It was expected of us that we would marry. Love, of course, does not have anything to do with these kinds of arrangements in families like ours."

A man like Valentino—so passionate, so alive—condemned to a loveless life? It made her feel furious at the system he was bound to.

"To my shame, now, I didn't feel my marriage had to have love. She's beautiful. I respected her. And liked her. We're good friends, which I suppose is a love of sorts."

A love of sorts, yes, Erin thought, but not the kind you married. And yet, wasn't that *exactly* what she herself had been going to do? Marry Paul without passion?

"I actually felt as if I'd done fairly well in the arranged

marriage department," Valentino continued. "Both kingdoms were in a frenzy of preparation for the engagement party."

Again, the parallel—she, too, had thought she had done fairly well in her relationship with Paul.

"But then she told me she didn't love me."

Just as Paul had told her. Not that he didn't love her, not exactly, but that something was missing.

"And I knew by the way she said it, that she already loved someone else. She said, of course, she would go through with our marriage. It was her duty. What she'd been born to.

"That's when I came to Touch-the-Clouds. I needed to think. There is something that cuts the legs out from under a man to hear a woman that you care for talk about marrying you as if it will be a trip to the gallows.

"I think I already knew in my heart what had to be done. But would I have had the courage to do it? Before I met you? Before I found out what I would be asking both her and I to miss? Maybe not. But, believe me, the first thing I did after I got down from the cabin that day after the storm was phone Angelica to tell her she was free.

"And then I was free. To ask you to dinner."

Erin was struck by the truth of it: they had both been on course to make a tremendous mistake. They had both willingly accepted less than they'd deserved from life.

She owed Paul a debt of gratitude that he had somehow seen that something was missing.

Valentino owed Angelica that same debt of gratitude that she had freed him.

They both owed it to the universe to embrace this second chance they had been given to get it right.

"Oh, Valentino," Erin whispered. "I called you an ass. I didn't even give you a chance."

"Well, given that my engagement was unexpectedly announced—equally surprising to me as to you—I can hardly blame you. Though I did at first. I blamed you. I was hurt.

"I thought you, of all people, should know who I was. My family—my mother, the queen—had gotten wind that I was with you. She rushed the announcement, thinking it would force my hand, force me back into the fold. She counted on me to be who I have always been. A man who put duty first.

"But when I left here, and I wasn't that man anymore, I couldn't put anything first, before what I had felt for you. So, I called it off. I tried to make it seem as if it had been my decision, hoping it would protect Angelica.

"Unfortunately, even having lived with the media all my life, I could not have predicted the ensuing circus."

He smiled wryly. "Angelica let me know, in no uncertain terms, she did not need my protection. And that she would make her own choices.

"Which were to be true to herself and show the entire world she was not afraid to marry the man that she loved."

"I've been a complete idiot," Erin said softly. And not just about getting angry with him, jumping to conclusions, but about accepting so much less from life than it wanted to give her.

"Yes, you have been," he teased her.

She slugged him softly on the arm and he pretended hurt. "At least I didn't blow up my own eyebrows."

They laughed and the laughter made something inside Erin sing back to life. She realized she had not laughed since he had left.

"What now?" she asked him. "Where do we go from here?"

"Before," Valentino told her, "I wanted you to come to my kingdom. I wanted to see if we could have a future."

She registered the *before*. Her heart fell. She had, it seemed, missed her chance.

"But now?" she said. "Why are you here if I have thrown away my chance?"

"Thrown it away?" he asked, astounded. "That's not it, at all."

"Then what is *it*?"

"Traveling to the kingdom right now is out. The press are on me like hounds on the fox. If you showed up now, they would never leave us alone. We would have drones buzzing us every time we tried to step out. I couldn't ask you into that, and I needed to escape it.

"And then I thought, *I know the perfect place to escape.*"

"That's why you're here," she said. "To escape."

"Why are you so resistant to the truth?" he asked her softly.

"Which is?"

"Erin, I want to be with you. I was dying without you. Yes, I want to escape. I want to get lost in your eyes. I want to dive into them as if they were a cool pond on a hot summer day. I want to let what I see in them fold over me and soothe me, to heal all the parts of me that are wounded.

"I want to see where this all can go. I want to spend a week up here, intensely with you, and nothing else. How many places in the world would allow such an experience?"

That was true. She had never seen the cabin quite like that. A sanctuary. A love nest, hidden from the rest of the world.

"I want to see if the universe brought me to a ski hill in

a storm so that I could change my destiny," Valentino told her softly. "So that I could know love instead of duty."

Love?

It seemed so wrong. It seemed too soon. It seemed so right. It seemed as if the rules of time were silly structures, not intended for them.

Destiny.

That is what this felt like. Destiny.

"Is it wrong to want to do so without the surprise of a drone shot of our most private moments being splattered all over the front pages? I admit I have sent the paparazzi on a bit of a wild-goose chase, worthy of their own devious devices, so that I could have time with you. Just you."

Erin carefully set down her hot chocolate.

And then she leaped into his lap, twined her arms around his neck and took his lips with her own. Homecoming.

"I plan to fit into your world," he informed her between kisses.

Didn't he know he already did? Wasn't it obvious?

"I brought books with me. So we don't get bored."

"I don't think there's much chance we are going to get bored," Erin told him. Still, if he'd brought books, she was hoping for the *Kama Sutra.*

Or maybe they could lie in bed and read Elizabeth Barrett Browning to each other.

"How do I love thee? Let me count the ways..."

"How to Build an Igloo," he announced, pleased.

CHAPTER THIRTEEN

As it turned out, Valentino discovered building an igloo, aside from needing perfect snow, required several elements that the book failed to mention.

For amateurs, building an igloo required a good sense of humor. It required puzzle-building ability. It required tenacity. Most of all, it required that he and Erin to work as a team.

If you wanted to get to know someone, he decided, building an igloo was nearly the perfect way to do that.

But that activity—and all else they did from cooking simple meals to making the bed together—was overshadowed by the awareness of each other that crowded out nearly everything else. Everything was complicated by it…and made better by it. His life had taken on a light that shone more brilliantly than the sun on snow around them.

Her laughter filled him.

Her touch healed him.

Her intelligence awed him.

Her strength complemented his strength.

Erin and Valentino had somehow happened on an activity that unveiled to them how, despite so many cultural differences, they were incredibly compatible.

And despite the fact they exhausted themselves on their project, they barely slept. Talking deep into the night, often falling asleep with the next word dying on their lips.

And yet they woke energetic, filled with excitement for another day spent together. Valentino had never felt so exquisitely and intensely connected to another human being in his entire life.

It filled a part of him that Valentino had not been aware was empty.

Finally, three days and six collapsed, abandoned, restarted, rethought, reconfigured igloos later, they stood staring, awed, at their completed project.

The polished snow blocks that formed the dome got their strength only from leaning on each other. There was no additional supporting structure.

There was a lesson about life here, Valentino thought.

"It's supposed to support the weight of a man standing on the roof, if we did it correctly," he announced.

Erin grinned impishly at him and crossed her fingers.

Like an ice climber, he scaled the rounded wall. On the top of it, he pulled himself to standing. It was a gorgeous, spring-come-early kind of day. He surveyed the clearing that had become his world: the cabin, smoke chugging out the chimney; the clearing still filled with the melting outlines of snow angels; closer, the cat in a basket they had brought for him, belly to the sun, paws pointed at the air, indifferent to their accomplishments.

Valentino crouched and held out his hand to Erin.

She giggled—that carefree, breathless sound he had come to live for—and took his hand despite the fact she was protesting.

"Does the book say anything about it supporting the weight of two people?"

"Let's live dangerously," he suggested and pulled her up beside him on the dome. It was a perilous balance on the slippery curved surface, but they clung to each other, as interlocked as the snow blocks.

Isn't that exactly what they were doing? Living dangerously? Challenging every limitation others—and themselves—had tried to put on them?

The structure—their salute, really, to forging their own way in a world that wanted to tell them what to do—held.

He kissed her and let go of her hand. Erin slid on her bottom off the roof and he followed her, the crystal-clear air of the clearing ringing with their laughter.

He gathered supplies they had brought—a blanket, a candle, a thermos of tea—and crawled through the ice tunnel that led to the interior of their snow structure.

Given how bright it was outside, it was fearsomely dark in there. He spread the blanket and lit the candle. Erin wiggled in, the cat in her jacket.

It was tinier than they had first envisioned, but that meant the candle they had brought in, plus their body warmth, heated the space, as the book had promised it would. There was just enough room to shrug out of their jackets.

"It's tight in here," Erin said.

"Cozy," he corrected her.

"Here's to cozy." Erin unscrewed the lid from the thermos, put it to her lips and then passed it to him.

He took a sip and offered his own toast. What had become *their* toast.

"Here's to surprises."

Four full days with her and she was still surprising him in the most delightful ways. He still loved his lips touching places her lips touched, like the rim of the thermos. Still lived for intimacy between them, small touches. Still was awed by the growing comfort, the heated looks, the moments of quiet contentment.

Harvey, on her lap, seemed quite crabby about the whole experiment. He glared back and forth between them, as if to say, *Uh, we have a perfectly good cabin... what nonsense is this?*

Nonsense of the best sort, Valentino thought.

And yet getting to know her better was an agony, too. Because, every day, his feeling that he could not live in a world without her intensified.

But this snowbound world was perfect. Here they could be private. And playful. Completely themselves.

Could he really expose her to the deep scrutiny that she would encounter in his world, a world completely alien to her?

Could what they had discovered about each other here stand up to the very unusual stresses of his life? At this moment, flushed with triumph and accomplishment, all his doubts fell away. In this moment, it felt as if what they had could stand up to anything.

"You have showed me your world," he told her.

She smiled. "That's not exactly true," she said. "You have showed *me* my world. Opened my eyes to it. Showed me a way of looking at it, and a way of being in it, that I did not have four days ago."

She reached out and touched his cheek. Her eyes on his face held an expression that was everything a man could ever hope for.

Valentino felt *seen.*

He slipped his own hand up to cover hers, slid her fingers to his lips and tasted the now familiar taste of her.

If two people could use nothing more than their intention, their intelligence, their willingness to learn, to build a structure that could hold their weight out of something as flimsy, as insubstantial, as snow, couldn't they do anything?

"Come to my world," he whispered. "Let me show it to you. Everything will seem new. Please say yes."

She looked at him deeply.

Valentino was aware that everything Erin knew was here. This was her world. Over these days together, he had discovered, as she'd talked about her life, how safe she had made it, how the turmoil of her childhood had made her cling to routines, long for safety and security.

Did he have a right to do this? To ask this of her? It was too late for doubts. He had done it. He was aware he was holding his breath.

"Yes," she whispered.

And Valentino began to breathe again.

Erin could not believe what was happening to her life. Was this how you were rewarded for toasting the universe with *to surprises*?

She, Erin O'Rourke, Canadian account clerk whose only claim to fame was her father's skiing career, was on a private jet.

A royal jet.

The aircraft, staffed with uniformed people, had more opulent furnishings than most houses she had been in. It was more luxurious than the presidential suite that Valentino had inhabited at the Northern Lights Hotel.

There was even a bedroom, a master suite she had glimpsed on their way to the main cabin area. It was a beautiful space of many cushions, gray silks and deep walnuts. It made her heart hammer to think of doing some of the things they had done up here at thirty thousand feet. She was stunned by how the exoticness of that possibility stirred something in her that she had not known she possessed.

However, on their last night in the cabin in her world—the one that had become their world—Valentino had briefed her a bit on protocol.

How to address his mother when they met. How to handle salutes, attention, the press. Reluctantly, he had informed her, there was one area of their life they would have to put on hold as they entered his world.

Even if he had not told her, she would have known as soon as they got on the jet. She would have known by the way he avoided taking her hand, touching her, that they had entered a place where he had to be extraordinarily careful. Where they would both have to be extraordinarily careful if they did not want to earn the censure of the palace and the clamoring of the press.

It might have all been a little overwhelming except for the fact Harvey was in a basket in her lap, letting her know he was mightily unimpressed with his first trip in an airplane and overseas. He yawned and licked a paw.

And, of course, Valentino was at her side. It was slightly unsettling to see he was addressed, always, as Your Highness, or sir. It was slightly unsettling to think all of this was his.

His hand found hers and gave it a quick squeeze before letting it go again as they prepared for takeoff. She realized, when he let go, that the unabashed passion they had for each other at the cabin would not be appropriate here.

Obviously, because of his position, the very physical part of their relationship needed to be reined in for appearances' sake.

For some reason, that made her nearly breathless with wanting him. Erin took his hand, surreptitiously ran her thumb over his wrist, until he looked at her with such heat, she thought she would melt.

A staff member came to speak to them. She slid her hand from his and looked out the window, smiling.

For all that he was a prince, Valentino was still the one who had given her a sense of discovering the new in her own world.

The one who was leading her now into this brand-new world. This was no time to be afraid. It was time to accept that life was an incredible adventure.

She had accepted the invitation.

She had to throw herself into it. There was no room here for that girl who harbored, always, the sense of not being good enough.

Indeed, it felt as if Valentino's attention to her had erased that part of her forever.

As soon as Erin stepped out the door of the plane, she knew she was in a magical place. The sun was warm but gentle on her face, like a kiss. The air held the mingled perfumes of spice and flowers.

From that first step, she entered the most extraordinary experience of her life determined to embrace every single thing about it.

A royal limousine met them and whisked them down narrow streets with whitewashed medieval buildings that seemed to lean over the streets, keeping the sun from reaching the cobblestones. Flowers cascaded out of the high window boxes that the sun touched. In places, colorful clotheslines, two stories up, spanned the street. Though the car was air-conditioned, Erin opened the windows to fully experience not just the sights but the sounds and smells of Valentino's home.

She could hear strains of music pouring out windows, laughter, a lovers' squabble, children shrieking, dogs barking. The air was redolent with scent: spicy cooking smells, exotic flowers, the sun on the white bricks.

It was fantastic.

The palace sat at the edge of those crooked streets, jumbled buildings, houses stacked up hillsides.

The cheerful chaos was left behind them as imposing wrought-iron gates swung open to lush expanses of lawn, gorgeous gardens, gurgling fountains. And at the end of a long, curving driveway, a palace.

It was not the typical "fairy-tale" palace, like Neuschwanstein Castle in Germany, but rather an imposing and majestic square. Constructed of huge white-marble blocks, the severity of the structure was diluted by the exquisitely carved detail around the doors and windows, the intricate designs on the caps that topped pillars, the lush vines that crawled up the walls, and the huge concrete vats of flowers that abounded.

Once inside the palace, Erin could not keep her mouth from popping open in astonishment. Though it was warm outside, the inside of the building was cool. As Valentino took her through to her suite, there was almost too much to take in: gorgeous gilt-framed paintings, chandeliers that dripped priceless crystals, hand-carved wainscoting, silk wallpapers, detailed tapestries and hand-knotted rugs.

Her suite was as ornate as the rest of the palace. She looked around, terrified to touch anything. It was his touch that grounded her.

By themselves, finally, he gathered her to him, covered her in kisses. Her ears, her eyelids, her neck, finally her lips.

"I've been longing to do that all day," he said huskily in her ear.

"Me, too," she said, taking his hand and pulling him toward the bedroom. "Should we—"

He backed away from her. "Sorceress," he said. "Sadly, there are no secrets in the palace. Your stay here will be a chaste one."

She looked at his lips and felt longing rip through her. Seeing him in this world—and their relationship being forbidden fruit—made her want to be exactly what he had called her. A sorceress, tempting him. She took a step toward him, but he laughed, shook his head and slipped out the door.

She found her way to her bedroom—a huge, carved four-poster was at the center of it. Tapestries hung on the walls.

Who does the dusting? She wondered practically.

There was a lovely pillowed bed for Harvey. The thought of a litterbox in this space made her wince, but still there was one, placed subtly in a closet.

She put Harvey on the bed. He sniffed it and settled himself approvingly on what she was fairly certain was pure silk.

Her suitcase had arrived before her—it had not touched her hands once since she had packed it—and now it had been unpacked for her! It made her wish she'd had time to invest in new underwear! She hadn't been prepared for the fact people would be touching her things.

She went through to the adjoining bathroom. The tub, veined marble, was large enough to swim in. The fixtures were gold—and probably the real thing.

She suddenly felt overwhelmed. The plane, and now this. Plus, unspoken rules around being with the man she had become so comfortable with. She felt she was being plunged into a world where she could never belong.

And yet when Valentino came to collect her, her

doubts were erased, again, by the look in his eyes. He stepped inside her room, took her face in both hands, and kissed her deeply and passionately.

"Don't do that and expect a chaste relationship," she warned him.

"You're right. It won't do to have you glowing with passion at the moment. Should we get meeting my mother over with?"

"Is it going to be horrible?" she asked.

"Of course," he said with a grin.

But it wasn't horrible. His mother was at a table in an ornate sitting room, which was a relief, since Erin thought she might be sitting on a throne with a crown on her head.

Instead, she was having tea, with a dog at her feet. She was also wearing a dress that might be called dowdy, if one dared to call the queen's dress dowdy, even in their own mind.

It was obvious where Valentino had gotten his good looks from.

They sat at the table with her, and a servant poured tea. Valentino introduced Erin as his friend. His mother, the queen, had obviously been putting people at ease her entire life and she was very, very gracious.

"I understand you love animals," she said, and Erin realized she had been *briefed*—given one detail about her—to make her feel welcomed. The queen was also good at not showing what she really felt. Though she was extremely charming, there was an impenetrable quality to her charm and her eyes were guarded.

They mostly discussed Harvey and the dog who snoozed at her feet.

"See?" Valentino teased her as they left the audience, "You survived."

"I feel kind of sorry for her," Erin admitted.

"For my mother?" he asked, incredulous.

"I get a sense of no one knowing her. Of deep loneliness. I—I'm sorry. I shouldn't have said that." There was probably a law against making observations about the queen!

But Valentino was looking at her, a small smile playing across his lips.

"You see, Erin? You see what others do not. They see her wealth, her power, her privilege, her station. Everyone wants something from her. It makes it impossible to trust, to be liked for herself alone. You see the heart she has never felt safe to show anyone."

His voice dropped. "It is the life you are saving me from."

After the audience with the queen, they seemed to be free, but with parameters. They had dinner that night in a small walled garden off her suite. Even though an exquisite meal had been left for them, and they were not interrupted, Erin was aware they were not really alone.

"Are there people everywhere?" she whispered to him. "Hovering in the shadows, waiting for you to need something?"

"I'm afraid so."

And so even after the delicious food, it felt as if they were starving. To touch each other. It was strangely tantalizing, their relationship suddenly fraught with suspense. Anticipation.

They got up from the table and Valentino led her to the darkest corner of the garden. He claimed, loudly, he wanted to show her a white flower that looked particularly stunning at night.

Instead, he pressed her up against the garden wall and ravaged her mouth, kissing her until they were both frantic with need.

Valentino yanked away from her when they heard the clink of dishware being cleared from the table in the garden. Erin giggled breathlessly. He ran a frustrated hand through the dark tangle of his curls.

"I thought my family left torture behind in the Dark Ages," he muttered.

The dishes clattered more loudly. They waited until the sounds stopped and then, like errant teenagers—and with all the same pent-up longing—went to their separate quarters.

As he showed her his country, they traveled in a three-car entourage. The first day they brought Harvey, but after that, to her shock, the cat agreed to tolerate Milo as his babysitter. She exchanged phone numbers, making Milo promise to call if there were any problems. She reminded herself—a little pathetically—of a nervous mother.

She had rarely been without the cat for over a year since his eyesight and hearing had started failing so badly, but she knew she was being silly. Milo had her phone number. She had his.

Valentino was an incredible tour guide, well versed in his country's colorful history, proud of its many accomplishments, passionate about the roads forward into the future. The country was amazing, but it was also amazing to see Valentino in this element. His element.

In the cabin, he had been exploring a new world. Eager, to be sure, but adorably inept at so many practical things.

Now, she saw the man that he truly was: confident, polished, comfortable with his position and power.

It heightened her already over-the-top awareness of him and a new tension sizzled between them. His hand reaching for hers nearly scorched her. Stolen kisses had the intensity of exploding rockets. His gaze resting on her could make her heart start beating so hard it felt as if it would break out of her chest.

After they had toured the ruins of one castle, they came out to find the road on both sides lined with people.

"Word must have got out that I was here," he said. "You don't mind if we stop, do you?"

"Of course not." Uncertainty hit her. "Do you want me to wait in the car?"

"No!"

She could tell his security team, who traveled in cars in front and behind them, especially Colonel Del Rento, hated this spontaneous stop as much as he loved it. It was evident he was admired and adored by the people of his country, and that he reciprocated those feelings.

He introduced her to the people as his friend. In some ways, it was not completely unfamiliar. At the height of her father's career, this is what it had been like traveling with him. People had recognized him, wanted his autograph, wanted to speak to him. Sometimes, quite a crush of people would form around him.

The big difference was that with her father, he had enjoyed the attention immensely because it had been all about *him*.

Erin noticed Valentino's utter and sincere interest in people. He smiled, clapped a shoulder, threw back his head and laughed. He would bend close to hear more clearly.

As with her father, when she sometimes had received reflected attention, mostly of the *Are you going to be a ski star, too?* variety, some people were very aware of her. Embarrassingly, one older lady curtsied. A little girl presented her with a hastily gathered bouquet of crushed flowers.

Her nose buried in those lovely flowers, Erin noticed Valentino being passed a baby boy. Something in her went very still as Valentino handled the baby with an ease that was unusual in a single man. He admired him and kissed his fat cheek before handing him back.

He, Erin thought, before she could stop herself, *is going to make a great father.*

The thought discombobulated her. He had made it clear, when he had come to the cabin, when he had brought her here, that he wanted to see what the future held for him.

He had introduced her to his mother.

Now, he was introducing her to his people.

Her future could be him. This land. His babies. A euphoria swept through her. It was quite unlike anything she had ever felt before.

It only grew as she watched him talk to one of the people in his entourage when they got back to the cars. Quietly, he was giving names and instructions: make sure we find out about crop insurance; send flowers to that woman, she's lost her husband; make sure that baby gets a teddy bear.

What she didn't like about traveling with him was the sense of constant surveillance—though it made those kisses stolen in that tiny cave at the base of the ruin even more sizzling—and the fact they were not free to be spontaneous. Erin longed to immerse herself in the noisy marketplaces, to have coffee and pastry at one of those outdoor cafés. But that was not his life.

Her favorite thing became the visit to the beach at the end of each day of sightseeing. While the front of the palace faced sweeping lawns and gardens, the back of it was perched on a rocky outcrop that overlooked the sea.

To Erin's delight, Valentino showed her a secret set of

stairs cut into the granite that led to a gorgeous, private, white-sand beach.

Here, finally—save for Harvey, who had yowled his dismay when she had tried to leave him yet again—they were alone. They were children again—as playful on that beach as they had been at her cabin. They built sandcastles. They played in the turquoise waters, running, splashing each other. There were snorkels, and Valentino showed her the magical world that existed right below the surface of the sea. They stole kisses and touched sun-warmed skin.

Today, after a long day of sightseeing, Erin lay on a blanket. She was wearing a bikini that a few weeks ago she would not have worn. But a new her—a bolder her—was confident in herself and her body, that confidence born of the fire in Valentino's eyes when he saw her in bathing suits. She found she quite enjoyed tormenting him, pushing him to break out of the chaste prison his position put them both in.

The waves came up and he grabbed a surfboard.

"I'll show you how," he said.

For all the age-old beauty of his country, for all that she loved every minute together, how could she not love these moments best of all? Alone. Playing. Touching each other.

Standing on the surfboard was a lot harder than it looked. Soon, they were both soaked, gulping down water as they gurgled with laughter. Erin had finally just managed to stand when she saw a little gray head, bobbing toward her. Harvey had fallen in the water!

"Valentino! Save him!"

Valentino hurled himself through the water, but as she watched the rescue, she realized her crazy cat was paddling around, perfectly content.

She was laughing so hard, she had to hoist herself up on the surfboard. “Have you ever seen anything like that before?”

His laughter joined hers, and he made it to the cat. He scooped Harvey, soaked, out of the water, came back and placed him in front of her on the surfboard she had straddled.

“Tigers swim,” he told the cat. “You wonderful old warrior. You are part tiger, aren’t you?”

Harvey preened.

And then Valentino put his hand on the back of Erin’s neck and tugged her mouth to his. The kiss tasted of the sea. And of sand. Of the sun’s warmth. Of things new. And of things ancient. The kiss tasted of promises.

It had a texture of its own: Erin could feel her future painting itself as his mouth claimed hers. The euphoria intensified until it was like a physical tingling inside her skin trying to get out.

They had been building to this moment for days, the anticipation of it razor-sharp between them. Now it was here, every physical longing, like too much water in a dam, suddenly bursting free.

She was hungry for him. Starving. And he was hungry for her. His mouth ravaged her willing mouth. He kissed the sun-warmed tops of her breasts, owning her, claiming her, letting his lips tell her *I need you. I can’t live without you.*

It felt as if she could not live one more moment without the beautiful intimacy between them. She drew his head from her breast, claimed his lips, tasted him.

And then a drone came overhead and swooped down toward them, buzzing like a bothersome fly. She lost her balance and the surfboard tilted, sending her and Harvey into the water. She surfaced, sputtering and gasping.

Valentino rescued them both, one arm holding the cat, the other protectively around her shoulder as he got them back to the sand.

As he broke away from her, he sent a fearsome glare to the drone and then gave her a look, impotent and furious, at the pleasure denied them once again.

CHAPTER FOURTEEN

VALENTINO AWOKE AND was aware of an ache of need within him. His first thought was of Erin and how his need to touch her, to kiss her, to have her, had been thwarted.

That drone, yesterday afternoon. He sighed. The reality of the world. His world.

Mostly, though, he loved showing her that world.

Loved her wonder, her enthusiasm, her delight. He was experiencing his realm through her and it seemed as brand-new and as shiny as a bright copper penny.

But he missed waking to her in the morning, as if he had done it his whole life, not just for a few days in a cabin in the middle of nowhere.

It occurred to him he was edging closer.

Not edging, really. Barreling. He had seen the look in her eyes when he had held that baby. He wanted to spend the rest of his life with her. He wanted her to have his children. He wanted her to be his queen.

There was a soft rap at the door.

Milo came in bearing a tray with coffee and a selection of local morning papers. Valentino would take breakfast in the garden, later, with Erin. He was aware that he was eager to see her, as if the gold of her hair and the green of her eyes were as new to him as that bright penny.

Today, they would go to see the olive groves in the south. He hoped to get her on a horse. She had never ridden before, and there was no better way to see the groves. He couldn't wait to share this activity that he loved with her. He hoped she would take to it, that someday she would ride as wonderfully as she skied…

Finally, he came out of his thoughts and noticed Milo was still standing there, a funny look on his face.

"Is something the matter?"

"Sir, the papers—" Milo looked so distressed.

Valentino picked up the first paper.

He looked at the front-page picture. It was of him and Erin in the water, just after they had kissed. Even though they had missed him lowering his head to her breast, it was a shamelessly intrusive photo.

The press—still hoping to milk a little more from both his and Angelica's lives—tried to follow them every time they stepped out of the palace. Thankfully, the staff had become masters at distraction, sending them in the wrong direction, dispatching decoy cars so that Erin and Valentino weren't always on display. No drones were allowed in the air within a mile of his entourage.

But yesterday that one had slipped in from the other side of the island, coming over that cliff before he'd been able to protect Erin from it.

Valentino frowned as he saw that something had been circled in the picture, and that an arrow showed an inset picture with a blow-up of the circled item.

It was Harvey, soaked, looking like a drowned rat, sitting between Erin's legs on the surfboard.

In his language, the headline blared *Crazy Cat Lady!*

There were several papers here, and he looked through them all. Each one had the same photo—sold, no doubt, to the highest bidders—and a variation of the crazy cat lady story.

It filled him with fury like nothing he had ever felt. How dare they miss her incredible beauty, her wonder at life, and expose something so banal? How dare they zero in on this minute detail about her, and blow it up cruelly and with such exclusive focus? Why wouldn't they see her love of an aging cat for what it was? Tender? Compassionate? *Good.*

His rage intensified when he realized he was powerless against it.

He looked at Milo. They had come a long, long way since that day when Milo had gleefully announced to Erin that Valentino was going to marry someone else.

Valentino was fairly certain that Milo was nearly as enchanted with Erin as he himself was. He adored the cat!

Milo gave him a look of pure sympathy, understanding the prince's position, maybe before he, himself, fully got it.

Valentino loved her.

He loved Erin O'Rourke madly and beyond reason. He would do anything for her. He would die to protect her.

He was suddenly and sharply aware of the demands of holding a position in a royal household. Could he invite Erin, someone he cared about deeply—that he loved deeply—into the kind of life where the public pressures could be so cruel and unrelenting? Angelica had rejected it, and she had been born to it. How unfair would it be to ask someone who didn't know the full weight of it to share this life with him?

Share this life with him?

He had become too caught up in it all. The passion had swept away his ability to be rational. The joy he had felt in her presence had made him, selfishly, just want more and more and more.

Of laughter. Of conversation. Of *wanting* with an unholy need.

How could he even consider the possibility of her and him together—forever—when he would never be able to protect her from *this*? From her life being put under a microscope; for her eccentricities to be exposed to a mean-spirited world.

She had told him about withdrawing from ski racing because she was so sensitive to her father's criticism, the expectations placed on her by the press.

How much worse would this be? A collective critical spirit aimed right at her. The person she was—who had grown up in the sanctuary of those beautiful mountains—could be destroyed by this relentless attention, this cutting meanness, this desire to focus on fault.

It was a repeating story within royal families.

The outsider was brought in. Some fool thought love would be enough. And it never, ever, was.

It had already started. With the cat. Then it would be her hair, or a dress she chose, or an extra pound put on, or a gaffe at a royal function. They would tear away at her like vultures on carrion, making her smaller and smaller…

He could not stand the pain of what he was seeing as her possible future if he brought her into his world. He threw down the paper and gave Milo a look.

"How can you love someone and do this to them?" Valentino asked, his voice hoarse with pain. "Ask this of them?"

He supposed he hoped Milo would have an answer, would hold out hope, would help him see things from a different perspective.

Instead, the man looked absolutely crushed—as if he had just seen a place of complete light turn dark—as he turned and left the room.

Erin looked at the note from Valentino. He had canceled their plans for today. She had been so looking forward to the olive groves. He had been going to show her how to ride. The thought was terrifying. And exciting. That was exactly what her feelings were of late: terrified and excited.

Every single thing they did together shone with a light.

He said he would be busy today, that something unexpected had come up, but if she would join him for dinner in the garden, he would be honored.

She had a lovely day. Despite being shadowed by security, she finally was able to go to a market. She had a rich and chocolatey cup of coffee and a sumptuous pastry at a local café. No one paid the least attention to her.

She felt as if she was absorbing Valentino's country through her pores. What she noticed was the softness of it, in stark contrast to her own home of harsh climates and landscapes.

Here, everything was soft: the light, the heat, the rolling landscapes, the flavors. She was falling in love with Valentino's beautiful island nation every bit as much as she was falling in love with him.

That truth warmed her, as rich and delightful as the drink she was sipping.

She loved him. Loved him. Loved him. Loved him.

The phrase was still repeating in her mind on an endless delicious loop as she entered the garden just as dusk was falling. The perfume of flowers was heavy in the air. A table had been set on the lawn. It was romantic, with a beautiful linen tablecloth, flickering candles, places already set. The stars winked like diamonds in the black-velvet sky above the garden.

Obviously, Valentino had planned a romantic dinner for two.

Her heart stopped as she saw him pacing back and forth near the back wall. He seemed nervous, and it was so unlike him. Her eyes went from him to the beautiful table setting.

He was going to propose.

He saw her and stopped. For a moment, she saw something in his face that terrified her—a sadness so acute, she wondered if someone had died.

"No Harvey tonight?" he said as he came and greeted her with the traditional kiss on each cheek.

"Milo is quite taken with him. The feeling seems to be mutual."

He glanced toward the sky. "Let's hope for some privacy," he said. "If a drone comes, we'll move inside."

The thought of the drone seemed to upset him, added to an almost agitated air about him. Something she was not accustomed to.

They sat and he poured wine. He drank his too fast, in two gigantic gulps. A feast had been put before them. It sometimes seemed as if the kitchen staff were trying to outdo themselves in their efforts to show her the wonders of their island cuisine. It was so endearing. She had made a point of going to the kitchen after every meal and discussing it with them. Thanking the chef.

Why was Valentino so not himself? Was he going to propose? Somehow, she would not have imagined it like this.

Had she imagined it? Him proposing?

Of course she had! She had imagined him on one knee,

his eyes—those oh-so-familiar deep brown eyes—resting on her face, filled with tenderness and hope.

Will you...?

Yet tonight his expression was anything but tender.

Finally, she could not get on with the pretense of enjoying dinner any longer. She set down her fork.

"What is wrong?" she asked.

He hesitated. He looked anywhere but at her. But then he did look at her, drew in a deep breath, set his shoulders.

"We've made a mistake."

Her mouth fell open. This was so far from what she'd expected.

"I'm sorry," she stammered. "What?"

"Not we. Me. I'm sorry. It's unfolded too quickly."

She stared at him, not believing what she was hearing. This was the same man who had trailed his fingers across the heated surface of her skin. Insatiable. Who had stood on top of an igloo with her. Who had swam, laughing in the sea with her just yesterday, splashing her, chasing her around through the waves. Who had stolen kisses as if he could not get enough of her.

The man who had held that baby and filled her with the most terrifying thing of all...hope.

"I don't understand," she said. His face was so remote, the Valentino she thought she knew replaced with the suave and distant stranger.

She said she didn't understand. But she was beginning to, she just didn't want to.

Her life was playing out in a constant, nauseating loop: she expected one thing and the exact opposite happened.

Twice now, she had expected a proposal and gotten this instead.

Why was she so surprised? Had she really thought she was a girl who could hold a man like Valentino's interest?

Even Paul, the most ordinary of guys, had seen her for what she was.

Beyond ordinary.

Boring.

Valentino wouldn't even look at her. He looked at his hand. He was grasping the stem of his wineglass so tight, it looked as if he might snap it.

He said, "Erin, there's someone else."

She heard shame in his voice. And defeat.

Love turned to hate in the blink of an eye. The euphoria that she had been floating on since she had arrived at Valentino's home hissed out of her, air out of a pricked balloon. She could feel everything inside her collapsing—as if a bomb had been dropped—into the space that had been filled with wonder, with discovery, with bravery, with a sense of adventure.

How could he do this to her?

How could he bring her all the way here to cut the legs out from under her like this?

The awful truth hit her. She had never known him. Not at all. She had believed what she'd wanted to believe, built a fairy tale around him.

The only part of the fairy tale that was true was that he was a prince.

She should have obeyed her instincts. They had warned her he was an ass. She would not give him the satisfaction of spitting those furious words at him, of letting him know how deeply she was wounded.

She got up carefully from the table. With her spine ramrod-straight, she walked away from him. She did not look back.

Valentino watched her go. Shored up by some innate dignity, by a strength she might not have even been aware she possessed, it struck him that Erin O'Rourke moved like a queen.

He turned away from the sight, from her absolute bravery in the face of his betrayal. He was afraid if he watched any longer, he would scream *No, I didn't mean it. It was all lies. Come back.*

He shouldn't have said the last part. The most awful lie of all, about there being someone else.

But he needed Erin not just to go but to never look back. He needed what had flashed through her eyes for him: pure and primal disgust. Maybe even hatred.

He needed those things because, if she looked back, he was not sure he would be strong enough to do what he had to do.

He needed to save her. And that meant letting her go.

If he loved her, truly, he needed to send her back to her old life before it was too late, before she was so notorious that—because of him—there could never be an old life to go back to.

CHAPTER FIFTEEN

ERIN WAS NOT even sure how she and Harvey got home. The journey was a blur. Somehow she had been back on that jet. Valentino must have arranged that in his eagerness to erase his *mistake,* to get rid of her.

For days after arriving at the resort, she felt as if she was in a fog. She could not bring herself to go to the cabin, to see if anything remained of their igloo and angels.

She went over the day before his horrible announcement with a fine-tooth comb. What had she said? What had she done that was so wrong? Why had he pulled the plug so suddenly? How could there be someone else when they had spent every waking moment together?

It must be someone from his past. Someone who had come forward after they had heard about his split from Angelica. It had to be someone more suited than her.

Erin also tried to figure out how she could be feeling one thing—she loved him, loved him, loved him—and he quite another. How was that possible without her awareness? And yet it was an awful, awful repeat of what had happened with Paul.

During the day, she was able to turn her mind to work, to other things, but in her dreams, she was with him, laughing. She would awake to a sense of grief.

Still, Erin surprised herself, too. She did not retreat from life. She did not hide out in her apartment going over things endlessly.

She found an almost shocking core of strength.

Each day Erin felt a little more certainty, a quiet confidence, that that she had never felt before. Increasingly, she was aware she might not be sure who Valentino really was, and in fact, it was quite likely she was never going to unravel the mystery of him.

But she was sure who she was.

Ironically, it was the time she had spent with him that had awakened this new confidence in her, a quiet sense of herself.

She became aware that her insecurities were rooted in her father's criticisms. She had developed a sense of not being good enough.

When he and her mother had split, she had taken on bits of that, too. What could she have done to save her family? If she had been a different person, a better person—if she had kept skiing competitively—would it all have turned out differently?

That is why she had accepted Paul, forgiving his slights, his insults, his lack of enthusiasm for her and their relationship. Because she had felt that was all she deserved. She had accepted what she thought she could get.

Despite the bad ending with Valentino, she had *grown* in the context of loving him. She had become *more* than she was before.

Even Kelly noticed the changes in her. "You're different," she said.

Erin didn't even have to ask her how. She could *feel* some basic difference in herself, born of shared laughter, of quiet talks, of heated looks and touches. Born of being with a person where she had become more completely herself than she had ever been before: silly, strong, adventurous, bold, shy.

And despite her new strength, she indulged one weakness. Erin scoured the tabloids, online and paper copies, looking for some news of him, a glimpse of him, a look at his new lover.

But each day passed with nothing.

How was that possible? He had done everything in his power to try to keep their budding relationship away from prying eyes and he had not been successful.

In fact, just this morning, there had been a text. It was the first she had heard from anyone from her days with the prince. Milo had her phone number because he had cared for the cat.

She'd been terrified—and hopeful—when his name popped up.

Terrified that he was sending bad news about Valentino. Or a picture of the new love that she told herself she could handle seeing.

When she looked at the photo—no text, no message—she was not sure why he had sent it.

It was a photograph of the front of a newspaper, from when she'd been there. That day that Harvey had swam with them. She vaguely remembered a drone coming over.

She wasn't able to read the headline—it was in their language. But looking at that picture, at both of them laughing, of Harvey perched on the surfboard, Erin felt exactly as she did when she first woke up every morning.

Grief-stricken.

She had closed the picture right away, feeling it robbing her hard-earned strength, feeling angry at Milo for sending it.

Partway through the day, it nagged at her. Why had

Milo sent the newspaper article? It wasn't as if she could understand it.

Still, on her lunch hour, she felt compelled to open it again. She stared at the picture. Such love! How could it—

She looked at the headline. Surely, in this day and age, she could translate what it said? Sure enough, she found an app on her phone and carefully typed in the exact lettering.

That didn't seem right.

The translation must be wrong.

Crazy Cat Lady!

Erin went very still. She got it. She got it completely.

The papers were making fun of her.

Valentino didn't have a new love interest.

He was doing what he perceived he needed to do to protect her. Just as with Angelica, he was willing to be the one who took it, who paid the price, who made the sacrifice.

For her.

To keep her safe.

She thought of his mother and the wariness in her; the loneliness she had seen in the cool shadows of the queen's eyes.

That was what Valentino was sentencing himself to. That was what he was prepared to do *for her.* That is what he thought love was.

And that was what he thought of her. That she wasn't strong enough. That he had to take it for her.

She saw Milo's sending the picture for exactly what it was.

A challenge to be more than she had ever been before: braver, stronger, more certain.

She saw it for its purpose.

To intervene like this, Milo must be extraordinarily worried about Valentino.

Erin knew what she had to do. She had to gamble that she was right. She had to trust that what had unfolded between them was real.

The most real thing that she had ever experienced.

She had to act more fearlessly than she ever had before.

Valentino was putting himself in a lonely prison because he thought she needed rescuing.

Oh, the irony. It was not her who needed rescuing! It was him.

She had to rescue the prince.

"Sir, there's someone here to see you."

"I'm not receiving today." Valentino saw the distress on Milo's face. It had been growing for days.

Valentino, on those odd days when he glanced at himself in the mirror, could see why. He looked awful. He was losing weight alarmingly. He was unshaven. There were dark circles under his eyes. His dreams were the dreams of a man tormented by what he had lost.

He knew he had done what he'd had to do.

But he had not expected to be haunted so completely by the look on Erin's face when he had betrayed her.

Surely, he could have done it differently? Surely, he could have made her see reason without hurting her so badly?

Milo left the room, shutting the door quietly behind him, and Valentino wandered over to his window. His beautiful land had been stripped of its color. He was blind to beauty now.

He should have just told her he was dying. It felt more true than what he had said.

He heard the door whisper open.

"Milo! Leave me! I don't want anything." Especially not him hovering with *that* look on his face.

Milo didn't answer and he turned to glare at him.

His world stopped. As he drank her in—the shining waterfall of her hair, the green of her eyes, the pale rose of her lips—he was aware of seeing color for the first time in weeks.

He could feel the weakness in him, as if he were a man drowning and a life ring was within reach. But what if you had to sacrifice someone else to save your own life?

He did not think he had any strength left. Not one ounce.

Yet he found just enough to lift an eyebrow at her, to strip the sigh within him from his voice. "How did you get here?"

"I flew. I had to bring my broom since I didn't have the private jet at my disposal."

Her words transported him back to the very beginning when he had teased her about her fairy-tale cottage minus the child-eating witch.

This was not the time for jokes. Though, when she said it, her voice so light, like music, he could feel himself leaning toward her, leaning toward the memory of their shared laughter, leaning toward a quiet strength in her eyes.

How was it she looked so much better than she ever had, when he was so much worse?

Really, just confirmation he had done the right thing.

"I had to leave Harvey," she said. "I couldn't figure

out the intricacies of traveling with him. Kelly is looking after him."

"You left Harvey?" A strange panic welled up in him. She'd only leave Harvey if it was an emergency. What if she had come to give him some awful news?

"I know. Your tabloids will be disappointed when they find out. Crazy Cat Lady with no cat."

"That was cruel of them," he said. "I'm sorry you had to see it."

She looked at him gravely then came and touched his arm. Her touch on his arm made him close his eyes and just drink in the way her closeness felt.

When he finally opened his eyes again, she was looking at him with an unsettling *knowing. A*s if the gig was up. As if she knew everything.

"It's okay," she said soothingly. "I'm okay."

He heard the truth in that. And wondered again at the unfairness of it. How could she be okay when he was not?

"This time," he growled at her. "What about next time? What about when they are tearing into you about your clothes, or your accent, or the fact you used the wrong fork at a state dinner? What then?"

She didn't seem to get the seriousness of this at all. She was smiling at him, ever so tenderly.

"Is that why you lied to me?" she asked.

He stiffened. "What makes you think I lied?"

"To protect me."

He made one last effort. He gathered all his strength. He said, "No! There is someone else."

"Uh-huh," she said with aggravating and patent disbelief.

"Don't you know who I am?" he said. "People believe me."

"Maybe people who don't know you."

Every moment they had ever spent together seemed to flash before his eyes. It was true. She knew him like no one else ever had. Or ever would again.

"Valentino," she said firmly, "there is no one else."

"How do you know?" he demanded with what was left of his strength.

She cocked her head at him. "Okay. Tell me the color of her hair."

But he could not think of any hair color except the sun-on-wheat color right in front of him.

"Eyes?" she prodded him.

Green. It was the only color he could think of.

"What do you feel like when she kisses you?"

His eyes fastened on her lips and the memories seared through him white-hot.

"That's what I thought," she said. "There is no one else. I know. I know by looking at you. I should have known right away that it was a lie."

What could he say? He couldn't very well produce evidence it wasn't a lie.

"I had to make you go," he whispered.

"Because of the story," she concluded. "You thought I would be hurt by the story, by being called names."

"It wasn't just that story. It was all the stories that would come. It would be watching, helpless, as they pecked away at you. It was what a life with me would steal from you."

"You understand what you're saying, don't you?"

"Completely," he said.

"That you love me. You love me so much, you would sacrifice your own chance at happiness to protect me."

He was silent. She was so smart. Why had he thought he could fool her for any length of time?

"The irony is, Valentino, that to be the woman worthy

of that love, I have to be willing to risk the arrows. I have to be strong. I can't let you protect me. I can't let you sacrifice yourself for what you perceive as my well-being.

"I don't think a life with you could steal anything of value from me. It would just give and give and give.

"Love and love and more love.

"And I'm not leaving you. No matter what you say or do, I can see your truth in your face. I can see it in how you've suffered—look at you—to protect me.

"Here's where you have it all wrong—you are not a prince riding in to rescue me. You will always be to me, first and foremost, a man not a prince.

"You will always be, to me, the one I would risk everything to rescue."

Her words poured over him like a warm balm over a raw wound. "You're turning the fairy tales on their head," he finally said.

She smiled at him. "I know, Valentino. I know."

And he could resist no longer. He reached for the life ring she had thrown him. He allowed himself to be rescued by her love. He went into her arms and laid his head on her shoulder, the warrior home from the war.

"Erin," he whispered, his voice hoarse and raw, the warrior's surrender complete, "I love you. I will love you forever."

Valentino watched Erin come across the meadow toward him. Summer had come to the mountains and the clearing, once filled with snow angels, was now filled with wildflowers. She wore a ring of them in the hair, which flowed freely onto her shoulders, bare to the sun.

She was wearing a white dress, though he was not sure he would have called it a bridal gown. She carried a basket, Harvey lolling in it contentedly, as if he, not she, was the star of today's show.

Valentino wondered: did all grooms feel this way as their bride came toward them? On top of the world? Like the luckiest man alive? Anointed by a mysterious force? Made strong and whole, not by their own power, but by love?

Erin could have had the wedding of the century. She could have worn a gown encrusted with jewels and a priceless lace veil that had been passed down for centuries. She could have had her wedding in a cathedral with a full children's choir, with a carriage waiting outside the door to carry them through the streets of the country that had come to adore her during the short days of their courtship.

Indeed, that wedding Erin had rejected, was what his mother had wanted. And her father, Enrique, would have been beside himself with delight if the wedding had been conducted with pomp and circumstance.

But this was Erin's day and she knew exactly what she wanted.

In the last few months, she had come into herself in ways that were as unexpected as they were wonderful. She *shone* with life. She had a unique ability to embrace the unexpected. The love flowed out of her and embraced everyone that she touched, which was why she had become so beloved to his people in such a short time.

But she had held firm about today.

She wanted to celebrate, not who they were publicly but what this cottage and this meadow had given them.

Whenever they were here, they were just two people and it was love that crowned them, love that lent them its glory.

In light of how difficult it was to keep a secret, to keep

things private, it was something of a miracle that they had managed to have only a few other people here: Milo, Kelly, Ricky and an officiant.

In a short while, a helicopter would whisk the visitors away.

And they would be home.

Not in this meadow, as much as they loved it, and not in the cottage.

Home was where they were, together.

Forever.

EPILOGUE

THIS, VALENTINO THOUGHT, was possibly one of the hardest things he had ever done. He held the cat in his arms, wrapped in a handmade blanket that had been a gift to Harvey from Milo.

Milo, who never stopped—even though more than a year had passed—trying to make it up to his princess, to Erin, that he had been the one who had delivered the cruel news of Valentino's engagement to Angelica.

Erin was at Valentino's side, the baby due any day, tears streaming down her face, as they made their way to the small walled garden where they still made time for each other every single day and shared romantic meals.

Even now it occurred to him how Harvey had protected Erin right until the end. Except for his increasing blindness and inability to hear, there had been no long illness, no injuries, no loss of appetite or interest in life.

They had just woken up this morning and Harvey had looked for all the world as if he was asleep in his basket next to their bed. In fact, they had gone out and had breakfast before noticing he had not joined them, as he usually would at the first sniff of food.

The cat had not been asleep.

Valentino had notified the gardener, who had dug a

small hole and now waited beside it, head bowed, shovel in hand.

The gardener must have told others because staff were now streaming into the garden, silent and respectful as Valentino knelt and laid Harvey in the tiny grave.

Valentino touched the blanket and said out loud, "Your work here is done, old warrior. You truly had the heart of a tiger. But it's my job now. You rest in peace, knowing I will make her feel safe. Cherished. Listened to."

If it was hard for Erin, in her condition, to get down, it didn't seem like it. She knelt by the grave, touched her fingers to her lips and then to that blanket.

"Thank you," she whispered. "My friend."

In her new language she whispered, *"Beloved."*

Valentino drew her to her feet and put his arm around her shoulders. She turned her face into him and cried as the gardener silently shoveled.

When he was done, Valentino lifted her chin and nodded over his shoulder to direct her attention to what was happening.

They were coming forward, the palace staff, one by one. Each of them held a single flower, which they laid on that small heap of rich, newly turned black soil until it was blanketed with bright blossoms.

Harvey had become quite famous. Rather than shirking the *Crazy Cat Lady* title the press had so maliciously branded her with in those first public days of their relationship, Erin had embraced it. Soon, Harvey had his own social media accounts and his own channel on the streaming service. At first, it was only the people of Canada and Lorenzo del Toro who embraced Harvey.

But then he had become a media sensation with millions of followers and millions of views of his videos, which were sometimes nothing more than him snoring softly on top of Milo's blanket in his basket. In the fall, they had allowed a charity to make a calendar of him and the sales had been through the roof.

The cat, according to experts in such things, had made the Royal family "relatable." The cat, and Erin, with her natural athletic grace, her easy way, her intelligence, her charm, her instinct for how to do the right thing, had brought his family out of the Dark Ages.

She had done it so gently, and with such humor and compassion, that it had not been a painful transition.

It seemed the last flower had been laid, when the garden gate swung open. Milo came through it, though you could barely tell it was him for the size of the giant spray of yellow flowers he carried. He was weeping noisily as he walked. He knelt before the grave, set his flowers on it.

This is who Erin was. Hugely pregnant, she didn't even hesitate to get back on her knees. She knelt beside Milo, put her arm around him and leaned her head against his shaking shoulder.

She was putting away her own pain to bring him comfort.

The staff—Milo—were here for the cat, of course. But it was really for her, to acknowledge the gift she had brought to this island and to his household. Humanity.

These people were not her staff.

They were the family she had always wanted. And they knew it.

Valentino knew it. He was her family. Soon, they would welcome a baby. Despite pressure to reveal the sex, the truth was they lived by their motto—*to surprises*—and did not themselves know whether the child would be a boy or a girl.

He looked at the two people kneeling by the small

grave. This was life then: one day you said hello and one day you said goodbye.

He could feel them rising to the challenge, dancing with the timeless, glorious, endless cycle of death and birth.

And love. That incredible force that Valentino had come to know.

That power that transcended it all.

* * * * *

COMING SOON!

We really hope you enjoyed reading this book. If you're looking for more romance, be sure to head to the shops when new books are available on

Thursday 6th January

To see which titles are coming soon, please visit

millsandboon.co.uk/nextmonth

MILLS & BOON

Coming next month

GREEK HEIR TO CLAIM HER HEART
Jennifer Faye

His eyes closed as his lips pressed to hers. He willed her to kiss him back. Surely he hadn't misread things between them. Had he?

And then her hands reached out, cupping his face. Her touch was feathery soft, as though she was afraid he might disappear in a puff of smoke. Her lips slowly moved over his as she took the lead.

Thoughts of his mother's estate slipped from his mind. Worries over selling the island were swept away. In this moment, his thoughts were only of Hermione and how right this kiss felt.

He wanted this moment to go on and on. Because a kiss was normally just a kiss, a prelude to something more. However, with Hermione, it was all by itself an earthmoving event. His lips gently brushed over hers. He didn't want to scare her off. He wanted to hold her in his arms as long as possible.

As he drew her closer, their kiss intensified. His whole body came alive with the rush of adrenaline. He'd never been so consumed with a kiss.

Hermione was unique in so many wonderful and amazing ways. As her lips moved beneath his, he wondered how he'd been so lucky to meet her.

The reality of their circumstances slipped away. The

only thing that mattered right now was him and her. And this kiss that was like a soothing balm on his tattered and torn heart.

He didn't want this moment to end. His hand reached up and gently caressed the smooth skin of her cheek. His fingers slid down to her neck where he felt her rapid pulse. She wanted him as much as she wanted him.

Buzz-buzz.

He didn't want his phone to ruin this moment. He didn't want anything to come between them. It vibrated in his pocket, distracting him from Hermione's tantalizing kiss.

She pulled away. His eyes opened to find her staring at him. He couldn't read her thoughts. Was she happy about the kiss? Or was she angry that he'd overstepped?

She glanced away. "You better answer that. It's probably important. And it's getting late. I'll see you in the morning."

Buzz-buzz.

"But I don't want to answer it. I want us to talk."

She shook her head as she stood. "We've definitely said more than enough for tonight. Good night."

And then she was out the door in a flash. Once more he was left with questions where she was concerned.